Tessa Barclay i
has written m
Hidden Beauty
Woman, the C ... *A Web of*
Dreams, *Broken Threads* and *The Final Pattern* (all
available from Headline), the Champagne series and
the Craigallan quartet. She was born and raised in
Edinburgh and is a member of the clan McKenzie.
Tessa Barclay now lives and works in south-west
London.

Harvest of Thorns is the third in the Craigallan
quartet – volumes one and two, *A Sower Went
Forth* and *The Stony Places*, are also available from
Headline and the final volume will follow.

'Tessa Barclay always spins a fine yarn. Her novels
are gripping and entertaining'
Wendy Craig

'[Her novels are] filled with fascinating historical
detail and teeming with human passions'
Marie Joseph

'Lots of intriguing detail'
The Sunday Times

'Takes up where Cookson left off'
Glasgow Herald

Harvest of Thorns

Tessa Barclay

HEADLINE

Copyright © 1983 Tessa Barclay

The right of Tessa Barclay to be identified as the Author of
the Work has been asserted by her in accordance with the
Copyright, Designs and Patents Act 1988.

First published in 1983
by Star Books

Reprinted in paperback in 1994
by HEADLINE BOOK PUBLISHING

10 9 8 7 6 5 4 3 2

ISBN 0 7472 4296 8

Typeset by Avon Dataset Ltd, Bidford-on-Avon

Printed and bound in Great Britain by
HarperCollins Manufacturing, Glasgow

HEADLINE BOOK PUBLISHING
A division of Hodder Headline PLC
Headline House
79 Great Titchfield Street
London W1P 7FN

Harvest
of Thorns

Chapter One

Rob Craigallan folded his copy of the *New York Times* with an angry gesture and threw it into a patch of wintry sunshine on the floor. The front page, with its elegant heading and date, 12th April 1914, fluttered and was crushed under the weight of the Sunday pages.

'You know what's going to happen?' he growled, throwing himself back in his armchair. 'There's going to be a war if that fool Wilson doesn't hold his horses.'

'Mmmm?' murmured Gregor, trying to keep his attention on the stock market prices. 'Hold what horses?'

'It's important, boy! Pay attention!'

'Yes, Father,' said Gregor, and raised his eyes from his copy of the *Daily News*.

Leafing swiftly through for clues about the wheat market, the president and vice-president of Craigallan Agricultural Products were in town for that important bi-annual event, the dealing on the Chicago Board of Trade.

The hotel was full. Dealers and advisors were in Chicago for a week or ten days of hectic business. After that the city would quieten down again to its usual steady rhythm. Chicago was never slow, but during April and August the pace picked up, the hotels were

1

crowded with out-of-towners, and everything was a whirl of activity.

But the Craigallans never needed to worry about finding a room for their stay in the crowded metropolis. The suite on the top floor of the Palmer House Hotel was held exclusively for their use. They dropped in whenever some event brought them to town — not always business, for the ladies of the family liked to patronise the opera and the charity balls, and sometimes friends would stay in the Craigallan suite. Mr Yarwood, for instance — Sam Yarwood was there now, still unshaven and with the marks of Saturday night's heavy drinking on his blotched face.

The year 1914 had been worrying so far for businessmen. United States marines had landed in Haiti in January, then in February setbacks had been admitted over that most important piece of engineering investment, the Panama Canal, due to open in the spring but delayed. Ships were now moving, but other anxieties had intervened.

War, his father had said. Gregor looked at him with incipient interest. 'What's the President up to now?'

Rob kicked the crumpled newspaper with a slippered foot. 'The editorial implies he may send the fleet.'

'To Turkey?' Gregor was at a loss. Why should the US Navy be sent to Turkey, where a war had just ended?

'Oh, wake up, boy! I'm talking about Mexico!'

Sam Yarwood, immersed in the long columns of *Tribune*, snorted. 'We're never gonna be at war with Mexico again,' he said. 'We taught 'em good when we took Texas and California from 'em in forty-eight.'

'That was a different bunch. Now they've got a rabble of revolutionary peasants in control, Sam. I tell you, if Wilson listens to the advice he's getting, there'll be a war.'

'Well, would that be so bad?'

Rob Craigallan shook his head. 'I don't like to think of fighting on the American continent,' he said. 'It's all right when those half-wits in Europe go at each other's throats, but you know war disrupts business communications, Sam. You remember what a mess we got in when we were supposed to be fighting the Cubans? Ships being commandeered, telegraph offices swamped with military traffic . . . No, no, I don't think we'd do too well out of a war with Mexico.'

'It'll make a difference to the dealing tomorrow, though,' Gregor put in.

Rob gave him a sudden smile. 'Good for you, Greg. You always like it when there's a bit of a flutter in the dove-cotes, don't you?'

'Nothing like a little nervousness among the dealers to make the Board of Trade lively, Mr Craig.'

'Yeah. What did you hear from Neil last night?'

'Said he'd bring us the latest forecast by eight on Monday morning. The weather on the whole has been in favour of the crops during the winter and the Department of Agriculture's figures for probable harvests are high.'

'Hm,' muttered Rob. He reached for the coffee pot, lifted it, and found it nearly empty. 'Ring for the waiter, Greg — no, on second thoughts, don't bother. We better go down to breakfast soon.'

They could have had breakfast served in the suite, but just before dealing began in The Pit, as the Board of Trade was called, it was necessary to see and be seen in public. To gather in private rooms for too long gave the impression of conferring, of anxiety and even of conspiring to affect prices. Rob Craigallan, his friend Sam Yarwood, and his 'ward' Gregor McGarth (known by most people to be his natural son) would saunter down to the breakfast room of the Palmer House and greet their colleagues. They would send for copies of the newspapers as though they hadn't already perused them from front to back. It was all part of the game, the grand game of dealing in futures on the Chicago wheat market.

Chicago was the greatest grain market in the world. Not even London, with its long history of brokerage, handled the amount of money that was gambled on the future price of wheat and corn and meat. Chicago was the bread basket of the world, the provision merchant from whom almost everyone bought the staples of life. Beef, pork, wheat for bread and cakes, grain for livestock . . . Rob and Greg foresaw the day when the sale of grain for horses might die away, as the automobile replaced the horse-drawn carriage. But then, as wealth increased, there would be an increase in the keeping of beef cattle and dairy herds which, in the uncertain climates of huge farming areas, had to be fed when grass died or was buried in snow.

Rob Craigallan sometimes said that the way to make money was to deal in something mankind couldn't do without. And the way to make even more money was to foresee how much of that commodity was likely to exist, and make bargains for it in advance. If there was likely to be a plentiful grain crop, then you offered low prices. The trick was to know if you had got your facts right — was there going to be a surplus of wheat and maize, or a scarcity? Would drought or insect pests damage the crop? Or, supposing everything went well, would there be some political upheaval which would cause the demand to soar?

For instance, if there really was going to be trouble with Mexico . . . Rob pictured the terrain in that parched, hot country. If armies were going to move about, they would need fodder for the transport teams — no fear of automobiles supplanting horses and mules in a backward nation like Mexico! Yes, if there was going to be a fracas, the demand for grain might rise.

'Telephone through to Curtis,' he suggested as he passed Gregor en route to his bedroom to dress for the day.

'But it's kind of early, Father—'

'But if you leave it till later they'll have gone to church.'

'Oh lord, yes.' Gregor made a grimace. Senator Gracebridge, the husband of his half-sister Ellie-Rose, had to observe the conventions. He and his wife and their two handsome children had to be seen to go to church regularly otherwise his voters in Nebraska might get to hear that young Curtis Gracebridge was becoming ungodly. Gregor felt that Curtis didn't mind the boredom of the long tirades from the Methodist preacher, but he often wondered how Ellie-Rose enjoyed them.

He asked the hotel's operator to get him long-distance and had the call put through to Washington. Ellie-Rose sounded a little breathless when she came to the telephone. 'Hello, Greg, what is it?'

'Anything wrong, Ellie?'

'No, we're just a bit at sixes and sevens this morning. Curtis got home in the wee small hours—'

'Partying?'

'Nothing like that. There was an all-night conference by the Foreign Affairs committee of the House.'

5

'About Mexico?'

She made no immediate response. Then she said: 'I'm not supposed to say anything but I won't disagree with that supposition.'

'Get Curtis to ring me when he wakes, eh, Ellie? We're having our usual planning session for the spring dealing, and we don't know how much credence to give to this speculation about Mexico.'

'I think you'll find that he can't discuss it, Greg. It's all under wraps.'

In effect, Ellie-Rose had more or less told him what he needed to know — that President Wilson was going to make some move over the disagreement with the Mexican government. What the step might be scarcely mattered — the mere fact of American intervention would affect the dealings in The Pit when it became known, and to have some early warning on that point would help Greg and his colleagues to decide on their buying and selling.

So now he said, 'How're you, Ellie?'

'Very well, thank you. Longing for spring. It seems awfully late this year.'

'And Gina and little Curt?'

'They're fine. Curt has taken up swimming at the suggestion of the doctor — he says it will improve his physique.' Ellie-Rose's son, Curtis Junior, had been a premature baby born under difficult circumstances which had affected his health all through his childhood. Now, at twelve, he was a stringy, gangling boy, all arms and legs and pale skin. Gregor was sorry for poor Curt, a continual disappointment to his father who had expected a rumbustious little adventurer of a son.

Poor Curt . . . It was the way everyone always

6

thought of him. It was a shame, because if you could disregard his thinness and his shyness, Curt was an engaging character with a wry sense of humour.

'We've decided on a school for him for the fall,' Ellie-Rose said. 'It's a place with a good record on things like sport and physical fitness—'

'I hope you're not writing off his brains, Ellie! He has some, you know.'

'Yes.' She sighed. Her husband thought little of Curt's intellectual abilities. True, he did badly in end-of-term examinations, but that was because he missed so much schooling due to ill health. And besides, he got exam nerves. If only it were possible to have a school where the children never had to sit down to examination papers . . . But if there were, Curtis certainly wouldn't let Curt attend it − he'd dismiss it as a crackpot place. Curtis liked everything to go on in the way he'd always known; new ideas on education, morals or politics offended him.

She changed the subject by asking after her father. Rob didn't need to make a parade of his affection for Ellie-Rose. She was one of the most important things in his life, a daughter who had lived up to all his expectations of her. Tall and slender and more beautiful now than she had been in her twenties, she graced the handsome home that Rob had bought for her in Washington and, with Rob's money, furthered her husband's career. A renowned hostess, a formidable ally to her husband's political ambitions, she was still a loving and attentive daughter.

When he had put down the phone Gregor glanced at his watch. Eight-thirty. His wife was probably awake by now. He moved quietly through the sittingroom and the vestibule to the room he and Francesca shared when

7

they stayed here. With a careful touch he opened the door and put his head round. Francesca was still asleep, her dark hair spread over the pillow like a fan of raven's feathers. He tiptoed in and stood by the bed, looking down at her. He would have liked to kiss her but didn't want to disturb her.

Since the birth of their child, Francesca had not been quite well. The doctors said it was due to some infection she had picked up during her childhood in Manila, some tropical germ which couldn't be eradicated from her blood.

'But I will not be an invalid!' she would insist. 'I live the same life as other American wives, no? I do not lie about on the sofa looking insipid!'

'You could never look insipid, *mi querida*,' he told her.

It was true. With her black flashing eyes and her lustrous hair, the imperious tilt of her head, her rare slow smile, she was an enchantress. Her illness only made her ivory skin more luminous and her eyes seem larger. Gregor watched over her with anxious but unobtrusive care. She was infinitely precious to him.

Their marriage had taken place against the wishes of Francesca's relatives. Out of respect she had written to them, far off in Spain, to ask their consent. Don Rafael, the senior member, had replied at once with a disdainful negative. How could a member of the Sagasta family ally herself with a nobody and moreover the illegitimate son of a nobody?

'Ha!' gasped Francesca, crumpling up the paper and throwing it on the floor to stamp on it. 'He takes me for some little pale *polilla* like those who live around him in Seville! He thinks I care about his approval and support. But where was his support when the bandidos

8

killed my parents? Which of them came to Manila to help me?'

She sent no reply. The wedding took place without the blessing of the grandees but in a Catholic church with the blessing of the priest who had taken Francesca into his care, and found her a quiet convent to stay in while she waited to become a bride. She came to the altar in the church all innocent and glowing, robed in fine lace and soft satin sewed by the devoted hands of the nuns. Greg felt his heart turn over as she approached him.

On their honeymoon in Europe he took her to call upon the Sagasta family in Seville, unannounced. One glance at their mouldering *palacio* told him there was more pride than money in their lives. Yet they received him with frigid politeness despite all the evidence of his wealth – the gleaming touring car under their *porte cochere*, the expensive furs on Francesca's shoulders.

Francesca, who had led a band of guerrilla fighters on Luzon, was treated as if she were a ten-year-old. They drank sherry from crystal glasses and ate stale ratafia biscuits. Regrets were expressed over Francesca's orphaned state and faint congratulations on her marriage. As they left Dona Isabella unbent enough to say: 'There is a branch of our family in California, America. I will write to Don Pedro to tell him of your marriage and give him your address – although whether he will wish to communicate with you, I cannot tell.'

'Thank you, Tia Isabella,' Francesca said. She curtseyed, Dona Isabella bowed, the servant ushered them through the hall, the door closed.

As they drove away, Francesca began to laugh. '*Que tal!* So those are my illustrious great-uncles and aunts!

9

Mama and Papa used to speak of them with such respect!'

'Respect they do arouse,' Greg agreed.

'Your family have more blood in their veins!'

'To say nothing of money in the bank.'

'Oh yes – they are so poor . . .'

'You want me to do something about that?' Greg asked.

She shook her head. 'Let them eat pride if they have no money for ratafia biscuits,' she replied.

In their hotel room a few hours later, he helped unhook the back of her soft voile evening gown. She glanced over her shoulder at him, smiling. 'You know, Gregorio – my great-uncles do not regard us as married. There was no family consent, no marriage settlement.'

He kissed the ivory skin at the turn of the neck. 'So what we're about to do is very wicked?'

'I fear so, my love. As for me, it is no problem. I merely confess my misdoings to the priest and receive absolution. But you, my Gregorio . . . What will become of you if you commit this sin?'

Swooping her up, he carried her to the bed. 'It's a great problem,' he agreed. 'Should I hire a separate room?'

'Ah, no, *mi alma, mi mundo* . . .' She wound her arms around his neck. 'Sometimes one must brave the displeasure of even great-uncles . . .'

'Displeasure?' he echoed. 'What does that word mean? At this moment I can't seem to think.'

He felt the gust of laughter against his cheek, then the whisper of love words in the language that seemed to sum up all that was most wonderful and desirable in his young wife. Only with Greg did she still speak her native tongue. Their love-making was still graced with the liquid syllables of endearments impossible to translate into the brisk, staccato notes of English. When their little girl was born, although Greg had been perfectly willing to have her called after Francesca's mother, Consuelo, she had shaken her head.

'No,' she said with firmness, 'she must have an American name.' She had heard university glee-club singers rendering *Sweet Adeline* and for a time insisted the baby should have that name. When Greg assured her it would be shortened to the unlovely Addie, she relented. In the end they settled on Clare, a reference to the colleague and helper of Francesca's name-saint, St Francis. Their little boy was called after Francesca's dead father, Luis, but spelt in the American fashion, Lewis.

Now the children were with their nurse in Craigallan Castle while Greg and Francesca made a short stay in Chicago for the opening of spring dealing. There would be one or two parties, a visit to the opera − these as token participation in Chicago society. Then, as the heat of summer came on, and the cities became unbearable, Francesca and the children would go to stay with Greg's mother in Colorado for a while. There, in the freedom she had become accustomed to during her years of lone fighting in Manila during the revolution, she would recover her complete health, he hoped.

Greg was debating whether to wake her with a gentle kiss when the telephone rang in the sittingroom of the suite. Sighing he returned to take up the receiver from the hook.

'Greg? You rang me? Say, Greg, it's a hell of a coincidence! Hooker and Sales and the others were just saying they needed a guy who spoke fluent Spanish and had his head screwed on the right way, and I mentioned you.'

'In what connection?' Greg inquired of his brother-in-law, puzzled.

'They need someone to go to Mexico and talk sense to these hot-heads in Vera Cruz. What d'you say, Greg?'

Chapter Two

The last thing Gregor McGarth wanted was to leave his wife in Chicago and go with a bunch of nervous diplomats to deal with the angry Mexicans. But the President made a personal request and it was impossible to refuse.

'They'll owe us a favour after this,' his father pointed out to him in cheerful tones as he angrily threw a few clothes into a bag in order to rush to Washington and be 'briefed'.

'I'd far rather stay here and get on with dealing in The Pit—'

'I know, I know, and I'd far rather you were here to do it. But with advice from Cornelius on the crop and the usual canny warnings from Sam I think I'll make out.'

'Oh, I didn't mean you couldn't do without me,' Greg said. 'I was just speaking from my own point of view. Mr Craig, look after Francesca for me, eh? She's shaken up . . .'

'She was going to Colorado anyhow, Greg. I mean, she was going to be parted from you—'

'But this is different.' Greg didn't point out in so many words that bullets might be flying in Mexico, and that it might be a very long time before good sense would prevail. Francesca knew that bullets could kill. She had seen them do so in Manila.

'I'll take her to Morag myself, boy,' Rob promised. 'Soon's we've finished bidding . . . three days, mebbe four. Meanwhile I'll see she doesn't find time hang heavy on her hands here — I'll try to keep her occupied.'

'Do you think if I asked Ellie-Rose to come to Chicago . . . ?'

'Dunno, Greg. Ellie-Rose has an awfully full schedule in Washington these days, you know.'

Ellie-Rose had immersed herself in career politics a few years ago. Greg had been surprised at her enthusiasm, for just before then it had seemed to him that she was losing interest in the Washington scene. Only her father knew that she had lost the man she loved, that the sudden interest in the Washington merry-go-round had been to distract herself from her misery.

She was waiting in the drawingroom of her elegant Washington house when Greg drove up, weary and vexed after an overnight train journey from Chicago. He had tried to sleep but his dreams had been disturbed by the picture of Francesca's trembling lips as she attempted to say a cheerful goodbye.

'Oh, you do look cross,' his half-sister greeted him. 'Come along to the diningroom and have something to eat. I've got hot muffins and coffee waiting.'

'Is that your recipe for soothing Curtis when he comes back from the Senate in a bad mood?'

'It doesn't do any harm,' she said, slipping an arm through his to urge him towards the diningroom. 'There used to be an old saying, the way to a man's heart is through his stomach. Maybe his heart isn't as vulnerable as all that, but his peace of mind is certainly improved when he has a decent meal inside him.'

'Where's Curtis?'

'He's on Capitol Hill. All hell has broken loose up there. The President is going to make some kind of announcement either today or tomorrow.'

'We're not really going to go to war with Mexico?' Greg said, sitting down slowly at the elegant table where sparkling silver and china invited his attention.

His half-sister seated herself at his side and poured coffee. 'I think it's sabre-rattling more than anything,' she soothed. 'The newspapers are making a big thing of it — "Mexicans insult the Flag", that kind of nonsense. So he's going to throw a scare into them, that's all.'

'I'm relieved to hear it. I want no part in negotiating with a bunch of beaten peasants. I'm not even keen on talking to them if they're trembling in their shoes.'

'Don't you see, Greg, that's why you'll be valuable. Curtis is no fool, you know. He can sense that there are a lot of people who want to get tough with "those damn-fool Mexes". He wanted to get someone with a sympathetic outlook into that team of presidential observers, and you're ideal with your pro-Spanish outlook—'

'I'm not pro-Spanish!'

'Well, you're pro-Francesca, and that's got to help, Greg.'

Greg drank his coffee and split open a muffin to butter it. 'I hated like hell leaving her in Chicago,' he muttered. 'She was looking forward to us all going to see Mother . . .'

'I know, I'm sorry. But Papa will look after her.'

Greg got up to put through a long-distance telephone call to her.

Ellie-Rose, passing the door of the study and hearing the rapid exchange of gentle Spanish endearments, felt a pang of envy. Why was it that she and Curtis never sounded like that when they talked? Could it be that all they seemed to talk about now was politics?

In Chicago, Cornelius Craigallan asked, 'You think there will be any actual shooting?'

'From all I hear, Mexico is poor in everything but ammunition,' said his father.

'But you're not worried.'

Rob shrugged. 'After today's dealing on the Board of Trade, I've a feeling there's bigger trouble than Mexico looming up, Neil. What the devil did all that shilly-shallying mean?'

Cornelius undid the stud that held his stiff collar and eased his neck. It had been a long, long day. First the early morning papers to devour for last minute clues about the grain crop and the political situation, then his own papers to check for the analysis of the growing season − present state of crop, possible infestation, success or failure of new strains, weather forecasts (mostly guesswork) and soil erosion. After that there had been the noisy and anxious session in The Pit. The dealers seemed to be at sixes and sevens − eager to buy one moment, anxious to sell back in the next.

Reading the futures market was always chancy, but today it had been almost impossible. Craigallan Agricultural Products had finished at a break-even point for the day's dealing but that wasn't the object of the exercise − they wanted to sell their considerable crops at a profit. Yet something was causing a background of uncertainty among the buyers. Prices were not exactly falling, they were hovering: the market was neither bull nor bear as yet.

After the day's business it had been necessary to dress and go out for the evening. Partly this was to entertain the forlorn Francesca, as they had promised Greg. But partly it was to get the feel of their environment, to hear what other businessmen thought of today's activity in the market.

Cornelius was surprisingly useful in this respect. He would sit quietly in a room taking no part in a conversation because, of course, he was deaf. Yet it could often happen that he would catch the words of a man on the other side of the room because that man, though speaking in a low and confidential tone, was facing Cornelius and could thus be lip-read.

'You know what Kossalof was talking about?' he ventured.

'No. I saw him having a long heart-to-heart with Brewster. Did you catch any of it?'

'I think he was repeating one word quite a lot. The Kaiser, the Kaiser . . .' To ensure that his father got it, Cornelius wrote it down on the pad he carried always in his breast pocket.

'Hm . . . Kossalof was buying this morning,' Rob murmured. 'I didn't check to see how much, but he was the only one who seemed sure of what he wanted to do and kept on doing it. I wonder if he's acting as agent for the German government?' He got up to pour himself a nightcap. 'Want something, Neil?'

'No thanks. Kossalof usually buys for the Russians, Papa, doesn't he?'

'But not today. When he's buying for Russia he waits for a fall, and today he just bought steadily for about an hour and a half at whatever price came along. I wonder, Neil . . . ? Could he have been buying for Berlin?'

'But why should the German government engage the man who usually buys for the Russians?'

'That's just it, boy! To prevent him from acting for the Russians. You know what those Slavs are like — they'll get in a hopeless muddle if someone's hooked their buying agent out from under their noses. It'll take them a week to sort themselves out and appoint someone else — and by that time Kossalof will have bought perhaps half of the wheat they would have bid for.'

'But why? I don't see it, Papa.'

'Nor do I, Neil, nor do I.' Rob sipped his whisky and thought it over. 'What I do see is that I'm going to have to put out a few feelers.' He sighed and set down his glass. 'Oh, I wish Greg hadn't had to go haring off to be a help to the President. Why can't that old woman in the White House collect a proper entourage and stop fishing men out of their careers to do his dirty work for him! Here we are, baffled by what's going on in The Pit, and my right hand man has been taken from me . . .'

Neil got up and moved towards the door. 'Sorry I can't be more help to you, Papa,' he said in his flat, toneless voice.

'Oh, it's all right, Neil, I'll manage,' Rob replied, and only realised after the door had closed on him that his elder son had been hurt.

For a moment he had an impulse to go after him, grip his hand and assure him that he was important in his own way. But almost at once he pulled himself back — in the first place he didn't go in much for sentimental gestures, and besides, it was more important to consider what to do about tomorrow's bidding.

He had to find out why the market was so unsettled.

To the outsider, there was nothing to worry about. Grain had been bought and sold today. But from long experience Rob knew that the dealers had been tiptoeing around the edges like bathers afraid of cold water.

He should ring Curtis to ask what was being said on Capitol Hill about Germany. He rose and made for the telephone. But then with his hand outstretched he paused. It was two-thirty in the morning. Even though Curtis kept the irregular hours of the politician, this was no time to be ringing him. After a moment's thought he picked up the instrument and dictated to Western Union's night clerk a telegram to be delivered at seven a.m.: *Telephone me when you have time to talk. Urgent. Craigallan.*

That done, he made for his bedroom. He was all at once aware that he was very tired. For years he had been accustomed to seeing to his own requirements, feeling that a personal servant was an effeminate luxury. But tonight he almost envied Cornelius his devoted valet, Larry Fitzgerald. Ever since he left university Cornelius had needed someone to answer the telephone and the door. Totally deaf, he would have found it very hard to manage on his own.

Neil seemed to have a talent for inspiring deep affection in those who could get past the barrier of his deafness and his strange flat speech. Rob had seen how the scientists at the Craigallan laboratories respected and liked him, some of them enough to have learned the deaf sign language to make things easier for him. The little girls who patted the typewriting machines and looked after the photographic equipment would have lain down and died for him. Even the Wagnerian Effie Mindingen, his secretary, seemed to have a gentleness for Neil hidden behind that stiffly starched shirtwaist.

Rob felt he himself didn't inspire real love. Business colleagues admired him and were a little in awe of him. His office staff regarded him with apprehension. Social acquaintances got along well enough with him – women even allowed themselves to be attracted, for he was still physically handsome, his russet hair only faintly sprinkled with silver threads and his face almost unlined save for a cleft between the brows. He needed glasses only for reading. His eyes often caught and held the flirtatious glance of a woman.

As to his family, Ellie-Rose loved him and he returned that love with an unquestioning affection. But she had her own family, her own life. If she had ever been deeply in love with Curtis – which he doubted – that was over, but in place of love had come loyalty, duty and custom. And her children, Gina and Curt, took up much of the time left over from being a social and political asset to Curtis.

Young Gina was a handful. Bright and wayward, she could twist her father round her little finger. Already she showed signs of coming out as a great beauty, which could only be harmful to a nature too demanding and thoughtless. Her brother worried Rob in a different way. A shy, reticent lad, painfully conscious of his thin arms and legs, depressed by the comparison between himself and Gina the beauty, he let her dominate him, of course. All the mischief that Curt had ever got into had been at Gina's instigation.

Rob wondered how the youngsters saw him. To them he was Grandpapa, a regular visitor from whom dollar bills could be expected as he left. Gina, he thought, found him perplexing: he couldn't be bent to her wishes no matter how she flattered and sparkled. Curt sometimes seemed on the verge of a genuine liking for him; but he got on better with the grandparents in Nebraska who saw in this skinny, large-footed lad the likeness of their son Curtis. From them Curt got the simple, undemanding love that his own parents seemed incapable of giving.

The parent-child relationship was difficult, Rob sighed to himself as he stooped to untie his shiny evening shoes. He himself had done the best he could for his children. He had made sacrifices for Cornelius's education at the School for the Deaf of Alexander Graham Bell in Boston. He had entered into a harsh financial contract with his estranged wife Luisa so that she would let him take Ellie-Rose with him out to the Great Plains. When he at last found his illegitimate son Gregor again, he had spared no expense in finishing his education.

Cornelius had spent too much time away from him to have for him that easy, unthinking affection that a son may have for his father. Gregor . . . well, it was difficult to know at any time what Gregor was feeling. Rob knew he was capable of deep emotion. He loved his mother with a protective passion that he kept carefully masked. Towards his wife Francesca his public manner was gentle and affectionate but Rob sensed a deep current of devotion between them. He suspected too that Greg adored his children although he never allowed that to appear in public.

And what Gregor felt towards Rob was a totally unknown factor. His manner with him was that of a close business colleague — friendly, frank, considerate and with enough deference to be flattering. Consider it how he might, Rob couldn't see it as filial or loving. But then, with Gregor, you never could tell.

21

The only person on whose love he could depend was Morag, Greg's mother. To her he could always turn for that ready, undemanding response that healed every wound, soothed every hurt. It was the one regret of Rob Craigallan's life that, led astray by ambition, he had married the wrong woman. If he had followed the inclination of his heart all those years ago, he would be sharing this hotel suite with gentle, devoted Morag instead of dragging himself wearily to bed alone.

Lonely . . . It had come to him recently that for all his money and for all the family ties so often spoken of in the gossip columns, he was lonely. Occasional visits with Ellie-Rose or Gregor and their families couldn't compensate for the many, many evenings he spent by himself. There had been years when he had enjoyed that solitude, planning how to extend his business empire, looking forward to next day's forays into the markets of the world.

But now it began to seem less of a compensation for his isolation. He longed to sit with Morag in the twilight, certain of her companionship and her sympathy.

He had a secret plan, not even so far put into words, for a plan once spoken of is somehow no longer a secret − especially in the world of finance. It only needed some slightest hint and it could influence the dealing on the grain markets, affect the price of Craigallan shares. Not that there were many of those available to public bid. Luisa held a few, and so did her brother Julius − these in acknowledgement of the contract Rob had made with her years ago before he set off to start again in the wheatlands. But neither Luisa nor Julius ever thought of selling them. Both his sons, Cornelius and Gregor, had a small block so that they could have voting rights on the board; and a few allotments of stock had been made to former employees. Sam Yarwood too had enough to put him on the board. But the vast majority of the shares were Rob's, and would always remain so, as long as he lived.

This gave him control of the corporation. But over the next two or three years he intended gradually to hand over control to Gregor. He had always meant Gregor to be his heir in the sense of managing the business, but now he planned to let him have it while he was still alive. It must be a gradual process so as not to cause any alarm but when it was done, Gregor would be the effective head of Craigallan Agricultural. With Sam Yarwood's wise old head to advise him on day-to-day matters and Rob still there in the background as a kind of *eminence grise*, Rob felt that Gregor would do very well.

It wasn't only for the sake of tranquillity in the world of big business that Rob intended to be discreet. He knew Ellie would fly to the defence of Cornelius if she realised he was being left out of his plans. Between Ellie and Neil there was a strong affection, going back to childhood days when she had been his only friend. Ellie wouldn't see Neil neglected or insulted. But if Greg took over by degrees, she probably wouldn't even notice.

Neil himself would make no outcry. He was happy enough as head of the research department. He understood, better than Ellie, how difficult it would be for him to control an agricultural empire like CAP. It was the dealing in The Pit that was so impossible for him. The shouting, the instant reaction to word or hint — for Neil these were a hopeless barrier. So it had to be Greg as successor to Rob Craigallan when Rob escaped to retirement.

Escaped . . . He had never thought the day would ever come when he would think of escape. But sometimes he longed now to be spared the need of always being on watch for the slightest alteration in the level of demand, the first sign of conflict either in business or politics, for changes in culture or weather or conditions that would affect the precious grain.

Sometimes he envied Morag in her retreat in the mountains. She was always busy, it seemed. She read, she went to meetings and concerts in the little resort town nearby, she listened to the phonograph records he sent. She walked endlessly on the slopes of her beloved valley. It sometimes seemed to him she knew every whippoorwill that called near the house. She cultivated her garden and was becoming quite an authority on high altitude plants — Alpine gardening, it was called. She never seemed to be in a fret over anything.

Once when he asked her if she ever grew tense or anxious, she smiled and patted his hand. 'Rob, when you've been as close to death as I was, you learn what's important and what isn't. Few things are worth getting in a fret over.'

Perhaps, if he retired and went to live with her on Pike's Peak, he'd be able to adopt that attitude too. His plan included alterations to the house, enlargements so that she wouldn't lose any comfort or convenience. He would ask her to change her name legally to Craigallan. They couldn't be married since his wife Luisa was still alive and well and journeying luxuriously to Europe and back each year, but it would be easier for them both if the inhabitants of Colorado Springs thought he and Morag were husband and wife.

None of this had been spoken of to anyone, not even Morag. He would make each move gently and imper-

24

ceptibly. In two years, three at most, he hoped to be a country gentleman, living in conditions not unlike the Scottish homeland that now seemed so misty and far-off to him. But he would be rich and comfortable instead of living at subsistence level as he had done as a boy in Glen Bairach. And he would make Morag a good and loving husband at last – God knows, somewhat late in the day, but none the less devoted for all that.

Smiling a little now, he got into bed and closed his eyes. He lay for a moment relaxing in the golden glow of his secret plan. Then he opened his eyes and frowned. He wished he had been less thoughtless with Neil earlier on. Sighing, he switched off the light and went to sleep.

The morning papers told him what Woodrow Wilson had decided to do about the Mexicans and their insult to the American flag. *US Navy en route to Tampico!* the headlines announced. *Ultimatum to be delivered!*

When Sam Yarwood came in for breakfast, as he always did during the bidding in the Chicago market, he found Rob deep in the editorials. 'Well, where d'you think Greg is at this moment?' he asked. 'On the high seas with the Navy?'

'No, they're still on their way to the border by train.'

Sam threw himself in a chair and poured coffee for himself: 'How're they going to be allowed in if the United States is at war with 'em?'

'Oh, come on, Sam, we're not at war. We're only making a fist at 'em. You know what it is – Wilson can't stand this guy Huerta who seized power and this whole thing's a scam to get rid of him.'

'You honestly think so?'

'Sure I do. And from the way I hear it, nobody in

25

Mexico loves Huerta very much, so he's likely to get a bullet in the back from one of his own compatriots.'

'Is that what they tell you in the papers?' Sam inquired with scepticism.

'No, it's what Curtis told me on the telephone this morning.' Rob sat back and lit his first cigar of the day. 'The way I see this Mexican foolishness is this — Huerta's unpopular, the Navy arrives in Tampico, boom boom with the big guns and Huerta sees he's likely to come to a nasty end one way or the other. I think they'll get rid of him. Whoever replaces him—'

'Will probably be just as bad!'

'Could be,' Rob agreed. 'So the Navy'll stay there until they put in somebody Wilson likes. It's this way, Sam. The US has got a hell of a lot of money invested in Mexico—'

'Are you telling me? My Mexican Railroad shares have taken a dive these last few days, I can tell you—'

'And Wilson always liked dealing with President Madero. What he wants is to get Madero back in power — though I doubt he'll actually achieve that no matter how many guns they shoot at Tampico.'

'Can't see it matters what figurehead they put in so long as he keeps the oil pumping. That's what matters, really, Rob — to get the oilfields in high production so we have fuel for our automobiles.'

Rob laughed. 'Remember how you protested when I said I was going to invest in automotive trucks, Sam?'

Sam coloured. 'Aw, well, anybody can be wrong once in a while.' He swallowed the remains of coffee in his cup. 'Come on, put your collar on and let's get down to the breakfast room. I'm starving.'

'No . . . If you don't mind, I'll hang on here for Neil. I'd like a word with him in private. But listen,

26

what do you think about Germany?'

Sam let his mouth fall open in exaggerated surprise. 'What do I think about Germany? You kidding?'

'No, go on – tell me what comes into your mind.'

'About Germany? Well, it makes good beer, it has fat opera singers, it's ruled by a guy with big moustaches.'

'The point is, Sam, you don't give a thought to Germany, do you?'

'Why the hell should I?'

'Because I think Kossalof was bidding yesterday on behalf of the German government.'

Sam, who had got up and moved towards the door in eager anticipation of breakfast, turned back and looked at his colleague with alert little black eyes. 'What makes you say so? Kossalof always deals for the Russians.'

Rob explained to Sam what Cornelius had discovered. 'You know the market was upset yesterday, Sam. And the funny thing was, it didn't know *why* it was upset.'

'Oh, come on, Rob—'

'I tell you, everybody I spoke to was puzzled. They went intending to deal, once they got the feel of the trading, but there was very little actual buying when you come to balance it out.'

'But why is the German government buying?' Sam pondered. 'It can't be because they have any problem with their own crops.'

'There are three possibilities, as I see it,' Rob said. 'First, they're going to need extra wheat. Second, they wanted to keep the Russians from buying by pre-empting their usual supplies. Third, they foresee a shortage for some reason on the European Continent.'

They considered these three ideas for a moment.

27

'Say, Rob . . . What you're implying is that the Germans are preparing for a war.' Sam shook his head in doubt. 'I don't see it, Rob. I can't believe those Prussian generals really want to have a go at the Russians. Look what happened to Napoleon when he tried it.'

Rob made no reply. He himself was dubious about his analysis. Yet some nerve in his body was tingling. He sensed that he had come on an important clue about a possible crisis.

'What did Curtis say, then?' Sam inquired.

'He pooh-poohed the whole thing. I didn't tell him all I've told you — I just said I'd got a notion Germany was up to something, stockpiling food supplies. He said the President regarded the whole of Europe as a powder keg but foresaw absolutely no trouble from the Germans.'

'There you are then.'

'Government intelligence has let us down before now, Sam.'

'All the same, Rob . . . this is all pretty vague.'

'I suppose so. All I can say is, I'm going to watch the dealing in The Pit today with a lot of care. I don't want to be caught with low stocks of future wheat if there's going to be fighting in Europe.'

'I suppose there's no harm in taking a look. But don't let's risk any money on it until we've got a lot more to go on.'

The discussion was interrupted by the arrival of Neil, with his latest information on the world grain crop. Winter wheat still only a few inches high, seed recently sown in the furrow, harvests now being brought in in the Antipodes . . . Neil had items of news on them all. He sat down with his father while Sam made off in the direction of his morning bacon and eggs.

'Listen, boy . . .'

'Yes, what?'

'About last night . . .'

'What about last night?'

'What I said . . . about Greg being my right hand . . .'

'What about it? It's true, isn't it?'

'It kind of made you feel you were unimportant, though — didn't it? I'm sorry, Neil. I didn't mean it that way.'

'It's all right,' Neil said. 'I know I'm only your left hand.'

'Don't say that! I couldn't manage without you, Neil.'

'Yes you could. You could hire someone to make an analysis of the probable harvests. It only needs good sources and good statistical arithmetic—'

'But nobody else would feel it so essential as you do, lad. You put your heart and soul into it for me. I appreciate it, even if I'm not so good at saying so.'

'That's all right, Papa.'

'I just wish . . .'

'You just wish I had my hearing, is that it?' Neil shrugged. 'I know, I understand. It's a terrible handicap if you're looking for someone to bequeath an empire to. Gregor's a better heir to the throne. I accepted that a long time ago.'

For a long moment they stood regarding each other. Then Rob put his hand on his son's shoulder. 'You're a good man, Neil. You don't even resent it, do you?'

Neil shook his head. 'One of the things you learn when you have to struggle with a handicap is that it's no use wasting energy on resentment. Besides, I owe

29

Gregor my life. If he hadn't come to look for me in Manila, I'd be dead by now.'

'So you don't mind letting him displace you as heir apparent to CAP?'

'I didn't say I didn't mind, Papa. I said I accepted it. Come on, let's get down to breakfast.'

He turned on his heel and went to the door. Because he was deaf, he didn't hear the sound of distress his father made.

For the next couple of days Rob watched the dealings on the Board of Trade. Slight hints made him sure that he had guessed right, that George Kossalof was buying through his assistants on behalf of some client other than the Russian government. On the Wednesday a dealer generally at the services of several clients came into the ring and seemed to be buying with a singularity of purpose and a haste which made Rob suspect he was the replacement of Kossalof hired by the Russians.

On the Friday Rob took action. Although he had sold much wheat, he now began quietly to re-invest in the future harvest. Sam Yarwood, uncertain, hovered about making deals and then re-selling, but in the end during the following week he took the same line as Rob. It was done so discreetly that few noticed it, and those that did were only slightly interested: Rob Craigallan off on some tack of his own, probably profitable but not worth following now that the main dealing had been done for the spring.

In June the New York newspapers contained a shocking and extraordinary report: the Archduke Ferdinand of Austria and his wife had been assassinated at Sarajevo by a Bosnian revolutionary. The item was read with interest by most people but soon forgotten. Rob, just back from a stay with Morag in

Colorado Springs after delivering Francesca and her children there, was as little able as anyone else to see where the event might lead. It was no use trying to make head nor tail of these Balkan politics – it was a mish-mash of little countries all seething with hate for everyone else.

Greg was back in town. He and the presidential team had had a lively time in Mexico. President Huerta had run off when the United States Marines landed, to be succeeded by General Carranza. The general, a sensible man, had realised there was no chance of winning if there was actual war with America and had begun peace talks at once. Greg had acted as interpreter and go-between where necessary; a document was now being drawn up by the legal department so his services were no longer required. Glad to get away from what he later described to his father as 'a hot and dirty madhouse', he was merely dropping in at Craigallan Castle to hear all the family news before taking the train for Colorado.

'I had a drink in the Biltmore with Sam last night, Mr Craig,' he said. 'He tells me you bought in a lot of wheat in April.'

'Yes, I had a feeling it would turn out to be a good idea.'

'The price seems to be fluctuating a lot?'

'It's a hell of a mess,' Rob agreed. 'And the Stock Exchange is uneasy too. I wish I knew what it all meant.'

'Are you going to go ahead with those new silos in Texas?'

'I think so.'

'That seems to mean you think we'll be storing grain in big quantities.'

31

Rob nodded.

'Storing it. Because we shan't be able to transport it?'

'I think there may be hold-ups – bottlenecks . . .'

'But why? What makes you say so? Transport's getting easier and cheaper all the time. Why should we think we'll be storing grain?'

Rob gave a little laugh. 'I don't know, boy, I really don't. I just feel it in my bones. We're going to need those silos because something's going to go wrong with the shipping of grain.'

Greg said no more for the moment. He had a respect for his father's instincts. In a few more days or weeks Rob would either be proved right or he'd take steps to rectify his mistake. All the same, the cost of the new silos was high – he hoped the cost was going to be justified.

Thankfully he took himself off to Pike's Peak next morning, eager to be re-united with his wife and children, and to see his mother.

Francesca ran down the path and threw herself into his arms when he stepped down from the wagon that had brought him up the mountain roads. '*Mi corazon!*' she cried, hugging him close to her. 'Oh, how thin and tired you are! It is almost the same as when we were prisoners together in Manila . . . Dearest, come in, Madre Morag is longing to see you.'

'How is she? How are the children?'

'All well, as I wrote you. Did you get my letters? I wrote every day!'

'I don't think I got all of them. I hope you got mine – the postal system in Mexico is hopeless but I was able to put some of them in the diplomatic pouch . . .'

The children, who had been held back by his mother,

broke free to throw themselves on him. Lewis wound himself round his father's legs. 'Did you bring me back a present?' he asked. After every parting, Papa always appeared with presents.

'Oh, what a mercenary! Well, well, let's go indoors and perhaps we'll find something for you. And you too, Clare – and Mother. How are you, Mother? You look well . . .'

The hubbub of arrival and the distribution of presents was over at last. The children sat down on the floor to play with their new toys, Clare already trying to discover how to unfasten the gaudy clothing of her Mexican doll, Lewis making his exquisitely made leather horse gallop all round the room.

'Are you here for the rest of the summer?' Morag inquired hopefully. Francesca found New York and Chicago unpleasant in the extreme heat of July and August, so that Greg often brought the family here. But sometimes they went to the coast instead, and last year there had been some talk of going to California. Among the ancient Spanish families who still held sway there, Francesca had a distant cousin who wanted to offer hospitality.

'I'd like to stay a while, Mother, that's unless Mr Craig needs me. I do feel kind of weary, I must admit. Vera Cruz is an uncomfortable place at the best of times, I imagine, but having to be up and about at all hours of the night and day while negotiations went on – or stopped short . . . Well, I can't say I fancy the life of a diplomatist, if it's always like that.'

'But you're pleased with the result.'

'Oh, sure. The President had us in the Oval Office when we got back and congratulated us. A man would have to be very cynical not to be pleased about that.'

'I have a high regard for Mr Wilson,' his mother said. 'I may be wrong, but I think he has a high moral standard.'

Greg grinned. 'Oh, Mother, you're so eager to think well of everybody! Woodrow Wilson is a politician, and probably no better than any other. But I admit he looks different, with those professor's glasses of his . . .'

At last it was time for bed. Gregor took Francesca into his arms in the quiet, flower-scented room and found solace for all the weeks he'd spent away from her. When at last they lay exhausted and comforted with her head on his shoulder, she murmured: 'You won't go away again, Gregorio? I missed you so.'

'I promise,' he said.

That was in the early hours of the morning of the 4th of July, a suitable day on which to be happy and to celebrate love and the joy of living. On the 6th, Greg took his family into Colorado Springs in a hired carriage, to spend the day. After ice-creams in the cafe of the resort hotel, the children elected to be taken to see the aquarium. On the way out of the hotel Greg paused by the newspaper stall to buy a paper. What he got was the Chicago *Tribune* of the previous day.

'Damnation!' he exclaimed.

'Greg!' scolded his mother, laying a hand on his sleeve.

'What's wrong?' asked Francesca, astounded by such an outburst from her normally self-contained husband.

He pointed to an item in the stop-press column. *General V. Huerta re-elected President of Mexico. Peace Treaty Jeopardised*.

His wife's hand tightened on his arm. 'You won't

have to go back, Gregorio?' Her great dark eyes were fixed on him, liquid with tears of foreboding.

He said nothing. He couldn't be sure what the government would decide to do now. He could only wait and see.

He made the trip into the town every day to get the newspapers. And as the month went on, the importance of events in Mexico began to fade like a flower in front of a furnace. Greater, more tragic events were taking shape.

As a result of the murder of the Archduke Ferdinand at Sarajevo, the Austrian government declared war on Serbia. Russia, allied with Serbia as a fellow-Slavonic nation, began to mobilise her army. Germany ordered Russia to cease this mobilisation. The month of July tottered to its close.

Gregor telephoned his father from the hotel lobby. 'What d'you think is going to happen, Mr Craig?'

He heard a snort of angry amusement on the other end of the line. 'Now you know what those silos were for, Greg.'

'You mean you foresaw this?'

'I didn't foresee how it was going to blow up. But I knew an explosion was near, yes.'

'Father, what's the United States going to do? What does Curtis say?'

'We're going to remain strictly neutral, my boy — thank God, because it's the neutral who inherit the earth.'

'You mean stand by on the sidelines and make money?'

'Can you think of a better way to handle it? None of it concerns us, after all. I don't care whether Russia fights Germany or Serbia fights Austria — do you?'

35

'No-o, I suppose not.'

'Damn right, you suppose not. You could perhaps feel a bit involved in that nonsense in Mexico because they were people whose language you spoke and whose traditions you shared to some extent through Francesca. But we've got nothing in common with that bunch of snarling dogs.'

'Do you want me to come back to New York?'

'I reckon it would make good sense, Greg. There's going to be chaos in the markets – a big upset has started already but it's nothing to what will happen when the armies really begin to move.'

Greg stood with the receiver to his ear, trying to imagine it. He had seen guerrillas in conflict in Manila, and Mexican troops whirling about in the dust around Vera Cruz. But great armies from great nations, marching and counter-marching on the great European plains – what would that really be like? He shivered.

'I'll have to talk to Francesca and Mother. They'll be upset. They were looking forward to a long holiday together.'

'I'm sorry. You've had almost a month. Unless you still feel run-down I'd like you here, Greg.'

Francesca, biting her lips on her tears, finally agreed to go with the children to her cousin, Don Pedro, in Monterey. Morag volunteered to go with her as companion and helper. The next day was spent packing. On the evening of the 2nd August Greg put them all on a train heading west from Colorado Springs for the eight hundred mile journey to Monterey. An hour later he himself set off for New York, fifteen hundred miles in the opposite direction.

When he stepped down from the train in Pennsylvania Station he saw the unbelievable headlines on the newspaper boy's placard: *Belgium Invaded. England Declares War on Germany.*

It was the 4th of August, only a single month since he had been reunited in love with Francesca. Then, he had been sure that his country had avoided a war, and had been happy.

He was wrong. His country, and the whole world, was heading towards a disaster from which it would never recover.

Chapter Three

Rob Craigallan wasn't by any means a good Republican. It was just that the Democrats seemed even sillier than the Republicans, and the Democrat President even sillier than most.

So it came as a considerable shock to him to find he was approving of Woodrow Wilson. *Total Neutrality*, the newspapers announced. That was to be the US line now hostilities had broken out in Europe.

'Do you really think we'll be able to stay neutral?' Cornelius inquired when they read the report. 'I mean, there are a lot of immigrants in America who'll feel strong ties with the Allies—'

'And a lot who'll feel strong ties with Germany. How many guys do you know who're called "Dutch"?'

'You going to talk it over with Curtis?' Greg asked.

'I thought we'd both go to Washington. We need to get the feel of government opinion. What d'you say?'

'Washington in August?' groaned Greg.

'Ain't life hell?' Rob riposted.

Greg hated the prospect of having to go the rounds of the political clubs, the bars, the restaurants and hangouts of the lobbyists . . . But he had to keep reminding himself that he had nothing to complain about. True, he was parted from Francesca and the children, but that was by their own choice and only until the summer heat on the eastern seaboard slacked off. There were men in Europe now, torn from their families and facing each other behind guns — that was what really mattered.

By now Ellie-Rose too would have gone with her children to the mountains. But because of the growing crisis she had sent Gina and Curt on without her. She was thankful to see her father and half-brother. Curtis had been quite hard to live with these last few days. He represented a farming constituency, which was having a hard enough time already without a war to complicate matters. His constituents were up to their ears in mortgage and foreclosure — yet he had to please the bankers of Nebraska too. So far he had not been able to sort out whether the European war would be a help or a hindrance — and the uncertainty made him fractious.

And there was something else, something more deeply personal. Ellie-Rose, who knew him as well as she knew herself, and perhaps better, was already aware of it. He was too courteous with her, too attentive. He brought her little gifts such as flowers and candies.

'Honey, you don't have to bring me a present just because you couldn't make it to the theatre,' she protested after the first few times. 'I understand — the debate went on longer than you expected.'

'This political merry-go-round sure plays the devil with family life,' Curtis said, looking apologetic. It was Sunday, they were just home from the obligatory attendance at church. He had stopped the carriage on the way home to buy her a dozen roses.

'But it's always been like that.' Unable to resist it she added wickedly, 'Why does it bother you all of a sudden if you miss out on one of our social commitments?'

He was flustered. His fresh-skinned face coloured up. He busied himself stripping off his yellow chamois gloves and putting his cane in the hall stand. He glanced about and gave a gusty sigh. 'I do appreciate the way you run this place, dear,' he remarked, side-stepping her question. 'It's so . . . so restful.'

'Of course, Curtis. You need peace at home, when you're so busy elsewhere.'

His colour became even rosier. He avoided her eye. She took pity on his consternation. 'I want you to be happy, Curtis,' she said, taking his arm and going with him into the drawingroom. She thought to herself as she sat down across from him: Yes, I want him to be happy. I don't want him to make a fool of himself. Please, Curtis, be very, very careful.

She had too much sense to be hurt over what she suspected. Nor would she condemn him, although she felt his present actions were silly and undignified. She only wished she could tell him that she understood. She too had known what it was to be drawn to someone outside her marriage — but she couldn't help believing that her husband's present involvement was a more shallow thing. Her own memory of secret love was harrowing, searing: she couldn't imagine that Curtis would ever experience anything that would sear him. Except, perhaps, disgrace or rejection at the polls.

'Darling, how would it be if we packed up and went on vacation?' she suggested. If she could get him away, perhaps the problem would die away.

'But . . . you know how tied up I am in the Senate.'

'But you've been working so hard—'

'Well, that's politics, Ellie.'

'Oh, darling, the prairie senators could manage without you for a week or so.' She knew this was true.

Curtis was a popular man — valued by his electors, respected on Capitol Hill, but not indispensable. She willed him to accept her suggestion, to step back from an involvement that would only do him harm.

But he shook his head. 'I don't think so, honey. It wouldn't look good if I shucked off the tariff opposition on someone else. You go, though, if you feel you need the break.'

The last thing Ellie-Rose wanted was to leave him alone in Washington. She smiled at him and picked up a Sunday newspaper. 'It was just an idea,' she said. But the casual manner hid a deep regret. She was fond of Curtis — too fond to want to see him make a fool of himself.

When her father came to her boudoir for early morning coffee with her the day after his arrival, Ellie-Rose told him straight out: 'He's having an affair.'

'Curtis?'

'Yes.'

'How do you know?' Rob was astounded. He'd never thought his son-in-law the type to stray.

'Oh, it's easy to tell. He's not very good at subterfuge.'

'Who is it, do you know?'

'An actress who came here in June with a stock company, Marie Marwood.'

'Oh, an actress. So it isn't serious—'

'I don't know whether it is on his side, but Marie's serious enough. She views Curtis as a meal ticket from now until she gets that starring role she knows is just around the corner.'

'Ellie!' her father said in reproach.

'What's the matter? You think I sound sceptical? Perhaps I am. I certainly don't think she's head over heels in love, if you want my opinion.'

'And Curtis?'

'Well, he's head over, but not quite heels up. He's got enough sense to keep it quiet. His voters in Nebraska would have him out at the next election if he were known to be going around with a scarlet woman.'

'So you're not worried . . .'

'No, but I'm depressed, Papa. Is this what life is all about? Holding a family together when the father is playing around with someone else? Furthering his career when he himself is endangering it?'

'Oh, poor little girl,' he said and put his arm around her shoulders. She was clad in a soft silk morning robe of the palest green. Under it she wore several layers of crêpe-de-chine petticoat trimmed with lace at every available point – neckline, hem and edges. On her feet were little block-heeled slippers of green velvet embroidered in silver thread. The notion that she was in any sense a poor little girl was absurd, and the words produced the laughter Rob had hoped for.

He and Ellie and Greg shared one talent: they could look real life in the face. If Ellie's marriage was less than perfect, she had the honesty to acknowledge she had never expected miracles. Morag had warned her in her gentle way that she ought not to be in a hurry, that some day she'd meet a man whom she could love with completeness and joy. In the end, Morag had been proved correct: Ellie had met and loved Tad Kendall. Yet that had not been until five years after her marriage to Curtis. Ellie knew she could not have waited that long as an unmarried woman, aware of the pity or amusement of her contemporaries at her failure to land a husband.

She had married Curtis because the time had come

for her, in her position in society, to be married. It had been in every way a good match: she could help Curtis's career with money and with the considerable powers to please which she could bring into play. She had liked Curtis well enough. Moreover, he had excited her physically, and she had had enough experience of physical love to know that this would be an important ingredient in her marriage.

It had been pleasant to know that Curtis had loved her almost to the point of adoration. He still loved her, she was sure of that. But more than fifteen years of marriage had brought them to the point where love had more to do with fitting into each other's ways, being the parents of their children, depending on each other for social standing and support, than with passion.

Every morning she had to make a conscious effort to begin to sparkle. Some foolish reporter had once named her 'the glowing Mrs Gracebridge', so now it was her role in life to be always full of gracious vitality. No one knew the effort it cost her − not even her father, not even Morag. These two were the people to whom she turned with her confidences and her occasional anxieties, but not even to them had she admitted the deepening depression that was creeping over her.

What was it all for, after all? To help Curtis campaign for or retain his seat in the Senate. Why did Curtis want to stay there? So that by and by he might stand for Governor of Nebraska. Because it was a useful step towards being nominated Republican candidate for President.

And if Curtis ever became President − what then? More speeches, more openings of exhibitions, more balls for diplomats and politicians, more hand-shaking . . . She would be by his side, always appearing delighted at his success, ready to cope with every little contretemps, making friends with the wives and sweethearts of the voters, bestowing kisses on the children, receiving deputations of anti-drink campaigners, women's rights supporters, soothing, chatting, smiling . . . Smiling, always smiling.

She had begun to feel she had nothing to look forward to. Other women would have ridiculed her — she, who might one day be First Lady of the Republic! Even if that prize eluded Curtis, he would almost certainly be a state governor. Surely that was worth looking forward to?

But for the moment everything else took second place to the events in Europe. 'Curtis is very worried,' she told her father. 'They all got a big fright, you know. I don't think anyone — not even Bryan, not even the President himself — expected the Germans to seize on the Sarajevo pretext in the way they did.'

'Oh, Bryan,' snorted Rob. 'What does he know? He's a hick, even if he is Secretary of State now. A man who stood — how many times? Three? — and never made it to the Presidency. All Bryan was ever good for was rabble-rousing speeches. I don't suppose he even knew where Serbia is!'

'Did you, Papa?' she put in wickedly.

'Well, no. But I'm not Secretary of State.'

'But you didn't expect the Germans to jump in like that, now did you?'

'As a matter of fact . . . yes, I did,' he replied, with some complacency. 'And in confidence I'll tell you something, Ellie. I stand to make quite a lot of money out of it. I foresaw they were up to something and I bought good stocks of futures in army supplies. Now I'm going to sell them on the rising market, and it'll make my banker very happy.'

'In other words you're going to profiteer.'

Rob grinned. 'I'm only a profiteer to a man who didn't have the sense to make a profit. To everybody else, I'm a very shrewd fellow.'

She shook her head at him. 'I won't make critical noises. I understand you didn't want this war nor encourage it. But I'd be careful who else you mention it to, Papa. Some of the liberal thinkers in the Democratic Party are very shocked at the way things have turned out in Europe. They're quoting that thing of Grey's, about the lamps going out.'

' "The lamps are going out all over Europe: we shall not see them lit again in our lifetime." ' Rob sighed. 'That's kind of a depressing thing for a man to say when his country's just going into a war.'

'Well, thank God at least we shan't be involved,' his daughter said.

She was wrong, however. As the weeks went by foreign envoys came to Washington to look for support for their cause. It became more and more clear that even if the United States intended to be neutral, the neutrality would be tinged with a rosier hue towards one side rather than the other. Everybody wanted to buy supplies – guns, ammunition, ships, trucks, horses, provisions.

Despite Ellie's injunction to her father that he might be accused of profiteering, she found that most American businessmen were only too happy to sell at inflated prices. And the government encouraged them. A faint hint came down from above: the President was better pleased if deals were done with the Allies than with the Germans.

Accounts in the newspapers, together with confidential reports from the embassies in both Paris and London, told of a growing anxiety in Europe about the food situation. Ellie heard that the radicals in London, furious at the lack of supplies at prices the poor could afford, were threatening to storm the elegant food stores in Piccadilly and Knightsbridge.

'It seems so wrong,' she murmured. 'When we have plenty here . . .' She thought of the food that went out of her own kitchen into the trash bin. 'Oughtn't we to send them some of our surplus at low rates, Papa?'

Rob shrugged. He wasn't going to talk hard cash to Ellie when she was in this sentimental mood. If she really imagined he had made a corner in the wheat market so as to dump the stores on the Allies at less than cost price, she was greatly mistaken. But there was no question that there was a great need in Europe, and that America was in a position to supply it.

He changed the subject momentarily. 'Curtis still seeing that actress?'

'Yes, though how he finds the time I don't know.' She smiled and shook her head. 'Love will find a way, they say.'

'You doing anything about it?'

'What should I do? Have a confrontation? I think that would only make matters worse.'

'Is it generally known?'

'I think not, Papa. No one has been nudging me about it and you know, there's always some kind friend wants to put you wise about a thing like that. So I gather Curtis has managed to keep it a dark secret.'

'Except from you.'

'Yes, except from me.'

Her father took a pace or two about her drawing-room. 'Are you worried about it?'

46

'Not for myself. I understand what's caused it. Our marriage has become a bit . . . mundane. It's natural Curtis should look about him for a little excitement. It's Marie Marwood who worries me. She doesn't want to let go—'

'You mean you think Curtis does?'

'I've no idea. I told you — we haven't discussed it. But I've taken the trouble to find out a little about her, and she's reckoned to be determined, clever and patient. She's only twenty-three so she can afford to wait and see how things go. If she were offered a big part on the New York stage or a chance in the cinematographic industry, I think she'd be off like a shot. But you see, Papa, the longer it goes on the more chance there is of discovery, with all the damage that could do to Curtis.'

'Yeah,' Rob agreed. 'I mean, lots of congressmen and senators have their little fancy pieces, and nobody cares. But Curtis has built up his reputation on the notion of the bright clean boy from Nebraska — his voters would burn him on a slow fire if they found he was cheating on them.'

'That's what I think.'

'I'll see what I can do, Ellie.'

'How d'you mean?'

'Well, I don't have any friends in the cinema world, but surely it can't be so difficult to find someone who'll offer her a part?'

'Preferably in a theatre in San Francisco, Papa!'

'I'll bear it in mind.'

But his efforts came to nothing. Although it wasn't difficult to scrape up acquaintance with theatre producers in New York, he discovered they were canny fellows. They would, of course, offer a part to a pretty and talented actress — but only if her friend or protector was willing to invest money in the show. Rob had no wish to throw money away on stage productions. He was prepared to take gambles in the world he knew, but the theatre was totally strange to him.

He thought it over for a week or two. By then, Christmas was coming on so that by comparison the news from Europe seemed darker and more tragic.

The German army had rolled through Belgium to Ghent and Lille, prevented from reaching the Channel ports only by the barrier of the River Yser. The battle to keep them on the far bank had lasted fourteen days; the casualties had been horrific. An American war correspondent, taken to visit a famous hotel in Paris transformed into a military hospital, sent back a report on what he'd seen. Christmas decorations put up by the mobile patients: *A Merry Christmas to our Doctors, Sisters and Nurses* spelled out with cotton wool stuck on a banner of green baize from the hotel's former stores. There was no heating; open braziers of coke had been brought in, extremely dangerous but necessary to make work possible in the bitter Parisian winter. A sad little Frenchman, his right arm gone, had told the reporter he didn't know what had happened to his wife and children. 'The Boches swept through our district — but I wasn't even there, I was in a trench at Ypres!' His story could be repeated a hundred times, the account noted, as could the story of the ugliness of war, the miseries of days under fire, the deafening bursts of the shells, the fear, the horror of seeing other men hit — killed or mangled by distant guns. The troops slept in trenches or gun pits, with little or no shelter from the rain that drenched the north of France that winter.

It was impossible to read it and be unmoved.

President Wilson read it, and many other reports coming through to him from diplomatic sources. He could not be involved in the actual fighting but he wanted to help in any other way he could. He didn't want to be accused by the opposition of risking American neutrality so it was necessary to have an all-party discussion on what could be done.

The upshot was that he suggested a delegation to go to Europe, to send back week-to-week advice on what to ship for the use of the Allies. Food, naturally, came high on the list. Informal feelers were put out to ask the advice of businessmen who knew the food markets.

Rob was approached. Would he come to a confidential meeting at the Senate Reception Room, to offer opinions on how to proceed? He surely would.

It was a long evening. What emerged at the end was that both Democrats and Republicans were invited to submit names for a bi-partisan group which would leave America early in the New Year for Europe. One section of the party would be based in London, one in Paris − or wherever else the French government settled, although at the moment it had returned to Paris after a frightened scuttle to Boulogne. Another group, less active, would go to Berlin.

Rob had no difficulty in getting Curtis Gracebridge's name included in the list. He was an eminently suitable candidate, the senator of a farming state interested in the sale of supplies to Europe. He could be spared: his seat in the Senate was safe, and though he took an honourable share in committee work none of it was nearly so urgent as knowing what to export to Europe and in what quantities. The demands from the buyers were enormous − but they mostly wanted credit. Part of the task would be to evaluate the credit-worthy status of the Allies and how much to believe them when they said they were desperate for meat or sugar.

Christmas came and went with its usual family gatherings. Gregor brought Francesca and his children to Craigallan Castle but this year Curtis went home to Nebraska with Ellie and Gina and young Curt. Rob didn't protest: in view of the fact that Curtis might be going overseas quite soon, it was only fair he should spend some time with his parents, who were getting old and crotchety.

Cornelius was at the Castle too, taking part in amusing the children with amateur conjuring tricks. Skilled in laboratory work, his hands were amazingly quick.

'Pity he doesn't marry and have kids of his own,' Greg remarked to his father, watching him mystify Lewis by the disappearance of a dime into the little boy's ear.

Rob shook his head. 'He's a settled old bachelor by now.'

'Don't say that, Mr Craig. Men have married at forty before now.'

'Who's he going to marry? He doesn't meet anybody worth making the change for.' Rob glanced towards Greg's wife, helping her little girl to master the intricacies of a new mechanical toy. 'You've been lucky, you found just the right girl. Neil did too — but that all went wrong.'

'Stephanie wasn't the right girl, Father. She was bound to fall apart some time — better that it happened before Neil persuaded her to marry him.' The events that had broken up Neil's romance with Stephanie Jouvard would never fade from their minds, for they had been bound up with an accident to Ellie-Rose that nearly lost her her second baby. His mind moving towards Ellie-Rose in this train of thought, Greg added: 'You didn't put up your usual snarl of annoyance when Curtis suggested Nebraska this year?'

'No, I had my reasons.'

'Really? Do tell!'

Rob grinned to himself and selected a piece of candy from the silver dish at his side. 'I think I'm getting him packed off to Europe.'

'What?' Greg started. 'On this bi-partisan delegation from the Department of Agriculture?' For a moment he couldn't take it in. 'But why? Oh yes — I see. You want him to keep an eye on the wheat interest for you. Yes, it makes sense. But what's Ellie going to say?'

'I don't think she'll mind too much. It's a great honour to be sent on a special Presidential delegation, after all.'

'Well, I guess so . . . All the same, it's a long way. I know Ellie and Curtis don't spend too much time clinging to each other these days, but are you sure she'll want a whole ocean between them?'

His father didn't confide that Ellie might be quite pleased to have a whole ocean between Curtis and Marie Marwood. That wasn't something to be discussed, even with another family member, even with a man as discreet as Greg. When the news was made official on the 4th of January, he felt that his daughter would have a sense of relief — that the Gordian knot had been cut, that Curtis would be removed from the scene of temptation without any scandal.

Rob had no doubt that Curtis would accept the post. He wasn't enough in love with Miss Marwood, from all he could gather from Ellie, to want to throw away a chance like this — a chance to stand out from his fellow

51

senators, to be reported not only in the American papers but in those in Europe. An international standing was no small help to a man with ambitions towards the White House.

No matter how attractive Marie Marwood might be, she couldn't match up to the chance of distinguishing himself in special government activities. Curtis would undoubtedly take the post abroad.

What Rob Craigallan had not foreseen was that Ellie-Rose would insist on going with him.

Chapter Four

They sat side by side on the sofa in the elegant Washington drawingroom, Curtis looking proud and happy as he held Ellie's hand.

'Ellie feels — and I think she's right — that if this mission lasts three or four months, or maybe even six, it's too long a separation. It was her own idea that she should come with me. But of course I'll be delighted to have her support and help while I'm operating in a totally strange environment.'

'Well . . . er . . . yes, I can see she'd be a help. There'll be entertaining to do, I suppose, even in a London at war. But . . . but . . . what about the children?' Rob faltered.

'That's no problem. We've talked it over — haven't we, children?'

Obediently young Curt said, 'Yes.'

'They'll be in school, you see,' Curtis surged on. 'So it's only having someone to supervise them and take care of them on weekends. I telephoned my parents but they felt it was a little too much for them at their age.' Gina made a sound which seemed to imply she was just as glad about that. 'So Ellie's written to Morag, and we've no doubt Morag will agree to come and act as foster-mother to our two chicks.' He gave a fond smile to the two chicks, who responded each after their own fashion — Gina pouted and Curt looked anxious.

'But Curtis, you know the climate in Washington doesn't agree with my mother!' Greg cried.

'Oh, come on, Greg — she won't be here during the hot weather, which is the time she can't endure the place — and who can? We always leave for the mountains ourselves in July. And of course by July we'll be back again and Morag can go back to her mountain hide-out while we carry Curt and Gina off to their holidays.'

Greg blew out a breath and went to stare out of the window at the fine sugar maples in the garden, bare and leafless now in the January wind, their twigs whipping to and fro.

'Everyone says the war will be over by the summer,' Ellie reminded them. 'So there's really nothing to worry about—'

'Everybody said the war would be over by Christmas, but it's getting worse, not better.' Greg turned back. 'I marvel at your agreeing to take your wife to a war zone, Curtis.'

'Ah, but it's London, you see, Greg. Nothing bad is happening in London. If it had been Paris, now . . . that would have been different. I shouldn't have cared to take Ellie to a city where the guns are so near. But London — what can happen to London? But I will confess I'd never have thought of asking her to come. It was her suggestion.'

Greg eyed his half-sister. He always suspected her of being clear-headed and cool rather than sentimentally affectionate. It could only be that she wished to snatch this excuse to travel — many American women had this feeling that Europe was the home of culture and tradition, that to be unacquainted with it was to be imperfectly equipped to lead society.

Certainly she could be a help to Curtis Senior, who had never left American soil and never expressed any wish to do so. Greg would not have thought to argue against it if his mother had not been called upon to care for the children. He knew she would accept the task, and that the children would benefit from her gentle but firm control. He simply felt that it would be tiring, and certainly not good for her if she stayed on into the sultry heat of Washington.

But, as Curtis said, they would be back by summer. Ellie was probably wrong in expecting a cessation of hostilities by then, but the US government wouldn't expect their delegates to stay longer than six months. So he said nothing more in disagreement at their plans.

It was Rob who pursued the argument when he got Ellie-Rose alone that evening in the interval of a play at Harper's Theatre. 'What's the idea, Ellie? Are you scared to let him out of your sight?'

She shook her head with some indignation. The diamond drops at her ears shimmered in the subdued light of the theatre box.

'Strange though it may seem to you, I feel it's my duty to go.'

'But why? The other wives aren't going, are they?'

'Perhaps they can't afford the expense. It means taking an apartment in London and of course paying for an additional passage.'

'I can understand that money might prevent Welboven from taking his wife, and Potter. O'Brien, of course, is a bachelor. About the others I don't know. They'll be sore as hell to think you're going and they're staying home.' He paused. 'Is that why you're doing it,

Ellie? To be one up on the rest?'

'No, Papa. I never even thought of it till this moment. Perhaps I've been tactless on that score . . . No, I really felt I ought to be with Curtis. He's never been abroad before. And you know . . . in some ways he's still a country boy at heart.'

Rob gave a snort of disbelief. 'Come on, don't try to kid me, daughter! You know as well as I do that Curtis can adapt himself to any circumstances. I agree you'll be a help and comfort to him in London, just as here, but he doesn't really need you all that much.'

'Has it occurred to you, Papa, that I need him?'

There was a little silence. From below came a rustling as the orchestra filed back into the pit. 'No,' Rob said, 'that hadn't occurred to me, I admit.'

A violinist below began to try out a soft series of notes on his strings. Ellie took her time before she went on.

'This thing with Marie Marwood shook me more than I thought it would,' she said at length. 'I hadn't understood how far we'd drifted apart. It's not that I'm jealous − I don't want you to think that! My feeling has been more . . . that I'm disappointed, puzzled. And when Curtis was offered this chance to do something a little special, I suddenly saw it as a chance to make a new beginning. Perhaps our marriage needs a shake-up like this, Papa.'

The steamship *Baltic* was waiting for them at South Street Pier, New York, busy with the loading of medical supplies and beset with eager young men in ill-fitting uniforms, members of an American volunteer ambulance corps. The band on the quay was playing melodies from the Lilac Domino. There was an atmosphere of urgency and optimism, almost of good cheer. Hardly anyone seemed to remember that the country to which they were sailing was a country at war.

Rob, who had come to the docks to see them safely to their stateroom, watched Ellie-Rose glance about at the bower of blossoms sent by friends. She took up the champagne from its cooler and poured three glasses, one each for her husband, her father and herself.

'Safe voyage and success in the job,' toasted Rob.

'Thanks, Father-in-law. This is a good time to say I've always appreciated all you've done for me.'

'Think nothing of it,' Rob replied, wondering what Curtis would say if he knew Rob had put him where he was, in this stateroom on this ship heading into the Atlantic where warships were on guard.

There had been a little flurry of naval activity at the beginning of January. The British battleship *Formidable* had been sunk in the English Channel. During the fall, the *Emden* had been sunk. But these were both in far-off waters, and no one was causing any anxiety or distress to merchantmen.

All the same, it was a little scary to be sending your only daughter off where cannons and fieldguns were in action, where grey ships hunted the enemy . . .

Rob wished with all his heart that he had not manoeuvred his son-in-law into this post with the Agricultural Commission. But it was too late to regret it now. He raised his glass in salute, shook hands with Curtis, hugged Ellie-Rose, and took his leave as the steward went his rounds chanting, 'All ashore that's for the shore, gangway clearing, all ashore that's quitting for shore!'

He stood on the quay to watch them come on deck to wave. Streamers were thrown from ship to shore, the band changed to *Auld Lang Syne*, there were cries of 'Goodbye, goodbye!'

Rob took off his hat. When Curtis and Ellie waved, he waved back. He stood watching until the *Baltic* had moved out of her berth and was edging out into the Narrows.

Then he turned abruptly and walked to his limousine. 'Where now, sir?' asked his chauffeur.

'How the devil should I know?' Rob snarled. 'Anywhere, so long as it's away from here!'

On board, Ellie and her husband turned away from the rail and made their way below to see if the stewardess had begun their unpacking. The cocktail hour was approaching and while it wasn't thought proper to dress for dinner on the first evening out, nevertheless it was only seemly that they should change into something appropriate for drinks with the officers. They were honoured guests, members of a governmental party and, as the shipping company's publicity manager had already warned, important in their own right as the son-in-law and daughter of Robert Craigallan.

They arrived at Liverpool on an incoming tide in the dark of a January evening. Their passage through the Customs shed was speeded by an anxious young consul. Baggage loaded aboard the southbound train, Ellie and her husband took their seats with his colleagues in the specially reserved compartment. There were five men including Curtis, but it didn't embarrass Ellie to be the only female. She had found the men easy to handle, eager to be courteous and considerate to this brave little woman who had elected to follow her husband in the wars.

And wars there certainly were. Terence O'Brien had

58

bought newspapers before boarding the train, which they now seized on as they waited for dinner to be served in the restaurant car. In the two weeks of their crossing from New York, during which time the captain had thought it advisable not to alarm his passengers with any unpleasant tidings brought to them by the ship's radio, two very disagreeable things had happened.

The most recent was the sinking of the German cruiser *Blucher* off the Dogger Bank. So far as they could gather, this had happened two days ago − while the s.s. *Baltic* was nosing her way into British approaches. It was a startling thought that had their ship been headed not for Liverpool, but for London, they might have been on the outskirts of a naval battle.

Worse yet were references back to events which seemed to have happened during the preceding week. Censorship made the accounts difficult to follow but it seemed that German airships had dropped bombs on the ports of Britain in an area known as East Anglia. 'Dropped bombs,' Ralph Potter snorted. 'It's a propaganda yarn! How on earth could an airship drop bombs!'

'I suppose they had someone in the basket-thing they carry underneath an airship, pushing them over the side.'

'But . . . good jumping Jonathan! Bombs are heavy! How could a lighter-than-air construction carry a bomb?'

'Darling,' Curtis said in Ellie's ear, 'don't let it frighten you. It's just some scheme to stiffen morale among the people by making them think badly of the Germans.'

'I'm not frightened,' Ellie-Rose said with perfect

truth. 'Even if it's true, I'm not frightened — I mean, who could possibly hit anything, throwing things down from the air — it's ludicrous.'

The train steward came by at that moment, calling second service for dinner in the first class restaurant. They rose and made their way along the lurching train. Ellie-Rose thought the carriages in the first class part of the train very elegant, and the restaurant even more so with its little shaded light at each table, its glowing napery and cutlery, and dark rose velvet chairs. If, when she found the cutlery not to be silver and the flowers to be artificial, she was a little disappointed, she was prepared to make allowances. After all, there was a war on. Whether or not the clever Germans had found a way to carry bombs in the air and drop them on land targets remained a dubious point, but the food served at dinner seemed proof enough that Britain was at war. Only three courses, and those with little choice between dishes . . . Well, one must be tolerant.

She slept well in the sleeping compartment, a compact and quite attractive little room she shared with Curtis. When she woke next morning, it was to find Curtis accepting a tray of tea and thin biscuits from the steward. She blinked, half sat up.

'What time is it?' she inquired, yawning.

'Six o'clock.'

She sat up, glanced in a mirror to make sure her boudoir cap was still prettily tied, and accepted tea from Curtis.

'Where are we?' she inquired.

'Nearly there. The steward says we get in at seven o'clock.'

That meant they mustn't linger over the early morning tea. It was surprisingly good. She was to learn soon that the same could never be said for the coffee, in almost any British establishment.

Curtis dressed first and went to join his colleagues in the day compartment. Ellie was still tying the tabs of her silk blouse into a becoming knot at her throat when the outskirts of London began to glide past the window. They didn't seem inviting — but then what could, in the steady drizzle now descending? The trees in the gardens were bare except for the evergreens, which showed almost black against the dark grey sky. There was no snow, which surprised her a little — New York had been deep in sidewalk snow-piles. The grass on the little lawns was a strangely vivid green in the dawn light. She was to learn later that the greenness of England conquers almost everything, even the surly, dismal weather of winter.

Euston Station was a surprisingly impressive place, older than the stations of New York and Chicago — almost cathedral-like in its architecture. It was thronged with people in uniform. The soldiers in their rough, hairy khaki she pitied at once — how uncomfortable that woollen cloth must be against cold wrists and necks! The sailors looked saucy and confident in bell-bottomed trousers and slim-fitted blouses, but it amused her to see how the trousers were creased in squares along the lines where they had been folded.

But what interested her more were the women. There were many of them in uniform too — brownish suits with flat peaked caps that made them look something like female chauffeurs. Or grey-blue raincoats, strictly tailored, with a velour hat trimmed with a band bearing a red cross. Or dark blue, with many buttons, and a wide-brimmed rather hard-looking felt hat — these, she guessed, were women policemen.

61

'Well, what d'you think?' Curtis said, as he took his wife by the elbow to guide her towards the ticket barrier.

'Aren't the skirts short!' she murmured.

If her husband thought it a strange first impression of London at war, he said nothing.

But though he didn't recognise the fact, Ellie-Rose had put her finger on a turning point in social history. If women wanted to 'do their bit', as the typical British understatement had it, skirts which dragged on the pavements or restricted the stride to only eight inches were an obvious hindrance. If one wanted to take a civilian job so as to free a man to join up, there would be a need to jump in and out of automobiles, clamber on and off omnibuses, run up and down stairs in offices. Shorter skirts became a necessity.

For the first time, women of the middle and upper classes adopted a style not because of the dictates of fashion but from sheer commonsense. If their menfolk objected they had the perfect answer — 'You're being unpatriotic.' So there was much twinkling of feet and ankles in sensible little low-heeled lace-up boots; kid gloves, until now *de rigueur* even in winter though helped on by fur muffs, were replaced by masculine-looking gauntlets. Dark colours were preferred for day wear, perhaps because gaiety seemed inappropriate but also because it implied less need to launder white trimmings and delicate fabrics. Hats, which until then had been rather small with much befurbishment of veil and side feathers and fur pom-poms, became broad-brimmed and rather severe because they kept off the rain and shaded the eyes while driving.

Ellie-Rose was astonished to see so many women driving cars. Each woman was of course releasing a man for the forces, but even so, the ease and mastery they showed was a revelation to Ellie. Her household in Washington owned two cars: it had never occurred to her to learn to drive either.

It took her two or three days to settle into the house taken for them in London. It looked narrow and restricted, with no garden in front and no porch, the door opening straight on to four steps going down to the pavement of Ebury Street, Victoria. But the rooms were unexpectedly well proportioned, high ceilinged and with windows that reached almost from floor to cornice. There was a small garden at the back, gracefully adorned with marble urns full now of rather dead-looking ivy but which could be brightened with geraniums for summer. The single tree delighted her by putting out clusters of little creamy-white blossoms while the weather was still chill and unrewarding in March.

The house had been taken furnished. The furnishing was rather sparse to Ellie's American eye, but good — mostly antique pieces, worn but fine carpets on polished boards, and dark rich curtains either side of deep window recesses, the windows themselves veiled by starched lace curtains looped up with satin bands.

For the first few days Curtis was seldom home. As informal chairman of an informal delegation, he went with his colleagues to be briefed at the Embassy, first by the Ambassador himself and then by the attachés — military, naval and commercial. He came home in the evenings ready only for a bath, a drink, and light meal, and a night's sleep.

Ellie used the interval to get staff hired: a cook-housekeeper, Mrs Towers, her husband as valet for Curtis, a superior housemaid, and a personal maid for

Ellie, Beading. At first Ellie was alarmed by Beading; she was older than the maids she generally hired to attend her, and talked very fast in an accent Ellie could make nothing of. But by and by her ear became attuned. She discovered that the accent was refined Cockney and that if you let the rapid rhythm guide you, you could catch the important words. Beading, for her part, seemed wary of her new mistress, 'one of them foreigners', as she'd remarked to Mrs Towers.

It was over clothes that they came together. Four days after settling into the house, with her belongings now unpacked and put away, Ellie went one morning to the cheval mirror in the bedroom. There she took hold of the wide frilly skirts of her negligee, folded them back against her legs, and raised them so as to expose her feet and ankles.

After consideration she decided there was nothing there to be ashamed of. She rang for Beading. 'Beading, I want you to bring in a dressmaker and have the skirts of all my day clothes shortened by four inches.'

'Oh, madam, you don't need a dressmaker for that. I can do it,' Beading replied, keeping her thin features under control so as not to show she was affronted.

'You can? But it would take forever! And I want to have something ready to wear this afternoon.'

'If madam will just show me which dress she wishes to wear this afternoon, I can have it ready by lunchtime.'

'Beading!' Ellie cried. 'Are you sure? I mean, haven't you plenty to do without that?'

'Madam, I am in the middle of pressing the clothes to refresh them after being in the cabin trunks. I can just as easily press them after taking up the hems, and as for

64

the needlework itself, I can do it by stages.' She drew herself up. 'I am a fully competent ladies' maid, madam.' She pronounced it 'lidies' mide', but worse was to come. '*Habile pour tout*, as the French say.' This came out as 'Abble por too' and caused Ellie some problems for a moment.

But she had gathered that Beading's pride was involved. She was struck by the fact that this thin little woman would rather sit sewing for hours at a time than admit she needed help in her work. Respect made Ellie give a little nod of agreement. 'Very well, Beading, I leave it to you.'

And in fact, the fawn walking costume was ready at two when she came upstairs after lunch to change for a visit to an Embassy wife who lived in country charm at Hampstead.

It took Beading two weeks to shorten the skirts. Ellie understood that to offer a money tip would be considered bad form. She thought it over and bought Beading a handsome umbrella with an ivory handle. The maid accepted it calmly, gave a little curtsey, and left. Ellie-Rose thought perhaps she had made the wrong choice. But glancing down from the front door steps later that day, as she left for an engagement, she saw Beading in the area outside the servants' entrance, the umbrella open to be baptised by a few spots of rain then falling – and the manner in which the other woman was flirting her shoulders to and fro told her that Beading liked the gift.

Now that the newcomers had been given a decent interval to settle in, invitations deluged down upon them. First there was an informal dinner at the Ambassador's, then a tea with the wife of the first assistant, then a soirée with other members of the ambassadorial staff. All the American set in London invited them. There were luncheons and coffee-parties and cocktails with Lady Paget or Mrs John Astor, invitations to shoot in the country from Lord Wolseley, to ride, to visit the coast from other members of society. Miss Phyllis Dare sent tickets for the theatre, Miss Olga Lowenthal left tickets for a concert conducted by Thomas Beecham. Ladies telephoned Ellie with suggestions for shopping expeditions or tea at Gunters.

The American Agricultural Delegation now had its own office in a building rented by the American Embassy for ancillary purposes. It was in Belgravia, convenient walking distance from the house. The other members of the group had rooms at Claridges which, though pleasant, was not like being at home. They tended to gather in Ebury Street in the evening when they had no other appointments, to talk long over bourbon and cigars. Ellie fitted up a room as a study with comfortable armchairs so that the men could be at ease. So it happened that she herself sometimes went out in the evenings on invitations to which Curtis felt no pressing need to give personal attention. These were mainly at the homes of women who interested themselves in good causes or women's rights. Such things were no part of Curtis's brief; he was glad to weasel out of them when he could.

She was at the London home of Nancy Astor on an evening in late April, to show willing over some charity connected with Nancy's hospital work. She had met this American bird-of-paradise soon after her arrival in London, for Nancy made it her business to contact every useful and influential newcomer.

The event had been described as a 'working party

with buffet'. The purpose was to arrange transport for wives and sweethearts visiting men convalescent after war wounds in the home set up for them in the grounds of Cliveden, the Astors' house near Maidenhead. When the business of the evening had been dealt with, Nancy waved them to a large, rather gloomy room where food was laid out with footmen waiting to serve.

Ellie selected some cold game pie and salad. The guests broke up into groups. Ellie found herself next to an elderly man with pince nez, who introduced himself as Walter Runciman, President of the Board of Trade. This title gave them pleasant conversation for a few minutes, Ellie explaining that in the United States the Board of Trade was not a government department but the place where trading in grain took place in Chicago.

He said politely, 'My work has little to do with dealing in that way, as I expect you know, but trade is the lifeblood of this country, Mrs Gracebridge. The Cabinet is very anxious that the delegation headed by your husband should be given every help in furthering—'

He broke off as raised voices were heard across the room. Their hostess was speaking to a woman a little above medium height, dressed in a dull evening gown of beige crêpe which did nothing for either her colouring or her figure.

'We must be austere!' Nancy was proclaiming. 'We must not increase the burden of the poor by indulging in luxury! No one can accuse me of being unaware of the plight of the poor—'

'Is this your idea of austerity?' inquired the young woman in beige. Her quick awkward gesture took in the sparkling array of silver dishes on the serving table, loaded with cold food of every kind. 'There is enough here to feed the women at my factory for—'

Two other ladies joined them to speak in soothing tones. The rest of the conversation was lost by the wall of bodies they presented, and in any case the argument, if it was an argument, seemed to have died away.

'Who is that?' Ellie-Rose inquired.

'Oh, Sylvia Pankhurst, of course, making a nuisance of herself as usual.' Mr Runciman hesitated. 'But perhaps you're a campaigner for women's rights too, Mrs Gracebridge?'

'Not at all. My husband finds activities of that kind unhelpful.'

'Quite so,' Runciman said, with a little smile of approval on his pale face. 'In that case, I'd advise you to avoid Miss Pankhurst, for she will talk you down until you feel like a trampled weed' – he recollected himself – 'that is, if anyone so beautiful could ever be thought of as a weed, dear lady.'

She decided she didn't greatly care for Mr Runciman, whose tone was patronising, although he was unaware of it. Since he'd warned her not to talk to Sylvia Pankhurst, she felt inclined to do so just to show him she quite capable of having a conversation with a politically minded woman without being talked down. So when a little later the ebb and flow of the groups brought her next to Miss Pankhurst, she introduced herself.

'Oh, dear me, Mrs Gracebridge, there's no need to tell me who you are!' exclaimed the other woman with a little frown between her high, fine brows. 'You are often spoken of among the people whose help I'm forced to seek.'

'Now that's irresistible. Why am I spoken of?'

'Because your husband has so much influence – he

and others like him. Are you aware, Mrs Gracebridge, that since the war began, the price of wheat has gone up to sixty-one shillings a quarter-ton, almost double the price? Can you imagine the dreadful impact this has had on the food budgets of the poor? A loaf of bread used to be fourpence-ha'penny – now it costs sevenpence, but wages haven't gone up, Mrs Gracebridge, not at all!'

Now Ellie understood what Mr Runciman had meant but she refused to give in to his view; this woman talked fiercely and without consideration for her hearer, but at least she was not just making conversation.

'Didn't I hear you speak of "your factory"? The wages you pay are up to you, surely—'

'Oh, good lord, we only pay what we can! It's almost a charity you see – a toy-making factory to give employment among the women—'

'Toys? You make toys? That can hardly be much help to the war effort?' Ellie interjected, glad to feel she would score a point.

Sylvia Pankhurst drew herself up 'But I, Mrs Gracebridge,' she said in her crisp, clear voice, 'I don't support the war effort.'

Despite herself, Ellie gasped. 'You – you don't?'

'Not in the least. I regard it as a huge, senseless waste that will bring nothing but tragedy, especially to the women I am pledged to help.'

'You're a pacifist?' Ellie was both shocked and puzzled. She was certain she had seen letters in the newspapers from Miss Pankhurst, calling on women to come to the aid of their menfolk in this gigantic struggle. 'I seem to remember reading in *The Times*—'

'Oh, that was my sister, Christabel. She is rabidly in favour of the war. She has influenced my mother in the

69

same way — it's rather like your Civil War, Mrs Gracebridge, when families were divided for and against.'

Ellie couldn't see the similarity. It seemed to her that Miss Pankhurst's view amounted almost to treason — and yet here she was, accepted with tolerance by the present company.

'You don't feel it unpatriotic to criticise your country's actions?'

'Oh, you know what Dr Johnson says!'

Ellie checked herself on the verge of replying that as yet neither she nor her husband had needed the services of a medical man. 'You mean Samuel Johnson,' she ventured. 'What did he say?'

'That patriotism is the last refuge of a scoundrel.'

'Oh!' Once again Ellie was shocked. 'Oh, I don't think that would be very popular in my homeland! We're kind of strong on patriotism.'

Miss Pankhurst glanced with dislike at their hostess. 'So I gather,' she said. Then recollecting herself, 'But it's understandable, perhaps. To be devoted to the flag is more necessary, in a young nation like yours—' She broke off, colouring a little. 'I beg your pardon. You have probably had that said to you rather too often since you came to London.'

'That my country is young? Why, no, I don't believe anyone has said it. But if they did, I shouldn't take offence. We're fond of saying it ourselves, you know — congratulating ourselves on how young and vigorous we are.'

'Indeed? We, on the other hand, continually congratulate ourselves on how old and proud we are — but it always seems to me we have little to be proud of if innocent women and children starve and their husbands

70

join the army merely to put bread into their mouths.'

'Miss Pankhurst!'

'You don't believe me? You should come to my settlement in Poplar, Mrs Gracebridge, and speak to the families there. It would open your eyes! But then, I daresay you have many claims on your time already, and have worked among the less fortunate at home in the States — you know the conditions.'

Ellie-Rose didn't want to admit she was only on the periphery of social work back home. She agreed that she was on the committee of various good causes and added: 'I've helped Gertrude Dorf of the American Garment Workers—'

'Ah, you know Miss Dorf? I've never met her, of course, but we've corresponded! She is a remarkable woman! Tell me, is she feeling better? Last time she wrote, she was suffering from an ailment brought on by dust from the fabrics.'

It struck Ellie now that she had sailed from New York without ever taking the trouble to look up Gertie. But she tended to keep her distance from that formidable lady, because to be with her reminded Ellie only too poignantly of their first few meetings, which had been in the company of Tad Kendall. Ellie tried never to think of Tad. It still hurt too much.

She confessed she couldn't give any recent news of Gertie Dorf and escaped from Miss Pankhurst. Nancy Astor descended on her, pretty and fair as Dresden china and lovely to see in a pale grey-blue silk dress.

'My dear Mrs Gracebridge,' she said in a tone of mock sympathy. 'I see you had a set-to with the redoubtable Sylvia. I'd have rescued you but you seemed to be holding your own.'

'She's all right,' Ellie-Rose replied, annoyed by the

71

other woman's assumption of superiority. 'She says people are starving . . . Can it be true, Mrs Astor?'

'Well, I imagine they aren't getting much jam on their bread. That's why I was saying I shall embrace austerity — it's only right that we should spread the problems of the war fairly among the rich and poor. I wish there was something I could do for poor dear Sylvia—'

'She could always use money, I imagine.'

'Oh yes, but then . . . My husband doesn't want me to be too bound up with her on a personal level. Her views about the war, you see . . . It's quite shocking that she speaks so strongly against it. She's almost pro-German at times.'

'What about this factory of hers?' Ellie said, avoiding personal gossip about Miss Pankhurst. 'It makes toys?'

'I believe so. I think, in fact, I've seen some of the products. Cut-out toys, you know — Noah's arks and dancing bears with jointed limbs — that kind of thing.'

'How about buying some of them? There's always some child you can give a toy to.'

'Oh dear. I don't know that I myself would . . . Well . . . perhaps if a group of us . . . But then if we go down to Poplar to look at the toys, she'll keep us there the whole day and introduce us to every socialist in the district!'

'Couldn't she bring the products here, Mrs Astor? Here we all are this evening, for example — if you had suggested she bring some toys, she might have sold quite a lot.'

'My dear, can you *imagine*! You can't exactly spring wooden toys on a Cabinet Minister and people like that . . . But it's a thought, after all. It's a thought, dear Mrs Gracebridge. I'll keep it in mind.'

A few days later Ellie-Rose received a note from Mrs Astor. She had spoken to Miss Pankhurst and invited her to bring a selection of the toys made at the Poplar factory to a weekend party at Cliveden, the Astors' country house. In view of the fact that dear Mrs Gracebridge had put the idea into her head, would Mrs Gracebridge and her husband like to be of the party? It would include Arthur Balfour and Lord Eustace Percy, among others.

'What do you say, Curtis? Would you like to go?'

'Well, the weather's improving and a break from the city would be kind of pleasant, Ellie. And I'd sure like to meet Balfour – he's a big wire-puller, from all I can hear.'

They went down to Maidenhead by a mid-morning train on Saturday and were collected by Mrs Astor herself at the station. Others who had come on the same train were also collected as they appeared – Ellie-Rose descried the upright, slender figure of Sylvia Pankhurst and a young woman of about the same age accompanying her, bearing between them a large cardboard box presumably containing the toys from Poplar. Nancy Astor waved at a footman to take it from them. It was loaded into the big motor car, almost as big as a small omnibus, together with the two young women, two young men in smart civilian suits, a young man in naval uniform, Curtis and Ellie, and Nancy herself.

The house was a magnificent place, about three miles out of Maidenhead. A flock of servants was waiting to help the guests out of the motor car and deal with their luggage. 'So much for austerity,' said Sylvia in Ellie-Rose's ear as they went indoors, where a huge roaring fire welcomed them.

73

There was a flurry of quiet conversation among the women of the house after the butler had spoken in private to Nancy. It was learned later, after Nancy and her sister had hurried away, that a telegram had arrived while the train was being met: one of Nancy's beautiful sisters had lost a friend at the Front. It cast something of a pall over the lunch that was served almost at once, at which Major Astor excused the absence of his wife and sister-in-law: 'Nancy's comforting her, you know.'

The afternoon was spent in listening to Sylvia Pankhurst explain the existence of her toy factory, the hard grey life of the East End which she tried to alleviate by giving employment and a small wage. 'You must understand there is almost no work for women, and what there is is of the lowest kind and so badly paid – they are household drudges, washer women, errand girls, charwomen . . . Yet they have talent, you know! All our toys are designed by them, we employ no designers, not because we don't want them but because we can't afford them. The women do it all themselves. This toy' – she held up a plywood ballerina, brightly painted in sugar-icing colours and worked by little tongs – 'this was designed by a girl who used to work as a sausage filler—'

The rest was lost in a little gust of laughter. The speaker coloured up but retained control of her temper. 'Yes, an amusing occupation, though someone has to do it if we are to eat sausages for breakfast. Ada, however, lost her job when her employer decided to close the factory so as to go in with a meatpacker working on government contract. So now she designs these little toys, and Carrie and Dolly and Aggie paint them and pack them and trudge round the big shops trying to sell them. What I'm trying to say to you is that these girls, these women, have unsuspected abilities. Inside their thin, poor bodies there is a sparkling spirit crying for release . . .'

Her listeners were touched. Ellie-Rose saw, looking round the big drawingroom of the country house, that the well-dressed women summoned here by Mrs Astor were enjoying the notion of helping the unfortunate denizens of London's East End. Sylvia had wit enough not to touch on politics or pacifism. She merely described the hardships she was trying to alleviate, and asked for the patronage of the audience in buying the toys or giving a donation.

Curtis had gone for a walk with some of the other male guests while this appeal to the good nature of the women was taking place. 'How'd it go?' he inquired.

'Pretty well, I think. How about you?'

'Oh, I had a long talk with our host. He's a nice guy — quieter than his wife, so far as I can see. She sure does talk up a storm, doesn't she? But it's tough luck about the boy-friend—'

'I wonder if Phyllis will join us for dinner?'

'Astor seemed to think so. He says she's being awfully brave about it. Gee, Ellie, I understand now why I've met a bit of anti-American feeling since we got here. They must think we're chicken, standing outside watching while they're in the ring getting killed.'

Ellie studied her husband's troubled face. He had put on some weight since their marriage but he was still a fine, tall, handsome man. His eyes were shadowed now by this close contact with the cruelty of war. 'That poor little girl,' he murmured.

Nancy's sister Phyllis appeared at dinner. Ellie-Rose was struck by the fact that both she and her sister had gone into mourning, black dresses of fine silk with exquisite ruffles of white chiffon which, by chance, enhanced their delicate flaxen fairness. Was it possible that they had mourning wear in their wardrobes, all ready for when the casualty lists were published? She shivered at the thought and was glad to busy herself with her dinner neighbours.

Next morning it was taken for granted that the house party would go to the parish church, although Mrs Astor was a Christian Scientist. They walked, since the spring day was very fine. Ellie-Rose was taken with the Anglican service, especially the singing of the choirboys who looked like angels in their white surplices. The singing in the Methodist church back in Washington left a lot to be desired, although the hymns were more fun. The sermon, of course, was about the duty to serve one's country. Names of local dead were given: Ellie was horrified to realise that in this small neighbourhood, six young men had died since the war began only seven months ago.

Lunch was another plentiful meal. In the afternoon they were all bidden to the nursing home in the grounds, where wounded soldiers were being cared for. Here, for once, Mrs Astor was stayed: the matron told her in sharp tones that the patients were resting and could not be disturbed. Even Nancy Astor could not get past her. 'Well, we'll walk around to cheer up those who are mobile,' she said with an airy gesture, and led her guests away.

Tommies, in the hospital blue suits that were already becoming only too familiar to Ellie, were sitting about in wheelchairs or moving cautiously on crutches on the lawn. Some already had visitors, either friends who had come from home or acquaintances of Mrs Astor's who made it their business to drop by when they could, in hopes of helping to pass time for the men.

One patient was sitting at a table in the sun, his head bent over a game of chess with a tall thin man in a dark suit whose back was to Ellie-Rose. The soldier moved his knight as Ellie drew near, so she paused while his antagonist pondered how to respond.

'Oh, now, I'm so glad you're heading this way, dear, because I've just remembered here's a fellow-American I ought to introduce,' cried Mrs Astor. 'Ellie-Rose, let me present Mr Thaddeus Kendall.'

The man playing chess rose and turned.

Ellie found herself staring at Tad, the man she had loved so deeply, the man who had turned his back on her all those years ago.

Chapter Five

A diversion was created by the soldier-patient, who tried to struggle to his feet in honour of the ladies. In doing so he jostled the little table so that the chessmen went over. Tad busied himself in a useless effort to keep them upright. By the time he straightened again, Ellie-Rose had regained her composure.

Mrs Astor had been occupied in cooing and scolding the patient to sit down again. Now she looked around. 'Tad probably wants to talk to you, Mrs Gracebridge – it's years since he was home.'

'Mr Kendall and I were acquainted back home, Mrs Astor.'

'Really? What a marvellous coincidence! It must have been a long time ago, though. You've been here for years, haven't you, Tad?'

'Quite right. I almost consider myself a Londoner these days.' He had given Ellie a little bow. 'I saw in the newspapers that you had arrived, Mrs Gracebridge.' He was waiting for Ellie to claim the degree of acquaintance.

'Mr Kendall and I knew Gertie Dorf,' she explained to Mrs Astor. 'We helped organise a benefit concert for her union.'

'Did you indeed! My word, Ellie-Rose, you have hidden depths! I never knew you were interested in public affairs to that extent.' She meant, in any way that didn't further her husband's career.

The danger point was past. It was now established that Ellie and Tad had known each other slightly in days gone by over matters of public interest. Ellie remarked that they ought not to interrupt the chess game any further and moved off. Her smiling farewell masked a feeling of shock and something like panic.

For the fact was that now she had seen his face again she knew that she still loved him.

He had disappeared from her life at the climax of a passionate affair which was rending them in two. Then, for the first time in her life, she was in love. She had given herself to Tad without reservation. But she didn't want to hurt Curtis, who at that time was a good and faithful husband. To run away with Tad Kendall would have meant a scandal, and the voters of Nebraska would soon have let Curtis know what they thought of a man who couldn't keep his wife in order. Moreover, even if she had had the cruelty to leave him, she couldn't leave her children. Little Curt had been so delicate and frail – he needed her more than Gina, but even Gina, sturdy and independent, held her rightful place in her mother's heart. Time and again Ellie went over the arguments and told herself it was wrong, it was unfair, to deceive Curtis. She must tell him the truth and go.

But time and again her heart broke at the thought and she kept her secret. She never knew that it was her father who solved the problem. He told Tad that he was killing her with the torment of indecision and offered him a job in San Francisco as some reparation for tearing them apart.

Tad had refused the offer. But a week later Ellie-

Rose received a brief letter. He told her he had been asked to go to London to do a study on the criminal courts of Britain for his law firm. He had accepted. The work would take him a year. But even if he came back at the end of that time, he felt they shouldn't meet. The relationship had to end. There was no alternative that he could see except misery for innocent people. He gave her no address to write to and though in the end longing overcame pride, her discreet inquiries resulted in nothing; she would have had to address her letters in care of his New York partners and that idea was abhorrent.

She had tried to hate Tad for leaving her. She had blamed him then, and blamed him still. He had made his decision without consulting her. Commonsense would murmur at this point that if he had consulted her she would have begged him not to leave her and they would have been locked once more into the agonising struggle of the previous months. His ruthlessness had put an end to an impossible situation. She understood but she could not forgive.

To see him again like this, so unexpectedly, was like putting out her hand to touch a twig and finding it a searing brand. The pain was intense. She got through the rest of the visit to the hospital with her face fixed in an interested smile that made her cheek muscles ache. Presumably she talked sense, for no one looked at her with surprise. But what she said she could never recall, nor how she managed to stroll unconcernedly back to the great house.

She was glad that Curtis had already said he wouldn't be able to stay until Monday morning, as some of the guests were doing. She got through the cocktail hour and dinner without betraying herself. At nine o'clock, with many cries of regret from Waldorf and Nancy Astor, they were put into a comfortable saloon car and taken to Maidenhead Station for the London train.

'My, she's some girl, that Nancy!' Curtis sighed as they settled in their compartment.

'Very capable,' Ellie-Rose muttered.

'And with those looks! Her sister too − there's a real American beauty!'

'Yes, the family deserves its fame for its looks.'

'The house is great, but a bit overpowering, wouldn't you say?'

'I expect it has more warmth in summer.'

'You all right, Ellie? I thought you'd be all a-twitter with interest over meeting two girls from the Langhorne brood!'

She roused herself to respond to Curtis's own interest in the weekend. But she was thankful when the short train journey was over and they stepped into a taxi at Paddington with their luggage strapped on top. She was able to admit then that she had a slight headache and wanted an early bed.

By ten-thirty she was lying between the sheets with the lights out. Beading had insisted on bringing her a hot drink with two aspirins but she had left them on the bedside table. Curtis was still downstairs enjoying a Bourbon-and-water and a last cigar. She heard him go to the telephone to arrange some matter with his colleagues for the next day. When he came upstairs at last she felt him lean over her. She pretended to be asleep. Satisfied, he moved away. She heard him in his dressingroom humming to himself as he got ready for bed. Soon his side of the bed was weighted down as he got in and not much later his steady breathing told her he was asleep.

The house was silent soon after. The light from a street lamp illuminated the room vaguely with a beam that lay across the windowseat and part of the floor. Above her, the ceiling with its Georgian cornices and central rose of plaster gleamed a creamy white. She heard a brougham draw up nearby, the sound of horses moving restlessly as the passenger alighted and then the brisk trot as they headed for the mews stables and rest. She rose from her bed to tiptoe to the window, to lean her head against the cool glass.

Inside her head Ellie could hear Tad's voice: 'Mrs Gracebridge and I were acquainted back home . . .' And then: 'I saw in the newspapers that you had arrived . . .'

So he hadn't forgotten her. He had been interested enough to take note of her imminent arrival. He hadn't intended to see her, though − he had been staggered when they were brought face to face in the hospital grounds. She had learned from Mrs Astor that he, together with other men who for one reason or another were not in uniform − for instance, their health didn't meet the service requirement or they were foreign nationals − had volunteered to come visiting. Their masculine companionship perhaps provided a change from the well-intentioned Florence Nightingale attitude of some of the women.

She gathered that he came every second Sunday. She must take good care not to accept another invitation to Cliveden on a Sunday, for he might be there, and if she saw him again she didn't know if she could support it.

But, surely, if he had any decency he would take steps to stay out of her way. It was he who had broken off their affair, he who had simply gone away − now it was up to him to keep things stable.

He had clearly settled down in some law firm — she had no idea where or how. Criminal law in England was very different from the States: he must have changed course since she knew him. Could he have done that simply so as to stay away from New York?

That argued a strong urge to be near her which he had to fight by tying himself down to work elsewhere — an urge sufficiently great that it needed him to change the basis of his career. Her heart gave a lurch at the idea, and she gripped the knob of the folded-back shutters convulsively. Did he love her still? He certainly wasn't indifferent — that had been clear from the pallor of his face when he recognised her.

She found herself praying: Oh God, give him back to me. But as soon as she became aware of the thought she crushed it down. She mustn't think like that! Hadn't she come to England with Curtis for the very purpose of putting the life, the meaning back into her marriage? And besides, she must never forget that Tad had walked away from her.

Why? Why? Perhaps his patience had run out — her continual struggle to weigh her family against their love for each other, her anguish and uncertainty . . . She knew that men could become bored with a woman who was always unhappy. Had she become too much of a burden for Tad?

She drew in a deep, unsteady breath. She wondered if she could survive the tension of knowing he was not far off and yet never within her reach. Perhaps she should tell Curtis that she was homesick or that she felt guilty at having left the children. Perhaps she should go home.

She had been here a little over two months. She could say that she had seen Curtis safely settled in, that she had done some entertaining for him, that it was time to go.

Yet they had accepted many invitations on the understanding that she would be here with Curtis all the time, and there were still many instances of hospitality that she ought to return. Curtis on his own would be unable to do it — and what, after all, was the point of his staying on in the Ebury Street house if she left? It was absurd for him to stay with a staff of four servants all alone in a town house when he might be more comfortable and certainly more convenient in a hotel. In a hotel, his entertaining would be limited.

He could always explain to the various ladies who expected dinner parties that his wife had gone home. How odd that would seem . . . As if they had had a quarrel, or as if she was so weak-kneed that she couldn't exist without her children.

No, she wouldn't have people thinking that of her. She had had to put up something of a fight to persuade others she should come to London. She couldn't make a fool of herself by packing up suddenly and going home.

She would stay, and she would avoid Tad Kendall. If he had the intelligence with which she credited him, he would take care not to accept invitations where they might be together. And if she did meet him, she would treat him with polite composure. An occasional hand-shake, a bow across a room or a nod in passing in the street — she could do that without coming to pieces with emotion. Now the first surprise was over, she was armed against him.

Oh, but if she had known he was still here in London . . . ! She would never have come with Curtis, if she had known. She had always presumed he had finished his year of special study and gone home, perhaps not to New York, although that was possible, for she moved in circles where he would seldom be. It was a long time since she'd ceased looking for his name in the law reports in the newspapers, or glancing through the passenger lists of arriving liners to see if his was there.

It was over. He had ended it. The fact that they happened to be Americans in London at the same time meant nothing. On her part there must be no longing, no looking back to what used to be. Just this one night, while her husband slept in their bed and she stood here in the yellow flicker of the gaslamp — she would think about the past and arm herself for the future. Then never, never again would she let Tad Kendall dominate her heart and mind.

This resolve took her through the next day, and the next, and the next. She busied herself with Curtis's affairs and played her part. There was much to occupy them, and there was news, bad news, about the war.

It had gradually become known that merchant shipping losses were increasing. Now it was announced that the German Navy had put a blockade around Britain using the submarine. Dreadful tales were told of the frightening craft surfacing to finish off a ship already wounded by torpedoes: some said crew and passengers in life boats were under fire from the submarine's guns. Ellie-Rose, influenced by Miss Pankhurst's convinced internationalism, at first refused to believe the stories. 'It's propaganda, Curtis, it must be,' she insisted. 'We know people back home of German stock — they would never do this kind of thing.'

'But we never knew them in a war, Ellie.'

'You mean you believe it?'

'It's not so much what I "believe". It's the hard evidence that they seem to have at the Embassy.' Curtis sighed and reached for the port, an English after-dinner custom he had embraced with pleasure. 'I reckon there must be something in it.'

Ellie shook her head. Sylvia Pankhurst was sceptical. She too would remain unconvinced until she met a survivor who vouched for those horror stories.

But soon after the lovely month of May had begun to turn London into a wonderland of blossom trees, she had proof. There it was in the *Times*. US vessel Gulfflight *sunk by U-boat without warning*. She gripped the newsprint convulsively. It must be true. The ship was named, the information came via the United States Mercantile Department.

A cable came from her father, via the diplomatic bag. *News very grave, much bad feeling here. Are you all right*? She replied at once that she was fine, though distressed. Should she come home? – for here perhaps was an excuse to leave London, with its dangers of an encounter with the man who had been her lover. Rob's reply came at once over the diplomatic cable: *On no account! Stay safe and sound in London. Letter follows*.

His letter never reached her. It was among the US mail loaded on the *Lusitania*. The British liner was sunk off the coast of Ireland with the loss of nearly twelve hundred lives, of whom a hundred and twenty-eight were American. A family known to Ellie-Rose went down with her – mother, father, and two children aged eight and nine.

A shock of revulsion seemed to go through the world. Curtis came home early from his office the day the news was given, and said in a tone of disbelief: 'The Ebbertons, Ellie . . . They were on her.'

'Yes, I had a letter from Morag last week telling me all the gossip and she said . . . she mentioned . . .'

'Us fellows here for the government have decided to go into mourning for a week, to show our respect and . . . well, kind of go along with the British on this, because they've lost a hell of a lot of innocent people on this one.'

'You want me to go into black too, Curtis?'

'I think it would be appreciated, Ellie.'

Now for the first time, she understood why Mrs Astor and her sister had black dresses in their wardrobe. If death could strike like this − out of the blue, clutching up innocent families as well as soldiers and sailors − then black would become a commonplace. Ellie had no black clothes, but the resourceful Beading sewed black braid on a grey day costume for the time being, and Ellie ordered a readymade gown in Debenham and Freebody's for that evening. A day dress would be made for her overnight, which she would wear tomorrow. These three items, with a black hat with black veiling and a black parasol, would see her through until the week of mourning was done.

As luck would have it, she had agreed to go down to Poplar to see Miss Pankhurst's toy factory. Wearing her black dress and with her parasol to protect her from the sudden sunshine, quite intense, of the May weather, Ellie daringly went out and took a bus. She had almost never used public transport and certainly not abroad − not until she met Miss Pankhurst.

'But my dear Mrs Gracebridge, if you go everywhere in a taxi or a limousine, you will never get to know anything about the real world,' her new friend urged.

'You say you wish to see something of my work among the poor — what will you understand of it if you merely come by car, look around, buy a few things and are driven away?'

'But I'd get lost if I came on a bus, Miss Pankhurst—'

'Are you so timid that you can't ask directions?' Miss Pankhurst frowned at her in reproach. 'All you need do is go to the bus stop, board a bus for Old Ford, and ask the conductor to put you down near No. 400 — he'll know the place if you say it's the women's factory, everyone knows it.'

It still seemed a hazardous undertaking to Ellie, but she was ashamed to shirk it. It was certainly true that since she came to London she seemed to be infected with a new sense of freedom. When she saw other women, often younger than herself, calmly swinging on and off troop trains, handing out travel passes to the servicemen, or ushering pedestrians across roads, or driving mobile canteens, she began to be irked by the narrowness of her own activities.

What did they amount to, after all? Each day she got up — early, it was true, because both she and Curtis had farming backgrounds — and had coffee in her boudoir while she prepared to face the world. Then she breakfasted with Curtis and read the newspapers so as to be able to discuss them with him and his friends and guests. When he had gone to the delegation's office, she saw the housekeeper to order meals for the day and give any necessary instructions. She might make alterations to the flower arrangements or take a stroll in the little garden. By about ten she would be out on the day's engagements, mostly with wives of other politicians or businessmen. Unless Curtis specifically said he would be home, she would take luncheon with friends.

In the afternoon, perhaps she would attend some gathering — a recital in aid of a good cause, a lecture . . . Or she would visit an exhibition, or be shown round a hospital or an orphanage or a hostel for business girls . . . By four she would be drinking tea, the inevitable afternoon activity of the British, and nibbling tiny triangular sandwiches offered on a lace-paper napkin on a silver salver. By five she would be home to change. Either there would be friends coming for drinks or she and Curtis were expected elsewhere. Then dinner, then bridge and conversation, or a theatre, or time alone in their drawingroom while Curtis mused over his reports.

It was a busy life. Yet it was sheltered. Never did she have to lift a finger if she didn't want to. When she wished to go out, she told the manservant, Shields; he would step outside and hail a cab, or telephone for a car which could be at the door within minutes. She didn't even know the way to the Post Office: Shields took the letters twice a day. Had she cut her finger, she wouldn't have known where to find sticking plaster without calling her maid.

Hitherto she had never thought to question her way of life. But wartime London seemed to put an invisible pressure on her to bestir herself, to change in some way — become more master of her own fate, less an adjunct to the fate of her husband.

It was such a new idea that she didn't wholly become aware of it at first. All she knew was that sometimes now, instead of waiting on the steps of a hotel for the doorman to whistle up a taxi, she would set out along the pavement and hail one for herself. Or even, like embarking on an adventure, make her way back to

Ebury Street on foot, feeling calm and self-possessed. It still had not struck her that she never opened the door for herself, that she had no doorkey — Beading or the housemaid was always on the alert to swing the heavy oak panels back and curtsey her indoors.

The bus journey to Poplar was an eye-opener. She had never realised that there were parts of London without shining windows, snowy curtains, wrought-iron railings and pretty window boxes. She stepped down in Old Ford very nervous and somewhat depressed. This area of London was as bad as the district in New York where Tad had taken her to see Gertie Dorf's garment workers.

Tad . . . She must not think about Tad.

She gave her attention to Miss Pankhurst, who hurried out to greet her. She was given a guided tour of the toy factory, which was simply a house given over to the making of toys. She tried to chat to the workers but could make little of their replies: they spoke like Beading only faster and less comprehensibly.

After the tour there was, inevitably, tea. This was poured from a brown earthenware pot into thick white cups, with plain biscuits as accompaniment. It was all quite different from tea at Lady Malvern's. Yet Miss Pankhurst came from a good family, so far as she'd been able to learn. It seemed strange to hear her going on about the wrongs of the poor, and socialism, and things of that kind. Of course, Gertie had talked in something of that fashion — but Gertie was a poor second-generation American, not a pillar of British society.

The talk turned to war news. Sylvia Pankhurst remarked on Ellie's black dress and supposed aloud it was for the *Lusitania*.

'Yes, but why do you say it in that tone, Miss Pankhurst? It sounds almost as if you disapprove!'

'To me it seems rather a pointless demonstration. It would have been better to prevent the ship carrying munitions of war in the first place, rather than put on mourning afterwards when it is too late.'

'It's neither here nor there what the ship was carrying! It was a passenger liner − it should have been safe from attack—'

'Come come, Mrs Gracebridge, your government must have known very well that the German Navy would be on the watch for her. Why, the German Consul in New York issued a declaration that she would not be permitted immunity—'

'The German Consul had no right to utter threats—'

'But it was a warning, not a threat. If the owners of the *Lusitania* disregard serious warnings—'

'What you are saying is, if a man warns me he is going to attack me when I step outside my door, then I must cower indoors? What becomes of law, of decency—'

'My dear Mrs Gracebridge, we are speaking of war. Nations must have regard for their people rather than their pride! If Britain and America would stop thinking about their nationhood and look upon their fellowmen as—'

'Love the Germans, you mean? I find it very difficult to love anyone who could be responsible for the death of twelve hundred innocent people—'

'And so you go into mourning black. A little theatrical, isn't it, considering you knew none of them—'

'But I did, Miss Pankhurst! I knew four of the people who were drowned!'

They sat staring at each other. Sylvia Pankhurst had the grace to colour up a little. 'I'm sorry,' she said in a low voice. 'But I'm forced to ask you – would you have put on mourning for them in the normal course of events?'

'No, but this is not the normal course of events, and I fail to see why you are so determined to find excuses for a vile act—'

'But more lives were lost in other naval engagements before ever we heard of the loss of the *Lusitania*. What I cannot accept is that you are making an outcry about this liner but you care nothing for the crew of the *Emden* or the *Blucher*—'

'Good God! Of course I am sorry for the loss of lives! But you must see it's different—'

'No,' Miss Pankhurst said stubbornly, 'that's just what I don't see. War is wrong. All deaths are tragic. And to single out some above others is . . . is . . .'

Ellie-Rose sprang up. They were having a real quarrel. She knew Miss Pankhurst was on the verge of calling her hypocritical. 'I had better go, Miss Pankhurst,' she remarked, setting down her teacup with a shaking hand.

'No, please, Mrs Gracebridge – you are vexed with me – don't go now—'

'I think it's best. Otherwise we may say things we shall regret. If you'll show me the way out . . .'

She made for the door and her hostess perforce had to follow. At the front door they bowed to each other. Ellie-Rose marched out, pink with annoyance, and was a hundred yards along the road before she realised she had not taken the parcel of toys she had bought, and moreover that she was walking in the wrong direction. She wheeled around, saw a bus with 'Strand' among the destinations on its painted board, and running for it, swung aboard. Eager hands helped her. 'There y'are, lidy! Quite a turn o' speed, eh? Enterin' the Derby?'

She laughed and was put into a seat, uncomfortable slatted wood. The bus was rather full. Office workers mostly, from the warehouses nearby at the docks, carrying messages to and fro about ship-lading and cargo. A few housewives with shopping baskets. Ellie looked out of the window, watching the grim grey buildings go by. The bus was lumbering towards a stop. A few people were waiting to board.

To her utter astonishment, she saw that one of them was Tad Kendall. She drew back but it was too late. Their glance had crossed. He frowned in surprise, raised his hat, was jostled by those behind him in the little queue. She saw him step aside to let the others clamber aboard, deliberately letting the bus draw away without him.

Ellie felt herself go hot, then cold. A new passenger sat down next to her, a large man taking up too much room so that she was pressed against the window — but she scarcely noticed.

Of all the people to see! What could he be doing in the East End of London? But then she checked herself — of course she had no idea what his business was these days. He probably had a better reason for being there than she herself. How it must have surprised him to see her on the London bus. Yes, and how it had shocked him: she had an immediate mental picture of his face, startled and pale at sight of her.

So it still meant something to him to see her. He couldn't disguise it at that moment, had no opportunity to turn away and hide his emotion as he had done in the grounds of Cliveden.

So much for staying out of his way. He had been the last person on her mind when she set off that afternoon, yet they had had this strange, silent encounter. Silent, yet so speaking.

She must at all costs avoid him. If she heard of his being invited to any gathering she herself must find an excuse not to go. This few seconds' meeting had warned her again — they were dangerous to each other. She drew in a deep breath and made her lips firm in token of this good resolution.

Which was entirely wasted, for Tad was a guest at the dinner party which she and Curtis attended that evening.

Chapter Six

The dinner was at the Howarths', an English family with interests in shipping. Curtis had become acquainted with them through negotiations about transport for supplies from America to Britain. Samuel Howarth had invited all the members of the Agricultural Deputation to dinner in the interests of furthering good relations and perhaps doing business. It had been necessary to accept.

Ellie had had no qualms. She had taken it for granted that in this English household, there would be no other American guests besides the members of the group.

Mrs Howarth's mind had worked differently. It had occurred to her that since the affair was largely to help with Samuel's cargo tenders, she would invite others who could be useful. She made up a dinner party of twenty with five other men and their wives or fiancées, and filled the gaps by inviting pretty unattached women as dinner-partners for the bachelors. Because she wanted Samuel's important guests to feel at home, she invited as many Americans as she could.

When Ellie and Curtis walked into the drawingroom, the other guests were mostly assembled. Somehow Tad's tall figure near the fireplace was disclosed to her without causing her a tremor. Perhaps the shock of that afternoon had inured her to surprise. She was ushered from group to group by her hostess, names were murmured, she bowed and said 'how do you do' in the accepted British fashion, and nodded when Mrs Howarth said, 'But Mr Kendall you already know, I believe.'

Almost at once the last guest was shown in, the last pre-dinner drink was served, and the butler came to announce the meal was served. They filed into the diningroom. To her horror, Ellie realised that Mrs Howarth had partnered her with Tad.

He offered his arm. She laid a hand on it, looking straight ahead, and walked unseeing after the hostess into the diningroom. They were seated. The butler was inquiring whether she would have the white wine poured now with the hors d'oeuvres. Only then did she regain her sense of what was happening. She covered her glass with her hand, the butler moved away, and the man on her left was saying ' . . . long in London?'

'Just over three months,' she replied.

'And how long d'you intend to stay?'

'We were supposed to be returning home at the beginning of June. But now that the war at sea has become so vindictive, my husband is worried about making the trip—'

'And he's right, ma'am! By golly, those Germans have no more pity than an alligator in a swamp! If Mr Gracebridge wants my advice, he should stay here until the British Navy gets the better of them dam' U-boats.'

The lady on his other side made fluttering sounds about the awfulness of U-boats. Ellie was left in silence for a moment. She felt her hostess's eye on her and turned obediently to Tad, to make conversation.

'What were you doing on that bus this afternoon?' he

demanded, in a tone that contained an almost proprietorial anxiety.

'I was coming from visiting Sylvia Pankhurst.'

'Ah, now I understand! And she insisted you must use public transport, because it's wickedly capitalistic to take a taxi.'

She smiled and pushed the smoked salmon about on her plate. 'You're acquainted with Sylvia Pankhurst?'

'Slightly. She and Nancy Astor sometimes team up for some piece of good work on behalf of the poor.'

'And of course you know the Astors.' She paused. 'I was surprised to see you at Cliveden.' Understood was the unspoken, 'and I would not have gone there if I had known you might be there.'

She thought she heard him sigh. 'In a small circle such as ours – expatriate Americans – it's difficult not to be in the same place at the same time occasionally.'

Her left-hand neighbour claimed her for a word, calling on her to tell the young lady next to him that in the United States their smoked salmon, from their own rivers, was every bit as good as Scottish fish. A short debate on the merits of Scottish and American angling then took place; the young lady, it appeared, was a keen trout fisherman.

When the plates were removed and the next course was served, Ellie turned back to Tad. 'It's my turn to ask what took you to the bus queue in Poplar,' she inquired politely.

'I was out on business. Since I settled here, I've turned to maritime law. I wanted to make a complete change, you know—' He broke off suddenly, aware that it was a dangerous way to have expressed it. 'I've joined a firm with a very high reputation for handling cases of international law concerned with the sea. It's a very complex area of jurisprudence and at present, of course, made a thousand times worse by the war. This afternoon I had been to the docks to interview a ship's captain on a neutral vessel whose company is claiming violation of sovereign rights . . . But you don't want to hear all this. The law of the sea is not only incredibly complex, it's incredibly boring.'

'Not as exciting as criminal law?' she suggested.

He didn't reply at once, and she knew he was remembering the case which had brought him to the hotel in Niagara to meet her for the very first time — the case of the assassin, Szolgozs. She felt a pang of sympathy for him. 'You regret giving it up?' she asked.

He shook his head. 'No, when I say maritime law is boring, I mean only to the outsider. To me it's fascinating. True, it doesn't have the same intense personal involvement as defending an accused man, but great issues are concerned — the wellbeing of merchant sailors, the rights of the vessels, the protection of lives and cargoes, the payment of dues and taxes, the pursuit of malefactors such as pirates or swindlers.'

'It sounds fascinating,' said she, consciously making it sound like a polite response from a dinner guest.

'Did I hear you tell Yelverton that you won't be sailing for home in June?' He was changing the subject.

'It seems unlikely, unless the British Navy gets control of the Atlantic by then. The sinking of the *Lusitania* has made everyone very nervous, naturally.'

'But if your husband's work is completed here?'

'I gather not. If we had gone home, others would have been sent out to replace us. So the President is suggesting it makes good sense if we just stay on until further notice.'

'But what about the elections? Curtis will have to fight his seat, won't he?'

She shook her head. 'You're a little out of touch, Mr Kendall. Curtis was re-elected last year and doesn't have to stand again until 1918.' She smiled. 'I imagine that by then the war will be decidedly over and we can sail for home! But seriously, Curtis has no anxieties over remaining here. There's a gentleman's agreement that his seat in the Senate is safe while he's on a Presidential mission, and the same for the others.'

There was a lull in the general chatter. Mrs Howarth, from her place at the far end of the table, called out: 'Now, please, everyone, no more talk about the war! I want to know who's seen this marvellous new film of Mr Griffiths'?'

Ellie followed her hostess to the drawingroom relieved and comforted. She had met Tad, talked with him, acquitted herself well. There was no more need to worry.

When the gentlemen joined the ladies it was no problem to stay with Curtis and further his conversations. Her hostess smiled upon her; she was doing the same thing for her own husband, within the confines of her duties to see that everyone was entertained. As the evening ended men exchanged cards and made notes in diaries about contacting each other. Rather to her dismay, she found Curtis making a note of the name of Tad's firm of lawyers. 'Might look you up quite soon,' he was murmuring. 'We've got to sort out some confusion about indemnities for cargoes lost through enemy action. Insurance sure is difficult at the moment! Perhaps you can advise us on how to route our cargo.'

'My firm would be delighted to advise,' Tad rejoined, with a bow.

On the way home in the car Curtis said, 'Sound feller, that.'

'Who?'

'Kendall. Seems like his firm could be just what we've been looking for to guide us through the jungle of international maritime law, now we're shipping to Britain.'

'You've recommended that?' Ellie asked, glad that in the darkness of the saloon car he couldn't see her face.

'About getting into contracts with the British — yeah, we saw no reason to turn business down, and now after this *Lusitania* thing . . . The neutrality boys aren't going to savage us for making deals with the enemies of the Germans now, are they?'

Ellie had meant a question about hiring Tad's firm. She couldn't pursue it now — it would seem too pointed. She let her husband talk on about the news he had gleaned over the port, nodding and throwing in a comment now and again to keep him happy.

Her own mind was taken up with examining the new situation. She had told herself again and again that she must stay out of Tad's way. Even if his firm undertook to advise the delegation on matters of law, that didn't mean she had to see him. The men generally kept business to the office, and if occasionally they brought negotiators to her home for a business dinner, on those occasions she took care to make herself scarce.

The sinking of the *Lusitania*, appalling though it was, had had only a limited effect on the British. Accustomed by now to horror after horror, with long casualty lists coming back from the Ypres battlefield and hideously awful stories about the use of a new weapon – poison gas – by the Germans, the loss of even a thousand lives on an ocean liner seemed a small tragedy.

But in America the reaction was cataclysmic. Ordinary people were shocked, politicians were outraged. That Americans, having no quarrel with either side, should be drowned when going about their lawful occasions in an unarmed merchant ship . . . It was beyond belief. American citizens of German origin began to have a hard time: some hastily changed their names. Business firms and shops put up placards: 'Our name comes from Poland' or 'We are third generation American.'

The Austrian Ambassador in Washington remarked to his First Assistant, 'Our sea-going brothers have effectively doubled the number of our enemies by this one act.' Austria, of course, had no navy and could not be blamed for this clumsy act of war. He was intensely alarmed: there was an influential 'war party' in Washington who might make wonderful use of the propaganda angle to get the United States into armed combat.

Greg Craigallan, hard at work among the foreign diplomats on a secondment to the Department of Commerce, listened to the outpourings of the French buyers who flooded into his office. 'Your government must let us have the *matériel* to beat these savages!' they cried. 'You see now how evil they are! You would not believe us when we told you what they did in Belgium – now do you understand?'

'Messieurs, the United States government is neutral. You must understand that the President has made no change—'

'Neutral? Neutral? *Quelle bêtise!* You let the Boches

drown your people and you remain neutral? Have you no sense of honour, you Americans?'

'They're determined to get us in with them,' Greg reported to his father. 'And of course I don't blame them. They're taking a hell of a licking on the Western Front.'

'They sound kind of hysterical to me,' Rob grunted. 'Do they always harangue you like that?'

'Frequently. I sometimes long for the peace and quiet of the Chicago Wheat Pit.'

'At least you're safe and sound at home,' his father remarked.

'Worrying again about Ellie? Listen, Father, if it bothers you so much, why don't you get them brought back? You could wangle it easy enough.'

They were in Greg's club in Washington, looking down the distant vista of Jefferson Drive towards the Smithsonian. Late May sunshine gleamed on the rosy-red brick of that turreted building, the ginkgo trees were in full leaf, and nowhere could a more peaceful view have been seen. Greg summoned a waiter with a jerk of his head to refill their whisky glasses.

Rob sighed, leaning back in his leather-buttoned chair. 'I had a long talk with the Secretary of Commerce yesterday — over a quiet drink, of course.'

'What did he have to say?'

'We're making money, that's for sure. Whoever is being harmed by this war, it sure isn't the good old US.' There was dry humour in his manner, but some distaste too. Rob liked to make profits yet somehow his conscience was bothering him a little. It had to do with his daughter being off there close to the line of battle. She might so easily have been on board a ship like the *Lusitania* . . .

'Did you discuss the trade commission?'

'Yes, we went into it quite thoroughly. The delegates are sending back all kinds of information and the detail we're learning opens up all sorts of avenues . . . Curtis has apparently got hold of a law firm that really understands the law of the sea. These round-the-glen routes we have to take with our shipments – he's getting the thing sorted out, what permits you have to have, which ports are sticky about strict neutrality, which officials expect to be bribed and which get on their high horse . . . All that . . .'

The waiter brought the drinks. They were silent until he had withdrawn. Greg took a sip and looked inquiringly at Rob.

'As to Ellie,' his father said, 'Redfield and I just talked in general terms about whether to recall the party, or replace them. It comes down to this. Redfield doesn't want to bring them home, and as to replacing them . . . It's kind of difficult, boy. Now that the sea war is hotting up, you can't *order* a civilian to set sail across the Atlantic and be drowned. The only way Redfield can replace the present delegation is if he sends government staff. But they wouldn't serve the same purpose, not at all. The whole charm of the present arrangement is that it isn't official, and it's bi-partisan. If foreign governments object, the President can reply that they're there on behalf of the Senate, not the government.'

'And so neutrality is preserved. I sometimes wonder if Wilson is as stupid as you like to think, Mr Craig!'

'All I know is that Redfield made it clear they'd like to leave the commission in place in London, because it's doing a fine job. Curtis is storing up laurels. As far as I could gather, if he wants to stand for the

103

governorship when he eventually gets back, it's a shoe-in.'

'Does he know that?'

'It's been murmured to him, I imagine.'

'So he isn't likely to start agitating to come home.'

Rob shook his head. 'In his letters to me he seems to be enjoying himself. You know what he's like, Greg. He enjoys being in the swim and somehow they seem to have been taken up by some very important people. That Langhorne girl seems to be important in British society.'

'Nancy Astor, you mean?'

'As a fellow-American she's taken Curtis and Ellie under her wing and that gives them the entrée to other important people . . . You know how it works.'

'What do you hear from Ellie?' he inquired. 'Do you get the impression she wants to come home? They would have been due about now, if the sea war hadn't got so bad.'

'I don't know, Greg, I really don't. She just says she'll abide by Curtis's decision. She worries about the children, of course, keeps asking for news of them. I wish they'd write longer letters to her!'

'We'll give Mother a hint on that, then.' Morag, installed in the Gracebridges' Washington house, was the gentle guardian of the children.

The two men would be on their way to dine with her after they had finished their whiskies. They might hear more news. Ellie wrote to Morag — Rob sometimes had a feeling his daughter confided more in her than anyone else. But what would Ellie have to confide? It was hard to say. Yet he had the feeling that his darling wasn't quite so happy as she tried to make it appear in the letters she wrote to him.

The sun was waning a little behind the graceful dome of the Capitol as they left the club to find a cab. The evening was mild. Soon it would be too warm for cloth frockcoats and high collars except on the most formal occasions. Instead white suits, popularised by the Southern politicians, would give ease and comfort to the male Washingtonians, and the ladies would be out in their gauzy muslins. Alas, for only too short a spell Washington would be delightful — and then would come the mosquitoes, and flies, and sticky heat, and mornings dimmed by a mist over the Potomac, and tar melting on road surfaces, and fractious horses running away with carriages, and soldiers keeling over on guard duty . . .

When they alighted at the house, Gina ran out to greet them. She knew she was a favourite with her grandfather, who expected a hug and a kiss each time they met. With Uncle Gregor she was on less effusive terms. She had a feeling he eyed her sometimes with less than complete adoration. Yet she admired him — so tall and fine-looking, a younger version of Grandfather and married to such a beautiful woman. Gina was somewhat in awe of her Aunt Francesca, whose exploits in defence of her home in Manila were occasionally mentioned in family conversation.

Gina longed to be allowed to stay up to dinner with the grown-ups. At almost sixteen, she was old enough, surely! But Granma Morag wouldn't allow it. 'The first time you stay up for dinner will be your seventeenth birthday, dear,' she said with gentle decision. 'And Curt will stay up too.'

'But that isn't fair! He'll still be only fourteen then! If he can stay up to dinner when he's fourteen, why can't I?'

'Because, darling, you know you'd taunt him with it if I let you have a privilege that he doesn't get.' Gina had been about to protest that never, never would she taunt Curt — but her eye caught Morag's mild look of inquiry and she dissolved in laughter.

It was only too true. She led poor Curt a terrible life.

So although she had been allowed to stay downstairs to greet the menfolk at eight, she was soon to be banished to her own room, where school studies and hair-brushing were supposed to take up her time until she went to bed at nine. She thought it very hard to be sent to bed at nine. Lots of girls she knew stayed up till ten, some longer. But it was no use arguing with Granma Morag. In fact, Morag never argued. She just listened, nodded or shook her head as the case might be, and then spoke her quiet decision.

Because her father wasn't there to be wheedled Gina always had to give in. She wished her father would come home. He was far easier to handle than Granma Morag.

Gina missed her parents more than she expected, but their absence in London gave her prestige with the other girls. 'Imagine!' they would say with bated breath. 'Out there where the war's going on!' They had an inexact notion of modern war, their ideas being based on epic paintings such as 'The Charge of the Light Brigade' or 'The Stand at the Alamo'. Banners waving, proud men standing with sabres in their hands, horses racing ahead while the rider shouted defiance — that was what it must be like all around London, and Gina's mother and father were there, brave and resolute for the sake of their President.

The London revealed to her by her mother's letters was rather different, but Gina never told her friends so.

She didn't exactly lie, she just didn't correct their misconceptions. When she read what her mother had written she was sometimes caught by envy for the reality – the outings with members of the British aristocracy, pictured by her as always elegant and articulate, like characters in an Oscar Wilde play. To be accepted by these aristocrats as an equal must be really something. Oh, wait, just wait, until Gina came out! – she would be as great a social success as Mama and capture a rich, handsome duke for a husband . . .

'And how's my little tiger-lily tonight, eh?' Grandfather said as he went indoors with her arm twined in his.

'I'm fine, Grandfather, and all the better for seeing you.' She knew he loved to be told that she looked forward to his visits. 'It's ages since you came to see us!'

'Well, I've been busy, chicken—'

'But you've been in Washington four whole days already! Why have you waited so long to come?'

They reached the porch. Morag was standing in its shadow to welcome them. She kissed Greg and linked an arm with Rob, the other side of Gina. Gina felt a little pang of annoyance – what right had Granma Morag to do that? But then . . . Granma Morag and Grandfather were special to each other. It was difficult to understand, exactly. Nobody talked about it and it was all quite taken for granted, yet it wasn't like other families.

For instance, Greg was Gina's uncle, and Grandfather's son, yet he didn't have Grandfather's name. And Greg was Morag's son, too, yet Morag wasn't Grandfather's wife.

This puzzle had recently been bothering Gina. All her

childhood she'd taken it entirely for granted but as she moved towards adulthood she found it coming back into her mind more and more. Only last week she had tried to question Morag about it, but Morag had said, 'You must ask your mother to explain these things to you, Gina.'

'But Mother's not here, and I want to *know* – !'

'Darling, it's not so important. You'll see.'

But Gina didn't see. Brought up in circumstances of luxury and ease, the hardships of real life had never yet touched her. She didn't even have the advantage of growing up on a farm, where so much about birth and death and physical need are taken for granted. Nice young ladies, well brought up young ladies, were reared to be virginal innocents. Time enough to discuss the rougher side of marriage on the wedding eve, or to let the groom initiate his bride into the mysteries of sex.

All Gina's friends were desperate to know what grown-ups kept so secret. They scanned books and magazines for clues, delved in Shakespeare or the Bible. The 'virgin birth' – what did it *mean*? That strange and thrilling story about Jacob and Rachel and Leah – what did it *mean*? When she tried to discuss it with the minister, he talked about God and favour and destiny. If she questioned the English mistress about certain lines at the beginning of *Othello*, Miss Carruthers coloured up and said it was poetic licence.

So because no one would explain, Gina and her friends speculated. Their theories owed much to high romance such as the *Morte D'Arthur* and the operas of Wagner. Passionate embraces, sleeping with a sword between a man and a woman, wearing a love token next to the heart – these formed part of their beliefs. But none of it explained where babies actually came from although several of them professed to understand it all on some higher plane.

Gina didn't understand, and it was becoming tremendously important. It was no longer enough to reduce a boy to adoration with a smile and a look of encouragement. She wanted to kiss and be kissed, to let some part of herself melt and merge — but how, how? And fighting against this unquenchable inclination was the knowledge that it would be wrong, that Mama had always told her to have high standards and not be a flirt.

She should ask Grandfather what it was all about. But she flinched away from that. This was something that had to be discussed between women, she sensed the importance of that. It would embarrass Grandfather to have such a topic broached — and it was very important to Gina to have a perfect relationship with her grandfather.

She went into the house with him, into the cool drawingroom where Francesca was sitting, a piece of needlework in her hands. She put up her cheek to be kissed by Greg. Enviously Gina watched them, saw how Greg's lips lingered against the cheekbone, how Francesca's hand came up to touch his hair in a momentary caress.

That was love, Gina knew. That was what the poems were all about, the poignant German *lieder*, the soaring duets at the opera . . . But how did it come, how was it nourished?

Granma Morag was offering drinks. 'You can have a small glass of sherry, Gina. Then it's off to your room. Mr Petrowski says your geography papers have been very poor so please try to do some work before you go to bed.'

'Oh, geography!' cried Gina with a toss of her head. 'Who cares about silly old geography!'

'Now, honey, that's not good sense,' Rob told her. 'If I didn't know something about geography, how would I know which countries can grow wheat?'

'Oh, yes, I can see it's important in that sense. But I don't see why I've got to learn all the provinces of China from north to south. What use is that ever going to be?'

'Might be very important one day. Cornelius says there's a lot of territory there that could grow good wheat.'

'Wheat? But the Chinese eat rice, Grandfather!'

'How's Neil?' Francesca put in. 'He does not come to see us these days.'

'No, he's pretty busy these days. Now the government's got Greg kind of tied up chatting with these Frenchies and all, Neil's had to take on a lot that Greg used to do.'

'He's managing well, too,' Greg put in. 'It's making him come outside the lab a lot more. Doing him a world of good.'

Rob sighed and said nothing. He was grateful to his elder son for taking on the added responsibilities caused by Greg's frequent absences in Washington, but he could never bring himself to consider that Neil could really cope with the big business world. His handicap, his natural reticence, and perhaps a lack of real appetite for the rough and tumble of commerce made Neil less of a partner than Greg.

Sometimes Rob was tempted to tell Greg to come back to Craigallan Agricultural and let the government find someone else to parley-voo to temperamental French buyers. Yet there were advantages in having

110

someone on the very inside in Washington. Special information, prestige, instant contact when it was needed. To tell the truth, the boy seemed to enjoy it. He might even say no if Rob were to tell him to turn his back on it. While Curtis was away, it made good sense to let Greg stay with the commercial work in Washington, and now it looked as if Curtis wouldn't be back for quite a while.

He mentioned this to the others when they were sitting down to dinner after Gina had gone upstairs. 'The President wants the commission to remain, for various reasons of suitability and safety. Of course he can't exactly command them, but then he can't command anyone to go in their place. So he's pitched it pretty strong about duty and honour and all that, and Curtis is inclined to go along with it.'

'Not to mention being unwilling to embark on a crossing beset by U-boats,' Greg murmured.

'Oh, Greg!' his mother reproached. 'You know the danger is very real. You wouldn't really like to see your sister on a ship hunted by a U-boat, now would you?'

'Reckon not. You hear from Ellie? What's she saying?'

Morag hesitated. Ellie's letters had been different these last few weeks; it was as if there was something she was longing to confide but couldn't put into words. 'She says she will accept Curtis's decision on the matter, as a dutiful wife should,' she told them.

'Well, I think they'll be staying on, in that case. Seems to me that means Ellie's found her niche in London society, Mother. Dutiful wife she may be, but if she was having a rotten time she'd find some way to persuade Curtis to come back.'

'I expect she worries about Gina and Curt,' Francesca put in.

'She knows they're in good hands,' Rob said with a fond glance at Morag.

Gina, listening on the stairs, clenched her fists in anger. As easily as that, she and her brother were disposed of! Of course it was only right that Papa should stay at his post, serving his President, but Mama could come home if she wanted to. All this nonsense about submarines! – everyone made out that every ship was in tremendous danger but it stood to reason there couldn't be nearly as many submarines as ships and anyhow Mama could have travelled on a roundabout route if she wanted to and avoided the submarines, and though it might take her a bit longer that way she would get home safe and sound, and the fact that she didn't proved, it just *proved*, that she preferred to enjoy herself in London with all those witty, handsome aristocrats!

For the moment Gina forgot that she liked Granma Morag, that there was a tranquillity and charm in the house while she was at its head. She thought instead of the dinners and parties that Mama would have given had she been here, how they filled each room with animation and laughter. And the picnics and outings Mama arranged for Gina and her friends – Morag didn't do that kind of thing in the same way, there was a sedateness to the occasions that devalued them to Gina. It had always been important to her to be a leader among her set. The longer Mama stayed away, the more her importance waned as a social asset. People would stop inviting Gina if all they got in return was tea-parties and cookie-bakes . . .

The talk in the diningroom had turned to dull old

politics. Gina got up and crept in bare feet back to her bedroom. As she came to Curt's door she debated going in and telling him what she had just learned. But he would be shocked that she'd eavesdropped — he was such a stick! She went into her own room where she threw herself on the stool in front of the dressingtable to stare moodily at herself in the mirror.

The reflection showed an oval face, framed in toffee-coloured hair held back by boudoir bows of pink silk. The complexion was creamy, very pale by contrast with the lashes of the wide-spaced eyes of gentian blue. She glared at herself, elbows on the table, fists against her cheeks. She was pretty, she was clever, she was fun . . . What use was it all if she had no mother to give her a coming-out party? No one to explain to her the mysteries of life and love?

If Mama didn't come home, what would happen in the summer months? The months they usually spent at Morris Mount in Virginia, with other families of good standing, where the boys called with a gardenia to escort you to an outdoor party, where in the dusk they would sing under the cottonwoods in languishing tones about Nellie Dean and Sweet Adeline . . .

Gina went to bed at last as she heard her grandfather leaving around midnight. She lay stiff with anger and resentment among her lace-trimmed pillows. He said he thought the world of her but he simply called a cab and went away, leaving her to months of aching dullness. Uncle Greg, too, and Aunt Francesca — they went into their room and into each other's arms, and never gave a thought to her, never cared that she was wretched, wretched! They were happy, they didn't care. Everyone was happy, even stupid Curt — everyone, except Gina.

Chapter Seven

When the Craigallan family remarked that Cornelius Craigallan was being forced to take a greater part in the running of the business, they were right. Cornelius Craigallan was coming out of his shell.

His deafness hadn't been so great a handicap to Cornelius as it would to a poor boy. He had had the best teachers, the friendship of the greatest of them all, Alexander Graham Bell. He had gone to schools where deafness was treated as a fact of life like hair colour or freckles — nothing to be ashamed of. A mixture of luck and inclination had brought him a career in plant research: anyone who knew anything about it acknowledged that Cornelius Craigallan was up there with Carver or Carleton.

So as he'd entered his late twenties he was a man of some confidence and distinction outwardly, though perhaps still troubled by insecurity. A stormy love affair with Stephanie Jouvard had given him experience of passion beyond anything he'd ever imagined, and to him the affair was of course the prelude to a normal, happy marriage.

That dream had been shattered by Stephanie's careless sexuality. It was bad enough that she took another love, but she chose his half-brother Gregor. In the awful, scrabbling, gouging fight that followed, Ellie-Rose had been badly injured when she tried to intervene. She almost lost her baby, little Curt. And for a time Neil had not only been blamed by his father, he had blamed himself. Banished, as he felt, from civilised life, he had gone to the war in Manila. It was Greg, untouched by the spirit of censure felt by the other men of the family, who had rescued Neil.

Neil came back very sick and exhausted. Months in captivity in the tropics under a callous guerrilla leader isn't the way to stay in good health. Almost a year went by before he was something like himself again physically and even then he didn't regain his former weight. He was destined to be thin and have rather yellowed skin colour for the rest of his life. His manservant Larry nursed him devotedly, and married rather quickly, conveniently importing a housekeeper to do the run-of-the-mill chores while Larry acted as nurse-companion.

It was Neil's interest in his work that brought him back into limited circulation again. A great debate was going on in the farming community about the use of sacks as the wheat came from the separator. 'Bulking' wheat had its advantages; it saved the expense of sacks, which brought with their fibres occasional mildews and diseases too. Handling them was a back-breaking task. Rats and mice gnawed them so that there was a loss from leakage and, when the sacks had to be moved again, the holes had to be mended. Many a farm-woman had skin coarsened by the unending work of patching sacks with a great needle and a leather-shielded left hand.

Neil's father was debating whether to go over entirely to bulk carriage and storage. It meant a huge investment in silos which, in their turn, had their drawbacks. Heat tended to build up in a silo, and any diseases taken in with the wheat could spread and damage great quantities within the protection of the container.

'There must be ways of dressing the seed so that we diminish the ravages of disease more thoroughly in the field,' Rob mused as he studied the cost for changing over to bulk storage. 'And if there was anything we could do at silo stage . . . How much is known about temperature control, I wonder?'

'I could do some tests,' Neil suggested.

Rob looked up from his papers. It was a long long time since Neil had shown any interest in the business. In fact, it was only fairly recently that the boy had begun to come to Craigallan Castle on visits. In general he stayed in his apartment in Chicago or went with Larry to the coast in summer.

Rob had been furiously angry with Neil for the harm done to Ellie-Rose. That was all behind him now, but he had said some things to his son that were hard to forget. Painfully, they were getting back to their old footing again. Even so, Neil knew — how could he not know? — that he wasn't the favourite child. Ellie-Rose was beloved because she was beautiful and bright and bonny. Greg was loved because he was a son to be proud of. Neil came a long way third.

But he had his value, and he was beginning to be aware of that again. The offer to help in deciding for or against the silo-building was a way of saying he was himself again, no longer an invalid, no longer a malefactor who had harmed his own sister.

His work in the laboratories of the Chicago head-quarters resulted in a report, painstakingly typed up for him by one of his adoring assistants. He and Greg and their father sat around chewing it over evening after evening, after the business of the day was done.

'Look, Neil, I don't really understand this well enough to make a judgement. In a sentence, what does it mean?'

Neil smiled. 'Can't say it in a sentence. Some of the words difficult too.' His flat tone could never convey amusement but there was a glint of it in his eyes. As he went on he sometimes had to resort to sign language to make himself clear but the other men were well accustomed to this kind of conversation. 'A big saving in manpower and other costs such as transport if we go over to bulk. Also means a cost factor that can't be ignored. Scrupulous cleanliness' − he paused to repeat it on his fingers, for he was never sure he was forming words correctly − 'must be in force round the silos. Many will hold their contents over two years—'

'Mebbe three,' Rob put in.

Neil nodded, catching the words from his lips. 'So temperature' − he spelled it with his hands − 'temperature of vital importance. Extreme cold not so harmful as extreme heat. For instance, silos at New Orleans a big problem. Yet it's an obvious port to site them.'

Rob turned to his other son. 'You've been mulling over those figures for days, boy. On a longterm basis, are we going to get our money back and make a profit?'

Greg pursed his lips. 'Those building costs are scary, Mr Craig.'

'Hairy?' Neil asked, astonished.

They went into fits of laughter. Greg signed the word for his half-brother. 'Oh, scary! I see. But we have a chance to be ahead of our rivals. We'd be able to deal in The Pit in April for September wheat, and know we could store the physicals *if we have to*.'

Rob drew in a breath and blew it out again. 'You seem to be more confident than Greg, lad.'

'I know more about it than Greg.'

'Ha,' said Greg. 'Test tubes and microscopes don't bring in profits if the money's gone to the wrong thing.'

Neil shrugged, said no more for the time being. Rob looked at Greg. 'What do you say, Greg?'

Greg took a moment before responding. 'I say Neil has to make the final decision. I really don't know if bulk storage is going to cost us more than we'll save.'

'Well then, Neil?'

To their surprise, Neil closed his report with a snap. 'I didn't do three months' work without coming to a conclusion. I say that in ten years, most of the wheat on this continent will be stored in silos.'

'Gee, listen to him. A prophet!'

Neil stared at him, misreading the word, then realised it wasn't 'profit' but 'prophet'. 'Yes,' he said laughing. 'I prophesy. And if I'm wrong you can send me back to Manila.'

'If you're wrong I'll be too broke to pay the fare,' joked Rob. That wasn't true of course. He wasn't foolish enough to sink more than he could afford into silo-building. All the same it was a huge investment.

Looking back now, ten years later, Neil Craigallan had a right to be proud of his courage at that point. His survey of the probabilities had been proved correct at every factor. Bulk storage was already the accepted mode, and those who had been in at the beginning had reaped the rewards of stabilising the market. Wheat was still volatile, God knows. Even the most scientific methods couldn't control the weather. But he, Neil Craigallan, had changed the means by which it was generally handled in the United States. And because

Craigallan Agricultural Products was in at the birth of the new business, they had made a killing.

Even so, Neil had made no demand for increased status. He liked his life in the laboratory. He had his own small circle of friends, mostly in Chicago and mostly to do with scientific matters. He would probably have stayed there, pottering around in the lab at CAP or in his own private one, making occasional useful contributions to scientific journals, settling down into an inevitable bachelorhood − except for the war.

Having two of the clan taken up with government duties − Curtis in London and Greg intermittently in Washington − Rob Craigallan turned more to Neil for consultation. He dragged his son out of his fastness in Chicago, made him stay at Craigallan Castle near New York, demanded that he play some part in heading the business. There was entertaining to do, there were meetings to attend. 'But, Papa, I can't hear! What's the good of going to the meeting?'

'Dammit, boy, you can read my lips and Greg's and Larry's − you damn well put yourself out to read Governor Bryan's!'

In favourable conditions, Neil could get ninety per cent of what was being said and guess the rest. Conditions weren't always good at business gatherings but as he became accepted he found he could nudge the man next to him and ask: 'What was that?' and have him repeat the missing phrase so he could read it. It became something of an accolade, something to be proud of, if a man could say: 'Helped that Craigallan feller − marvellous, really − he's quick, you know.'

Neil couldn't deny it was pleasant to be so well accepted. It had come rather late to him, but he was enjoying something of a success. But better was in store. And once more it was because of the war.

Neil had a natural sympathy for others with hearing deficiency. As the dreadful conflict built up on the Western Front, men were invalided home with eardrums destroyed by blast damage, ears deformed by shell fragments, delicate internal balance unhinged by sound waves too vast for the human senses to deal with. Most of the injured got only the most elementary treatment. Neil, reading in scientific magazines about the work being done for them, understood that when this war was over there would be vast numbers of newly deaf — men who had never learned to cope with the disability, men embittered by lack of help or sympathy.

He was visiting the Volta Bureau for the Deaf in Washington with Dr Bell and his family early in 1915 when they had an important conversation. It began with Dr Bell talking to Miss Keller, the blind-and-deaf author, saying aloud the words she was telling onto his fingers. 'It is possible to come back to life after being almost dead. Who knows it better than I? Those poor men brought back from the trenches . . . we must do more for them.'

'Aye, my dear girl, I agree with you,' said Bell. And then to Neil, 'I'm thinking of setting up some sort of fund . . . The Europeans have most of their money tied up in killing each other, y'see. How'd it be if you and I and a few others got something going to finance the re-education of those poor fellows?'

Miss Keller let it be known she thought it an excellent idea. In a multiple conversation that would have amazed most people since it relied so much on understanding without the voice, the group in the lecture room at the Volta Bureau decided to see what donations they could depend on, and how to convey the money to Europe. It was their wish to send funds to both sides of the hostilities, because both sides would have a large number of men with damaged hearing.

Even Dr Bell, the great inventor of the telephone, couldn't persuade the American public to give money to help the Germans. If he had made his appeal before the sinking of the *Lusitania* all might have been well. But that disaster brought out an anger and an antagonism that could not be quelled. They had to content themselves with appealing on behalf of the Allies only.

'Damn right, too,' said Cornelius's father. 'I don't mind putting my name on the subscription list for a substantial sum if I'm going to get good publicity out of it. But I'm not going to make myself unpopular by giving money to the Huns.'

'Oh, Papa,' Neil groaned. 'You know as well as I do that when the war's over the problems on both sides will have to be solved before the world can get back to normal. What's the good of having handicapped men left to rot? It'll only cause unrest!'

'Let 'em deal with their own unrest,' Rob said. 'But I'm prepared to do something handsome for the cause if you limit it to the Allies.'

That being the general feeling, Dr Bell and his committee settled on an association to help the wounded with hearing damage on the Allied side. After much thought they settled on the title Deaf Veterans' Aid Society. Alexander Graham Bell, after being a moving spirit in its inception, withdrew: 'I'm on so many committees, lad,' he said to Neil. 'But I leave it in good hands. I've recommended that you should be chosen as President.'

'Me?' Neil croaked in horror. 'You mad? President have to make speeches. I can't make speeches!'

'Try,' advised Dr Bell.

'Try? I'll drive off more supporters than I attract!'

'Don't be silly. You can actually speak – it ma come out a bit flat and toneless, but you can be heard Think of Helen Keller! She doesn't mind making publi appearances and she can't speak, can't see, can only communicate with a hearing person through a thir party. Come on, lad. Have you less get-up-and-go than Helen?'

Still Cornelius resisted. He had no wish to be a figure-head. He had work to do for Craigallan Agricultural Products. There were other people much more suitable . . . and so on and so on.

Dr Bell said to Rob: 'I wish you'd encourage him to take on the Presidency of DVAS. There's a lot in Neil that's never had expression. I've known him a long time, and better than most people . . .'

'You can say that again,' Rob agreed, remembering when he had taken the little deaf boy to the great speech expert in Boston. 'But he's always been rather reticent. The laboratory is his favourite place.'

'How old is Neil now?' Dr Bell asked. 'Thirty-nine, forty?'

'About that. Why?'

'Seems a waste, doesn't it? My Scots nature goes against that. Here's a decent man, clever, kind, capable. He's just the right fellow to head up our organisation. Besides, it'd do him a world of good.'

'He doesn't feel the need to have good done to him,' Rob suggested. 'He's happy enough as he is.'

'Happy enough . . . Aye, I suppose he is. But he could be happier. That's why I want him to do this. The more he's out in the bigger world, the more chance he has of being happier.'

Rob had no great feelings for or against his son taking the Presidency of the new charity. If Neil wanted it, fine. If not, what did it matter? But Dr Bell's words stayed with him.

It was true, Neil's life was a bit restricted. It was confined to the Craigallan clan and its money exclusively. Perhaps the old teacher was right: it might be good for Neil to go out in public.

Besides, it would look good, wouldn't it? To have a Craigallan as head of a big public charity?

So Rob urged him to take it on, and Greg supported him, and a letter came from Ellie-Rose saying how delighted everyone was in London to hear that her brother was working at the head of this new, important voluntary organisation. Because he couldn't think of any more arguments except that he thought he'd put his hearers off, Neil gave in.

He had to get the organisation going first. The funds had rolled in, besides which he knew his father would put his hand in his pocket to remedy any deficiencies. So he took offices in major cities: New York, Washington, Boston, Chicago and San Francisco. He got together a team of Vice-Presidents whom he sent out to hire staff enough to get the office going. He hired an advertising agency to do posters calling for voluntary helpers. The agency came up with a phrase that was to become famous, on a poster of simple design – a man in a war-stained uniform straining to understand as he gazed out at the beholder and across the top: 'He can't hear so . . . *show* you care!' That, and an address to which to send donations, was enough. Neil had decided to make Chicago the headquarters of the Society, because it happened to be where he spent most of his time. Here he chose offices on the north side, in a block where Adolph Zukor had been making cinematic films until he took off for Hollywood. He asked a couple of the devoted young ladies in his CAP office to transfer to the charity's office at the same salary. The rest of the staff, he hoped, would be volunteers.

This was how he met Bess Gardiner. She bounced into the headquarters soon after the first appeal was published in the newspaper interview with Dr Bell. One of the things that attracted him to her was that she at once sat down in the chair facing the window and held her head up so he could see her lips.

'What made you think of offering your help?' he inquired, as he did with every candidate. Some applicants had let him see they expected to get a seat on a gravy-train.

'I work with deaf children,' Bess replied. 'I've been doing it for about four years now – downtown in Calumet. My family wouldn't let me train to be a teacher, you see – thought it was unsuitable for a Gardiner.' She paused, hesitated, and smiled. 'I suppose I ought to say straightaway that my family are a pretty prim bunch. Grandmother was a Brewster and we're connected to the Marshall Fields, and they'll want to ensure that everything here at the Deaf Veterans' is high-tone.' She looked at him anxiously, clearly relieved when he smiled.

'I think they'll be satisfied. There's quite a lot of blue blood among our supporters, although you're the first who's personally come to volunteer for actual work.' He studied her. 'Why did you, in fact?'

'Because two days a week teaching little ones to do

124

their sign exercises isn't enough to keep me sane!'

He couldn't hear the explosion of annoyance in her voice but it was there in her heightened colour, her half-smiling half-frowning glance. She was rather a plain girl if one took her to pieces to examine her item by item, he supposed. Tall, rather angular in her afternoon gown of braided green serge under a matching short cape, she had a wide mouth, freckles and green eyes behind gold-rimmed spectacles. Her hair was drawn back somewhat carelessly into a small hat with a green feather. She looked as if she had put on her clothes in a businesslike mood, with no wish to fascinate or impress. Yet there was something very likeable about her. Compared with, for instance, Greg's wife Francesca, she was a dim star. Yet she had her own kind of inner illumination.

'We're just setting up here,' Neil explained. 'You perhaps know we have offices in other cities, but this will be HQ.'

'I beg your pardon?' she said, having failed to catch the last phrase because she was expecting a word.

'HQ. Headquarters.' He said it full-out. 'I'm sorry. You have experience with the deaf, you tell me. I have no hearing, it affects my speech.'

Her expression changed but she didn't make exclamations of pity or admiration, which he would have hated. Instead she said, 'Oh, I'm so sorry – I should have guessed that by the tone of your voice.' Then she gave him an anxious glance to see if that offended him. When he took it calmly she rushed on: 'You can see I'm flustered. I haven't much experience of being interviewed for a job.'

He was surprised she hadn't seen in the gossip columns some hints about his disability. Journalists, especially lady journalists, would from time to time remark that the son of Robert Craigallan played his part in his father's business and social activities 'despite drawbacks that would deter lesser men'. But they felt it would be gauche to say outright that he was deaf. He said: 'What have you read about us in the papers, Miss Gardiner?'

'Oh, lawk, I don't read the papers much,' she burst out. 'Mommy is always trying to read things out to me but I avoid all that. Except for the serious things − but then I get that more from educational magazines and so on.' She clasped and unclasped her hands. 'Makes me sound real earnest, doesn't it? Perhaps I am. But all the bits in the social columns that Mommy reads are so boring.'

'Well, I daresay some of the work for Deaf Veterans will be boring too. There's a lot of administration to get the thing on the road. Funds are coming in well, but we've got to arrange for the money to be transmitted to organisations in London and Paris who can make proper use of it. Then we want to get information about the latest techniques for helping adults newly made deaf . . . Dr Bell says there's a lot of work going on but it needs to be collated.'

'You know Dr Bell?' she breathed.

'Yes, I've known him a long time, since my childhood. You've never met him?'

'Oh, heavens, no . . . Not in my little poky school . . . Besides, why should I be introduced to him?' Colour came into the freckled cheeks. Bess had been taught to have a low opinion of herself by an ambitious mother and two pretty sisters.

The interview ended with Neil telling her that she would hear from DVAS. She left with no great hope of being selected. She couldn't typewrite, nor take short-hand, nor do book-keeping. She had had what she considered a useless education which had given her the ability to play the piano a little, sing French chansons in a breathless soprano, embroider flowers on silk, and write acceptances of invitations in a pretty, legible hand. She had then been put on show for a husband to take up, but no husband had been forthcoming.

Her elder sister married, her younger sister was engaged . . . Her two brothers had married well – girls with some money and some looks. Bess remained, 'hopping about like a brown thrasher', as her mother was wont to say. As if it wasn't enough that she was homely, Mrs Gardiner sometimes thought her middle daughter was downright simple. If a young man showed even a polite interest, Bess was apt to scare him off by talking about things he didn't want to hear about. Of course it was right to be worried about the poor and the sick, but not at a ball! Not at a soirée!

'But Mommy, I've said all I have to say about Mrs de Mayer's potted ferns,' Bess would groan when chided for frightening off yet another escort.

'I declare, Bess, you go out of your way to misunderstand me. Of course I don't expect you to talk all evening about Mrs de Mayer's conservatory. But did you have to tell Johnnie Perpacks that a family among the coalminers could live for a month on what he spent for cigars?'

'It's true, Mommy—'

'True or false, it's unsuitable and inconvenient of you to mention it. What am I to do with you, Bess?' And throwing up her hands in despair Mrs Gardiner would retire to her boudoir with lavender water, a clean handkerchief, and her address book, to see if there were any mothers of unattached young males to whom she could appeal.

Bess solved the problem of what to do with herself by taking up actual physical work. Mrs Gardiner was horrified. Arnold Gardiner took it with more philosophy. 'If it's what she wants to do, Lucy, why not let her? It keeps her out of mischief.'

'She'll be an old maid!' wailed his wife. 'Only old maids devote themselves to good works—'

'The orphanage is a decent enough place, dear. She won't come to any harm there. Seems to me it's better than to have her sitting at the edge of a dance floor, an obvious wallflower.'

'How can you speak so, Arnie! No daughter of mine ever sat waiting for partners. I see to all that beforehand so her *carnet* has names enough—'

'That's just it, isn't it? She hates all that. If working with these kids makes her happy—'

'But how is she going to meet a man she can marry?'

Arnold Gardiner sighed. 'Has it ever occurred to you that our Bess might be a born spinster?'

If he had suggested Bess might be a Hottentot witch-doctor, his wife could not have been more shocked. 'Arnold! What a thing to say!'

'Dear, we may have to face it. She doesn't seem interested in boys and boys don't seem interested in her. I sometimes feel we should have let her take teacher-training—'

'Now, Arnie, you know that was absurd! No daughter of mine—'

'I know, I know. And in any case, she seems to have found something that appeals to her at the orphanage. Seems to me, Lucy, we must just leave her to it, because if you keep on pushing her face to face with young men she'll only talk to them about the needs of parentless children—'

'Oh, dear heaven,' wept Lucy Gardiner, 'what did I ever do to deserve a daughter like this?'

But her husband's words stayed with her. Bess might quite possibly be one of those aberrations of nature, an unmarriageable girl. Her coming-out had been a disappointment, no sudden flush of beauty had succeeded the grooming and the gowning that took place then. Her social programme over the succeeding years had led nowhere. Perhaps it was time to stop giving herself sick headaches about Bess but to concentrate instead on the plans for Enid's wedding next spring.

Left to her own devices, Bess had worked her way into the running of the St Ursula's Home for Abandoned Children so that she became accepted as part of the fittings. She turned up two days a week, fetched and carried and wiped runny noses. Little by little she began to identify groups which needed her more than others.

Children who are abandoned by their parents fall into two classes – those who are left because their parents can no longer afford to keep them, or those whose parents don't care about them. Children with handicaps come into this second category. Several of the children at St Ursula's had been cut off from their parents by an unacknowledged deafness, and it was to these that Bess was drawn. The doctor of the orphanage explained their predicament – unable to hear, they didn't learn to speak. Unable to speak, they were written off as stupid – 'dumb'. 'They need special tuition, but we don't have the funds to hire special teachers nor to send them to special boarding schools.'

Bit by bit Bess began to attack the problem. She tried at first to establish personal communication. Then when she discovered that each child was adopting a personal style of 'speech' she took it upon herself to learn the Visible Speech language. This she taught to the children at St Ursula's with help from a visiting expert. At twenty she was to some extent trained in handling deaf pupils but with no certificates or official qualifications. so when she came to offer her services to DVAS she expected to be told she wasn't wanted.

Her mother was not displeased when a letter came inviting Miss Gardiner to join the staff of the charity. It was better than being buried in an orphanage in a poor neighbourhood, certainly. Mrs Gardiner, who made it her business to keep track of the great or the wealthy, knew that the famous Dr Alexander Graham Bell had been party to the formation of the new charity and that the son of Robert Craigallan, the wheat millionaire, was to be its nominal President. People of good quality would flutter round such an organisation: rich old ladies would give it their patronage, and the male relatives of the rich old ladies would be pressed into service to help. It was Mrs Gardiner's hope that one of the male relatives would take a fancy to Bess.

For her part, Bess was delighted. She hadn't really expected to be chosen. What pleased her was the idea of doing something really useful and on a larger scale than teaching a handful of handicapped children, although she intended to keep up her visits to St Ursula's. It also gave her pleasure to discover she would be working in the main office, which Mr Craigallan would visit on several days a week. She had taken to him during that interview. He was capable, unselfpitying, and pleasant to converse with. If she also thought him very goodlooking in his grave, tall way, she kept that to herself.

Neil needed to get firsthand information about what was happening to the deaf-wounded from the battle-field. Statistics and hospital reports were not adequate: they tended to deal with the more spectacular injuries, the amputations and lung damage from poison gas. The injuries to the head and ear were of course well catalogued but what was unclear was the fate of the patient after discharge. Who kept track of him? Who taught him to come to terms with his loss of hearing? And there were those whose deafness was not obvious, those whose injuries were to the inner ear alone with no outside symptoms. Many of those seemed to be entirely missed, or counted as malingerers.

Neil wrote to doctors and specialists and heads of hospitals. He wrote to teachers of the deaf, to the directors of institutes. He wrote to friends of his own and of Dr Bell's. He also wrote to his sister Ellie-Rose.

'No doubt there's a lot of voluntary work going on among the ladies you know, on behalf of the wounded. Please find out, if you can, whether any special care is taken of the deaf-wounded. I know of course there is an organisation in Britain for the purpose of helping the deaf but their resources must be stretched at this time. Many men must be left with no help, no one to turn to in a new and frightening situation. For some reason, those blinded in battle attract very great sympathy but those who lose their hearing are not considered at all. Dear Ellie, if you hear of any way in which we can bring influence to bear so as to get more information, please let me know.'

Ellie-Rose read this aloud to Curtis over breakfast. Curtis, munching toast with English marmalade, nod-ded in agreement. 'Yes, there must be a lot of chat among the men themselves about things that never get to their commanding officers.' He hooked another spoonful of marmalade on to his plate and became thoughtful. 'All the same, Ellie, you don't want to waste too much of your time gossiping with private soldiers . . . We've more important things to do.'

It was true that Ellie had many calls on her time and attention, few of which brought her into direct contact with privates or able-seamen. She made token appearances at tea-parties and smoking concerts for servicemen, as did many other women of society, but at such affairs conversation was mostly limited to stilted remarks. 'How are you, private?' 'Fine thanks, missus.' 'Can I pour you another cup?' 'Thanks, mum, and two spoons of sugar.'

She couldn't picture herself asking any of those men whether they had difficulty with their hearing because of gunfire or shell-blast, nor whether any of their comrades were suffering. But she wanted to help Neil, who seemed at last to have found something to do that brought him into the limelight a little. She thought about it, and it occurred to her that such a woman as Sylvia Pankhurst would know how to get just the kind of undocumented information that Neil was asking for.

It troubled Ellie that she and Sylvia had quarrelled. She still couldn't accept the other woman's notion that the Germans could be whitewashed, but certainly there were some very wild rumours circulating. It was said — and the newspapers published such reports — that the airships known as Zeppelins were appearing over the coasts of England and dropping bombs on innocent civilians. Ellie couldn't really bring herself to believe it. How could any apparatus, flying yards up in the sky, launch missiles with any hope of hitting any selected target? And as to simply choosing towns and emptying bombs on them — that was absurd. What would be the point of it? Margate, for instance — why should the Germans attack Margate, which she gathered was a seaside resort something like Atlantic City?

Ellie had no doubt that there was misunderstanding or exaggeration, and perhaps both. It grieved her to see how these misunderstandings swelled the tide of anti-German feeling in London, where even such people as the Rothschilds heard harsh remarks directed against them.

Now she had a reason to visit Miss Pankhurst and make peace with her, using Neil's request for information as an excuse. So on the evening of the 31st of May she set out to visit the toy factory in Old Ford. It was a decision quite suddenly arrived at; Curtis was out at some all-male affair, she had had a light meal by herself and had settled down to listen to a new record of Caruso on the gramophone, as the British eccentrically called the phonograph.

It was a fine evening. The lilac in the garden at the back of the house was fading, filling the air with perfume as if to leave a remembrance of itself when its blooms were done. The leaves of the little tree threw a pattern of shadow over pansies and pinks grown in tubs. At eight o'clock the light was still strong from a sun sinking behind little lambskin clouds. Restlessness seized Ellie. The full, passionate tones of the great tenor seemed to beat inside her head. She wanted to be out, doing something, not sitting by the open window watching the golden evening die away.

She took a taxi to Old Ford. Although she had learned to use the bus, she saw no reason to prove her emancipation by travelling so far on it at this time of day. Miss Pankhurst was surprised to see her, but

133

pleased. She too had had second thoughts about some of her remarks the last time they met.

'How nice of you to call, Mrs Gracebridge! And as it happens, I have a countryman of yours here too. Do come upstairs to meet him.'

Somehow, even as she went up the uncarpeted stairs behind Miss Pankhurst, Ellie-Rose knew it was Tad Kendall in the room above.

In the small house used as a factory, voices carried. He had heard Sylvia exclaim on greeting her and was ready to face her. 'Good evening, Mrs Gracebridge,' he said, getting up from the table where he was examining the toys.

'Oh, you two know each other?' said Miss Pankhurst.

'We both know Gertie Dorf, whom I believe you have some dealings with, Miss Pankhurst,' Tad said. Then, turning to Ellie: 'I'm here at the behest of Mrs Astor. She wants to see if I can interest some of our clients – ship-owners and the like – in financing an expansion of Miss Pankhurst's work.'

'Mrs Astor is so beneficent,' Miss Pankhurst remarked, with just enough acid in her tone to let Ellie know that she thought Mrs Astor was something of a poseur. 'Well, let me offer refreshments, Mrs Gracebridge. We have no coffee – shall I make you a cup of tea?'

'No, no thank you, I only came to ask your help.' Ellie explained her brother's project and his need for direct information. She could see Sylvia Pankhurst was impressed. 'If you could speak to the women of the neighbourhood, or to their husbands as they come home on leave . . . ? Neil wants to know how accurate the government statistics are, and what is done for the deaf or partially deaf in the services. Just a general impression, although if you could note regiments or ships' names, it would help.'

'Certainly, what an excellent scheme! I'll do all I can.' Miss Pankhurst then turned her attention on Tad, asking for names of businessmen whom she might contact for funds. He parried her direct questions with skill, suggesting instead that he should speak to the men himself and see if he could persuade them to make a donation. He bought some toys as a gesture of goodwill, then it was time for him to go.

'You had better go with him, Mrs Gracebridge,' Sylvia said in her direct, no-nonsense way. 'I can telephone for a taxi for you if you prefer, but it may take some time to fetch one. Whereas if you go up to the main road with Mr Kendall, you should be able to hail one without much difficulty.'

Ellie hesitated. Kendall, with a faintly ironic smile, offered his arm. Miss Pankhurst saw them to the door, where she stood issuing instructions about which direction to take. They walked off, arm in arm, and turned into Roman Road, where, sure enough, a taxi soon cruised up. Tad handed her in.

Ellie said nothing. She would have liked to get rid of Tad as soon as possible, not be in his company all the way back to Victoria, but she could scarcely give her reason — which was that to be with him was an agonising embarrassment. She stiffened her spine; if he could bear it, so could she.

They had reached the junction of Bethnal Green Road and Shoreditch when a curious sound made them all turn their heads, passengers and driver alike. A swishing, whining noise seemed to go by overhead and to their right. At the same time a light arrowed over in

135

the now-dark sky, like a shooting star.

'What the devil's that?' exclaimed the driver. He swerved into the side of the road, where two or three pedestrians were standing with their heads thrown back.

But the shooting star had gone down behind the tall buildings of Shoreditch. The taxi driver was just about to steer away from the kerb and continue on his way when another flicker appeared in the sky.

'God Almighty!' he cried. Then, 'Beggin' your pardon, lady!'

'What on earth is it?' Tad asked, opening the door and leaning out.

An ominous sound came to Ellie's ears – a steady, humming throb, deep and strange, like a great cat purring. The driver was out of the cab now, staring up into the sky, shading his eyes against the street lamps so as to see what was above.

'It's a Zep! It's a Zep!' The cry was taken up by the people in the street. They gathered in little groups, gazing up at the darkness beyond the lamps. Ellie got out to stand beside Tad on the pavement.

Against the grey-blue of the May sky a long, fish-shaped object could be seen, moving slowly and inexorably above the buildings. From time to time little flickers of light seemed to drop from it. The airship was to the right of them, over the district of Hoxton. But as they watched, it changed course, seemed to drift south so as to be almost overhead in a frighteningly short time, and once again the flickers of light appeared below it. The very air seemed to vibrate with the sound of the engines.

Almost simultaneously came a series of crashing detonations. The pavement under Ellie's feet shuddered. Spouts of orange flame erupted on the roof of a building twenty yards off.

Something black hit a house wall and clattered down on the street. Almost comically it bounced . . . once, twice. The second rebound brought it down on an elderly man standing in amazement by a bus stop. It felled him. He seemed to vanish for a moment, cut almost in two by the object. Then suddenly he was a mass of flame, and so were the road and the post by which he was standing.

'Oh, God!' shrieked Ellie, rushing towards him to save him.

The flame rushed across the cobbles in a strange orange stream. Tad grabbed her shoulder and pulled her back, falling with her in a headlong heap. The ground shuddered under them. Another bomb had fallen nearby. Running feet. Screams. Suddenly everything was a scarlet glow as the buildings caught alight.

Ellie and Tad were helped up. Ellie was sobbing with fright and shock. 'He . . . he . . . caught fire . . . !'

'Incendiary bombs,' someone shouted. 'Take cover!'

The thunder of the Zeppelin's engines almost drowned the call. There was another whining fall and another, two detonations as the bombs hit. Tad dragged Ellie into a doorway and held her within its shelter. The threatening thunder of the airship's propellers vibrated through their bodies. The flames outside grew in intensity of colour and heat. There was a babel of screams, shouts, curses.

'Oh, don't!' sobbed Ellie. 'Don't − please don't let it—'

'It's all right, Ellie. You're quite safe. Don't be afraid. I'm here, Ellie darling.'

They stood clinging to each other in the middle of the

maelstrom of fire, prisoner in the moment, and prisoner to each other once again.

Chapter Eight

Although the first Zeppelin raid in London seemed to go on for ever to those who lived through it, the duration was only a little over ten minutes. The capacity of the bomb-bay was limited and when the cargo had been released the great airship moved slowly away, unchallenged by any defence force.

Tad released Ellie, shivering with reaction. She swayed and almost fell, but caught at the jamb of the doorway in which they'd taken shelter. Tad ran out into the street. The flames were luridly red and orange, smoke billowed like a great sea-fog. 'Tad!' Ellie screamed, and lunged after him.

Farther up the street a house was on fire, flames surging from the upper windows like the tongues of some multi-headed monster. People were running towards it, calling to each other. 'There's someone in the bedroom! Ladders — fetch ladders! Call the firemen!'

Already the clanging of the fire engine's bell could be heard. Whistles were blowing as police constables summoned help from other streets. Ellie picked up the front of her brown silk suit and ran. A little girl and a woman came staggering out of the house next to the one in flames, coughing and weeping in the smoke, their night-clothes already turning grey with flinders and dirt from the fire. 'Auntie Edie, Auntie Edie!' the child was sobbing. Her mother pulled her close, tried to hide her face against her nightgown to prevent her from seeing the raging fire-storm that was consuming the neighbouring house.

The fire engine careered up, crashing to a halt with a jarring of equipment. Men leapt down, others ran to help. The mother and child were pushed hither and thither in the crowd. Ellie put an arm round the woman and guided her away. For the moment she had lost sight of Tad. Through the confusion in her mind one thought had come clear and cool – the burning house was going to fall, the woman and child must be got away.

They retreated to the edge of the crowd of fire-fighters, eager hands took charge of the pair. Ellie took off her jacket to wrap round the little girl who was shuddering with shock. A man gave his topcoat to the woman. A sudden rush of sound and a flare of orange light told them that in another street another building had been consumed by fire. A shout of horror and anger went up.

The scene was like a nightmare – there was frenzied activity in an effort to prevent the fire spreading, to get out whoever was in the house. Helpers came running from side-streets. But it was useless, the heat was like a furnace. Afterwards Ellie learned that the substance in the bombs was phosphorus, impossible to combat once it is alight except with special techniques which the London Fire Brigade had not as yet learned.

The air was hideous with sound – the strange swishing roar of the flames, the cracking of fire-expanded bricks, the falling of masonry, the shouts and curses of men, the clanging of bells as other fire trucks raced towards other fires, running footsteps, the gushing of water from hoses, car horns, breaking glass, screams for help, weeping, moaning . . .

At length the noise diminished. The roofs of the houses had caved in, the fire began to die a little in the first house and was brought under control next door. The crowd drew forward to look. The firemen tried to hold them back. 'Now then, now then − there's bodies in there, we've got to get 'em out. Clear the way, please, clear the way . . .'

Ambulances had appeared further down the road. The people looked about now, their attention at last diverted from the holocaust. A strange growl began. 'Bodies . . . They killed 'em . . . Them Huns, them bloody Huns . . .' As if they had been stirred by a giant hand, the crowd eddied and re-grouped. A confused shouting began. Ellie couldn't make out what it was.

The woman and child from the fire-damaged house were taken into an ambulance. Ellie saw Tad threading his way towards her between the exclaiming, arguing groups.

She ran to him, grasped his arm. 'Is it true − there were people inside the house?'

He nodded. 'A man and a woman in bed upstairs, an elderly woman sitting downstairs. We heard her screaming but we couldn't get to her − she was at the back of the house.'

'Oh, Tad!'

He was pale, his face streaked with sweat and dirt. His stiff white collar had been pulled adrift, he had a tear in his sleeve and a burn on one hand. 'Tad, you must get that burn seen to—'

'It's all right, it isn't much—'

'The ambulance men will put on a dressing.' She pulled him towards a stationary vehicle where two men were giving first aid to those hurt by flying sparks or falling masonry. Tad stood in line at Ellie's insistence. Five minutes later, just as he was rejoining her, the crowd in the street suddenly took off in a rushing tide of movement.

Ellie was knocked to one side. Arms flailing she fell against the side of the ambulance. A first-aider grabbed her. 'What the hell—'

'Signalling! They was signalling! Get 'em boys – get the Huns!' The crowd were yelling and gesticulating, rushing by like a torrent.

'What're you doing – stop! – you're hurting people—' But it was no use. The first-aider was swept aside, Ellie and the minor casualties were crowded into the wall of a warehouse as the mob dashed by, hot for blood. They were calling something to each other, something Ellie couldn't make out. Only next day did she learn they had been shouting 'Lippermann, Lippermann!' – the name of an innocent German baker whose premises were wrecked and who was dragged out of his bed to be beaten up in revenge for the Zeppelin raid. The supposed excuse was that he had signalled to the Zeppelin.

Dazed and shaken, she pulled herself to her feet. Tad, crushed against the bricks so that his face was grazed, came towards her wiping blood away with a grimy handkerchief.

'Come on, Ellie, let's get the hell out of this!'

Arms about each other, they breasted the crowd and came to the crossroads where they had got out of the cab. It was still there. The driver was moving about the kerb, stooping.

'Hi, there!' Tad called. 'Can you take us on now?'

'Just let me find my cap, guv'nor — some idiot knocked it off.' He found it, opened the door for them, and bowed them aboard. 'Fun and games,' he said gruffly. 'Dunno who's worse — the Gerries or the Bowboys. D'jever see the likes?'

'They're angry,' Tad said. 'It's understandable. But I don't want to hang around here — let's get going.'

'Right you are, guv.' He got in, started the engine, then turned to look over his shoulder. 'Where to, like? If you don't mind me saying so, sir, the lady seems shook. Don't you think a drop of something would do her good?'

'Right! But not here — drive on out of the area.'

'I know just the place, guv. Hang on.' The rate at which he drove was hardly safe, but it scarcely seemed to matter. Traffic was in chaos as people struggled to reach the area where the raid had taken place and others hurried away from it to safety. Reporters and sightseers were cramming into taxis and buses, passersby were diverted from their homegoing journey to turn about and look at the results of the bombing attack.

Near Liverpool Street Station he drew up alongside a handsome public house with engraved glass windows and brass swan-necked lamps outside. 'Here you are, sir.'

Ellie drew back. She had never been in a public house and didn't want to start now, smoke-stained, jacketless, hair in a tangle, skirt crumpled. 'How about if you bring us out something, driver?' Tad suggested, sensing her feelings. 'And get one for yourself.'

'Thank you, guv, that's handsome of you.' He took the money and went in. Within a few minutes he was back with three double brandies, grouped between his

143

two hands. 'Here you are, sir, madam. Your change is in my pocket, sir.'

'Keep it. Here's your good health.'

'Yours, sir. Same to you, lady.'

With shaking hands she raised the glass to her lips. But after the first sip she choked, a storm of weeping seized her. The brandy went all down the front of her frilled silk blouse.

'Oh, God,' she wept, 'oh, God!'

Tad took the brandy glass. He said to the taximan, 'Soon's you finish, let's get on. The lady's had enough for one night.'

'I get your point, guv. Righty-oh, hang on.' He swallowed the rest of his drink, took the glasses from Tad, and ran back with them to the pub. In a moment he was in his driving seat and they were on their way again.

The rest of the journey was never clear in Ellie's mind. She sat huddled in a corner with Tad's arm about her shoulders. She didn't look out of the window, was quite unaware when at last the cab turned into Ebury Street. She was helped up the front steps. The door was flung open. She heard voices: Beading exclaiming in horror, Curtis full of anxiety and bewilderment.

'Happened to meet at Miss Pankhurst's . . . Zeppelin . . . Mob scenes . . . She's very shocked . . . A good long sleep . . . No thank you, I must get home, I have to be up in the morning.'

She was led indoors and upstairs. Kindly hands undressed her, she was put into a soothing bath, her hair was brushed and tied back, her nightdress was slipped over her head. Next moment she was in bed. She was asleep, worn out by an emotion she had never before experienced. Terror . . .

She woke in the grey of early morning. She was alone in the big double bed. Out of consideration Curtis had slept in his dressingroom. The bright clear light of the first day of June was turning the old plaster of the ceiling a gentle ivory-white.

She lay on her back, hands clutching the sheets in fear as she recollected what she had seen last night. Gradually, calmness came to her. Her grip relaxed. She sat up among her pillows.

She had been near to death last night. She had seen a man die, wrapped in a garment of flames. The incendiary bomb could quite as easily have hit herself, or Tad.

Life was unsafe, it seemed. Death could rain down from a starlit sky. Any moment an end might come to this existence that had seemed so secure, so certain.

What a fool she was to concern herself with dignity, with pride, with avoiding Tad for what was past. What did it matter that he had left her without explanation all those years ago?

What mattered was that they were alive, here, together, in a city of war. To hesitate over trifles, to diminish their need of each other, was madness.

He loved her. She had known that the moment he put his arms about her in the doorway while the bombs fell. And she loved him. She had never ceased to love him, and never would. Everything else was nonsense — mere convention, self-regard, childishness. Who knew how much life they might have to live? However much or little it was, she would give it to Tad.

The birds were singing outside in the little garden. A thrush in the hawthorn tree was calling. What was it Browning said about the thrush — that he sang his song two times over for fear he couldn't recapture 'the first fine careless rapture'. Her heart went out to the thrush, sending out his message of courage to the world. A fragile little thing, yet full of defiance and music, among the faded blossoms and thorns of the tree.

She would speak to Tad today. She would tell him she had realised they must waste no more time. They had been given a second chance – to recapture the first fine careless rapture. They must accept their chance, seize it with both hands. Nothing must be allowed to stand in the way, not the thorns of war that beset the peaceful fields.

She knew he would understand and agree. Whatever the reason he had for breaking up years ago, it couldn't be allowed to matter – not now they had found each other again. Providence had given them this second chance: it would be wrong to refuse it.

That settled, she closed her eyes and fell asleep again. Curtis, peeping in at eight o'clock, nodded his head to see her being healed by a long deep sleep. He told Beading not to wake her, but to wait until she rang and then ensure that she took breakfast in bed. Quietly he let himself out of the house to go to the office. It was Tuesday the 1st of June 1915, the day on which his marriage was suddenly heading straight towards the rocks – but he was quite unaware of it.

Ellie-Rose was sitting up in bed eating honey on little fingers of toast when Beading came in to report a phone call. 'Shall I tell him to call back later, ma'am?'

'Who is it, Beading?'

'The gentleman who escorted you home so kindly last night, ma'am.'

'I'll speak to him,' Ellie said. She swung herself out of bed so hastily the tray nearly went flying. Beading saved it just in time, but was so busy with it that she was

146

unable to prevent her mistress's getting up. Dragging a negligee around herself, Ellie ran to her boudoir.

'Hello? Tad?'

'Ellie! I didn't expect you to come to the phone — I just rang to ask how you were.'

'I'm all right, Tad. Listen, I must speak to you—'

'I don't think so, Ellie.'

'But I've got to, Tad!' Her voice broke. 'After last night—'

'Last night didn't change anything. All that happened was that we got caught in the middle of a disaster—'

'But you said — you said—'

'Whatever I said, you have to put it down to a flare-up of nerves. The circumstances—'

'The circumstances made us come to our senses, Tad! Don't pretend about it—'

'I'm not pretending. The point is, nothing's changed otherwise. We happened to be together in a spot where I — lost my head a little. Now I'm ringing to make sure you're recovering all right. That's all there is to it, Ellie.'

'I won't let it be like that!'

'That's the way it has to be. I'm going to put the phone down, Ellie.'

'No!' But it was too late. She heard the click the other end, then the vague sound that meant the exchange was connected, and then the operator's voice saying: 'Hello, caller? Can I help you?'

'No, it doesn't matter.' Ellie said in a dead voice, and replaced the receiver.

Until he spoke to her, she had been so sure she understood how things would be between them after last night. It had not entered her head he wouldn't see things as she did. She sat down by the unresponsive telephone and bowed her head into her hands. There Beading found her a few minutes later, put it all down to reaction after being caught in an air raid, and insisted on guiding her back to bed.

At midday Ellie got up. She ached, she had bruises on her elbows and knees and a scrape on her knuckles. She dressed for a luncheon engagement with Theodora Treventine at the Savoy but didn't go. Instead she found herself walking in Green Park, head bent, eyes on the path and the pigeons scuttling out of her way. She walked on, into St James's Park. The sun shone on the lake. Ducks swam about energetically, some of them followed by little wedge-shaped parties of ducklings. Children threw bread, nannies rocked their prams.

At four o'clock she went into a tea-shop to rest. She ordered tea and toasted tea-cakes, but ate nothing and drank little. Her body seemed to be at a low ebb. She was physically tired, spiritually tired, perplexed, lost.

About half an hour later she realised the waitress was hovering, wondering why she didn't consume the food she'd ordered. She asked for the bill, paid her, left a tip, and went out. She had little idea where she was. The afternoon was warm now, the streets full of the smell of flowers from the flower-stalls, dust, horses and harness. She passed a church whose door stood open. 'Turn to the Lord!' commanded a placard pinned to its noticeboard. She went in, sat on a hard rush-seated chair, and tried to turn to the Lord. 'Help me,' she pleaded. 'I don't know how to go on.'

But no tranquillity came, no unvoiced answer from on high. When she came out she looked about helplessly. A taxi was passing. She hailed it and was taken home.

Beading was at the door as she came up the steps. 'Madam, where have you been? Mrs Treventine rang from the Savoy to say you never turned up!'

'I . . . forgot, Beading.'

'Now come along, Mrs Gracebridge,' the maid said in a soothing tone. 'You shouldn't ought to have gone out in the first place. Not up to it, that's what it is.'

Curtis came home early, anxious about her because she had apparently gone missing when he rang from the office. She reassured him. She was quite all right, just a bit tired. She felt she couldn't face their evening engagement at the Cecils. It was just that she was afraid they'd ask her about the raid . . . He must go without her, make her excuses.

They argued for a few minutes. He didn't want to leave her alone. But truth to tell, he wanted to keep the date at the Cecils — a very important family. And it was only upsetting Ellie to think he'd give it up on her account. So he dressed and went out at seven-thirty.

Ellie was still in the day clothes she had put on to lunch with Mrs Treventine — a loose, softly draped dress of dark blue silk tissue with a white collar, over which went a blue and white cape-coat. She accepted a tray of soup and cold chicken in her boudoir and toyed with the food for a time but the idea of eating was unthinkable. Everyday details had receded from her. Nothing made any sense.

Suddenly she put the tray aside and got up. In Curtis's study she found his desk diary. Tad's name and address were noted, but only his office address. She closed the book, put it back in its place. For a moment she stood at a loss.

Then she found the London telephone directory. She looked up Tad's name. His address was a block of mansion apartments in Gray's Inn. She picked up her handbag and coat from her bedroom and went swiftly downstairs, making no response when Beading called out: 'Madam? Is that you?'

A short taxi ride took her to Gray's Inn Crescent. She went into the echoing foyer. On a board on the wall she found the names of residents and their apartment numbers. Tad's flat was on the second floor. There was a lift with an iron cage and gilt handles. She went in, pressed the button, was taken up to the second floor.

Once she had stepped out, her courage failed her. She looked around. The doors stretched away on either side, heavy mahogany with the numbers in ivory. A dim light filtered in through stained glass at the far end. She suddenly shivered and turned back to the lift.

It had gone down to the ground floor after she stepped out. Now it rose again to the second floor. The gates were pulled open.

And Tad himself stepped out.

He was the only passenger. They stood staring at each other in the dimness. She put out a faltering hand.

'Oh, Ellie . . .' Tad said and, putting an arm around her, guided her to his door.

Chapter Nine

News of the Zeppelin raid sent cables rushing to and fro between Craigallan Castle and London. Rob took it for granted that his daughter would want to move out of the city to a safer area. 'Sure, she can't come home to us, I see that — there's more danger from those damned U-boats than from the Zeps. But I don't think she should stay in London.'

Greg, staying for a few weeks of the fine early summer with his father, merely shrugged. 'London's a pretty big place, Mr Craig. The airship hit on the East End. It was just sheer bad luck Ellie happened to be there at the time.'

'I want her in a safer place!'

He wrote at length, urging her to move out. He had looked at maps of England and thought that a pleasant cathedral city such as Bath or Winchester — in the centre of the country, away from industrial targets — would be good. He had set about buying the great house in the glen of his birth, Castle Bairach. When the purchase was completed, Ellie must go there.

He couldn't understand why Ellie resisted the advice. She stubbornly refused to leave London. 'I really can't, Papa. What would the British think of us Yanks if we ran away to the country the minute things got a little uncomfortable?' She described how even elderly ladies refused to budge. 'They have this thing called "stiff upper lip" — and don't they just despise anyone whose upper lip gets a bit soft!' Her letter played down her experience in the East End. 'I discovered afterwards that the damage was really not very great — the police cleared the crowds away and apparently within days there was nothing to be seen.' She had to agree that six people had been killed but refrained from telling what she herself had seen. She was glad now that she hadn't blurted out to Curtis, or even Beading, the awful nightmarish scenes she had witnessed.

To Curtis she brushed it all aside. She had been shaken, yes. She had fallen, collected some bruises, got her clothes soiled, yes. But it was nothing, really. Nothing to make a fuss about, and certainly not worth all the upset and inconvenience of removing to a manor-house far from the capital.

'How would you manage, Curtis?'

'Well, I reckon I'd stay in Town all week and come home on weekends . . .'

'But that's not why I came to Britain with you, is it? To live in a different place most of the time.'

'No, honey, that's true.' Curtis was touched by her steadfastness. When he wrote to his father-in-law he sided with Ellie. Everything was really quite safe here in London. You were more likely to be knocked over by an automobile than hit by a bomb. It would sure be a loss if he and Ellie had to have separate existences — Ellie's charm and warmth were so helpful when he entertained important guests, and brought them so many invitations in return.

Ellie felt a cheat. But it didn't matter. Nothing mattered, except staying in London.

152

'Well, if she's bound and determined, there's nothing I can do about it,' Rob mourned. 'And after all, she's no fool — if she thinks the air raid danger is slight, I suppose I must accept that.'

The truth was, he could do nothing. His favourite child was thousands of miles away across the Atlantic, beyond his control. Not that he had ever had much control over Ellie, if the facts were faced.

Ellie's children were quite impressed to get letters telling them their mother had been involved in an air raid. It made her into a heroic figure. Gina thought it would have been even better if Mama had tended the wounded, going to one prone figure after another in a snowy white uniform and a cap with a red cross on the front, like the illustrations in *Harper's*. But photographs reaching them, after long delays due to problems with sea-mail, showed Ellie in fashionable London clothes at fashionable London events.

'Do you think she looks different?' she asked Granma Morag, holding out the latest one to her.

Morag put on her glasses and studied it. She saw a tall, shapely woman, looking younger than her years, in a gown of Grecian inspiration by Worth, high-waisted, loose-skirted, the lovely throat rising from the gold-trimmed square neckline. Her hair, showing darker in the photograph than in real life, was piled up in loose curls on top of her head and held in place by a gold cord, after the style of dancers shown in Greek frescoes. Her hand rested lightly on her husband's sleeve. Curtis, about the same height but heavier, thickening in the middle, looked somehow much older than Ellie — stuffy, self-satisfied, mundane.

For no reason that she could think of, Morag felt a prick of alarm. You looked at the picture and you knew they were man and wife — yet somehow they were separate beings, the one not dependent in any way upon the other.

But then, many marriages came to this, Morag told herself. Settled, middle-aged — held together by convention and habit. And Ellie had never been head over heels in love with Curtis to begin with.

'She's really beautiful, isn't she?' Gina murmured.

'Yes, very beautiful. And you take after her, Gina.'

'Did she have lots of beaux when she was my age?'

'Of course. The boys were around her like bees around a honeypot.'

Gina longed to ask how Mama had handled it. She herself was constantly in a state of temptation. Other girls boasted they'd let boys kiss them or put an arm round them. Fanny Lebener even said she'd gone on the Ferris Wheel with a boy and let him grab her real close against him.

At the school soirée, boys from the neighbouring military academy had been invited. The windows of the school's assembly hall had been open to the recreation grounds since the evening was warm. More than one couple had disappeared out into the shadows beyond the tennis courts. Gina had let Arthur Loomis take her into the darkness among the laurels to kiss her.

But his breath had smelt of the whisky he'd been sipping from a hip flask, and his chin had lumps and bumps from acne, and his hands in their cotton gloves had been hot and disgusting, like living creatures crawling over her. So she'd shoved him away hard and he'd fallen into the bushes and emerged later angry and dishevelled.

He'd called her a rude name. Gina was shocked. If men were like this, how did you ever come to love one?

How did you ever come to the moment where, according to suspicions she was beginning to have, you had to take your clothes off in front of each other? She had never yet met a boy who didn't bore her or embarrass her — the idea of being alone with one in a bedroom, and doing mystifying things together unclothed, was sickening.

'Granma Morag, when a boy is allowed to invite you out . . . it's all right to kiss them?'

'If you feel you want to, dear.'

'What if they want to, and you don't?'

'Then you say no.'

'But what if he wants to a lot, and . . . he won't let you say no?'

'Gina, I hope you haven't had any boys behaving like that with you!' Morag was shocked. It was her duty to supervise Gina's life in Ellie's absence. She took her role seriously and was beginning to realise that it was time to have what was known as 'a serious talk' with the child.

'Arthur Loomis kissed me,' Gina blurted out. 'And he was awful!'

'What happened? Gina, tell me?' But Morag's momentary alarm died almost at once. At the soirée of the finishing school, no mishaps had been reported. No one had been missing from the 'ballroom' for more than a few minutes at a time. The games mistress had been patrolling the grounds to make sure that everyone got shooed back into the main assembly. There had not been the slightest hint of anything happening to Gina.

'Oh, it was nothing, I suppose. He was a bit pickled. He carries whisky around with him in a flask.'

'Oh, does he indeed?' The information would be passed on among the Washington matrons. From now on Arthur Loomis would not be invited to respectable homes without the strictest supervision.

'I don't really like him anyway. He can't dance worth a nickel.' Gina sighed. 'Granma, why are boys so *disappointing*?'

Morag didn't laugh. 'I think it's because they take so long to grow up, my dear.' She nodded towards the window, beyond which Gina's brother could be seen amusing himself by doing acrobatic tricks on the swing below the cottonwood.

'Ye-es,' agreed Gina. True enough, Curtis always seemed a lot younger than Gina. Much more than two years younger. She'd always thought this was because as a child he had needed special nursing that seemed to keep him in his babyhood longer than others, but perhaps all male children were the same — children indeed, until the world forced them to grow up.

Perhaps she might find it more agreeable to be in the company of older men? Like most girls, she had a yearning for the handsome young French teacher, and admired various actors she saw in the theatre. But for the first time it occurred to her — perhaps she might be able to find friendship and understanding with a man who had gone past the callow stage of youth.

She pictured herself with such a man. He would be tall, dark, with deepset eyes and an air of hidden sadness. He would discuss with her the things that boys never seemed to know anything about — poetry, especially the poems of Lord Tennyson, and the music of Frederic Chopin, and plays such as *L'Aiglon* . . .

She sighed to herself. Well, for sure, she wasn't going to meet this fascinating stranger in the next couple of months, for at the end of the week Grandfather Gracebridge arrived to take her and Curtis to

Nebraska for a long duty visit.

She viewed the prospect with dread. Grandfather and Grandmother Gracebridge were so *old* . . . They weren't any older than Grandfather Craigallan, she supposed, but they acted old, and seemed so . . . so past the enjoyment of everything except small talk and prayer meetings. Her brother quite enjoyed the visits to the Nebraska farm. He was glorying in a new-found, almost-perfect health – out all day at school where exercise and physical prowess were the rule, and then at home always on the move – climbing, walking, helping in the garden. In Nebraska he'd be out on horseback or clambering about on the bluffs. They had never been companions because of his poor health, and now that he was fit they seemed even further apart.

At school the teachers gave their students little lectures about not wasting the vacations and long lists of books they ought to read. Morag took Gina shopping on the Thursday for the books. Among them was a study of sculpture by Addington Symonds, *The Renaissance*. As she paid for the pile of ornate volumes Morag was thoughtful – perhaps at last she had been given the opening she had been seeking.

That evening she came into Gina's room to cast an eye over the trunks packed by Gina's maid. The girl herself was putting personal items into a cut-velvet valise. Morag took it from her hands and led her to a settee. 'Sit down a moment, Gina. I want to talk to you.'

Gina looked at her with a pout of her full lips. It was going to be a lecture about being good at Sandhill and not plaguing Grandmother Gracebridge.

She was surprised at Morag's first words. 'You

remember the other day we were talking about boys, Gina?'

She nodded. A sudden anxiety seized her. What was Granma Morag going to say? She had done nothing wrong — even if she had let Arthur Loomis kiss her, she had pushed him away.

'You said you wished they weren't so awful. Has it ever occurred to you why they're so important — why it matters if they're nice or nasty?'

'Well . . . A girl has to get married to one . . .'

Morag suppressed her smile. 'Exactly. "Male and female created He them." You've never wondered why?'

Gina went a dull red and looked down at her clenched hands. 'It's to do with . . . babies,' she muttered.

'Quite right.' Morag paused. 'Do you and the other girls talk about that?'

'Oh yes. A lot!'

'Where do they say babies come from?'

'Sally Hagermeir says it happens if you sit in a chair immediately after a man's been sitting in it. But that's not it.'

'And how do you know that?' Morag asked gently.

'Because I tried it!' Gina looked up, red with embarrassment, tense with defiance. 'It's just not true! I told her it wasn't and she dared me, and I did it, and nothing happened — but I knew it wouldn't.'

Morag nodded and gave her a smile of approval. 'I'm glad you've got so much sense that you can see nonsense when it's put before you. But all the same, don't rush to prove the truth of what other people say about important things. Sex isn't a thing to be in a rush about.'

'*I* don't want to be in a rush about it. It's everybody else − they get in a kind of fever over it − I think it's because we don't really *know* . . .'

'I understand, Gina. So let's think what you do actually know so far. You remember the day you first started to have your monthly cycle?'

'Oh yes.' Hateful day! Frightened and disgusted and shocked, she'd hidden from the maid, from her mother . . . Ellie-Rose had found her in a closet at the top of the house, huddled into herself in fear at her own body.

'What did your mother tell you then?'

'Oh . . . that it would happen regularly from then on, that it was what made me different from a man, that it shouldn't be talked about but had to be endured . . .'

'Yes,' Morag agreed, sighing. It was all too true. 'What else? Did she tell you about babies?'

'She said . . . she said when a woman is having a baby, all that kind of thing stops.' The panic that had ensued when Gina herself had had a cessation for three months! − due as it later was shown to anaemia. Her mother had laughed at her when she blurted out at last that she thought she must be . . . 'with child'. She had wanted then to know why Mother was so sure it couldn't be so, but Mother had said, 'We'll talk about all that when you're older.'

Morag now began the talk that Ellie-Rose had intended to have. A wide generation gap separated her from Gina, but she tried to cast her mind back to her own girlhood, even more sheltered than Gina's, for she had been raised in a church orphanage where the word sex was never even mentioned. She tried to recall her own mystification and fear. Clinical words she had none, for no one had ever said them to her. She had learned from experience — first with rapture and love for Rob, and then with horror and disgust after an assault by a gang of drunken men.

She spoke to Gina of her own body, of how it was made and what it was intended for. She opened the book on sculpture so that, by means of its illustrations, she could show Gina what she meant. Gina listened avidly, clothing the older woman's simple narrative with veils and splendours borrowed from poetry: the girl in 'The Eve of St Agnes' undressing, 'her silken garments rustling to her knees'; Cleopatra's 'baby at my breast that sucks the nurse asleep'; the mysterious words of Donne's 'Holy Sonnet', 'Immensity cloistered in thy dear womb'. As Morag painstakingly mentioned the aspects of womanhood and tried to explain them, Gina seized on the information to make it fit with her romantic visions.

It was summed up for her in the words of a madrigal she'd espied in a collection from which they were learning in the music class at school. Miss Happer had never let them see it, restricting them instead to songs about Maying and Bright Gloriana. But Gina had read it and felt as if a door were opening to her. 'No beauty she doth miss, when all her robes are on. But beauty's self she is, when all her robes are gone.'

Now as Granma Morag spoke, she understood it. The mystery and beauty of the female body were for the purpose of enchantment, of mastery over men. In some way, that body became the temple in which the baby grew and was cared for, afterwards to lie in his mother's arms as she, like a painting by Giotto, smiled down on him.

Morag had been brief. She had no great taste for the

160

task she was performing and felt she had no skill at it. The most difficult moment was approaching. She turned the pages of the book until she came to the illustration of Michelangelo's David, that poem of praise in marble to the male body. With hesitation, but calmly, she went on with her instruction.

Gina looked at the illustration and listened at first, but after a bit she sought once again for poetic images to veil the facts. Yet there seemed to be none. None of the poetry she had ever read celebrated the harsh details she was hearing now.

'Is there anything you want to ask me?' Morag said, ending the lecture with relief.

Gina shook her head. It was more a negation of what she had been told than an expression of satisfaction. After a moment she said, 'Isn't it . . . what you've just said . . . more like animals?'

Morag was going to say, 'Not when there is love.' But that was hardly an honest reply, for many a woman had borne children without ever loving their father. After a moment's thought she said: 'Human nature has a side that we try to hide. Whether it's animal I don't know, if you mean it in the sense of being low or beastly. But let me remind you of the Bible — "Male and female created He them". It's God's creation, Gina. If he intended it so, how can it be wrong?'

'But . . . how can a person . . . a *lady* . . . bring herself to . . . do that?' She remembered Arthur Loomis, hot and smelling of whisky and heavy against her own body. What was the use of all these wonders Morag had just been explaining about womanhood if all they were for was to take part in a brutish act?

'Dear, it's too difficult to explain all at once or for you to understand all at once. What I've been talking

161

about is the physical side — I sensed a restlessness in you, an impatience, and as you're going to be away on holiday I thought I'd speak to you about that and you would maybe think it over. But there's more, you know, Gina. There's desire, and passion . . .' Morag fell silent for a moment. 'There's love, too.'

'But love isn't like that!' Gina pictured her damsels in their moated granges, her fleet-footed nymphs hunting with silver bows in the moonlight, Juliet sighing on her balcony. To imagine that when Romeo climbed up and clasped her in his arms they went on to . . . to *that* . . . It was impossible!

'Love is all kinds of things, my love,' Morag said. 'You'll see. Now it's getting late. I want you to finish your packing and get a good night's sleep. Grandfather Gracebridge will be here early but you won't be leaving until the afternoon, so if there's anything worrying you tomorrow morning you come and talk to me about it.'

Gina would rather have died than have any further conversation with Morag on the topic. She was busy holding together the cloud palaces in which her dreams were kept. She was sure that there was some mistake in what she'd been told. In bed and unable to sleep, she let her mind go back to Morag and her words, and she remembered something. Morag had had a baby, because Greg was her son. But Morag wasn't married. So it followed that Morag had an imperfect knowledge about that side of life. Everybody agreed that to have a baby and not be married was very wrong, and though she couldn't quite believe that Granma Morag had ever been wicked, all the same she wasn't to be relied upon. She wasn't like Mama and Papa. Gina thought of her mother and father in each other's arms, engaged in the activity that Morag had been trying to describe — and she shuddered with horror. Impossible! Impossible! Mama and Papa would never lower themselves to behave like that!

Grandfather Gracebridge was fond of saying that his 'old bones' deserved consideration, so the long train journey to Lincoln, Nebraska was broken by two overnight stops. The first was at Chicago, where they stayed with Uncle Cornelius in his big apartment overlooking Grant Park. This was enjoyable, because his housekeeper, Mrs Fitzgerald, was quite young and liked to chat. She took Gina shopping after dinner in the grand shops on Michigan Avenue for an hour or so, even let her try on a grown-up gown with batwing sleeves like a Japanese kimono.

'My, you do look different with that on, Miss Gina!'

'Well, everyone says I'll be goodlooking, Mrs Fitzgerald. Do you think I will?'

'I sure do, darlin'. Now you change back into your proper things and while you do that, I'll just go and buy some yarn to finish those socks for my Larry. Meet me in the lobby. We'll be thrown out with the trash if we hang around any longer — they're just on closing.'

Gina unwillingly divested herself of the ivory silk dress. She knew that with her dark hair and great green-flecked eyes she looked wonderful in it — almost like some exotic butterfly. She said to the salesgirl on an impulse, 'I'll take it. Send it to my uncle's apartment — Mr Cornelius Craigallan, on—'

'Oh, we have Mr Craigallan's address in the delivery room, I'm sure, madam,' the girl said in a tone of awed respect. Everyone in Chicago knew the Craigallans. 'Shall I charge it to his account?'

'Yes,' Gina said casually, 'do that, will you?' Later, as she was saying goodnight to the menfolk, she said in a low voice to her uncle, 'I bought a dress while I was out, Uncle Neil — had it put on your account. Was that all right?'

Neil, unaware that she was telling him all this almost in a whisper, smiled and nodded as he read her lips. 'Quite all right, kitten.' Manlike, he never thought to ask if it was a suitable dress for a young lady who was not yet 'out'.

Next day the parcel arrived and was incorporated without comment among Gina's luggage except that Curt, who had been put in charge of it by his grandfather, complained. 'Gee, haven't you got enough to lug around with your old books and valise full of hair-ribbons and stuff? What d'you want to buy something else for?'

'Oh, I'll carry it myself if you're so simple you can't look after it—'

'I never said I couldn't look after it. I only said why . . .' The porter at the depot came up, touching his cap, and began to put the bags on his trolley. 'Fourteen pieces now,' Curt said, putting out his tongue at his sister as he counted them onto the loader.

The train from Chicago westward was a slower one than the express from New York. They were to stay overnight in Des Moines. This proved to be a one-horse sort of town as far as Gina could make out in the dusk of Saturday evening. They piled into a horse-cab and were taken to the Des Moines Plaza Hotel where they had rooms booked. Although Grandfather Craigallan would have paid any expenses for his daughter's children, Grandfather Gracebridge was sturdily independent, so that their accommodation was nothing like the luxury and comfort Gina was used to. However, she was better off than Curt. He had to share a room with his grandfather. Gina at least had a room to herself.

After dinner Grandfather Gracebridge fell asleep over the newspaper in the hotel lounge. He had the habit, willingly adopted, of taking forty winks after every meal except breakfast, a habit Rob Craigallan would have scorned. It made for dullness for the youngsters, but at least there was a quartet dispensing light music in the Plaza's tea-room whither Gina and Curt repaired to pass the time with a soda until bedtime.

Next morning, Sunday, they were to spend in Des Moines. It was against Grandfather Gracebridge's principles to travel on a Sunday except for business. Taking his grandchildren home for the vacation was pleasure, according to his view. So they wouldn't resume their journey until Monday.

Sunday morning was spent listening to a tedious sermon from a Methodist preacher in a nearby church. After lunch Tom Gracebridge settled down with an improving book for his customary nap. Gina and Curtis examined all the amenities of the hotel, swung for ten minutes or so in the canopied seat in the garden and were then at loose ends.

'Well, I don't know about you, but I'm going out!' Gina announced.

'Where you going?'

'How do I know? Out!'

'Well, I guess I'll come with you.'

Gina didn't really want him, but in decency she could hardly say no. They set off after they had collected the necessities without which no respectable person could venture out of doors – gloves, hat and matching purse for Gina, gloves and boater for Curt. Out they strolled, into the hot June sunshine of the prairies. There was a park, which they entered. Soon Curt had been tempted off to play baseball with a crowd of boys who yelled an invitation. Gina walked on, and noticed a placard advertising a band concert.

She followed the pointing arrow. Soon the strains of a soprano rendering 'Hark, hark, the lark' assured her she was on the right path. She came out into the band arena. A fourteen-piece orchestra under a pagoda canopy were playing the coda to the song. The soprano bowed to applause and began on 'I'll sing thee songs of Araby'. Gina looked about for a seat.

'Please take mine,' said a voice.

She turned. A tall man in pale grey worsted was rising to offer his place. 'Oh, no, I couldn't deprive you—'

'Not at all, please sit down. I prefer to stand.'

She sat, aware of him at her side. He was tall, his clothes were well tailored to show his broad shoulders and slim hips. He carried a malacca cane and held his hat with the tips of his fingers on its brim. His hair was black, thick and glossy.

Gina sat half-listening to the song, pleased that she was wearing her Sunday clothes. At school it was necessary to wear what was known as 'student dress', loose blouses with a sailor collar or a shawl neckline, pleated skirt coming to above the ankle, boots with medium heels and thick black stockings. At Sandhill Farm she would wear print dresses of similar style, loose shirtwaisters and perhaps a sunbonnet to protect her hair. On Sundays it was permitted to be more individualistic, so that Gina was this day wearing a suit of pale blue cotton patterned with a darker check, a white blouse with a frilled jabot, and rather elegant little pale blue boots with high heels.

There was no reason to care greatly what the citizens of Des Moines thought of her appearance. All the same, she felt happy at not looking like a schoolgirl.

On the platform a board was changed to advertise Number Eight. The tall man at her side offered her a printed programme. 'Number Eight,' he murmured, '*Moment Musical* by Schubert.'

'Oh, thank you.' She put up her hand to shield the sun from her eyes as she acknowledged his help. He at once shifted position so as to give her shade with his body. She was delighted. What a considerate person . . .

By the end of the concert he had introduced himself, Alexander Bebbeker. 'Call me Alex. Everyone does.'

'My name is Gina Gracebridge.'

'How do you do. Say, it's great good luck to run into someone as interested in music as you are. Usually I never find anyone to talk with.'

They were threading their way with the rest of the audience out into the park. 'Would you like a cool drink or some coffee? I noticed a good drug-store just down the street.'

She knew she should say no. But the alternative was to go back to the Plaza Hotel and kick her heels until dinner, so she accepted.

Over their coffee and cake he told her he was in Des Moines for a seminar at Drake University. He was a post-graduate student. She was thrilled. He must be at least twenty-five years old. He was much older than the boys she met in Washington, and much, much more interesting. 'An older man . . .' Hadn't Granma Morag said the boys she knew were boring because they hadn't grown up enough?

For her part, Gina told him enough to account for

herself — she was passing through Des Moines on her way to stay with relatives in Lincoln, she would be leaving next day, how very pleasant to meet someone who shared her interest in music. Not a word about a boring younger brother and a grandfather asleep in the hotel lobby, not a word about her almost total lack of interest in music.

When it was time to go, Mr Bebbeker took her hand and held it a moment too long. 'Must we part?' he asked, with a wistful look in his brown eyes.

'I'm afraid we must. I'm expected back for dinner.'

'I couldn't persuade you to have dinner with me?'

Gina was shocked but thrilled. Dinner with a man? Unthinkable. She shook her head. 'I'm afraid not.'

'Afterwards, then,' he pleaded. 'You say you're leaving tomorrow — don't deny me your company this evening.'

'Oh, I really couldn't—'

'There's a recital of dramatic readings in the lecture hall of the university this evening. Please let me take you?'

'No, really, Mr Bebbeker—'

'Please! I know you would enjoy it. You are just the kind of companion I would love to have for that occasion.'

'I mustn't — I have only just met you—'

'And perhaps never will again! Oh, Miss Grace-bridge, don't you think it's a pity not to enjoy this transient communion of spirits? I'll be so lonely if you don't come! The recital begins at eight o'clock, with a reading of "Oenone", by Lord Tennyson—'

'Oh, but he's my favourite poet!'

'You see? It was meant! Say you'll come!'

'No, no, I mustn't!'

But they both knew she would, and when Al Bebbeker went to the fraternity house to change for dinner he was delighted with himself. A pretty, eager, dainty little light o' love . . . and he'd thought Des Moines was going to be as dull as dishpans.

All through dinner Gina was telling herself the idea of going to the concert was impossible. All the same, as soon as Grandfather Gracebridge fell asleep over the newspapers, she told Curt she was going to bed. It was about seven-thirty. Curt said, 'What, now?' and she snapped, 'It'll be more fun asleep and dreaming than awake!' and strolled out.

In her room she changed into the dress she had bought in Chicago. It was almost as if fate had intended her to buy it for just this occasion. She did her hair up in a soft chignon and tied it with a satin bow of pale yellow. She didn't have an evening bag but she took a satin handkerchief sachet which was elegant enough to pass muster.

She stole down the stairs expecting Curt to erupt from the lounge crying, 'Where on earth do you think you're going?' But Curt was out in the hotel garden trying to climb up to a mockingbird's nest. The doorman summoned a cab for her without comment — she was thrilled to think she must look so entirely grown-up that he didn't find it strange.

At the lecture hall people were drifting in. Alex was standing on the stoop looking for her. He drew her arm through his with a smile of gratitude. He really was extremely handsome; so tall and broadshouldered.

The poetry was mostly dramatic narrative. 'Macgregor, Macgregor, Remember our foemen!' and 'She stood upon the castle wall, Oriana: she watched my crest among them all, Oriana!' Some of it was quite harrowing. Alex put his arm around Gina in protective comfort.

The last poem, recited to the music of a phonograph recording was 'The Swan's Nest' by Mrs Browning. The actress who read it didn't need the book. 'Little Ellie sits alone, Mid the beeches of a meadow . . .' The steady rhythm in the smooth, rich contralto surged on. The music from the phonograph was of violins almost crooning.

> *'He will kiss me on the mouth*
> *Then, and lead me as a lover,*
> *Through the crowds that praise his deeds*
> *And, when soul-tied by his troth,*
> *Unto him I shall discover*
> *This swan's nest among the reeds.'*

By mere chance, the phonograph music ran out before the speaker had reached the disillusioning end of the verses, so she stopped and made her bow. The audience, who hadn't heard the poem before, applauded with enthusiasm, the actress bowed and blew kisses, and the curtain descended.

Outside in the warm darkness of June, Gina let Alex retain his arm about her shoulder. She was still thrilling to the verses she had heard: 'He will say, "O love, thine eyes, Build the shrine my soul abides in, And I kneel before thy grace!"'

'Wasn't it beautiful?' she breathed.

'I'll say it was. Glad you came?'

'Oh yes, so glad.'

'Let's go somewhere and talk. We don't want to say goodnight yet.'

'All right.'

He took her to a cafe near the campus. He ordered wine and though she felt she should protest, she didn't. She had had small amounts of wine at home, on special occasions, but she had never drunk it unwatered before. Her head began to swim.

When at last she looked for a clock, she found it was after eleven. She was on the verge of blurting out, 'It's long past my bedtime,' but stopped herself just in time. 'I must go,' she exclaimed. 'Will you call me a cab?'

'Oh, let me walk you home? Please?'

'Very well.' She too wanted to prolong the evening. What Morag had suggested was quite correct − men were more interesting when they were older. She let him lead her into the street, quiet now, for to this plains town, eleven o'clock was owl time.

'This way,' he urged, taking a street that led to the park. 'It's so much more romantic under the trees.'

That was the signal. She should have understood that the word romantic meant love-making. She, thinking of her beautiful poems, agreed. They went into the park.

She was not really surprised when he stole a kiss. It was what boys always did, she supposed. This time, she responded. The wine made her feel warm and dreamy. His arms were strong around her. His cheeks weren't pocked with acne like Arthur Loomis. He didn't smell of whisky but of the same rich, rounded wine that she herself had been drinking. It was pleasant to cling to him, to let his lips touch her throat and her eyelids, and then the skin in the wide neckline of the Japanese dress.

Somehow they sank down on the grass in the shadow of the trees. Then his caresses began to be frightening and she said, 'No, no − don't—'

'Oh, come on, honey! You'll like it!' He held her fast

beneath him, then kissed her with lips that seemed to fasten on her like leeches.

She gasped, 'Oh, *don't*!' and threw herself to one side. Her soft silk dress was caught so that it rode up over her thighs in her movement. His hands were there, pushing and exploring. She drew in a breath to scream in outrage, but her head was turned to avoid his kiss and the sound seemed to be muffled by the very ground.

'Keep still, you little fool,' he said in a strange voice, strained and urgent. When she tried to clutch at his hands to stop them, he slapped her arms and then leaned heavily on her so that all the breath went out of her.

Now she was frightened, disgusted, horrified. She writhed to get free, and he captured her arms and held them above her head. He was heaving in a strange rhythm. She felt a searing pain somewhere in the very midst of her being. She wailed in agony but he smothered the sound with kisses that were savagely unloving, teeth against her lips, hard bones of his jaw grinding into her mouth.

For a moment her senses seemed to reel in a red mist of pain. She could hear panting, a groaning sound. Then the attacker rolled off her and she was free. She heard him gasping in satisfaction.

A great sob burst from Gina. She scrambled up to her knees, clutching her soiled gown close about her. 'You filthy beast—'

'Oh, shut up a minute, honey!'

'How could you! I thought you were nice—'

'I was nice, dear. I taught you something good, didn't I?' He had suspected she was a virgin, and the thought had been a teasing target all through the

172

afternoon and evening. He was known to his fellows as Break-'em-in Bebbeker — never known to fail if he went after a girl. He got up now, tidying himself, and held out a hand to help her up.

She shrank away from him. 'Don't you dare to touch me!'

'Oh, don't be like that about it. It's got to happen some time, you know, dearie. All okay now? Ready to go home, eh?'

'Stay away from me!'

'Come on, I'll see you home—'

'Keep away!' She got up painfully, swayed and almost fell, but gathered herself together. As she felt Bebbeker take her elbow she lurched forward out of his reach. 'Don't ever come near me again!' she cried, and ran off through the park.

By the time she reached the Plaza, she had brushed off the grass and twigs from the outside of her gown. The stains inside were not visible, thank God. She went up to her room remarked, but not exceptionally so, by the night porter. She ran a bath, scrubbed herself all over, and sponged again and again those intimate parts that the man had violated. She went to bed about one o'clock, but didn't sleep. She was caught in the horror of what had happened.

All that Morag had implied was true. There was this awful, animal side to men. Gloss it how you might, that hideousness could never have any affection in it. It was a cruel joke to say so.

When she left with Grandfather Gracebridge and Curt next morning, all the clothes she had worn the previous night were in a trash bin in an alley behind the hotel.

Chapter Ten

Curt Gracebridge looked back at that summer afterwards as one of the oddest in his life. It seemed as if his sister Gina was mad at the world in general and him in particular. Nothing he said or did pleased her. At first he was distressed by her bad moods, for he had always admired her − older, brighter and more lovable than he, she had been his exemplar of all that was worth aiming for in life.

But he had his own compensations that summer. The new school had taught him to use his body. He spent long days in the saddle with the farm manager, or swam in the Boon, a tributary of the Platte River, with the neighbourhood boys.

Gina, on the contrary, seemed to shut herself away. She wouldn't go on the hayride, she wouldn't attend the barn-dances. Her grandmother said to her grandfather, 'I declare, the Devil has got into the child.' To which he replied, 'It's just a phase, Mother.'

The reason was kept wrapped in secrecy by Gina. When her body failed to fulfil its normal cycle towards the end of the month she was in a panic that took away her appetite, made her head swim, gave her many of the symptoms she dreaded. After all, hadn't Granma Morag just explained to her that was how babies were

174

made? And had said it need not have anything to do with 'Love'?

She had no inkling of the fact that psychological elements played a part. Shock and revulsion had frozen her body. At last, two weeks late, the longed-for signs appeared. She was wildly happy – relieved, delighted, delirious. But then she was racked with pains and cramps. Grandmother Gracebridge dosed her with womanly remedies but nothing helped. For a week Gina was quite ill, and hated everyone because of it. She hated Alex Bebbeker because it was his fault. She hated Grandmother Gracebridge because she kept saying soothingly, blandly, 'Just sip this, dear, it'll put you right.' Why couldn't she open her arms and take Gina to her bosom, murmuring, 'Tell me all about it, dear?' She hated Curt, too, because he was innocent and carefree, keeping out of her way after the first few attempts to coax her out to enjoyment.

If she could have seen Morag during those days, she might have been able to blurt it all out. But Morag was off in Colorado Springs, enjoying herself. Morag was with Rob, as it happened, and was too happy and busy to notice that the duty letters from Gina were skimpy and flat. There were certainly no questions as a follow-up to the conversation they had had the night before she left for Nebraska – but perhaps she was saving all those up for when they were back in Washington in the fall.

Not so. Gina never referred to the conversation. It was as if it had never happened. Yet there was a change in Gina in other directions. She no longer sat for hours reading poetry or tales of historical romance. She didn't shine with that flower-like radiance. She was still beautiful – perhaps more so, but it wasn't the beauty of the young girl any more. She was much less talkative, and sometimes there was a bitterness in her manner that troubled Morag.

Gina was in her last year at school now. She worked hard, did well in her studies, took part in the school production of Dion Boucicault's *The Colleen Bawn* with resounding success and had more partners than she could put on her dance programme at the cotillion which closed the spring semester. When next day her friends came by invitation to a hair-ribbon party, Morag arranged to have them served with a pretty little snack in Gina's room. She looked in to see that all was going well, to find them chattering together as they looked through Gina's trinket boxes.

All except Gina. She was sitting aside, watching them with such a look of contempt that Morag felt her breath catch in her throat.

What was wrong with the child? That evening, when Gina's guests had gone, Morag went in search of her. She was standing in the twilight garden, staring up at the cloudy sky.

'It's time to change for dinner, dear.'

'Yes, I'm coming.'

'Your friends enjoyed the party.'

'They seemed to.'

'But you didn't, Gina.'

The girl turned. 'Of course I did,' she said calmly.

'No, you didn't. I saw the look on your face. You seemed — almost angry with them.'

'Oh, they're such fools!' she burst out. 'They don't know anything about anything!'

Morag held out her hand. 'Come and talk to me about it,' she suggested.

But Gina turned away. 'Oh, talk,' she said, with a

dismissive shrug. 'I don't think there's anything to say.'

'That's pretty sweeping, isn't it? If something is bothering you, perhaps I could help.'

'No, thank you,' Gina said. Her tone was quite polite but cold. 'I don't think anything much is bothering me.'

It was so patently untrue that Morag almost exclaimed in impatience. But scolding would do no good. Confidences can't be forced – either Gina wanted to tell her something that was troubling her or she didn't.

Later that evening she discussed it with Nellie, the black maid who had been her companion for many years now. They were together in the sittingroom set aside for them when they stayed at the Gracebridge house.

'She's soul-sick, Miz Morag,' Nellie said, her wrinkled face sad. 'Who kin tell what caused it? Mebbe she fell in love and it didn't work out. You know how hurtful puppy love can be.'

'I wish her mother were here.' Morag sighed. 'She'd be able to talk to her better than me.'

Nellie shook her head. 'I don' think so, Miz Morag. Ellie and Gina ain't so close. I reckon both Ellie and Mr Curtis been too busy all they lives, gettin' up-in-the-world. They ain't never had enough time to get close to they children. Curt, he had lots of care for his health – Ellie grieved over him, many and many a night when he's been poorly. But she ain't really got to know him. It don' matter so much because he's sort of self-contained – know what I mean? But Gina – Gina needed something she's never had from her Mama.'

'I wish it was something *I* could give her.'

'You doin' you best, and you know it. Nobody kin

177

get close to that chile for the time bein', but she gonna get over it, whatever it is.' Nellie patted Morag's hand. 'You know time's a great healer, now don't you?'

'Yes, dear, I know.' No one knew better. Despite everything — the war, the absence of Ellie-Rose and Curtis, problems with Gina — Morag was happy. Time had healed her hurts. She had a role to play in the Gracebridge family and, more important still, was an essential factor in the life of Rob Craigallan. Though still legally married to Luisa, Rob was Morag's husband, almost openly acknowledged by everyone within the inner circle of the Craigallan world. Even Curtis's parents — rigid Methodists, easily shocked — accepted without complaint the fact that Rob was the father of Gregor, Morag's son, and that she was not in any sense to be thought of as a 'fallen woman'. To tell the truth, good sense dictated a certain politeness when dealing with Morag. Anyone who insulted her was likely to feel the weight of Rob's wrath.

A letter arrived from Luisa Craigallan, Rob's wife. She had been in Europe when war was declared and was at first quite scared, as the German troops marched through Belgium and into France. She had been staying with friends at Aix at the time. Somewhat hastily she removed herself to other friends in Italy. Italy was neutral. It was quite pleasant to be trapped in Naples by the difficulties of sea transport — of course Luisa couldn't travel back to America, it was much too dangerous. No one had argued with her; in fact, no one missed her, for she had been abroad so much that Grandmother Craigallan was almost unknown to her grandchildren.

Now, incredibly enough, Italy had declared war on Austria-Hungary. Luisa took it as a personal affront.

'This stupid war! What is the point of Italy getting involved in it? I hope it isn't going to make difficulties in getting money to me, because it would be extremely embarrassing to be among friends and not pay my way . . .'

Rob, to whom this was addressed, took the hint and made sure that her allowance was detoured via Switzerland. 'Not that I can see her risking a sea voyage home if the money ran out,' he remarked to Morag. 'She'd stay where she is, cadging off the latest Italian count who's courting her.'

'Oh Rob,' Morag reproached. 'You're always so cynical about her. She's past the age where she's taking lovers, surely.'

'You want to bet? Joe Ranselaer from the Rome Embassy was home on leave a month ago, and he told me she's had her hair dyed Titian-colour and found a dressmaker who can make her look quite slim. These new slender styles from that little French girl – Chanel – they've made the European ladies give up over-eating, it seems.'

'If it makes her happy, Rob, it's a good thing.'

'I can't help thinking that when these middle-aged dandies of hers find out she's on an allowance and can't hand over a million, they must be damned disappointed.' He paused. 'If she ever found one she wanted to marry, it'd be different. We could get divorced and then you and I . . .'

'Darling, don't even think about it. Luisa is never going to want to marry anyone else – you know that.'

'Yeah . . . She'll never marry anyone with less money than me, and rich Frenchmen and Italians have too much sense to be caught. I sometimes think, though, that she might take a penniless duke or baron — for the title.'

Morag shook her head. 'She might have, in years gone by. But I think she knows she'd never be accepted into the best society now, even if she were married. Besides . . .' She fell silent. They both knew that Luisa would always reject divorce so long as it opened the way for Rob to marry Morag. Luisa hated Morag as fervently now as she had done when a young woman.

'It's just that I'd like to be able to walk into a room with you on my arm, dearest, and introduce you as my wife,' Rob murmured.

'I know, I know. But it's not as if I went into society much, Rob. It doesn't really matter.'

'And Greg, too — I'd like him to have my name. I wish now I'd taken out legal adoption papers when he first came to me . . .'

'Too late now, Rob. He wouldn't agree to it. He'd think it disloyal to me, to give up my name.'

'And he'd be right, I suppose. And his own children — they'd have to change their name too — it would mean a big upheaval, it simply wouldn't be worth it. I often wonder if he holds it against me, Morag — the way I let you struggle without help for so long.'

'Perhaps he used to, darling.' She linked her arm through his and led him on a gentle stroll through the garden, pausing to examine favourite plants and flowers in the sunshine. 'But you know, being happy does away with many resentments. Greg's happy now. He and Francesca have a good marriage.'

'What's he doing this summer?'

'I thought I'd invite them all to the ranch-house,' Morag said. 'Gina refuses pointblank to go to the Gracebridges in Nebraska and I don't think Curt is all that keen either, so it seems to me the best thing is to take them there. And if I can persuade Francesca to come with Lewis and Clare, it ought to make a nice happy party. Might cheer Gina up.'

'Yes, say, what is wrong with that girl?'

'I don't know, Rob. I wish I did. Annie Wilson suggested to me she was miffed because she can't have her coming-out as long as Ellie-Rose is away—'

'It can't be that, can it?' Rob interjected. 'Surely a few balls and parties aren't all that important? I thought she had more sense!'

'You're quite right. Yet in a way, I feel that may be part of it. I think it's to do with her mother being gone so long.'

'She's missing Ellie-Rose?' Rob strolled beside Morag, absently pulled a leaf from a lavender bush and rolled it between his fingers. 'And Curtis?'

'I sometimes get the idea she feels she's been . . . let down, somehow. That they deserted her when she needed them.'

'Stuff and nonsense!' he grunted. 'You're here! Gina's got nothing to complain of while she's got someone like you.' He gave a little snort of laughter. 'Tell the truth, you're a lot more patient with her than Ellie might have been. If Gina had been smarty-pants to her mother the way I've sometimes heard her with you, she'd have been given the rough side of her tongue!' He hesitated. 'Perhaps you should be a bit tougher on her, Morag.'

Morag pressed his arm against her side. 'I can't be tough, dear. I haven't got it in me to be hard on her. Besides, I brought up Greg without ever having to put him on bread and water or take a stick to him!'

'Yes, dear, but Greg was always a lot less self-centred

181

than Gina.' He shook his head. 'Mebbe that's what's wrong – she hasn't enough to keep her occupied.'

'She has as much as other girls of her age, Rob. And it isn't as if she's complaining of boredom or anything like that.'

'Um . . . If it wasn't for this damned war, we could send her travelling in Europe, give her a wider outlook.'

'Instead, we can only offer her Colorado Springs.'

'Well, perhaps we ought to do something more than that, darling. How about if we have a little tour to see a few sights and cities?'

'Where, for example?'

'New Orleans – no, that'd be hot and sticky in summer.' He mused over it. 'Montreal? Boston? Or how about if we all go to see the Bells in Nova Scotia?'

'I don't think Gina would enjoy the Bells. Although she's fond of her Uncle Neil, I don't think she's in the mood to cope with a gathering of deaf people – and you know that's what tends to happen there.'

'Okay, suggest something.'

'I'll think about it, Rob.'

The question was settled for them quite suddenly, for Gina ran away from home.

Chapter Eleven

Her absence wasn't known until two days after she had gone. She was supposedly staying over a weekend with a high school friend in Alexandria but when she wasn't brought home on the Sunday evening Morag telephoned to inquire about the delay.

'But, my dear Mrs McGarth, she hasn't been with us,' cried Mrs Conrad. 'She told Dorothy at school on Friday that you had said you wanted her home with you after all, because you were expecting visitors.'

'But . . . she left for the college on Friday morning with her overnight bag, Mrs Conrad! And she didn't come home!'

'She isn't with us, Mrs McGarth. We had Jessie Oliphant and Marie Poursuit here — they left for home about an hour ago in our limousine and of course if Gina had been here she too would have . . .' An indrawn breath. 'Mrs McGarth, where can she be?'

'I've no idea. Forgive me, I must ring off and find out what's happened.'

Morag ran upstairs to Gina's room. She looked everywhere for a note but there was nothing to be found. She looked in the closet but only a few things were gone, such as Gina might have taken for a couple of days at the house of a schoolfriend.

Her brother was unable to shed any light. 'Aw, she never talks to *me*,' he said.

'But, Curt dear, have you no idea what she might have done? No idea at all?'

'Oh, only that she's making a fool of herself as usual. She moons around like a tragedy queen, if you ask me. What's she got to be so sore about, anyhow?'

'Is that how she's seemed to you? Angry? What about?'

'I told you, she doesn't talk to me. All I know is, a couple of weeks ago when we were discussing whether to spend the summer in the mountains or at the coast, she sighed and said life was empty anyway so what did it matter where we went . . . I told her to put a sock in it and she got tears in her eyes and said I was a boor.' Curt looked anxiously at Granma Morag. 'I'm not a boor, am I, Granma? I mean, just because I don't get twined up over every little thing, it doesn't mean I haven't got feelings same as everyone else.'

'Don't let it worry you, Curt,' Morag soothed.

'But say, she hasn't run off because I told her she was all wet?'

'No, I'm sure it's nothing to do with you, Curt.'

But what did it have to do with? And where could she have gone? Morag sat down to contact every friend and acquaintance who was on the telephone and to send messages to those − still quite a large number − who had refused to be connected. She sent for Rob and Greg. Rob was in New York but caught the next train. Greg was in Washington so arrived almost at once.

School friends were cross-questioned until they became almost tearful. 'I tell you, Mrs McGarth, I really don't know where she's gone! She never talks to me any more. We're not best friends the way we used to be.'

The picture that emerged was of Gina isolating herself more and more over the preceding year, offending former friends by her critical manner, by her assumption of superiority. Only a few girls had remained relatively close, and even they were friendly more by habit than by encouragement.

'Boy friends?' Morag suggested. For Nellie had murmured at once that she felt Gina had run off with a sweetheart. But all the girls shook their heads with apparent conviction.

'She's not interested in boys, Mrs McGarth. Honestly, she's awfully down on them — and on any of us who were going steady or anything. She kept saying we were fools, didn't know what we were letting ourselves in for.'

By midday Monday everything had been done that Morag and Greg could think of. They waited only for the arrival of Rob to call in the police. The uniformed sergeant who came was soothing and reassuring. 'Young ladies often run off,' he said, 'if their feelings have been hurt or that kind of thing. Don't you worry about it, ma'am. She won't be far off.'

'Sergeant,' Rob said in annoyance, 'don't talk to Mrs McGarth as if she were an idiot. She's already tried everything that seems possible among our immediate circle. Gina is not with any friend or relation.'

'Quite so, sir. She have any money?'

Rob looked at Morag.

'Her allowance of course. It's the beginning of June so she's still got most of it.'

'How much would that be, ma'am?'

'Fifty dollars.'

The policeman looked as if he might say something about a young girl with more pocket money than most men earned, but merely made a note in his notebook. He also listed all the friends and relations already contacted. Rob learned afterwards that the police followed this trail again, only more quickly and less tactfully than Morag. Tuesday came and no one could say where Gina had gone. The police ascertained that a young lady answering her description had bought a ticket at the railway station on Friday afternoon about four o'clock.

'Going where?' Rob asked, incredulous.

'New York.'

'New York. That seems as if she was coming to see me at Craigallan Castle—'

'But she didn't turn up there, sir?'

'No, indeed. I didn't even know she'd left Washington until Mrs McGarth telephoned me on Sunday night.'

'Ah, well . . . New York is a good place to go if you want to hide, sir.'

'But why should Gina want to . . . to hide? From whom? From what?'

'I can't answer that, sir. But I can set investigation in motion in New York.'

Nothing could be learned. It was as if Gina had disappeared off the face of the earth. At first, the inquiries were kept private but as day followed day without word of her, the police suggested it would be a good idea to inform the press. 'They can get people looking around, keeping an eye open for her. She's a pretty, well-dressed young lady – likely to have been noticed, I'd say.'

Morag shivered at the words. It was a secret dread of

hers that Gina might have come to harm because of her appearance of wealth and good breeding. She let Rob take her hand to comfort her but soon withdrew it. 'I must send a cable to Ellie,' she said. 'I didn't want to worry her, if this turned out just to be a childish escapade – but it's getting serious now.'

The cable was written but the friends in the State Department were unable to give it priority, as they usually did for the Gracebridges. The presidential election campaign was in full swing, the nomination conventions were being held, and official attention was on them. Such diplomatic activity as was going on outside the matter of canvassing support for Woodrow Wilson was mainly concerned with Roger Casement, who had been arrested in Ireland earlier in the year and whom the Irish faction in the States wished to save from hanging. Domestic matters like troublesome adolescent runaways had to go to the back of the queue.

Morag therefore sat down to write an ordinary letter, which might arrive almost as soon as the cable if the diplomatic lines were not cleared. She tried to keep the anxiety at a low level – Gina had left home without informing anyone of her intention, she had clearly made plans beforehand so that she would not be missed for a day or two, but everything was in hand.

The butler came in with the evening paper. One of the headlines was: *Gracebridge Debutante Runs Away*. The item was written in terms that suggested the solution would prove to be an elopement. Quotes were given from Gina's friends, to the effect that she was a great beauty and that the boys were always after her. What was not stated was their conclusion – that while boys were interested in Gina, Gina was not interested in them.

Morag re-read her letter and realised it was as dishonest as the newspaper report. She had pretended to Ellie and Curtis that she wasn't worried. But she was dreadfully worried and growing more so with every hour that passed. Why had Gina gone? That was what burned like a hot iron in her thoughts. Why? Gina was not running away *to* anyone, of that she was almost certain. So was she running *from* someone – or something?

Once more she surveyed Gina's home surroundings. Surely there was nothing here to make the child so unhappy she felt she must escape into no-man's-land.

The next day the morning papers had the story. The Gracebridge family, because of its links with the rich Craigallans, was news. Friends rang from New York and Boston to say that they had seen it, to express their good wishes or perhaps simply to get titbits for coffee-table gossip. Morag deputed the butler to take the calls: 'Thank you, madam, I shall pass on your concern to Mrs McGarth. We have no further news of Miss Gina.'

'Damn fool child,' he said to the cook, 'she deserves a good spanking!'

About lunchtime a call came through. Jordan came to the drawingroom, where Rob and Greg were discussing whether to offer a money reward for information and if so, how much. 'Mr Craigallan, sir,' he said, 'I think there's a call you should take.'

'Oh? What is it? The police?'

'Oh, Rob!' Morag cried, grasping his sleeve as he rose.

'No, sir, it's a lady. Mother Aloysius, she says she is.'

'Oh, a religious crank,' Greg said. 'That's all we need!'

'She may be a crank, sir. I never thought of that,'

Jordan said, colouring a little. 'But she sounds quite sensible.'

'I'll come,' Rob said, and walked wearily into the study to take the call. Into the receiver he said, 'This is Robert Craigallan.'

'Grandfather of the missing young lady?'

'That's right. And you are — ?'

'Mother Aloysius of the Revived Order of Poor Clares, Mr Craigallan.'

'Poor Clares? I beg your pardon?'

'It's an order of nuns, sir. Do you remember on the occasion of the wedding of your son Gregor and Miss Sagasta — her wedding veil was made by our convent and you sent a large donation to our funds? I was not the Mother Superior then, Mr Craigallan, it was Mother Fabiola.'

The name rang a faint bell. He began to understand the call was genuine. 'I believe I recollect the matter, Mother Aloysius. Why are you telephoning?'

'I believe we have your granddaughter here, Mr Craigallan.'

'*What?*'

'The gardener, a layman, drew the attention of the housekeeping sister to the item in the newspaper, sir. On Saturday a young lady arrived at our gates begging to be given sanctuary—'

'Sanctuary?'

'That was her word, Mr Craigallan. She was very distressed, very unhappy. She said her name was Jane Smith. We could get nothing more out of her, nothing about her home or her family. There seemed to be no alternative but to give her a bed and let her stay a while, to see if she would regain her emotional balance. When I saw the newspaper today, and thought about the

189

quality of her clothes and shoes, and compared her appearance with the picture that was published . . . I felt it to be quite likely that it was Miss Gracebridge.'

'Good sweet Jesus!' exclaimed Rob. Then, recollecting himself, 'I'm sorry, Mother Aloysius.'

'Quite all right, my son. I approve of the appeal if not of the tone.'

'Let me speak to the girl,' he said. 'I'll soon tell if it's Gina.'

'She doesn't know I'm telephoning,' said the nun. 'I believe she would disapprove and might even run away if she knew of it. Not that it is easy to run away from our convent, as it happens — but we could not exactly stop her if she wished to go.'

'She's a young fool,' Rob snarled. 'I'll put her over my knee when I get to her! The anxiety she's caused us—'

'She herself has been in some anxiety, I judge,' Mother Aloysius said. 'Otherwise she would not have had to run away to sanctuary.'

'Sanctuary! I don't get that at all!'

'It's what a fugitive seeks when he is pursued.'

'But nobody's pursuing my granddaughter!'

'Not that you know of, perhaps. But the human soul has pursuers that others don't suspect.'

'Demons, you mean? But . . . Gina doesn't believe in that kind of thing.'

'People say they don't believe. Yet they experience demons — guilt, remorse, anger . . .'

Rob remembered that young Curt had spoken of Gina being always angry. Yet he couldn't bring himself to believe that pretty, bright little Gina had been hounded to look for sanctuary by a bunch of imaginary evils. It was so unlike her! Yet what did he know of her, really? Who would ever believe that she would run away from the comfort and luxury of her home to, of all places, a convent of Poor Clares?

If it was Gina, of course.

'The only way to find out if it's my granddaughter is if I come and see her,' he suggested.

'I think you are right. But, Mr Craigallan, don't come in a mood of reproof. The girl we are sheltering needs help, not disapproval.'

'Huh,' Rob grunted, and after ascertaining how to reach the convent offered his thanks and hung up.

Morag insisted on going with him. 'You can't be expected to feel at home in a convent, dear,' she said calmly. 'You need a woman with you, and we can't ask Francesca to take this on. It's my responsibility, after all.'

'It is nothing of the kind! She's a grown girl and it's her own responsibility—'

'That's not what I mean, Rob, and you know it. I stand in the place of her mother, and a poor job I seem to have made of it if she has to run away asking for sanctuary. I must be there to understand what has gone wrong, before we bring her home.'

The convent was in Massachusetts, it was a long train journey to Holyoke. Rob knew the district a little; a friend owned one of the big papermills in the town itself. They hired a brougham and were driven out north-eastwards towards Granby, admiring the Connecticut River as it gleamed in the fine June day.

When they reached the convent Rob glanced anxiously at Morag, worried in case the travelling had tired her too much. But she met his glance with a firm little shake of the head. He rang the bell at the thick wooden door. A spyhole opened and a hooded figure looked out.

Rob introduced himself and Morag. 'Ah yes, Mother Superior told me to expect you. Please wait.' There was a long pause while locks were undone and then the door swung open to show a wide stone path bordered with lawns and leading to a sombre building of newish grey stone. 'This way.'

Their guide was a thin elderly nun, in a brown habit with a white coif. She kept turned away, not as if she were under a vow of silence but as if she were unaccustomed to company. They followed her into a large hall, stone-flagged, and with a very uncomfortable wooden bench as almost its only furniture. 'Please take a seat. I'll tell Mother Superior you are here.'

She went through a door at the side of the hall. By and by she came out again, slightly behind a taller, more imposing woman with a beautifully engraved wooden crucifix attached to her rosary. 'Do come in,' she said. She led them into her office. It was a businesslike place, surprising Rob with its typewriting machine and telephone. Then he told himself it was absurd to think they would use quill pens and packmule to carry out the business of the institution, which seemed quite large to judge by the building he had so far seen. He had made inquiries and learned it was an offshoot of the Franciscan order, devoted to relieving the sufferings of the poor.

'Have you told Gina we are coming?' Morag inquired of the Mother Superior after introductions had been effected.

'No, I didn't think that was necessary. A convent is a place of discipline and order, you see. And as your granddaughter has put herself in my charge, I am empowered to make decisions on her behalf.'

'May we see her?'

'I have sent the almoner to tell her I want her in my office.'

The door opened, the almoner came in, ushering Gina in front of her. At sight of them she stopped short. 'Oh!' she cried, clenching her fists and with a piercing look at Mother Aloysius. 'You've betrayed me!'

'Sit down, my dear,' said the Mother Superior.

Gina turned as if to run out. The other nun stepped in her path. No one said a word. There was a moment when it looked as if the girl might launch herself on the almoner with her fists, but then her shoulders drooped and she came further into the room, towards the desk where her grandfather and Morag were seated. She took the plain chair the almoner set for her.

'Now, Gina,' said the Mother Superior, 'you lied to me when you first came here—'

'No, I didn't! I told you I was in spiritual torment—'

'Tut, tut, don't dramatise. You told me your name was Jane Smith and that family troubles had forced you to leave home. You said it would cause great problems if you were sent home again and begged to be given safe harbour here in our convent. Now, none of this was true.'

'I only told you a false name because I didn't want to be found—'

'Gina, why on earth did you do a thing like this?' Rob burst out. 'You've had us out of our minds with anxiety!'

'Oh, how can you say a thing like that! You don't care about me! All you care about is making money, or where to spend the summer vacation — you never give a thought to me!'

'Gina!'

'That's no way to speak to your elders,' said Mother Aloysius. 'And the fact that they do care is demonstrated by their immediate presence here, once I had contacted them—'

'And I thought I could trust you!' Gina wailed. 'I never thought a nun would turn telltale—'

'That is quite enough, Gina,' Morag said with more sharpness than she usually allowed in her tone. 'Mother Aloysius took you in and gave you hospitality. Calling her names is a poor reward for her kindness.'

'Oh, you're all alike — you think because you're older you can order me about and make me do this and that but you've no real interest in me, none of you! You only want me back because it would look bad otherwise!'

'I can't make out what's got into you!' Rob exclaimed. 'To run away, without a word — you must have known we'd be worried—'

'I was just so sick and tired of being taken here and there and told what to do. Nobody ever asked me whether I wanted to go to Montreal or San Francisco—'

'And so you ran off to a nunnery? Oh, dear me, all you had to say was, "I'd rather go into a convent"!'

Morag put her hand on his sleeve to beg him not to sneer. 'What is it you came here to find, Gina dear?' she asked.

'Peace! Peace and reparation — a chance to clear my mind of everything that's been battering at me so that I could think straight again!'

The nun exchanged a glance with Morag. Morag

remained silent, leaving it to the other woman to speak. 'What torments you then, child?' she asked, in a voice of surprising gentleness.

'Oh, everything! The awfulness of life, the pointlessness – the hurrying about from here to there, being just like everybody else and never really *understanding* the way the sword is hanging over us—'

'Sword? What sword?'

'Oh, Grandfather, you would never understand! Nobody does, nobody could, but at least here I thought there would be no one to keep telling me I must dance with Arthur Loomis or be polite to Mrs Bretherton when all I want is to be left in peace.'

'My dear child,' Mother Aloysius said, 'you misunderstand the life of a convent. We live by a rule here. It is true we have peace, but we also have duty. If you expected to spend all day sitting quietly looking at the sunshine through the stained glass, you are mistaken.'

'What you're saying is that you don't want me here,' Gina said, and she sounded like a small child who has been told she cannot go to the party.

'You are right. A religious order is a place for a man or a woman who has a vocation. You have no vocation, my dear – only needs you thought we could fulfil.' Mother Aloysius shook her head. 'We cannot.'

'You want me to go?'

'You never seriously thought about convent life,' the Mother Superior said calmly, 'or you wouldn't have brought your overnight case with silver brushes and a crêpe-de-chine nightdress.'

Morag got up and put her arm round the weeping girl. 'Gina, Gina, you've been acting out one of your romantic poems, that's all. Come along now, we'll go home.'

'No, I don't want to — I want to stay here!'

'No, dear. You don't belong here, you'd only be a disturbance. Besides, what would your parents say if I wrote that you had gone to retreat in a convent? Now come along, fetch your case and we'll go.'

The almoner came to Gina's side to accompany her to her room and fetch her belongings. When the door had closed behind her Mother Aloysius said, 'I should have a doctor to see her when you get her home. She's very tense and unhappy — but we aren't equipped to deal with girls in a fit of hysteria, I'm afraid.'

'No, thank you, you've been very forbearing.'

'Yes, ma'am. I surely appreciate the way you've dealt with this. If I can show my appreciation in any way . . . ?'

'Thank you, our work is carried on with the aid of charity so I won't reject your offer. But I would like you to believe I didn't contact you and return the child to you simply to be given money.'

'Of course not.'

'I don't know how to handle her problem, whatever it may be. I think it is a problem of the world and can only be solved in the world. That's why I think you should seek advice — medical advice for her nerves, in the first place.'

'We'll certainly do that,' Rob assured her, although a certain grimness in his manner warned that he was much minded to spank her.

They were offered lunch but Rob said he thought they had better find a hotel and eat there. He was writing a cheque for the convent's funds when Gina came down wearing her jacket and hat. 'What's that?' she inquired in a flash of anger. 'The thirty pieces of silver?'

They were all shocked at the comparison. Then Mother Aloysius closed her eyes, bent her head, and clasped her hands. 'Forgive our inadequacies, Lord,' she prayed. 'We fail each other, but You never fail us. Help us in our difficulties.' She ended with some words in Latin, kissed Gina lightly on the cheek and turned her towards Morag. 'Go back into the world where you belong,' she urged, 'and ask yourself — when half the world is at war, why should you think you can easily find peace?'

Gina made no reply. Her mutinous expression said she didn't want to be lectured. They went out, the gatekeeper escorted them to the door, and they were ushered through.

'Goodbye, go with God,' said the nun.

'Goodbye, and thank you.'

The driver of the brougham looked at them with a lively curiosity as they came out into the country road. He opened the door, Morag got in and then Gina. Last came Rob. 'One on guard either side in case I run away again?' she queried.

'By God, if you go on like this I'll not only be glad if you do run away, I'll give you a one-way ticket!' her grandfather growled. They drove off.

They returned to Holyoke for a meal and a short rest. Then they travelled by train to Boston and thence to New York. Once safely installed in Craigallan Castle, Rob called the family doctor. Sorensen gave Gina a bromide, which ensured a good sleep of fourteen hours. While she slept Rob cancelled the cable to his daughter and son-in-law in London — no need to worry them now they had the child back safe and sound and, as far as he could tell, suffering from nothing more than a girlish attack of romantic pessimism.

Morag re-wrote her letter to Ellie, trying to describe what had happened. 'You'll recall in your own girlhood, dear,' she suggested, 'how you were restless and unsettled. Do you remember coming to see me in Long Island?' This was a reminder of Ellie's misery over not being able to fall in love like everyone else — her feeling of disappointment and frustration over the inadequacies of life. Morag went on to explain that Gina had sought for peace from her restlessness in a convent, but not with any idea of becoming a nun. 'I think she merely saw it as a place of peace and tranquillity. Perhaps we were prattling on too much about sightseeing and travelling for the summer — I dare say it seemed frivolous.' Unanswered was the question: why should Gina be averse to frivolity when all her friends of the same age embraced it with eagerness?

Almost simultaneous with this letter, Ellie-Rose received one from Gina which her grandfather had insisted she write. It was an apology for having caused so much trouble, a plea for forgiveness which sounded more like Rob than Gina, and a promise to behave better in future. 'Grandfather Craigallan has arranged for me to go to a residential college for ladies for a year's tuition of my own choice. I asked to study theatre so I'm going to the Classical School of Speech and Drama. I look forward to it very much and promise to work hard.'

Baffled and anxious, Ellie-Rose handed the letters across the breakfast table to her husband. As he read he made little explosive sounds of annoyance and bewilderment. 'A Catholic convent?' was his eventual query. 'What the devil prompted her to go to a Catholic convent?'

'It's probably the only one she knew of, dear. Francesca sometimes mentions it.'

'That's not what I'm asking. I'm asking why Gina would want to have anything to do with Catholics! Dammit, we're a Methodist family, always have been!'

'Methodism isn't as romantic as nuns in cloisters, Curtis . . .'

'So you think it was just Gina playing up the sweet poetic maiden bit, do you?' He leaned back in his chair and pushed away his plate of eggs and bacon. 'Damned if I understand it.'

Ellie-Rose felt the same. 'I wonder . . . Perhaps we've been gone too long, Curtis. Perhaps we should go home.' Yes, take me home, she was saying within herself, with a part of her mind. Save me from this love affair which is consuming me more and more. Help me to free myself by making me go back to Washington.

In war-time London, it was very easy to carry on a love affair. Everyone had their own work, their own preoccupations. No one stopped to inquire what Ellie-Rose Gracebridge was doing. Curtis was busy, and more so as in America the election campaign gathered momentum. Requests came by every mail for Curtis to supply information that might help to sink the chances of Wilson's re-election – inside information on how badly he was handling international affairs, for instance, or hints that would justify the rumour, growing back home, that the US President intended to declare war on Germany.

Curtis looked thoughtful for a moment, leaned forward towards the table, and sipped his coffee to give himself time before replying. He wanted, of course, to be a loving and concerned father. But there were other things besides Gina's escapades to consider.

'See, Ellie,' he began, 'I want to hang on here in London if I can. It's important − '

'Because of this foreign-relations background you're sending home to Hughes? So far as I can tell, Curtis, he doesn't make much use of it in his speeches.'

'Not yet, but he will − when he counters Wilson's No-War claims. That's the main plank in Wilson's campaign, right? − that he intends to keep the US neutral. If Hughes can spring it at just the right time, in just the right place, it will stop Woodrow Wilson right in his tracks − he'll be shown up as more or less a liar, because so far as I can tell, he's no more neutral than a national flag. He's on the side of the Allies and I don't give a damn what he's saying now, if he gets back into the White House, he'll bring Americans into the war.'

'Yes, but Curtis . . .'

'Well, what?' he demanded, frowning at her.

'What I was going to say is . . . Shouldn't we have other priorities than catching Mr Wilson out in duplicity? After all, Gina *is* our daughter—'

'Oh, she's just playing games. She always liked to be the centre of attention, you've said so yourself.'

'But this seems kind of different, dear. And this letter of hers . . . She doesn't account for what she did, not a bit. She . . . it's almost as if she didn't understand it herself!'

'I reckon that's the truth of it. She got some silly notion into her head, went through with it, and sees now what a fool she's been.'

'I can't help feeling there's more to it,' Ellie-Rose said, shaking her head in anxious doubt. 'Don't you think we ought to mention to the Department of Agriculture that we've been here a good time longer than we ever intended?'

'And go home in a convoy that might end at the bottom of the sea?'

'I don't think we ought to be afraid to face it if we're needed back home—'

'Oh, needed! Your father and Morag are coping okay — you can see that in Morag's letter. I mean, she ran off, but they got her back in no time at all.'

'You don't understand, Curtis. What's worrying me is why she should want to run off in the first place.'

Her husband grunted, rubbed his newly shaved chin a time or two, then said, 'You spoke of priorities. Okay, I'll tell you a priority. I want to stay in London because, if Hughes makes it to the White House, I'm certain to make it to Grosvenor Square.'

She gasped. She stared at Curtis, bereft of speech.

'Yes, honey — the ambassadorship. His Excellency the United States Ambassador to the Court of St James — how's that for a handle? And I'll get it too. If Hughes is President, I'll be Ambassador.'

'But . . . But . . . Curtis!'

'I'm the man on the spot here, see? I know the ropes, I've made a lot of contacts in the British government, I could be a lot of help to a Republican President. And, too, there's your money, darling. I mean, we have to face it — being Ambassador costs money. I reckon your father would invest quite a lot to see his daughter the wife of the Ambassador to London, wouldn't he?'

'He . . . I . . . Of course he would support you financially, Curtis. He always has. You really think . . . ?'

'I do, I really do. I tell you, honey, to go back home now for family reasons would be the most damn-fool thing I could do. I'm useful to Hughes here, he gets stuff from me he couldn't get any other way. If he pulls off the Presidency, he's admitted he'll owe a lot to me for keeping him alongside of the war situation. The White House plays it mighty close to the chest, you know — the Embassy here doesn't put itself out to help the President's opponents with any inside information. So I'm Hughes's white-headed boy in London, and if he wins the election I get the ambassadorship.'

'I see.'

'Do you, Ellie? Do you see that I can't let Gina's nonsense wreck everything for us? This is a plum post. I can go home after a stint as Ambassador and the Governorship of Nebraska will fall into my hand.'

She nodded, wordless in face of the naked ambition in his voice and eyes. He wanted the ambassadorship — the desire for it was as clear on his face as a longing for sexual fulfilment.

Something Ellie-Rose had valued withered at that moment. She had always been fond of Curtis even after the first flush of sexual attraction had faded. She'd wanted to see him do well, had furthered and protected his career at all times.

To her he had always seemed young, almost boyish. But somewhere along the way that boy she liked so much had changed. In his place was a middle-aged selfseeker, avid for advancement at no matter what cost. He didn't care that Gina was in some adolescent misery, that young Curt might feel the lack of his father's company. He didn't care that his children were growing up without them. Nothing mattered except that the Presidential candidate was holding out a carrot — donkey-like, Curtis stretched out his neck to it. He couldn't even see that his wife was in torment. He was too blinded by ambition.

So they would stay in London. They would tell others

and themselves that they were 'doing their bit' as the British phrase had it. But Ellie-Rose knew Curtis was here because he felt he was on the threshold of his throne-room — the room where high office would lead on to the chance to be a Presidential candidate.

She could hardly bear to see his disappointment when November came and with it the news that Woodrow Wilson had been resoundingly re-elected on a No-War platform.

Another wartime Christmas came round. There was a party at the Embassy to which all expatriates were bidden. Tad was absent, off on business to do with liability for loss of shipping. His work took him around Britain, to ports such as Liverpool and Glasgow, to Dublin and Cork, and every now and again — subject of great anxiety to Ellie-Rose — to St Malo or Bordeaux. Over Christmas he was in Ireland. There had been a vast sinking of merchantmen off Queenstown during an action by U-boat 'packs'. In fact, the Christmas presents which Ellie and Curtis sent home went down with those very ships, although they didn't know until months later that the parcels never arrived. So much in wartime was wrapped in mystery due to delay and censorship.

Ellie-Rose missed Tad, yet the social round held her attention. She had to give parties and be entertained in return. On Boxing Day she honoured the strange British tradition of a visit to the pantomime. This was her second viewing of this strange form of theatre and she still couldn't understand its attraction for the British. She thought it vulgar, illogical and silly. 'Well, now that's over, we can have a lull until New Year's Eve,' she remarked to Curtis as they drove home to Ebury Street.

'What's the matter, Christmas getting you down, honey?'

She sighed. 'It's hard to be very merry when everything's so gloomy, isn't it?'

'You mean that damned election,' he grunted. 'Gee, that was a let-down!'

She had meant the war news — the launching of a British offensive in Mesopotamia which friends in high circles murmured was doomed from the start, the losses to the Allies on the Meuse, rumoured strikes in Welsh coalfields with the implied terrors of socialist revolution, the scarcity of food even in London, the whispers among the diplomats that Russia was tottering towards disaster . . .

But now that Curtis could bring himself to mention the disappointment, she said with a hand on his arm: 'Darling, don't you think you should reconsider going home? There's no hope of the ambassadorship for at least another four years—'

'I'm not going home with my tail between my legs!' he broke in with a burst of annoyance. He shook her hand off his sleeve. 'Half the Republican party must know I thought I'd get that post. What would they say if I closed up shop and went back to Washington the minute I knew it was a bust? No, I'm staying. You can go home if you want to, if you're really worried about Gina.' He stopped to think that over, having said it in a moment of pique. He added: 'I wish you wouldn't though, Ellie. The other guys on the mission keep saying what a disadvantage they're at, not having a proper household with a hostess. They rely on us to do a lot of their entertaining for them. It would be a lot different if you left.'

It was as if he were begging her to keep contact with

her lover. She felt like a moth in a collector's net — fluttering in desperation, imagining because her wings still moved that she could be free. Why couldn't he understand! If she were forced to leave England, her affair with Tad would end.

Almost, she burst out with it. 'Let me go home! I'm growing more and more in love with another man. Soon I won't be able to bear it any more.'

But she stifled the cry. She couldn't be the wreck of all Curtis's ambitions. She and Tad had discussed it often and often, lying in each other's arms: 'Tell him, Ellie, let him get a divorce. The children are older now, they don't need you in the same way, and Curt is fit and healthy. It's only Curtis who stands in the way. Tell him and be done with it.'

But a divorce would still cause the voters of Nebraska to turn their backs on him. It was hard for her to admit that the strengthening of his ambitions, to which she had given so much of her life and energy, really meant nothing.

She said to Tad that the longer they could delay it, the better. The war was changing things: perhaps in a year or so, convention even in the Mid-West would be less rigid. Time was the escape route — let time pass, and perhaps she would see a way to end her marriage without harming Curtis. Who could tell? He might be offered some post in the administration for services rendered, a post that would make his aim of Governor of Nebraska unimportant. Woodrow Wilson was taking a few Republicans into his confidence as advisers — perhaps Curtis would receive an invitation of that kind. Perhaps, perhaps . . . perhaps something would make it possible to confess their liaison and all would end well.

But she really didn't believe in that fairy tale. Nor, though part of her longed to be an honourable wife and mother, could she bring herself to end the affair. She was too deeply in love. She had tried to force Fate to end it − if Curtis had agreed to go home, she would have tried with all her strength to break off with Tad once and for all. But Fate had declined to help her.

So they had drifted on without taking any decisive step. After all, they were happy. It was a stolen happiness, but none the less real for all that. By and by events would force them to a choice. If Curtis were sent for to return to Washington, Ellie guessed she would never be able to accompany him − she would have to stay with Tad, and confess her unfaithfulness.

But until that time came, she and Tad must seize what they could out of the hazards of life and war − they were not alone in doing so and that very fact seemed a justification for their attitude.

Ellie was expecting Tad back in London in time to celebrate part of New Year's Day with him. She had a party in her home to look forward to on New Year's Eve. On the morning of the 31st she got up early as usual, to start work on the final details of the party. She was feeling a little unwell. She hadn't been quite well since Christmas − all that heavy, rich British food. All the same, it was strange how the queasiness continued, because since Boxing Day she had been very abstemious. 'Good Lord,' she muttered to herself as she sat at the little table in her boudoir, pencil at the ready to check menus while she drank her early morning coffee. 'I hope I'm not turning into a dyspeptic middle-aged lady!'

Beading put a pretty shawl across her shoulders, protection against the draughts that seemed to penetrate despite all the heavy curtains at the window. 'Cream, madam?' she inquired. 'I think you should take cream this morning — you've a heavy day ahead.'

Ellie watched the maid pour thick cream into the black coffee. It formed on the surface, swirled around in a lazy brown coil. Tiny little globules of fat formed at the edge of the whirlpool.

Ellie got up hastily, knocking the table, dropping the shawl. She hurried to the bathroom, where she was retchingly sick.

When the spasms had passed, she straightened to stare at herself in the bathroom mirror.

She knew the signs well. She was pregnant.

Chapter Twelve

Curtis couldn't possibly be the father of the child. It was Tad's. At the thought a surge of fierce joy shook Ellie-Rose. At this late stage in her life, when she had thought such blessings were gone by, she would bear Tad a child.

She must let him know at once. Forgetting how early it was, she ran to the telephone and asked the operator for the number. But the phone rang and rang without answer and she had to remind herself that Tad wasn't expected back from Dublin until the next day.

She went back to the boudoir to find the cup of coffee poured by Beading still awaiting her. She poured it away in the bathroom and refilled her cup with strong black coffee, well sugared. She'd attended first aid classes after the scenes at the Zeppelin raid, and she knew that a hot sweet drink was good for shock.

And she had had a shock, no doubt about it. As her mind began to assimilate the facts, she realised that a crisis had come upon her.

It was many months now since she and her husband had shared the same bed. Curtis had let her sleep alone out of consideration for her state of nerves after the air raid, and for several days thereafter. Then things had returned to normal but even so, they had not made love. Curtis was tired physically and troubled mentally by his work in London for the trade delegation. Moreover, although he was still deeply attached to Ellie-Rose, and proud of her, his sexual taste turned now towards younger women. Ellie was well aware that he found diversion among the pretty ladies on the edge of London society, and bore him no ill will on that score.

For about the last twelve months he had taken to sleeping regularly in his dressingroom, a room smaller than the master bedroom certainly but comfortable and pleasant. It meant he could tiptoe in without disturbing her after a night out with the boys, a night of too much whisky and too many cigars. It meant also that there was no danger of his wife asking for his husbandly attention when he had spent himself with a girl from the chorus of *The Bing Boys*.

Perhaps Curtis had been surprised that Ellie-Rose made no complaint. But he had too much sense to query the way things had fallen out. They were both satisfied with their arrangements.

Ellie-Rose must speak to Tad as soon as possible, to tell him her news and ask what to do. She had better not confess to Curtis until Tad had been told. The coming confrontation would be unpleasant enough for Tad without the additional distress of being taken by surprise.

She wrote a note for Tad, begging him to get in touch the moment he returned, and turned her attention to the day's routine. She had twenty people coming to dinner, and then they were going on to a restaurant for a late-night party to welcome in the New Year. At the thought, she sighed, and had a moment's longing to withdraw from the whole thing. She need only tell Curtis she didn't feel up to it; she had been under the

209

weather since just after Christmas, Curtis would understand.

But then she straightened her shoulders and shook her head. No, she was going to behave exactly as usual. The fact that she was pregnant could not be acknowledged until Tad had been told and Curtis faced. Until that time, she would be Mrs Ellie-Rose Gracebridge, star of the American constellation in London.

If she seemed a little less brilliant than usual at the New Year's party, no one noticed in the hubbub of celebration. Glasses were raised: 'Here's to 1917! Victory this year!'

Next day, New Year's Day, she waited at home for a call from Tad. The servants were surprised to find her up and about soon after six as usual. But nine o'clock came and went without a telephone call. Ten o'clock, no call. Eleven o'clock, the phone began to ring — but only with New Year wishes from friends. By midday she had had eleven telephone conversations, none of them with Tad. At one Curtis came home to eat a light lunch and complain of a hangover due to the previous evening's festivities. 'I shan't be home for dinner, dear — Tom and Al are taking me to meet some members of the new Cabinet at the House.'

She was thankful for the news. It meant she could hurry to Tad's apartment to see him when he got back from his office. Generally he left the firm at around five-thirty; she would be waiting when he got home, they could have a talk, and then she must be back in Ebury Street to dress for an evening engagement which she herself couldn't evade since Curtis had cried off — the insult to the hostess would be too severe, especially since the concert was in aid of Belgian refugees.

By five-fifteen of the very cold New Year's Day, she

had let herself into Tad's apartment. There was no central heating in this old-fashioned building and no fire had been lit for over a week — not, in fact, since their last passionate evening together before he left for Ireland.

'That's when it happened,' she told herself with a little laugh of guilty pleasure. She went into the bedroom to sit on the bed and recall the storm of desire that had swept them away. 'Oh, Tad, hurry home — I'm waiting for you!'

But he didn't come. She became so cold that she wrapped herself in the bed-quilt, but the minutes ticked by and he didn't come.

At seven o'clock, by which time she was already very late to get home and change, she went downstairs in search of the porter. 'Are you expecting Mr Kendall?' she inquired.

'Dunno, mum. He's away on business.'

'Wasn't he due back yesterday?'

'Yes, but he never turned up.' The porter, a disabled ex-serviceman recently given the job, had no great interest in the tenants.

'You haven't had word from him?'

'Me, mum? No.' He seemed to think the idea absurd.

'Thank you,' she said, and went upstairs to prop her note, delivered yesterday, in a prominent spot against the clock in the livingroom.

He had been delayed, obviously. The crossing between Dublin and Holyhead was notoriously difficult because of weather conditions. It wasn't the first time Tad had been held up on his way back from an investigation in Ireland. He would be home tonight, perhaps, or tomorrow. He would telephone as soon as he read her note.

211

But all next day she heard nothing. About four o'clock her anxiety forced her into an action she knew was indiscreet, but she had to know why he had not been in touch. She rang his law firm.

'Noble, Derring and Kendall,' said the reception clerk at the other end.

'Good afternoon. May I speak with Mr Kendall, please?'

'I'm sorry, Mr Kendall is not in the office today.'

'Is that so? Do you expect him tomorrow?'

'No, madam, we don't.'

'Why not?' she asked sharply.

'I . . . er . . . Mr Kendall is away on business, madam.' Ellie could hear the young man saying to himself, 'Careless talk costs lives.' The work of the firm, concerning as it did shipping losses and cargo values, might give aid to the enemy if it became known.

She took a deep breath and set to work to charm him. 'I don't understand it,' she said in a hurt tone. 'Mr Kendall had an engagement to dine with my husband last night and he didn't turn up. He didn't even send a message of excuse! It's too bad.'

'Oh. Er . . . who is that speaking?'

'This is the wife of Senator Gracebridge, of the American Agricultural Delegation. As a fellow-American we thought Mr Kendall might be lonely on New Year's Day so we . . .' She let her words tail off in reproach.

'Oh, I see. Quite so, madam. I'm very sorry. Mr Kendall is overseas on a maritime inquiry.'

'I believe I knew that – but he was expected back from Ireland at the end of December, surely?'

'Oh, you knew he'd gone there? Oh. Well . . . One moment, madam.' He left the telephone. She could

212

hear the faint echoing sounds of voices in the old office in New Bridge Street. Then the phone was picked up again. 'Mrs Gracebridge? I asked Mr Robert Noble if I might tell you facts and he says he sees no reason why not, in the circumstances. Mr Kendall was expected back from Dublin as you say, but the circumstances of the case made it necessary for him to go on to Lisbon.'

'Lisbon!'

'Yes, madam, it's an extremely difficult case concerning a compensation claim against the German government by two neutral nations, and can only be conducted from a neutral country.'

'I see. Thank you,' Ellie said in a breathless voice.

'I'm very sorry if Mr Kendall seemed impolite over the dinner engagement. Mr Robert sends his apologies. He'll mention it to Mr Kendall when he writes to him in Lisbon.'

'No, no − please don't − it's not important − I don't want to make a fuss now that I know − thank you for telling me. I'm sorry to have troubled you.'

'No trouble, madam.'

Lisbon! As Ellie put the phone down she was shivering with reaction. How was she ever going to get in touch with Tad in Lisbon? She didn't even know what hotel he would be at. She would have to wait until he wrote to her, and then reply at once.

Meanwhile, she must be patient, stoical.

And stoicism was what she needed. At the end of that month Germany announced a policy of unrestricted naval warfare, which meant that no ship on the high seas, enemy or neutral, was in future safe from attack. In a way this only formalised what had been going on during the autumn of the past year, but it sent a shudder through the world. Then in early February bread rationing was introduced in Britain. For months now food had been growing scarce yet the scarcities had hardly touched Ellie-Rose. Now she found that a simple thing like toast for breakfast was unattainable. Like any other rich, pampered woman, she was shocked into attention to the miseries of the poor, who relied on bread as a staple food.

The very next day Curtis came home from his office in a state of muted anger and excitement. 'Do you know what that fool in the White House has done, Ellie? He's broken off diplomatic relations with Germany!'

'What?' she gasped. That was like the preliminary to a declaration of war. But Wilson had campaigned on a No-War platform. 'What does it mean?'

'It means he's going to welch on his election promises, that's what it means, dammit! Why, the devious prosing squit—'

'But he can't, Curtis! He got back into office by promising to keep us out of the war!'

'What difference does that make?'

'It'll all blow over,' she said hopefully.

But it didn't. A few days later the President was ordering the arming of United States merchant ships to meet the U-boat menace. 'Oh, great!' groaned Curtis. 'It only needs one ship's captain to open fire on a submarine, and we're at war.'

Ellie was in a state of depression by now. The news was unremittingly bad. Almost as difficult to bear, she had heard nothing from Tad. She lived from day to day, hoping for a letter, but nothing came. Instead there were rumours of wholesale sinkings in the Bay of Biscay by U-boats. She began to be afraid that Tad had not even reached Portugal safely.

And all the time the baby was growing within her. At present there was no visible change in her figure, but she was more than two months pregnant now, and soon she must speak out. She rehearsed the phrases she would use to Curtis: 'I would have told you at once but the baby's father is overseas . . .' No, that sounded as though Tad were in the services. 'I would have told you at once but I wanted to talk it over with the baby's father first—' But that sounded as if she scarcely knew him . . .

In the middle of March she was preparing to go out to a morning meeting of a women's charity when Curtis arrived home with the other members of the delegation. 'Honey,' he said, 'us fellows need to confer in private and have access to the phone. Will you tell the servants to clear the line as soon as they can if anyone calls? And we'll be here a while − we'd like a meal around − say − one o'clock?'

'Of course, dear. Do you want me to stay home? I'm only going to the Women's Hospital committee—'

'No, this is all pretty confidential and the less people around the better.'

Frowning a little, Ellie-Rose welcomed the men into her home, led them to the study they knew so well, arranged for coffee to be served at once and a meal of whatever was available at lunchtime. All the time she was at her own committee meeting her mind was worrying at the problem − what was so confidential they couldn't discuss it at the office in Victoria Street?

The answer came to her. It was an anti-Wilson, anti-Democrat plot of some kind. They couldn't discuss it at the office because that was in a building housing pro-government, pro-Democrat diplomatic staff.

She got home soon after three. The men were still

closed in the study. She could hear the rumble of voices, smell the cigar smoke. She had tea taken into them, and later went herself to see if there was anything else they wanted.

They looked exhausted – angry, frustrated, dishevelled, with cigar ash down the fronts of their waistcoats. It reminded her of secret meetings among party wheeler-dealers at nomination time back home. What could they be up to?

When cocktail time came, she sent in the whisky decanter and the soda siphon. Half an hour later she tapped on the door to remind Curtis they had a theatre engagement. 'Ring up and cancel, Ellie.'

'At this late hour?' she said, aghast.

'All right then, you go – say I've got the grippe.'

'Curtis!'

'I can't go. Sort it out how you like.'

She decided to keep the theatre engagement, which was with a young couple related to the Curzons. Luckily in their box it was easy to mask the fact that one of the party was missing.

When she got home, it was about eleven o'clock. The door of Curtis's study stood open, to reveal a scene of chaos – remains of sandwiches on dirty plates dotted about, ash-trays full up, sticky glasses and used cups on every surface, crumpled sheets of paper, files of reports. Curtis was sitting by his desk reading through a hand-written report.

'What was that all about, Curtis?' she inquired, coming in to stand at his shoulder.

'I'm not supposed to tell you, but we've been arguing about whether to make a public challenge to the President over his intention to declare war on Germany.'

216

'Curtis!'

'Yeah — how's that for a circus elephant?'

'Declare war? Is Wilson going to declare war?'

'All the signs point that way. We got a heavy hint this morning from one of the diplomatic corps in our building that it's only a matter of days.'

'But he can't!'

But the fact was that he could.

Two days later Curtis was called to the Embassy to receive a special message from the Secretary of State. In view of his very active interest in the war situation, the US Government would like him to go with a small party of Americans to visit the Western Front. This was not an order, he was to understand — it was a request.

'See, they want to get me involved in supporting the Allied forces by visiting them,' he muttered to Ellie. 'I feel I ought to refuse as a way of showing I'm against the whole damn thing. But you don't refuse a request from your President, now do you?'

She could see he was talking himself into accepting. 'When would you be going?' she asked.

'Day after tomorrow. What d'you think, Ellie-Rose? Should I tell the Secretary of State to go to hell?'

'No, dear, I think you should accept,' she said, because she knew that was what he intended to do anyway.

When he comes back, she told herself, I must tell him about the baby. I ought to have told him before this, but it wouldn't be fair to upset him when he's going on an important trip with officials from other governments. When he comes back, I'll perhaps have heard from Tad. Any day now, there *must* be a letter from Tad. She had written to him at his London firm — marking the envelope 'Personal: please forward' — but whether he had ever received it, she had no way of knowing.

The continual anxiety was having an effect on her. She was thinner in face and body, except where the thickening of lines told of the baby's existence. But that, thank God, was masked by the loose pleated skirts that were now in fashion. For another week or two she was safe from discovery. But not much longer than that.

I'll wait a day or two after Curtis is home, she told herself, and then I'll speak to him.

But she never did. By one of those freak accidents that make war seem like a lottery, a sniper saw a party of eminent gentlemen being escorted around the lines at Argonne. From his vantage point high up in a budding chestnut tree he drew a bead on the tallest of them.

He shot Senator Curtis Gracebridge stone dead.

Chapter Thirteen

Rob Craigallan tore the telegram apart with his two hands and let the pieces flutter down to his desk. 'God curse the Germans!' he shouted, throwing his fists in the air. 'God damn them and destroy them!'

'Rob, for God's sake!' Sam Yarwood jumped out of his chair, sure that his old friend was having a seizure. Cornelius scooped up the two pieces of paper and read aloud the message.

'Regret to inform you Senator Curtis Y. Gracebridge killed by German action Wednesday 25th of March while visiting Allied lines. Deepest condolences.' The name of the Secretary of State was appended.

'Christ,' Sam whispered.

They were in the office at Craigallan Agricultural in Chicago, having preliminary discussions about May wheat bids. The secretary had buzzed through on the desk fitment to say a telegram had arrived and had brought it in on Rob's command. No one had thought it would concern anything except wheat or corn.

Cornelius saw that his father was pale with shock. He went to the concealed cupboard among the bookshelves, took out the brandy decanter, and poured a measure into a glass. When he took it to his father, Rob waved it away with a gesture that sent it flying.

219

'I'm all right,' he said. 'I just thought immediately – my poor Ellie-Rose!' and then: 'I wonder what the hell happened?'

'A shell came over, I suppose—'

Rob picked up the telephone to start finding out the details, but the first to have information were the journalists. They made the most of it. The way it appeared in the newspapers, it seemed almost as if the sniper had picked out Curtis *because* he was an American.

Indignation ran high, when the story broke on the 30th of March. Cynics afterwards refused to believe that grief for the loss of this faithful servant caused Woodrow Wilson to summon his cabinet.

But a few days later a special congress declared war on Germany.

Rob walked into his Chicago office one evening soon after. He threw himself into a chair. Sam and Neil were with him, sheafs of notes in their hands on phone calls they had to make to the brokers to finalise certain points. Rob stayed them with a wave of the hand.

'I'm going to London,' he said.

Sam stared at him. Neil frowned. 'No,' he said.

'Yes, boy. I'm going. My little girl needs me.'

'How you gonna get there?' Sam inquired. 'You read in the papers – shipping taken over for troops—'

'I'll go on a troopship.'

'Gee whiz, you gonna join up? At your age?'

'Don't be so funny, Sam. I can swing it. I'll get on a ship, don't you worry.'

'No,' Neil said again.

'Yes, Neil, I will. I've done enough for this country, paid enough into charities and political funds to earn myself some goodwill. If that don't work, I know things about some high officials they sure don't want mentioned in public.'

'Why, Rob, that's blackmail,' Sam protested, in pretended reproof.

'Damn right it is. I'll be on the first troopship going to Britain or I'll know the reason why.'

'No.' Once again Neil said it, and this time he shook his head and slapped his hand on the desk for attention.

'What d'you mean, no? I tell you, I'll manage it somehow.'

'Not that,' Neil said. 'I'm thinking about Craigallan. Who's going to mind the shop if you go?'

There was a pause. Sam looked at Rob. The answer ought naturally to have been Gregor. But Gregor was once again in Mexico at the behest of the administration, soothing down touchy and unreliable negotiators. But in Mexico everything takes longer than you expect. He was still there, five months after his departure from Washington.

'You're going to take over, Neil,' Rob Craigallan said to his elder son.

'Me?' It was a gasp of disbelief.

'Yes, why not? You've shown yourself a fair administrator setting up this deaf charity. You always play your part well over the dealing in The Pit.'

'But you know people don't understand me when I talk, Papa—'

'Sam understands you. Sam will help you. Sam's been dealing a long time, delivering puts and calls. Listen, son, perhaps I wouldn't have made you shoulder this if things were normal. And perhaps I'd have been wrong . . . I've begun to think I should have made you play a greater part all along, but there you are — that's hindsight. Any rate, from now until I get back from England, you're head of Craigallan.'

'No, Papa, I don't want to.'

'Dammit, lad, do you think *I* want to? I wouldn't leave you and Sam to manage on your own if I had a choice. But Ellie's over there in London alone. I don't know what's happening — the mail's all to hell. The only thing left is to get over there.'

'Papa, what will Gregor say?'

'What does it matter what Gregor says? My mind's made up. Get yourself ready to move in here in the next couple of weeks, Neil, for I'm going to be on a ship London-bound by the end of the month.'

Neil didn't believe that even Rob Craigallan could achieve this miracle. The official attitude was that only troops, necessary civilians, and military supplies could be given transport. Yet by the end of the month, as he had foretold, Rob Craigallan was being waved goodbye from South Pier by his family.

'You are head of the family now,' Francesca told Neil as they turned away after the liner had disappeared from view. 'It is a great responsibility.'

Neil shook his head. 'I'm not taking on the family, Francesca! Craigallan Agricultural is enough to wrestle with. Someone else will have to deal with domestic problems.'

'Such as what to do with Gina?'

Gina had taken the news of her father's death with strange calm. Rob himself had gone to the Classical School of Speech and Drama in Concord, New Hampshire, to break the news. 'It says he was killed by enemy action, my dear. We don't know any more than that.'

'Oh, he died a hero's death, I've no doubt. It couldn't be anything else.'

'Well . . . yes . . . I expect that's right.'

'He heroically left his home and family to serve his President in England. He heroically stayed there among the dangers of weekend parties and visits to the theatre. He heroically went to Flanders to see how the soldiers behave. And he heroically died by some accident, probably with a runaway horse and cart.'

'Gina, what's the matter with you?' her grandfather cried. 'You sound as if . . . you're making fun of him!'

'Perish the thought!' For a moment she looked directly at Rob, her dark eyes luminous with pain. 'I'm sorry he's dead. But he's been gone so long, I can't really feel as if I've lost him.'

'Do you want to come home with me to Craigallan Castle?'

'Why? Is there to be a funeral service there?'

'No, we think he'll be buried with military honours in France . . .'

'So what is the point of coming home, to New York or Washington?'

'I thought you'd . . . like to be with the family.'

'No,' she said in a judicious tone, 'I don't think so, thanks. I'll go into mourning, of course. Will you let me have some money extra to my allowance, Grandfather? I'll need to buy black dresses.'

Baffled, he took out his pocketbook and counted out bills. She accepted them with self-possession and put them in the pocket of her skirt.

The doctor had said there was nothing physically wrong with her — he called her over-strung and under-occupied. Rob had wanted her to train for something useful, like secretarial work or nursing, but she chose to study drama. It didn't make any difference — all she needed was to be kept with her nose to the grindstone for a year or so.

He had half expected her to rebel, because the school was devoted to Shakespeare and Greek drama – she'd been expecting something more 'bohemian'. She'd wanted to shock her grandfather by choosing theatre instead of a worthwhile training, but she realised when she settled in at the Classical School that it was respectable in the extreme.

Young ladies were housed in a boarding establishment supervised by Madam Dorabella Doran, ex-Titania, ex-Juliet, ex-Juliet's nurse and now retired. The young gentlemen were housed in a dormitory building attached to the college. Strict segregation was the rule except during classes, and even then embraces and kisses were not permitted even when called for by the text. Only Bowdlerised Shakespeare and Greek tragedy were studied. Racine and Corneille were permitted entire, in cool translation. Victorian melodrama was much approved of; its moral tone made it very suitable, and its veiled allusions to evil-doing avoided the need for difficult explanations.

Gina set herself with grim determination to work her way through this year of exile. Her fellow students were divided into two types: those who, starry-eyed, saw themselves as Bernhardt or Tree, and those who looked forward to a career in the pulpit or the missionary hall. Gina was 'interestingly different'. When Madam Doran asked why she had chosen to study drama, she replied that it was to improve her voice and carriage. And in fact, one of the few things she learned at the school was how to speak well and hide whatever turmoil she might be experiencing behind a suave exterior.

In these hothouse circumstances, it was inevitable that romance should flourish no matter how the staff tried to quell it. Some of the girls had a passion for one of the voice teachers, but most of them were in love with Helmer Ziegler, a third year student bound for fame as a *jeune premier*. He, the same age as Gina but somehow seeming much younger, fell desperately enamoured of her. He kept tucking quotations from love poems into her text books.

'I wish you wouldn't, Mr Ziegler,' she admonished him.

He seized her hand. 'I want you to know how much I admire you, Miss Gracebridge! Your cool beauty, your reticence and tranquillity . . .'

'But I'm not the least bit tranquil, Mr Ziegler,' she said with amusement.

'But you are reticent, you can't deny that. What secrets do you guard behind that quiet charm?'

He began to be almost a persecution. The other girls at Miss Doran's couldn't understand why she wanted to avoid the adorable Helmer. If he chose her, she ought to be honoured and swoon into his arms.

'Swoon into his arms,' laughed Gina. They were such innocents! She didn't remember when she herself had thought that was what a love scene consisted of – a slender youth, a languid maiden, and a kiss or two on the hand.

The fact was, his persistence disturbed her. She found herself wanting to teach him a good lesson. So she thought, why not accept his invitation – why not go out with him one evening, for what was then known as 'eager necking'. She would scare him to death! It would be the end of his romantic daydreams.

It didn't work that way. When they sat down

together in a swing hammock looking out from the hotel's garden on the starlit Merrimack, she was ready to lead him on and laugh in his face. But at the first touch of his hands, she froze.

The teasing words died in her throat. She thought she was going to suffocate. She began to shake. Little broken sounds of panic broke from her.

Helmer, thinking it was natural maidenly modesty, soothed her by stroking her hair. 'Don't be afraid, my lovely flower,' he murmured. 'You know I wouldn't do anything you didn't like—'

'Don't,' she shuddered. 'Don't touch me! Don't touch me!'

'But . . . Gina . . . I only want to touch you with a butterfly's kiss—'

'Oh, be quiet, go away!'

'Darling, if you knew how much I love and respect—'

'Take your hands *off* me!' It was almost a shout. Other couples, wrapped in gentle embrace elsewhere in the summer garden, roused and looked about.

'Ssh, Gina, everybody's looking!'

'I don't care! Leave me alone! Don't touch me!'

Helmer got up, so astounded that he almost lost his balance. 'But I . . . I didn't do anything—'

'Go away! I can't bear you near me!'

'But . . . Gina . . . then why did you come?'

'Oh, let me alone, you stupid, stupid fool!'

Hurt, taken aback, wounded in his young romantic manhood, he turned and stalked off. He didn't even pause to consider how Gina would get back to college. She took a hackney and sneaked indoors unobserved.

The next day, Sunday, all her fellow-students at Madam Doran's were agog to know what had happened. The outing with Helmer had been supposed to be secret but it was impossible to keep secret a thing like that. Gina avoided all hints and direct questions. It became clear that something very bad had happened, that Helmer Ziegler had acted in a very ungentlemanly manner. He, poor fellow, didn't know what he was accused of and, moreover, believed in a code of honour that forbade him to defame a lady. They stayed away from each other with ostentatious care.

In the eyes of the other male students Gina became all the more desirable. She was unattainable — therefore they all wanted to 'attain'. Gina had to develop some armour very quickly. She chose to turn herself into a kind of mixture of Portia and Lady Teazle — cool, quick-tongued, always in control. Now and again she looked at herself in the mirror and asked her reflection: Where is the real Gina Gracebridge?

And sometimes she thought the answer was, there never has been a real Gina Gracebridge. Between the dreaming girlhood and the arid present, no real personality had ever emerged.

What did it matter? She would pretend. She need only hold out until her year at the Classical School was up.

When that ended, the responsibility for Gina devolved upon Cornelius, as head of the family. He solved the problem quite neatly by giving Gina a job in the offices of the Deaf Veterans' Aid Society. This was quite convenient, because now that so much time would be taken up with Craigallan Agricultural Products, he had decided to hand over the work of administrating DVAS to Bess Gardiner.

Bess had become quite invaluable to him over the past year. Her quick grasp of essentials, her commonsense in a crisis — he liked them very much. Moreover, she could speak with him in the mixture of speech and sign that was familiar to him. From the very first there had been no awkwardness between them in working together. In fact, he was going to miss her greatly when he ceased to see her regularly at the charity's headquarters.

She was overwhelmed when he asked her to take over the work. Her freckled face went pink, her eyes sparkled with unshed tears behind the goldrimmed glasses. 'Oh . . . Neil . . . I wonder whether . . . I mean, I've never been asked to take control before. I'm not used to responsibility.'

'Nonsense, Bess, you've been taking responsibility for ages without noticing it.'

'But . . . But . . . To sit in the office with the name "Administrator" on the door — that's different.' She paused. 'I don't know if my parents would approve.'

'Why on earth shouldn't they?'

'They might think it was . . . unwomanly.'

He shook his head at her. Nothing Bess ever did could be unwomanly. He thought her tremendously attractive, with her slight figure and quick movement. He couldn't understand why she had never married. Some women were like that, of course. If Bess had chosen that route, he thought it a pity. She would make some man a wonderful wife.

'Talk it over with your parents,' he suggested. 'Tell them that we need you. I'll still keep the title, if that would make them happy — but you'd be the one doing the work.'

'I . . . shan't see so much of you, though, shall I?'

'I'm afraid not.' He sighed. 'My father going to London leaves me head of everything — family, business . . . I don't like it much. Like you – not used to responsibility.'

'Oh, goodness!' she cried. 'I say the same to you as you said to me. You've been taking responsibility for ages without knowing it! Ever since your brother went to Mexico, you've been so terribly busy.' She had noticed it. He had not been able to come into the charity's office so often. She had missed his frequent visits.

'Shall be busier still, for a while. Please say you'll take on DVAS for me, Bess.'

'Yes, I will,' she replied, clenching her fists at her side in resolution, determined to withstand any objection her mother might put up.

Cornelius wrote to his father in London to reassure him: so far all was well, August was coming up and the reports on the visible supply seemed encouraging. Markets were jumpy but business was good because of the demands brought about by America's entry into the war. Dealing in The Pit was expected to be high.

Rob scarcely paid attention to his letters. The business of his great agricultural empire had receded from him after the shock of what he found in London.

He had cabled beforehand that he was on his way but had been unable to give a definite date of arrival. He took a taxi from Waterloo Station to Ebury Street without pausing to telephone. When Beading opened the door to him she was in no doubt as to who he was – his face was familiar to her from photographs in Ellie's room. 'Mrs Gracebridge is upstairs lying down, sir.'

'Lying down? Isn't she well, then?'

'She's been under the weather, sir. I'll just go up and prepare her—'

'Prepare her! Don't be an idiot. The best remedy for

whatever ails her will be to see me.' He bounded up the stairs ahead of her and by instinct chose the correct door. He threw it open and went in crying, 'Ellie-Rose, sweetheart — here I am.'

And drew back in startlement.

His daughter was lying on her chaise longue in a silk wrapper. Her hair was loosely brushed, as if she had not been out at all so far that day. Her face was lined and drawn. She was much thinner than when he last saw her. There were shadows under her eyes, her skin was without that blush of colour that made her features so appealing.

Yet her smile of greeting was rapturous. She held out her arms to him and hugged him close, whispering, 'Papa! Oh, Papa!'

'Dear child . . . whatever is wrong with you?' For she looked so ill. And yet she was happy — her eyes were luminous with joy, her lips trembled with delight.

As yet she couldn't confess the reason to him. First she had to explain to him, confess her wrongdoing. Yet she had the courage for that because she had at last heard from Tad. A bundle of letters had arrived two days ago — seven letters held up by inefficient Portuguese postal officials, delays over arranging convoy escorts, muddle over landing mailbags at wrong ports . . . A dozen factors had contributed to keeping Tad's letters from her. Now at last she knew he was safe in Lisbon, worried at not having heard from her, desperate for news.

She had written at once. With luck, in a week or so he would know everything that had happened.

She threw back the soft cashmere shawl that had covered her and sat up. She heard her father exclaim.

'Yes, Papa. I'm expecting a baby.'

'But . . . but . . . why didn't you let us know?'

'I'll explain it all in a minute. First let me have something brought for you — would you like a drink? Something to eat?'

'I'd like a big pot of coffee and a sandwich, Ellie, if the household can run to that.'

'Oh, we're not entirely without food, no matter what you've heard.' She rang for the housemaid and ordered the snack. She parried all her father's worried questions until it had come, then she told the maid they were not to be disturbed.

'The baby's due in late September, Papa. I didn't write about it because . . . it isn't Curtis's child.'

'Ellie!'

'Don't be angry. Wait till you hear who the father is. Papa — do you remember Tad Kendall?'

'What?' Rob gasped. He remembered only too well. It was Rob who had sent Tad away when the affair had become a torment to his daughter.

'The lawyer, you mean?'

'I met him soon after we arrived. He's been living here in London ever since he left the States. We . . . we couldn't help ourselves, Papa. It seemed as if it was meant for us to be together. I mean, it must have been meant, for why else would Fate have brought me here to meet him once again?'

'Did . . . did Curtis know?'

She shook her head. 'I was summoning up courage to tell him when he was invited by the President to join that visiting delegation to the Allied lines. I intended to tell him when he came home — but he never came home, Papa.' She bent her head and a tear trembled on her lashes. 'Don't blame me too harshly. I didn't want to harm his career. But when the baby started, I knew I was going to have to do it. But I put it off because Tad is overseas — his work takes him away and at the moment he's in Lisbon. I've been so anxious,' she said, clasping and reclasping her hands. 'The mail's been all to pieces — we haven't been in touch with each other since before January — until two days ago.'

'You mean he doesn't know about the baby?'

'Not yet. I wrote as soon as I got his address. As soon as he gets my letter I expect him to get passage back to London.'

'And then what?' Rob asked, trying to come to grips with this vista of events.

'Then we'll get married.' She laughed and touched her midriff. 'It can't be too soon, can it?'

'Oh, good God — but everyone thinks it's Curtis's baby, I suppose?'

She nodded. 'I haven't said anything, but I feel so awful — people are so kind and sympathetic and I feel a . . . fraud. And yet I do grieve for Curtis, Papa, I really do.' Suddenly she began to cry. 'Oh, it's all such a muddle! I feel I ought to be in the depths of misery at what happened to my husband, but I can't be unhappy, I can't — not now that I know Tad is safe and well. I'll see him soon, and we'll be married, and the baby will have his name—'

'Ellie, people will know—'

'I don't care! It's Tad's child, and it has to have his name!'

'Well, well.' He sat beside her on the chaise longue and put his arm about her. 'You sure have taken me by surprise, kitten. It's going to take me a while to get used to the idea of a new grandchild.' He hesitated. 'Is it all right, Ellie?'

'You mean, at my age?' She mopped at her eyes. 'I

don't know. I've been awfully sick, yet I think that's been because I was so worried over not hearing from Tad. And remorse over Curtis, you know. And uncertainty . . . things like that. Now I know I probably will have Tad here beside me soon, perhaps in a few weeks. Everything is going to be all right now. I've heard from Tad, and you're here . . . Oh, Papa, I'm so glad to see you!'

He sat with his arms around her, thinking back to the days when she was little and needed him. She'd always been so sure he could cure every ill. Things were different now, but he would help her, shield her, support her until the man she loved came to stand at her side.

Another letter from Tad arrived a few days later. It was dated May 9th. She read it avidly then gave a little cry of distress and went paler. Rob, who had run upstairs to her boudoir with it on seeing the Portuguese stamps, caught her hand.

'What is it, Ellie? What's wrong?'

'He's enlisted, Papa!' She handed him the sheet of paper.

Tad began by saying that he still had not heard from her after an absence of four months and was beginning to wonder if she had decided, since events had forced them apart, to make a final break. 'You often reproached yourself for being unfair to Curtis − I could quite understand it if you had decided to end it between us. But, oh, Ellie, I wish you had done it by some means other than silence.'

He went on to say that after hearing the news of America's entry into the war he had felt the least he could do was put himself at the disposal of his country. Because of his special knowledge of maritime law he had been sworn in as a member of the United States Navy with the rank of captain. He was waiting now for his posting to the Legal Section of the Navy Department.

He ended with a plea for a letter. 'Even if it is only to tell me what I begin to fear, that everything is over, send me word; I shall never cease to love you whatever you decide.'

'This damned war!' Rob said under his breath. Then, taking Ellie's hand, 'It's all right, daughter. Your letter will have reached him by now, or at any rate it'll get there any day. He'll know you still feel the same—'

'But he's in the Service now! Papa, don't you see? He may be sent anywhere!' She was dry-eyed, pale with shock and anxiety. Beads of sweat had come out on her forehead.

July turned towards August with no further news. Ellie's health didn't improve. On a hot August night, with the moon's first quarter silvery in a clear dark sky, Ellie gave birth to a boy, five weeks premature.

'Is she going to be all right?' Rob asked the sister who brought him the news.

'Oh, it's *he*, Mr Craigallan. He's tiny, of course, but he's full of fight.'

Rob had meant his daughter. 'Mrs Gracebridge,' he insisted. 'How is Mrs Gracebridge?'

'As well as can be expected.'

They sounded ominous words to Rob, but Ellie improved within a few hours. It was as if, with the arrival of Tad's baby, she felt she had something to live for and fight for. At the end of the month she was sent home to Ebury Street – they might have kept mother and baby longer but the hospital was strained to its utmost by war-wounded from the Second Battle of

Verdun. Rob wanted to take them to some quiet country spot so that Ellie could rest, but she refused.

'No,' she said, her pale lips set, 'if Tad gets to London he'll expect to find me here.'

But less than four weeks later she was made to change her mind. German aircraft came thundering over London, Zeppelins and aeroplanes. The first fullscale air attacks of World War One were launched on a helpless target. Bombs rained down on the city. Even though a blackout had been enforced after the first Zeppelin raids, the full moon and the curve of the Thames were guidance enough. For three nights in succession the aircraft reigned supreme in the London skies, audacious, cruel and unassailable.

Warning rattles were sounded as soon as spotters announced them, but to take shelter in the tube stations was almost as bad as risking injury above ground. The Gracebridge household sheltered in the basement of the Ebury Street house, feeling the ground shake as the bombs impacted, hearing the sound of falling wreckage, calls for help, screams of pain and terror.

In the early hours of the 2nd October, after the third raid, they came out as the all clear was sounded. Ellie had her baby, Bobby, in her arms. Her maid Beading had wraps and shawls. The newly engaged nanny carried the basket of baby things. The butler had a hamper of vacuum flasks and cups. The housemaid carried rugs and blankets. The cook had a tray of little savouries she had made to take with them if the warning drove them to shelter. Rob came last with an armful of pillows and cushions.

The night sky was not quite completely dark but the stars could still be seen. What was unusual was that they could be seen through the rafters of the house. At the far end of the street there was a bomb crater. The houses, shaken and battered by flying debris, had suffered damage to a greater or lesser extent. Water was gushing from a broken main in the pavement outside. The taint of gas was in the air.

'That does it,' Rob exclaimed in fury and resentment. 'We're going! Get some things together, Beading. Shields, see if the telephone is working. If it is, send for a couple of taxis. If it isn't, go round to the hire-car agency in Belgrave Street. I want two cars here in an hour. We're leaving.'

'But where are we going, Papa?' Ellie cried.

'For tonight and tomorrow, we'll find a hotel in the country − I don't give a damn where so long as it's outside the city limits. Then we're going north to Glen Bairach, Ellie. It's time I went home.'

He had bought it on the death of the two remaining heirs to the earldom in the Battle of the Somme, to prove to himself he was the equal of the lairds who had ruled the district in his childhood.

Now he was taking his family there, not to lord it over the peasantry, but to find refuge.

Chapter Fourteen

At long, long last Ellie got the letter she had been living for. It had been forwarded on from the London Sorting Office and bore an American postmark. She tore it open with trembling hands when she saw the familiar handwriting.

'Darling, your letters have at last caught up with me after long delays, although of course I now understand that you couldn't write to me at first because you had no address. When I think what you've been through, I don't know what to say! I learned of Curtis's death as soon as I reached Anapolis but that was the first I'd heard of it — the Portuguese papers carried no mention. I don't know what to say to you. Poor Curtis, it seems so unfair somehow. Your other news fills me with joy. I've arranged a posting to London by means of some backstage diplomacy and hope to be with you soon after you receive this letter.'

It was dated August 25th, had taken six weeks to reach her at Glen Bairach via London.

'I must go to London,' she told her father. 'He may be there, looking for me—'

'Daughter, use your head,' he reproved. 'If he goes to Ebury Street he'll see the house is empty. Everyone knows where we can be reached – the local police, the Embassy, all your friends. He'll find you sooner than you'd find him.'

It was true. Tad contacted his former partners in the law firm, to whom Rob had given Ellie's address in Scotland.

Ellie was in the nursery, watching her baby being bathed ready for bed at six o'clock on a glowing evening of late autumn, when she heard a flurry of activity in the hall below. She rose from her knees beside the baby-bath, and was going to the door to inquire the cause when she heard footsteps coming up the stairs. Quick, striding footsteps on the stone steps. She knew that stride . . .

'Tad!'

He swept her into his arms and whirled her round. She was crushed against the buttons of his uniform overcoat. His peaked hat went sailing from his head as she flung up her arms to embrace him.

'Oh, darling, darling! Oh, God, Ellie! Are you all right? I've been so worried—'

'Yes, yes, I'm all right – fine, now you're here – Tad, how different you look in uniform! Oh, darling, thank God to see you after all this time. Tad, it's been torment – Oh, no, never mind all that, it's over, past and done with! Tad, dearest – oh, come and see your little son!'

The nurse was just slipping the embroidered nightgown sleeves over the little flailing arms. The baby was howling lustily at being put into these restraining layers after the joys of his warm bath. His little red face was creased in fury, his tuft of dark hair stood up damp and straight like a blackbird's feather.

'This is Robert,' Ellie-Rose said, and took him from

the nurse. 'Hush, now, baby . . . your daddy's here to see you.'

As if by magic, the baby stopped crying. He sobbed a couple of times, filling the narrow chest and then relaxing. The creases smoothed out of his face. He opened his eyes, blue eyes, and stared about at the lighted room, at the vague shapes moving there.

'Robert . . .' Tad leaned over Ellie-Rose and put a finger on the child's cheek. The touch startled him. He waved a fist. Tad put his finger against it and he folded his hand around it. It was the first move of the baby, any baby, folding its hand around the finger and the heart of its parents.

'He's – he's beautiful. I didn't expect him to be so . . . so sweet and complete. When was he born, darling?'

'Two days after you wrote your letter saying you were coming, Tad. I think he's like you, my love!'

'Me? Heaven forbid!' But he laughed and hugged her.

When Rob came in from a visit to a neighbouring farm, he found them tête-à-tête in the drawingroom. Shields had already told him of Tad's arrival so he hurried in with his hand outstretched. 'Boy, am I glad to see you!' he cried. 'It's been like a jigsaw, trying to get you two together in one place. Well, feller, you look fine in your uniform. How d'you like your son, eh! Cute as a June-bug, isn't he?'

'He's marvellous,' Tad said with a blush of pride. 'Finest baby I ever saw.'

'Among the hundred you're acquainted with, you mean. Oh, don't look embarrassed. All new fathers are the same. Well, now, we've some talking to do, eh? But you two want to have some time together first so we'll defer the family conference until after dinner, shall we? I'll go smoke a cigar and change.'

Tad only had a three day pass. He had to be back in London on Friday and it had taken him the whole of Wednesday to get to Glen Bairach. He would have to set out in time to catch the night train at Carr Bridge for the fourteen-hour journey to Euston, so they only had about twenty-four hours in which to talk.

The two lovers tended to be attracted away on non-practical topics. It was Rob who kept them to the point. He had ascertained that to be married under Scottish law, three weeks' notice had to be given. The banns would have to be called at the local registry office or parish church. The ceremony could be as quiet as they liked but it could take place no earlier than the 21st of November. Tad said he didn't think he would get leave again so soon; recently arrived in his new post at the Naval Law Section at the London GHQ, he couldn't expect any preferential treatment.

'No, and we don't want to attract special attention by pulling any strings, I suppose. How long d'you think before you get a leave pass, Tad?'

'I don't know. You have to understand this is all fairly new to me, this service life. But I reckon I can get my chief of section to give me a week when I explain I'm getting married.'

'Well, look, the nearest phone is at the pub in Kinselloch — you'd better make a note of the number, they'll bring a message up to the house any time.' Rob had ensured that service by liberal bestowal of pound notes. 'Or you can send a wire — the post office is at Kinselloch too and the boy'll come up on his bicycle with it.'

'Couldn't you have arranged to come to a more accessible place, Mr Craigallan?' Tad groaned.

'Sorry, perhaps I made a mistake in bringing the

household so far north. But after that third air raid I just wanted to get my womenfolk into a damn safe place.'

'Quite right,' agreed Tad.

Ellie went with him in the limousine to Carr Bridge and clung to him until the train steamed in. To the onlooker, she was any wife saying goodbye to her husband in uniform – a common enough sight in Britain after three years of war. He let down the glass of the train window and held her hands until the guard held up his lamp for the departure and the whistle blew.

'I'll be back before you know it,' he called as the train lumbered away. 'I love you, Ellie . . .'

'I love you, Tad . . .'

Letters began to come for Ellie almost every day. The application for a marriage licence had been safely signed and delivered at the registry office. The formalities were completed. Tad thought he could get a pass for the first week in December. Ellie-Rose had merely to choose where the ceremony was to take place.

'I'd like it to be in church, Papa,' she murmured. 'Do you think that's wrong of me?'

'Wrong? How can it be wrong to ask for God's blessing?'

'But Tad and I . . . We already have a child . . .'

'Good Lord, kitten, do you think you're the first to be married to the father of the baby? God understands all that,' Rob said with conviction.

He looked at Ellie now and thought that he had never seen her look more beautiful. She was still thinner than of old, and it might be she would never regain the rounded curves of youth. But her skin was fresh and smooth, her eyes sparkled, all her old vitality had returned. When she leaned over the baby, she looked like some painting of the Madonna – serene, loving, gracious and comely.

The date was at last settled. The wedding would take place on 7th December, a Monday, a day when few people were likely to be hanging about in the parish church of Kinselloch. Tad's leave began on the Sunday: he would take the night train on Saturday, reaching Carr Bridge at midday on the Sunday. Rob volunteered to meet him there but Tad ruled against it – trains were so undependable because of troop movements that he might be late. He would get a taxi at Carr Bridge or a pony and trap. He expected to be with them in time for tea at latest on the 6th.

But tea time came and he didn't arrive. Ellie began to grow anxious. The weather was bad, there was snow falling and drifts were beginning to pile up. She felt sure the train had been blocked by snow-drifts.

Rob went down to Kinselloch to ring the station at Carr Bridge. True enough, the weather had caused some upset to the timetables, but the London train had come in right enough – two hours late, but it had got through. Had the stationmaster seen a naval officer alight? No, no such passenger.

'He's missed the train, that's all, Ellie,' Rob said. 'He probably had work that kept him late at his desk. There *is* a war on, you know, sweetheart.'

She flashed him a look that made him sorry for his foolish tone. 'He would have telephoned to Kinselloch,' she insisted. 'If he just missed the train, he'd have got a message through.'

'Perhaps the lines are down somewhere, dear—'

'Did you inquire about that when you rang Carr Bridge Station?'

'No, I never thought of it.' He heaved himself to his

feet. He was tired, he had had a bad drive in the automobile to the village in a snowstorm and a bad drive back. 'I'll go and do that now—'

'No, no, Papa.' She flew to him and put her arms round him in apology. 'The weather's rotten. Don't go out again. There's some simple explanation. Tad will be here, it's all right.' She summoned a smile. 'After all, the wedding isn't until three in the afternoon. It doesn't matter if he arrives in the middle of the night or first thing in the morning.'

The trains were such that Tad was going to be hard put to it. Having for some reason missed the night train on Saturday, he had only two chances on Sunday, and the second of those would bring him to Carr Bridge about ten on Monday morning. Even so, he could make it to Glen Bairach by noon, or failing that could telephone to say he would be at the church at Kinselloch by three.

There had to be a telephone message — that was the long and short of it. But no word came. By midday Monday, the snow had stopped, the weather was cold and sunny with an eggshell blue sky. Perfect weather for a December bride. Ellie-Rose in her dark brown broadcloth coat trimmed with fur and matching hat looked lovely, though her face was clouded with anxiety. She went with Rob in the limousine to telephone from Mr McFadyen's pub.

There was no telephone at the billet Tad occupied in London. They had the number of his office in Upper Brook Street. Getting through was a problem but at last Rob had the exchange in the building and asked for the extension.

'Hello? Hello? May I speak to Tad Kendall, please? Captain Kendall?'

Ellie stood beside her father, watching his face as he waited. She could hear distorted sounds from the other end but no distinct words. 'He has? You're sure? Thank you. Yes, thank you — it must be some problem on the journey. Many thanks.'

He put back the receiver. 'That was some feller works in the same room. He says Tad left on leave Saturday midday.'

'What?' Ellie shook her head. 'I don't understand it. Where is he? Why hasn't he telephoned if something has delayed him?'

'I don't understand it either, Ellie. What d'you want to do? Go back home or go on to the church?'

She clasped and unclasped her hands. 'I don't know . . . If we go home we might miss each other. He knows the ceremony is at three o'clock in the church.'

'Shall we go there, then?' he asked, his heart aching for the worry and embarrassment she was undergoing.

'I . . . I think so. If he . . . if he doesn't come, we'll have to explain to the minister, anyhow.'

'Yes.'

They went to the plain little church in Kinselloch High Street. The village consisted of only some twenty houses, cottages mostly although the dwellings of the schoolmaster and the minister were more substantial. Kinselloch boasted a post-office-and-store, a public house, a school. Most of the people were engaged in sheep-farming. No one was about by the church as Ellie and her father went in. The minister was there, and the verger. The verger was to have been a witness, together with Rob.

The time was half past two. The church was cold. They waited and waited, but no one came. Three o'clock arrived, three-thirty. 'I'm sorry,' said the

Reverend Donald Watson, 'but I have to leave. I promised to visit a parishioner over at Cromachy by four o'clock.'

'Yes, of course, Reverend,' Rob muttered. He shepherded his daughter out of the church and into the waiting car. They drove back in the swiftly gathering darkness to Glen Bairach.

'I don't understand it,' Ellie-Rose said at last. 'Something must have happened.'

'Sure, honey. There's an explanation. Just hold on to your good sense. Tad would be here if something hadn't prevented him.'

'But what?' They were both thinking of air raids, Zeppelin raids, on some east-coast town during his journey. Could the rails have been damaged near Newcastle-on-Tyne or Edinburgh? But no, the trains appeared to be running.

'What we'll do now,' Rob said when they were indoors at last, 'is we'll wait till daylight tomorrow, and then I'll go down and telephone and I won't come back until I get some information. I mean — I'll go if Tad hasn't arrived in the meantime.'

'Yes,' Ellie-Rose said. She gave him the ghost of a smile then went upstairs to stay with her baby. He didn't see her again until next morning, and it was clear she had not slept at all. God damn the boy, swore Rob to himself. Why doesn't he get in touch? If he can't get through on the telephone, why doesn't he send a telegram?

He set out in the car soon after eight. The road was icy, he skidded about like a drunken stork, but he made it to Kinselloch by ten. Mr McFadyen opened the door of the pub to him. 'Still nae word?' he asked with concern.

'Not a thing.'

'Ah, poor leddy,' McFadyen remarked, and ushered Rob to the phone.

By one of those vagaries that seemed to seize the telephone system he got through at once, with a clear connection. He asked for Tad's extension and was speaking almost at once to the same young voice that had answered him before. 'Mr Craigallan? Yes, I hoped you'd ring. I should have asked how to get in touch when you rang before, but I didn't imagine it would be necessary.'

'What's happened?' Rob said, his heart contracting at the misery in the other man's tone.

'I'm damned sorry, sir . . . I don't know how to tell you . . .'

'What? For God's sake, lad, spit it out!'

'We just got the news this morning, sir. It must have happened after Tad left here on Saturday. It's funny, I remember now, he *said* he felt peculiar − put it down to wedding nerves.'

'Oh, sweet Christ, will you tell me what's happened?' Rob cried.

There was a tiny pause at the other end. Then the young officer said, 'I'm very sorry, sir. Captain Kendall collapsed at King's Cross Station on Saturday night and was taken to hospital. He was in a fever, delirious I gather − they couldn't discover who they should contact so they sent word to our section commander this morning.'

'Sent word? What word?'

'Captain Kendall passed away soon after midnight last night, sir.'

'Passed away? How could that − don't be absurd! Tad Kendall was a fit healthy man!'

'I'm sorry, sir. It's this influenza epidemic. We've had four deaths in our department since last week. Captain Kendall is dead.'

Rob stood with the receiver against his ear, unable to believe what he was hearing.

'Sir? Sir? Are you there?'

'Yes, I'm here.'

'I'm sure Admiral Johnstone would want us to offer our deepest sympathies. Captain Kendall was on his way to be married, we know that.'

'Yes.'

'Would you please tell . . . tell the bride . . .'

'Yes. Thank you. I . . . I must hang up now.'

'Yes, sir. I understand.'

Rob replaced the receiver blindly. The innkeeper, seeing his face, backed away on the point of inquiring if there was news. Rob went out to the car, put his hand on the door handle, then suddenly leaned against the car roof in a spasm of grief.

How could it happen? In four days?

But Tad Kendall was only one of millions of victims of an enemy who killed more than all the weapons of man in World War One.

Chapter Fifteen

The two girls were discussing the next in the sequence of Welcome Home balls for the troops. 'I don't know how you find the energy,' Bess Gardiner said. 'This will be the fourth in a row you've attended.'

'Oh, it helps brighten up the post-New Year gloom. Everything always goes so dull in January, doesn't it? I can never understand why we don't have Thanksgiving in January.'

'Probably because it's difficult to imagine the Pilgrim Fathers giving thanks for anything on the east coast in January. I do wish you'd think again about going tonight, Gina. I hear that last ball at the Cleveland Hotel ended in a fight.'

Gina Gracebridge shrugged and concentrated on studying her features in the mirror of her powder compact. She smoothed down the sides of her bobbed hair against her cheeks and pursed her lips to see if they needed more lipstick. Bess watched her with uneasy concern. 'The trouble is, there's too much drink at affairs like that,' she went on. 'Ex-servicemen seem to have acquired a taste—'

'Oh, good heavens, if that stupid Volstead Act really comes in, it'll mean no alcohol anywhere. You can hardly blame them for wanting to get in as much drinking as they can, beforehand.'

Bess felt that you could. She hated to see people staggering about, quarrelsome and noisy, just because they'd taken too much liquor aboard. But such scenes had become only too frequent in Chicago as home-coming servicemen hung about waiting for their discharge papers.

Because she was the chief administrator of the Deaf Veterans' Aid Society and therefore Gina's titular employer, Bess felt a responsibility for Gina. Gina was supposed to give three days a week to the office of the charity. She did in fact show up on three days a week, because she had a strong suspicion that Uncle Cornelius was capable of cancelling her allowance if she didn't, but her heart wasn't in it. Despite all Bess's coaxing, she refused to take the job seriously, wouldn't attend to correspondence or stay by the telephone to answer enquiries. Her only value was that she knew a great many young people, thus providing contact with their parents when a fund-raising drive was in view.

Bess tried to be friends with her. Her view was that anyone who was a niece of Cornelius Craigallan couldn't be all bad. But sometimes it was hard going with Gina. She could be very cold and abrasive. Yet occasionally there were flashes of vulnerability which let Bess have a glimpse of a different girl – sensitive, responsive. Why Gina hid this other self so effectively was a mystery. But it was another reason why she persevered in trying to be friends with her.

'You won't be coming to the office next week, of course,' she remarked as she began to tidy her desk for the end of the day. Outside in the general office, the stenographers were already putting the covers over their typewriters. She and Gina were the last to be leaving –

Gina because she had changed into her dance-dress in the ladies' powder room and was preparing for the evening's gaiety, Bess because she was always last to leave.

Gina rose and put her cosmetics into her gold evening bag. 'Of course I'll be here,' she said. 'What makes you think not?'

'But . . . surely you're going to New York for the family reunion?'

'Oh, the great Craigallan Homecoming? No, I think I'll give it a miss.'

Bess stifled a gasp. 'But Gina! You've got to be there—'

'Oh, they'll get on all right without me.'

'That's nonsense.' The rebuke burst from her. 'Gina, your mother is coming home after a long absence and your grandfather too—'

'I think you attach too much importance to family ties, Bess,' said Gina in a nonchalant tone. She smoothed down the skirt of her gold-tissue dress, fluffed up the little godets of tulle at the sides, surveyed the little gold shoes at the end of legs clad in sheer silk hose.

'But she'll be terribly hurt!'

'My mother?' Another of Gina's expressive shrugs. 'I don't think so. She's hardly bothered to write more than six lines to me in the last twelve months—'

'But she's been so ill, Gina—'

'Oh yes, heart-broken over the death of my father . . . I don't mind her being heart-broken so long as I'm not expected to let her cry on my shoulder.'

'I never get the impression from what your uncle says that she cries easily—'

'No, and that's what makes this depths-of-despair

business such a bore. And as if that wasn't enough, I'm expected to drool over the new little brother.'

'Well, he does seem very sweet, from the pictures I've seen.'

'I think it's disgusting!' Gina burst out. 'At her age! And when Curt and I are all grown-up—'

'Oh, is that what's wrong?' Bess inquired, her angular face creasing in amusement. 'You feel it makes you look foolish — injures your dignity?'

Gina recovered her composure at once, as she always did. 'Babies don't interest me one way or the other. The whole business of family life is vastly overrated. I've thought so for a long time and I'm certainly not going to Craigallan Castle to be boxed up with Mama and Grandfather Craigallan and Grandfather and Grandmother Gracebridge and Uncle Gregor and Aunt Francesca and Clare and Lewis and Granma Morag and Curt and Uncle Cornelius and Nellie and an English nanny and God alone knows what else. It's like a roll call for a sitting of Congress!'

She picked up a cloak lined with white fur from the back of an office chair. Bess thought she looked very beautiful — too beautiful, perhaps, because she used it as a weapon and a shield. After she had opened the door she paused, to swing the cloak over her shoulders and pose for an instant in the opening, for effect. 'So long, Bess. Don't listen to any hard luck stories!'

'Goodnight. Have a nice time.'

'Oh, I will.' With that she was gone. Bess heard the sound of her high heels passing through the outer office and the opening and closing of the outer door, and later a faint whine of the elevator. She sat for a long moment with her elbows on the desk, staring at the glass-fronted bookcase across the room in which her reflection could

251

be seen. It passed through her mind that an entomologist would have said she and Gina belonged to entirely different species – Gina a gorgeous bright butterfly, herself a workaday little cicada.

Perhaps she ought to drop a hint to Neil that his niece was intending to stay away from the family reunion. He would see to it that she changed her mind. In his quiet way, Neil could be quite awe-inspiring when he wanted to and certainly when Gina first arrived, bursting with plans to enjoy herself after a dull year of Antigone and Portia, he had kept her in order without too much trouble. She wondered if he knew what Gina got up to these days. The girl lived in the suite kept by the Craigallans at the Palmer House Hotel, where the hotel staff kept an eye on her. Yet she was so quick and deft that Bess didn't doubt she could slip out to whatever entertainment she liked.

For instance, Bess knew that Gina had taken to frequenting the jazz clubs that had sprung up all over Chicago in the past year. She wondered if it was her duty to tell Neil . . . But she shrank from acting as informer. That wasn't the sort of role she wanted to play with Neil.

Well, no use sitting here moping about it. She sorted the papers into piles for attention next day and put them into the relative baskets – For Attention, Immediate Action, Filing. She looked through her diary at tomorrow's engagements: a meeting with the Benefits Committee, a delegate from New Orleans to plead for a deaf school for adults, and a talk to a church group on the theme, *He that hath ears to hear* (*Mark IV, 9*). She was developing quite a skill as a public speaker. At least she had value to Neil in that – she could take on this task he dreaded.

She heard the whine of the elevator and looked up. She caught a glimpse of herself in the bookcase glass and realised she was smiling. The elevator was probably bringing Neil on a visit; he sometimes came at this hour of the evening, after the day's work at Craigallan Agricultural was over. If she was honest with herself, this was why she waited about after the others had gone . . .

She heard his footsteps cross the outer office. He tapped on the door of the inner office. He always did so, as a token of respect for her title − although he could never hear if she were to call out, 'Come in!' After a fractional pause he opened the door.

'Good evening,' he said. 'I rather hoped you'd still be around.'

'Nice to see you, Neil.' She smiled and rose, offering him her chair at the administrator's desk. A few times a month Neil glanced over financial reports and signed cheques. He took the chair after waiting for her to perch on Gina's desk. 'There are two cheques needing your signature,' she told him, facing him carefully. 'We had to have glass replaced in the partitions after the new filing cabinets fell as they were being moved in.'

'Yes, I remember. What happened about the liability?' One of the workmen had been hurt and had claimed DVAS was responsible.

'We're settling out of court. We're not really liable but Deneuve thinks it would look bad for a charity to go to court over an injured man.'

Neil nodded, satisfied. He never queried anything Bess did. He had complete reliance upon her and, besides, he didn't really come here to keep tabs on her. It was just an excuse to see something of her. Now that he spent almost all his days at the office, chances to meet Bess were few. Tonight he had come with the idea of inviting her to an exhibition of war paintings to be held at Covici's bookstore. Now that he thought about it, it was absurd − you didn't take a nice girl like Bess Gardiner to look at paintings of legless corpses and barbed wire.

'Everything looks in apple pie order,' he remarked after reading through the day-book and casting an eye on the press cuttings. 'I want to thank you, Bess, for keeping this in such great trim.'

'Oh, there's nothing to it,' she said, jumping up and moving restlessly about. 'I just follow the routine you laid down.'

'You're better at it than I was,' he said. 'And I know you're going to work even harder now the men are coming back. Simmonds of the Veterans' Association will be in touch with you soon − they want to set up lines of communication−' He broke off, wondering if he had enunciated the last word clearly enough. When speaking to Bess he sometimes didn't bother too much about word formations − she seemed to divine what he was saying.

'Yes, he telephoned at the end of last week. We're going to set up a conference.'

Neil nodded. Dozens of voluntary bodies were recognising the need to collaborate in the gigantic task of undoing the damage of the war. Sometimes he regretted having too little time to give to the charity for he felt it had great things ahead of it.

'Gina pulling her weight?' he inquired. He had a feeling the answer was probably 'No.' He had few illusions about his niece.

'She put me in touch with two businessmen who have

promised a substantial donation, Neil.'

'Yes, she's good at that — but I wish she could get herself together and be more . . . well, more like you, Bess.'

In her restlessness Bess had moved behind Neil. She said now to the back of his head, 'Oh, darling, darling Neil . . .' safe in the knowledge he couldn't hear her burst of gratitude for his compliment.

What she had forgotten was that she was standing facing the glassfronted bookcase. Neil, sitting looking at it, saw her lips form words and automatically translated them. Then he gave a little jerk of astonishment and tried to make them read as something else. But they would not.

He turned to stare at Bess. 'What did you just say?' he asked.

It was a common enough question from him, and usually elicited a common enough reiteration. It was what he expected this time. He knew he must have got it wrong the first time.

But to his incredulous amazement, Bess went scarlet with embarrassment. 'No . . . nothing . . . I didn't say anything,' she stammered.

Neil frowned. He got up. He came to her, took her hands in his, and looked down into her face. 'What did you say?' he insisted.

'Nothing.'

'Did you just say . . . "Darling Neil"?'

'No.'

'Bess, did you?' And then, as she bowed her head and he saw the tips of her darling, embarrassed red ears, he knew he had got it right the first time.

'But it's impossible!' he exclaimed, his voice very loud because his surprise startled him out of control. 'I mean, a marvellous girl like you, who could have anybody . . .'

She said, her face hidden, 'Oh, *Neil*!'

Neil was unaware she had spoken. 'I've been crazy about you for months,' he said. 'I've wanted to tell you but it seemed so presumptuous . . .' He knew he had made a mess of the word and was about to attempt it again when Bess put her fingers on his lips. She was looking at him now, and her eyes were bright with unshed tears.

'Oh, you idiot,' she said.

Neil's breathing had got in a hopeless mess. He tried to say, 'You mean, you care about me?' but his always unreliable voice had deserted him.

Bess held his hands firmly with her own and looked up into his face. 'I love you,' she said with great clarity.

'Oh! Gee! Oh, Bess!'

If anything, she went even more red. 'You ought to say you love me,' she told him. 'I mean . . . darling . . . I'd like to hear it.'

Neil grabbed her and hugged her against him. Then he kissed her with all the pent-up strength of months of longing. Bess, who had never been kissed in her life other than a gentle peck on the cheek, threw her arms around him and responded with a sudden fire that startled her when she thought of it afterwards. They stood for a long time wrapped about each other in a passionate embrace. Then Neil, suddenly aware that this was no way to treat a well-brought-up young lady, let her go. He took her hands again.

'Could we get engaged?' he inquired, taking care to say the words clearly.

With her fingers she wrote on his: 'Yes, please.'

Chapter Sixteen

Cornelius Craigallan was walking around like a man who must be very, very careful not to drop and shatter a fragile piece of glass. He and Bess were engaged. He had gone to see her parents to ask for her hand in the proper fashion.

Mr Gardiner had been in his study when he called by appointment. Mrs Gardiner had been banished upstairs to her private sittingroom where she sat and worried: had the difficult and tactless Bess done something wrong at the office? Was Mr Craigallan here to tell them he must dispense with her services? If so, perhaps it was for the best. Mrs Gardiner had hoped her unmarried daughter might meet some suitable young man there, but nothing had come of it. All Bess's fault, of course. She just wouldn't make the *effort*.

'Well, now, Mr Craigallan, what can I do for you?' Arnold Gardiner inquired, nodding Cornelius towards a chair.

'Ah . . . I'll stand, if you don't mind. My secretary told you this was important, I hope?'

'Well . . . yes . . . she did. Though I can't imagine . . . ?' Mr Gardiner was seeking a cigar in the fumidor.

'Excuse me, Mr Gardiner, would you look at me

when you speak? I can't understand what you're saying otherwise.'

'Oh – of course – I'm sorry. Cigar?'

'No, thank you.' Cornelius sighed. Men smoking while they talked made life very difficult for him. 'Mr Gardiner, I'm here to ask your permission to marry your daughter.'

'Eh?' said Mr Gardiner in astonishment.

'Bess and I would like to get engaged.'

Bess's father gaped at him. After a long moment he said foolishly, 'Does Bess know about this?'

Cornelius smiled. 'Oh yes. I know it's fairly sudden. We've been falling in love a long time but we only discovered we each felt the same last night.'

'Upon my soul!'

'I beg your pardon?'

'Nothing, nothing. You and Bess . . . ?'

'Yes, sir. I take it you have no objections?'

'Objections? Good God! My dear boy—'

'No, wait,' Cornelius said, putting up a hand. 'First of all, there's this.' He put a finger to each ear. 'It's not hereditary, in case you've ever wondered. It's just an accident of birth.'

'Oh. Well, I must say I never . . .' It had never crossed his mind to wonder, because he had never been all that interested in Cornelius Craigallan.

'Then there's the difference in our ages. I'm twenty years older than Bess, Mr Gardiner. That's a big gap—'

'Oh, yes . . . I suppose so . . . I must say . . .'

'We talked about that, she and I. What she says is, marriages are arranged all the time by influential families who don't think it's wrong for an older man to marry a younger girl—'

'My dear Mr Craigallan—' Arnold Gardiner stopped. 'Cornelius—'

'People close to me generally call me Neil.'

'Er . . . Yes . . . Neil. I don't make an issue of the age difference.' God, no! Bess, married? And to a Craigallan? Lucy would be in seventh heaven. If Cornelius Craigallan had been a seventy-year-old lame dwarf, Lucy would have welcomed him as a son-in-law so long as he was morally upright and had money. Whereas this tall, slim, handsome fellow with his whole appearance breathing wealth was beyond her wildest hopes.

'Then we have your permission to announce our engagement?'

'Of course! I'm delighted. I can't tell you how delighted . . . Surprised . . . and delighted!' He heard himself babbling on like a demented parrot and pulled himself up. 'Well, now, we must tell Mother the good news. I'll just—' He reached for the bell and when the maid came in commanded, 'Go up and tell your mistress I'd like to speak to her in the study. Oh, and Agnes, when I ring again in a few minutes, go up and fetch Miss Bess.'

'Yes, sir,' said the maid, and went out.

Mrs Gardiner flew downstairs so fast that she had to draw up outside the study door to get her breath back. She was consumed with curiosity and alarm. What could be going on?

'Dear,' her husband said, 'I've some very good news for you. Mr Craigallan has just asked for the hand of our daughter.'

Lucy Gardiner heard the words but they made no sense. She began, 'But our daughters are all married—'

'Mr Craigallan – Neil – wishes to be engaged to

259

Bess, dear,' her husband said very firmly.

'Bess?'

'Yes, Mother.'

'Are you sure?' gasped Mrs Gardiner.

'Quite sure, Mrs Gardiner,' Cornelius said, smothering his amusement. From Bess he had already heard enough to know that her family totally underestimated the worth of the marvellous girl who had told him she loved him.

'Well,' she said in a faint voice, and sat down on the nearest chair.

'You join with me in welcoming Neil to the family, Mother,' her husband said in warning tone.

'Yes, I do. Of course.'

He rang the bell. They sat in frozen joviality until Bess came in. She too paused just inside the door, but the way she then went straight to Neil's side and took his hand made her mother draw in a breath in surprise. 'Why,' she thought, 'they're in love!' And then, 'Why, she's quite pretty!'

'Daughter,' said Mr Gardiner, 'Neil here has just told us your good news and your mother and I unhesitatingly give our blessing. Don't we, Mother?'

'Oh, yes,' said Mrs Gardiner with fervour. 'Yes, indeed!'

Bess went to her and kissed her on the cheek. Then she went to her father and did likewise. 'Thank you, Father. I felt you would be happy for us.'

'I am indeed. Yes. I am.' Arnold Gardiner looked from one to the other of the happy pair and felt a pang of envy. How long ago was it since he had been as close to Lucy as these two were to each other?

Wine was brought, a toast was drunk, Neil and Bess went off to the wintry garden for a few minutes' private bliss. When they came back, Bess was wearing her engagement ring. It was a diamond chosen earlier that day. It took Lucy Gardiner's breath away by its single sparkling purity. 'My God,' she thought at last, 'a Craigallan! She's landed a Craigallan!'

'Bess darling,' she said, 'have you given any thought to the wedding?' St James's Episcopal Church, banks of gardenias, a soprano from the Met to sing 'Oh Promise Me', a honeymoon in Europe now that the war was over . . .

'No, Mother, we haven't gotten used to being in love as yet,' Bess said. 'And perhaps we wouldn't even have told you about that only Neil has to go to New York next week on family business and he felt—'

'I felt I had to make it official in case when I got back I found it was all a dream.'

Mrs Gardiner got up and went out hastily. Bess was beloved . . . It was such an unexpected thought that it made her quite faint. Perhaps *she* had dreamed it all? But no, that fourteen carat diamond on her daughter's left hand was no dream.

Cornelius escorted Gina to New York two days later after spending almost every intervening moment with Bess. Her uncle's quiet authority had quelled her intention to refuse. Gina at first imagined that the lack of conversation on the journey was her idea, but it dawned on her after a while that her uncle was wrapped in a kind of dream all his own. It annoyed her, so she became talkative. But Cornelius knew how to counter that. He closed his eyes, and pretended to doze off – and of course with his eyes closed he could not 'hear' her.

The same proved to be the case at Craigallan Castle. Gina had thought that her marked reluctance would be noted. But no one bothered about her. Perhaps it was because there were so many people in the party, perhaps it was because all attention was on Ellie-Rose and Rob.

Gina had been determined to be cool and unforgiving to her mother. But her resolution was shaken by sight of her. Gone was the confident beauty of the portrait photograph sent home from London. The dark blonde hair was ashen now, and carelessly arranged. The gaze of the hazel eyes was listless, almost blank at times, like that of a statue. Gina's mother sat quietly, taking little part in the conversation, hands folded in her lap, summoning up an unmindful smile when she must make some response. She was thin, with the thinness that comes from a complete lack of appetite. At lunch she pushed her food about so that it looked as if she had eaten, but anyone who cared enough to pay attention could see that she had not swallowed a mouthful.

If Ellie-Rose had made a grand gesture of affection to Gina, Gina would have rejected it. But Ellie-Rose gave her a cool kiss on the cheek and seemed to forget her almost at once.

Gina couldn't bear being forgotten, being ignored. Pent-up anger against her mother demanded some outlet. Determined to punish Ellie-Rose for the years of absence and neglect, Gina sought her out in her part of the castle.

The ostensible reason was to coo over the baby. People were asked to drop in singly or only a couple at a time, because Rob had decreed that too big a commotion would upset his new grandson. He lay in his cot, a little dark-headed boy, dark eyes fixed on the play of light on the ceiling.

His mother was busy with some needlework. It shocked Gina. She'd never seen her mother with a needle in her hand. There had always been ladies' maids and seamstresses to do such chores. Yet for this new baby son, Ellie-Rose Gracebridge was willing to come down to the level of hired help.

As always, Gina masked her feelings. 'Busy?' she asked.

Ellie-Rose nodded. 'There's always something to do, around a baby.'

'I don't see why,' Gina said, sauntering to the cot to study the occupant. 'There's plenty of others to do the chores.'

'I like to,' her mother said.

Conversation died. It seemed Ellie-Rose had nothing to say to her daughter. And all the accusations Gina longed to utter were dammed up behind the barrier of nonchalant reserve.

For a moment she was tempted to walk out again. That would be enough to demonstrate her hostility. Yet she wanted her mother to know why she was hostile.

'Going to stay in mourning long?' she asked, the casualness of the tone an insult in itself.

All my life, Ellie Rose said within herself. But instead of speaking aloud she gave a faint nod.

'It doesn't suit you, you know.'

'Well, it doesn't matter.'

'You don't care how you look?'

Ellie-Rose shrugged.

Gina was appalled at the things she was saying. She, who had always been so deft, was like a brigand wielding a cudgel. And it was having no effect. That was what made it so awful. Her mother simply didn't care what she said to her.

Ellie-Rose heard the words but their meaning was unimportant. As to the tone in which they were spoken, she knew it meant resentment, bitterness, misery. And this was her daughter, firstborn of her children. She ought to hold out her arms to her, comfort her.

I will never hold out my arms to anyone ever again, she thought, except to Tad's child. That's all that matters, to see that his boy thrives and grows up strong and well. If Tad had lived, he would have wanted Bobby to be well and happy — and he shall be.

For herself, she felt she had no strength left for living her own life. All she cared about in the world had gone out of it with Tad. She looked back now to the day she heard of his death, and it was all a blank. Her father's voice, saying carefully, 'Now, daughter, I want you to be very brave . . .'

And after that, nothing.

Days later — she knew now that it was about a week — she had come back to reality. She was sitting by the fire in the great old house in Glen Bairach, with a quilt about her knees and a book in her hands. It was a copy of the poems of Thomas Moore, open at page 175. Her eyes focused on the lines:

> '*Sail on, sail on, thou fearless bark*
> *Wherever blows the welcome wind,*
> *It cannot lead to scenes more dark,*
> *More sad than those we leave behind.*'

They made no sense. Why was she reading them? With a shudder she closed the volume.

Her father's voice said: 'Had enough, dear? Ready for bed?'

She glanced at the wall clock. Twenty minutes past one. In the morning, obviously, otherwise why was Papa talking about bed?

'Yes, I think so,' she agreed. She rose. He hurried to clear away the quilt as if she were an invalid. She went up to her room, stooping over the cradle at the end of her bed to say goodnight to her baby. Then she undressed, and went to sleep.

Two hours later she awoke. It was dark, the shutters were closed at the window. She sat up. Her hand automatically found the matches for the shaded candle on the bedside table. She lit it, rose from her bed to look at the baby. But he slept soundly. It wasn't his cry that had roused her.

She sat down on the end of her bed. Something had happened. Some dreadful, unbearable thing. Yet she had borne it, going on living, functioning, behaving apparently almost as usual.

She would have to cast her mind back. They had come to Glen Bairach after the house in Ebury Street was destroyed in an air attack. Tad had got leave and come to her at last . . . They'd talked and planned. They were to be married.

Her finger touched the ring on her left hand. Married . . .

But this was the thick gold band she had worn for almost twenty years now. This wasn't the ring Tad had written of, chosen without her help in a jeweller's in Bond Street, London, of pale gold with an oak leaf motif . . .

Where was her new ring?

Bewildered, she looked for it on her dressingtable, taking the shaded candle with her. But though its flickering flame gleamed on crystal jars and bottles, on silver backed brushes, the ring was nowhere to be found.

Nowhere, nowhere . . .

It had never been placed on her finger. If it had, she would never have taken it off.

Like the sudden opening of a pit under her feet, she knew. 'Tad!' she gasped. She fell forward across her dressingtable, knocking crystal fitments to the floor. She grasped the struts of the gilt mirror. 'Tad! Oh, dear God . . . Tad!'

Her father came hurrying in, summoned from his light old-man's sleep by the fall of the bottles and jars. He gathered her in his arms as if she were a little girl. She was weeping, at last. Thank God, thank God — he'd thought the pent-up grief would kill her.

He held her against his shoulder and rocked her. If he could, he would have gone like Orpheus to reclaim Tad for the living. But that was impossible so he did the only thing he could. He held her and he let her weep, and when at last the storm was over, he held her yet, safe in his arms, until the wan light of morning crept in at the cracks of the shutters.

Ellie-Rose had been uncaring about the return to the United States. She had come because her father wished it. She was just as indifferent to what anyone thought or said. Gina's scarcely veiled antagonism didn't reach her. She sat in the nursery with her baby and plied her needle while Gina tried now to find a weapon that, needle-like, would prick that shell of indifference.

The way to hurt her was through the baby. 'He's not like any of the rest of us, is he?' Gina remarked.

He's like his father, Ellie-Rose said inwardly, he's like my darling. But she merely shrugged and made no reply.

'This seems a funny place to choose to bring him. Are you going to stay here, Mama?'

'I suppose so.'

'Not much fun for little Bobby, especially if you get involved in the social whirl the way you always do. He's going to be lonely.'

'I'll see to all that when the time comes.'

'He'd be better off in Nebraska, wouldn't he?'

'Nebraska?'

'You always said it was good for us, on Grandfather Gracebridge's farm.'

To Gina's astonishment these words seemed to strike home. Ellie-Rose sat up straight, looked away from her sewing. 'Bobby doesn't belong at the Gracebridge farm.'

'No? Not going to be a farm-boy, then. An intellectual, perhaps?'

Ellie-Rose picked up the fine flannel garment she was working on. She made no reply.

'If he turns out an intellectual he'll be different from the rest of us. Curt and I were just about average in most things. But then so was Papa, wasn't he?'

There was a pause. Then Ellie-Rose said in a quiet tone: 'Average or outstanding, death ends it all.'

'And what about the living, Mama? Average or outstanding, shouldn't they be considered?'

'Considered?'

Gina lost her temper. 'All those years you were gone – did you ever consider anyone except yourself? Did you ever bother about Curt and me? You wrote letters home telling us to be good and mind our studies, and told us all about the fine times you were having with your aristocratic friends! What did it matter to you that we needed you?'

She made herself stop, waiting full of anger for a defence from her mother that she knew would be inadequate, halting. She was ready with a hundred other accusations.

Ellie-Rose looked perplexed. Then she said, 'I'm sorry.'

'Sorry?'

'For failing you. I see I did.'

'You're sorry? Is that all you have to say?'

Ellie-Rose seemed to consider this. 'I don't know what more I can say.'

'You think that if you just say you were to blame, I'll forgive you?'

'I don't know.' It really seemed as if her mother couldn't sort out the answer. 'Do you forgive me, Gina?'

'No, I damn well do not!' cried Gina, and stalked out, slamming the door behind her as hard as she could.

When she was walking away she heard her new brother begin to cry, frightened by the uproar she had caused. Good, she thought, serve her right, now she'll have to pacify him.

But before she reached the head of the staircase, she realised her mother would have forgotten her the moment she picked up her frightened baby.

Ellie-Rose was just as cool with Curt but he, unlike Gina, took care to sit near his mother, tried to foresee her wants and supply them – an additional cushion, a nearer position for her coffee-cup, anything that might summon up a ghost of a smile.

Gina and Cornelius had been the last to arrive. Greg and Francesca with their children had already come from Washington, Morag and her companion Nellie had been there for two weeks getting Craigallan Castle ready for the family gathering. Rob's legal wife, Luisa, would arrive the following week from Italy: she would never be in the same house as Morag or Gregor so had timed her visit for the day following their departure. Luisa intended only a short stay. 'You know I'm no good with sick people and besides I've promised to tour Greece with Baroness Tuza.'

There was a big family dinner that evening. When Ellie-Rose had gone upstairs to take a last look at the baby on her way to bed, Rob glanced at the rest of the family still in the drawingroom. 'She was so ill,' he said. 'I tried everything — I had friends to stay up at Glen Bairach, I took her to London . . . None of it helped. She didn't seem to know where she was or why. The only time she came to life was when she was tending the baby. She wanted to send the nurse away, do everything for him herself, but I wouldn't let her. I thought it was getting to be an obsession, you know?'

'She is very much altered,' Francesca said, her dark eyes sad. 'It is strange. I did not think she was as greatly devoted to Curtis.'

Rob drew on his cigar and said nothing. No mention had ever been made to anyone of Tad Kendall and he intended to keep it that way. As far as the rest of the world knew, Robert, named for his grandfather, was Curtis's posthumous child. Ellie-Rose, in one of her rare flashes of emotion, had protested that she wanted the child known by Tad's name, but he had been stern with her. 'If you want a memorial to Tad, put up a headstone in the cemetery,' he had said with brutal force. 'Don't make that poor kid carry all your memories for you.'

'But he's Tad's son!'

'Listen, Ellie, don't you think I've regretted almost

every day of my life that Gregor bears a different name from mine? It would have made everything so much easier for us — for him and for me — if he'd been a Craigallan. No explanations, no excuses — he'd have been accepted without comment. Don't do that to Bobby, Ellie.'

She had said no more and the matter was never referred to again. In truth, she didn't really care enough to make a fight of it. All that mattered was that her little boy should be cared for and happy.

The length of the family reunion had not been planned. Two or three days, perhaps — long enough to become acquainted again after the absence caused by the war. Curt had leave from college. Cornelius had made arrangements to be away until the end of the week. Gregor was somewhat at liberty now that his most recent task for the government had been accomplished, the smoothing down of international indignation after the nationalisation of the Mexican oilfields. Rob looked forward to long talks with his sons, to getting back into harness with them again.

He would spend a year or eighteen months with them ensuring that Craigallan Agricultural Products was ready for the bad times he sensed ahead — busy, rewarding months, settling his two sons into the part of the business they handled best. And then, at last, the retirement he'd been promising himself. Ellie-Rose was his only anxiety. He couldn't go off to live with Morag near Pike's Peak if Ellie-Rose wasn't cured.

He was about to find there were other obstacles.

Gregor sought him out the day after the first family dinner party. 'There's something we have to discuss, Father,' he said.

'Of course.' Rob waved him to an armchair in his

study. The morning papers were spread around him. It was part of his scheme to get back into the swim — the necessary background to American life that he had missed during his stay in Britain. 'You want to know when and where to go back into Craigallan Agricultural. I realise there's a slight problem, since Neil's been at the head so long — but I don't think he'll make any difficulty about stepping aside. He—'

'No, Father, that isn't what I want to say.'

'You want a bit of a vacation? I can understand that. You do look kind of peaked. That climate in Vera Cruz is kind of hard to live with—'

'Father, please let me speak.' Greg's natural authority asserted itself, even over his father. Rob was silent, looking at him in surprise. 'What I want to tell you is, I'm not rejoining CAP.'

Rob stared at his son. Tall, straight, russet-haired. Skin a little tanned by the Mexican sun, face a little too thin from anxiety over negotiations with too-touchy officials or perhaps from the unappetising Mexican food. Not rejoining CAP? What the hell did the boy mean? He couldn't turn his back on a whole agricultural empire!

'You don't say anything?' Gregor said. 'Have you been expecting it?'

'Christ Almighty, no!' It exploded from Rob in rejection, incredulity. 'That's the last thing I would expect. What do you mean?'

Gregor leaned back in the big leather armchair. His attitude showed that he expected this to take a long time. 'I've been giving this a lot of thought over the last six months—'

'You never said anything to me in any of your letters!'

'No, well you had enough on your plate with Ellie-Rose so ill . . . Besides, I hadn't quite got it sorted out. And I wanted to talk it through with Francesca—'

'I should think she'd have something to say about your planning to throw away your place in—'

'Yes, she had,' Gregor put in, over-riding him without raising his voice at all. 'She and I haven't seen enough of each other over the past four years. I've been off on some little chore for the White House or I've been cooped up in committee rooms and boardrooms talking to foreign businessmen. Don't misunderstand me, Father. Compared with some, I've had an easy war. But if you think about it, Francesca and I have *never* had a real home of our own, never put down any roots—'

'Roots? What the hell are you talking about, roots?' Rob cried. 'Your roots are with the Craigallans—'

'Yes, where? In Chicago, at the headquarters offices? Here, at the Castle? At the house you rented for us in Washington? Where?'

His father threw himself back in his chair with annoyance. 'Good God, if it's simply the matter of having a house—'

'Don't be absurd, Mr Craig,' Gregor said. There was just enough reproof in the tone to make Rob colour up. But he held his peace as Gregor went on: 'While I've been working in Mexico trying to smooth down their ruffled feathers, it's dawned on me what a bad attitude we Americans take towards them. And remember this, Father. My wife is Spanish, my two kids are half-Spanish. It came to me during last year that Clare and Lewis will grow up here on the eastern seaboard without ever being in proper contact with their heritage—'

'Heritage? What kind of nonsense is this? Their "heritage" is their share in a forty-one-million-dollar corporation—'

Gregor nodded. 'Of course. I'm not belittling it. You want your grandchildren to have their share of what you built up. But Francesca has things to hand on from her side of the family, and they're being swamped, disregarded. What you just said about money is pretty typical — it's the way the US deals with other nations. "We have all the money in the world, who are you to disagree with us?" '

'Now look here, Greg—'

'I hear it all around me, Mr Craig. Americans talking about the Mexes, the Wops, the Kikes, the Swedies — and it worries me. Seems to me we're storing up trouble. So I talked to Frannie and she agreed.'

'Agreed what? What, for God's sake?'

'I've been offered a government post out in California—'

'California? Are you mad? Nothing's going on in California—'

'That's a typical easterner's view, if I may say so, Father. A lot is going on in California, and some of it is mighty interesting. The government wants someone to head up a new office out there — Department of Hispanic-American Research—'

'Research? What you going to do, dig up old Spanish missions?' Rob was angry, disbelieving, eager to trample on this day-dream that his usually sensible son was spinning.

'Research into inter-cultural relationships, the preliminary study calls it.' Gregor refused to rise to his father's baiting. 'There's a lot of friction between the

Spanish-speaking inhabitants and the more recent American influx—'

'Recent? What are you saying? California was settled by the covered wagon pioneers—'

'Father, California was discovered by Juan Cabrillo in the fifteen-hundreds and was a Spanish settlement until 1822, when it declared its independence from Spain and joined up with Mexico. I know,' he held up his hand, 'you don't want a history lesson. But I'm telling you, until gold was discovered there, no east-coasters ever bothered with the place. Well, it became a state of the union seventy years ago but that doesn't mean everybody suddenly became a patriotic English-speaking American. There are families out there who feel they've been betrayed by the government, forced to give up their language and traditions and even their religion for a way of life they despise. And that's not to mention the flood of Mexicans who swim over the Rio Grande or trudge across the desert to escape from the poverty of their homeland.'

'Yeah, great, it sounds like heaven on earth,' Rob said in disgust. 'So why do you want to go out there?'

'Two reasons. First, I've discovered I have a talent for dealing with difficult people. Second, the climate out in San Francisco is better than Chicago or New York. Francesca doesn't thrive in either of those places, Mr Craig. Whatever it is that happened to her health due to her hardships in Manila, it's not helped by the kind of life she's been leading—'

'She never said anything – ?'

'No, she's not the type to complain,' Gregor said with a faint smile. 'Well, that's it. She has some distant relatives out there, in Monterey. She's Spanish by birth and tradition. I have a good understanding of the kind of problem that's involved through my work with the Mexicans. I speak the language. The job attracts me. I'd like my children to have some appreciation of their heritage. That's the story.'

Rob got up stiffly and moved from his desk, causing the pile of newspapers to cascade to the floor. He ignored them. He went to the window to look out at the January snow on the gardens of the Castle. In California, he had heard, it never snowed except high up in the mountains.

He turned. 'And being president of Craigallan Agricultural in due course doesn't weigh enough against all that?'

'I thought about it a lot, Father. I know I'm giving up something other men would give their eye-teeth for. But . . . I want a life of my own. I want a family home with Frannie and the children. I have the feeling that it's time to gather them to me and start again.'

'You'd never even have thought of this if you hadn't taken on those damned jobs for the government! They took you away from the excitement of dealing in The Pit, of being bound up in the needs of the grain market—'

'That's true, perhaps. Now that I've tried something else, I realise there are other things in life besides doing clever deals on the Board of Trade.'

'Don't do this, Greg!' Rob said in sudden anguish. 'All your life — since I first found you again when your mother was so ill — I've thought of you as my heir. Don't tell me you can turn your back on all I want to give you.'

Greg got up from his chair and came to stand opposite him. He put a friendly hand on his shoulder. 'I know it's a shock. I'm sorry. But you've got Neil —

he's your true heir, after all.'

'Neil . . . Greg, don't go! There's a lot of work needs doing at CAP. Life isn't going to be so darned easy now that peace has come. I need you here!'

'But Neil has done well, Father. You know he has. When you went rushing off to London and I was in Mexico, Neil took over, without a tremor. He's made money—'

'Goddammit, boy, a man who couldn't make money with the whole world crying out for bread-wheat and feedstuffs would deserve a place in a waxwork museum! Of course he made money! But it's not going to be so easy in the next five or six years.'

Gregor shook his head and turned away. 'You underestimate him, Father. Besides, you'll be here – you and he will make a very formidable team.'

No, Rob cried in unvoiced despair, I want to hand it over, to settle down with Morag . . . Aloud he said: 'I'm not young any more, Greg. I won't see sixty again.'

'Oh, come off it, Father! You look fifty, you've got the energy and determination of a twenty-year-old, and you know you love the excitement of the battle in dealing with grain! Perhaps you feel a disappointment now, but once you get used to the idea that I'm going to be elsewhere, you'll settle into a partnership with Neil that will be just as much fun as the old one with me.'

'Fun?' Rob said. 'Fun? With you the other side of the continent? California's a hell of a long way away.'

'Oh, nonsense. The new fast trains make the trip in three days – it isn't as if we can't get to each other if we want to. Once Frannie and I are settled, we'll expect you out for Thanksgiving and Christmas – any time the weather's terrible in the east, you'll be coming west.

And we'll come and see you too.'

'Greg!' Rob begged. He could hear in his son's voice the goodbyes that become ever more final. He made a last try. 'What does your mother say to all this?'

He saw his son hesitate. 'That's another thing, Mr Craig . . . I've asked her to come with us.'

'What?'

'The climate would suit her too. Of course she's happy at Pike's Peak but the only reason you settled her there was because of the need for pure air. Frannie and I will find a house in some good spot, out of the city proper, among the foothills . . . I want her to come, Father.'

'No,' Rob said. He didn't want Morag to go. He couldn't bear it. 'What does she say?'

'She's thinking about it.'

'You've talked this over with her without consulting me?'

'Only a few hours ahead of talking to you, Father. I assure you − I only spoke to her last night.'

There was nothing more to say for the moment. He needed time to get used to the idea that Greg, the son he had thought of as his right arm, his natural heir, was turning his back on all he could offer. And that Morag might be lost to him too.

Greg went out. A little later Rob sent the butler to fetch a coat then went out for a walk in the wintry grounds. He felt the need of physical activity to banish the numbness brought on by Gregor's blow.

He marched quickly along the icy paths, the snow crunching under his boots. It was a grey day and cold, but with no bitter wind for the moment. From beyond the ice-bound Hudson River, a skein of geese came flying, in search of winter feeding, circling as they

277

looked for green blades and turning to head on south for milder terrain. He watched them go. Every year, from north to south and then back again from south to north . . . Humans could not take wing and change their living place so easily. If Greg went to the West Coast, over two thousand miles would separate them. Useless to say the train service was excellent, they would often see each other. It wasn't the same. And as for Morag . . . God help him if Morag went away. He had missed Morag more than he could express, while caring for Ellie-Rose in Scotland.

He came to the frozen lake. The grandchildren had been skating there earlier in the day, swooping and gliding, calling to each other with whoops of delight. Even Gina had been there, twirling like a ballerina, head back — forgetting in the pleasure of physical skill the spiritual unrest that teased at her. Young Curt's college scarf had been left behind on the back of a bench. Rob took it in his hands, sat down with it as a kind of token link with his family.

He was still trying to come to terms with what Greg had told him when he heard footsteps. He look round. Cornelius was treading his way towards him over an icy patch. He threw himself on the bench with relief. 'Tricky!' he said. 'You could break a leg.'

'Yeah, it thawed and re-froze overnight.'

'Should you be out here without a hat, Papa?'

'I'm all right.'

'I came out hoping to get a moment alone with you. There's something I have to say to you, Papa.'

Rob hunched himself in his thick nap overcoat. 'About Greg?' he asked. 'He's told you?'

'Yes, he just—'

'He'll change his mind when he thinks it over,' Rob

broke in. 'He's a businessman, not an administrator.'

'I think you're wrong. Greg's always known his own mind. It's one of the things that makes him so formidable.'

'Yeah.' It was a sigh of agreement.

'But it wasn't about Greg that I wanted to speak. It's about myself. I've something important to tell you—'

'Oh, God,' groaned his father. 'Don't tell me you've decided to withdraw from the firm and devote yourself to charity!' As he said the words the possibility seemed very real, and he gazed at his eldest child with supplication. Don't go away from me, he was begging. Ellie-Rose scarcely knows I exist, Greg's off to start afresh without me, Morag's going – don't go, Neil, don't go!

Cornelius had always been quick at catching slight alterations in facial expression or body movement. Lacking the ability to hear tonal inflections, he had had to find other methods of reading inner meanings. Now he saw that his father was in despair. He put out both hands and took Rob's.

'No, it's good news,' he said, smiling widely. 'I'm getting married.'

In the frosty air his father's sigh of relief was quite evident. Then Rob said, 'Married?' He was so used to the idea of Neil as a confirmed bachelor that he could hardly believe his ears.

'Married,' Neil said again, and as he said the word his fingers moved to repeat it.

'By God!' said Rob. Then, 'Who to?'

'You can't guess?'

'Damned if I can! I never saw you around with a girl.'

'It's Bess – Bess Gardiner.'

279

Her image sprang up at once in Rob's memory. Tallish, angular, freckled, sandy hair . . . No beauty, but then . . . 'Congratulations, boy,' he said in hearty acceptance, and shook both Neil's hands with gripping fingers conveying his pleasure.

'Thank you. We . . . we only found out we wanted to be married a couple of days ago. You know how it is . . . I thought I wasn't good enough for her and she didn't want to make the running—'

'Too well brought up,' Rob suggested, while thinking, poor lamb, she wouldn't know how. It occurred to him that his son thought himself a very lucky man to have got such a girl. Well, well . . . real love? And Bess? He tried to summon up Bess in his mind, other than her appearance. Not backward to speak, business-like, sensible . . . Had she accepted Neil because she couldn't land anyone else? But she hadn't struck him as that kind of girl. Not a husband-hunter − if she had been she'd have got a husband by now with the help of that steel-trap of a mother. Perhaps it was love on her side too. Why not? Stephanie Jouvard had loved Neil, no matter how inconstantly. And the man was good-looking, impressive. And all those little girls in his office looked at him with such devotion. Why not a real love match on both sides?

'Come on, boy,' he said, hauling him to his feet. 'Let's go and open a bottle of champagne to celebrate!'

'What, at this hour of day?'

Rob got out his watch. 'Eleven-thirty − just the right time to open it for lunch. Come on!'

As they made their way back to the house, Cornelius gave his father a few more details about his romance: her parents approved, they thought of getting married in April, quietly, no fuss. Rob nodded, thinking the while that if they got away with a quiet wedding with Mrs Gardiner playing the role of bride's mother, he'd eat his hat.

'Papa, will you tell Mama?' Cornelius said with discomfort in his face. 'She doesn't like having conversation with me and this is important. I don't want her shrinking away from me while I tell it.'

'Leave it to me,' Rob said. He could just imagine what Luisa would say, that Bess Gardiner was the best her handicapped son could be expected to get for a wife. Luisa, expected in three days' time, had been a cloud on Rob's horizon until the much worse news of Gregor's going made it seem unimportant.

The champagne was produced at lunch, the reason for it was given. Congratulations were called out. Even Ellie-Rose seemed to wake from her trance of withdrawal for a moment. 'Is she nice?' she said to her brother.

'She's wonderful!' Neil declared.

'I'm so glad, Neil.' She got up from her place, went to him, and kissed him. 'I look forward to meeting her.'

'Well,' Gina remarked under her breath to Curt, 'it seems some things really do make an effect on her.'

'Cut it out, Gina. I just wish there was something I could do.'

'Don't waste your time, little brother. Mama's order of importance doesn't include either of us.' And, she thought to herself, when Mama sees plain old Bess Gardiner, she'll be a lot less enthusiastic about her sister-in-law-to-be.

The next piece of family news was Gregor's intention to move to the West Coast. This brought little or no reaction from Ellie-Rose. Already she had sunk back into her passivity. 'See?' Gina said, nudging Curt.

For his part Rob was watching Morag. She took no part in the conversation. It was hard to tell from her expression what she was feeling. Gregor made no mention of taking his mother with him to San Francisco. As he had said to his father, 'She's thinking about it.' He didn't want to jump the gun, but he was longing for her to intervene and add, 'I shall be going with them.'

The Gracebridge grandparents did their best to share in the family news, but they had little to contribute. They had come to Craigallan Castle to welcome back their widowed daughter-in-law, to be a comfort to her in her bereavement. They couldn't penetrate the thicket behind which, like Sleeping Beauty, she dwelt in quiescence and resignation. They turned instead to the grandchildren, cosseting Gina and Curt, but receiving little encouragement from their granddaughter. Mr Gracebridge was wont to say to his wife that he thought they could have made a better job of bringing up Gina, safe in the knowledge that she would never have submitted to their guardianship.

When the luncheon party broke up, rather belatedly to the minds of the servants, Rob had telephone calls to make to Chicago with Cornelius standing by to give opinions. That done, Cornelius asked his father to telephone a telegram for Bess: *News announced, all went well, see you soon, Fondest Love*. Rob asked to be allowed to insert three more phrases of his own. *Father very pleased, invites parents to dinner Palmer House, date to be arranged*. 'That'll be some event,' Cornelius said. 'Mrs Gardiner will tell the society columnists, you can bet. We'll have reporters watching every mouthful we eat.'

282

'Let 'em,' Rob said, and clapped him on the shoulder. But he sighed to himself. He would have to take Luisa to the dinner. You could hardly have a celebration over an engagement without the mother of the groom. He dreaded the thought. She could be so hurtful . . . And what on earth would the Gardiners make of her?

He was sitting over some long-term reports Cornelius had brought so that he could catch up on the dealings of his year's absence. There was a tap on the door. 'Come in,' he called. The door opened and Morag entered.

'Am I intruding, dear?' she inquired.

'Oh, don't be so silly . . .' He met her, took her hand, and led her to the most comfortable chair. The fire in the big grate had sunk low. He stirred it up for her, and put a footstool at her feet. She leaned back in the big chair, her dark green dress edged with a soft grey chiffon collar that just picked up the grey strands in her dark hair. Her feet were in little slippers of black lizardskin, each with a strap and a silver button. She wore no ornaments, except for the case of her reading glasses pinned to the bosom of her dress, a handsome engraved gold case, the gift of Rob last Christmas.

'Well?' he said, taking the armchair across from her.

'I've come to talk about the move to San Francisco.'

His heart sank. The move to San Francisco − did that mean she included herself in it? He said nothing, merely looked at her inquiringly.

'Greg told you about asking me?'

'Yes, he told me.'

'He's very anxious for me to go, you see, Rob. He's always been very protective towards me, and he feels that I've been doing too much the last few years −

moving into the Washington house, coping with Gina, then travelling back and forth looking after Curt—'

'Curt's no trouble,' Rob broke in.

'That's quite true, and of course now Ellie is back it's not my place to go on acting as mother to him. Though, mind you, I shall miss all that . . .' She sighed a little. She was fond of both of the children although Gina perplexed her. But Curt was so straightforward and boy-like . . . In many ways he reminded her of her own son at that age, except that he seemed very susceptible to falling in love.

I shall miss all that. Rob heard the words and saw that they meant she was going to California. 'You'll have Gregor's children to fuss over,' he said.

He thought there was surprise in the glance she gave him.

'They're lovely children,' she said. 'But of course I miss out on some of what's going on – when Frannie speaks Spanish to them.'

'Oh, you'll soon learn Spanish, if that's all that stands in your way.'

'I suppose so.' She hesitated. 'What did Greg say to you exactly?'

'That he'd asked you to come and you were thinking about it.'

'What do *you* think about it, Rob?'

'Me? Well, I hate the whole idea,' he burst out. 'I can see Greg's got his mind made up so there's no use trying to change it. But San Francisco's so far off, Morag!'

'Yes,' she mused, 'it's a good deal further than Pike's Peak.'

'Twice as far! When will I ever see you, Morag?'

'Well, the train service is very good. And we could always telephone one another.'

'Oh, Lord, it all sounds so . . . empty!' He sprang up and paced the study. 'I'd move out there myself, but San Francisco's a nothing place so far as business is concerned. I can't run CAP from San Francisco — I have to be in Chicago to deal in wheat, and the New York Stock Exchange is the next most important place. Besides . . . there's Ellie-Rose.'

'She's going to live here, I take it?'

'Yes, and since she's lost so much . . . I think the least I can do is be with her here, at least until she comes around a little more.'

'You're right, dear.' Morag nodded. 'There's really no way it would fit your life, to go out to the West Coast.'

'And yet—'

'What?'

'If *you're* going—'

'Who said I was?'

He stared down at her. 'Why, you did!'

'Did I? I said I'd come to talk about the move. I didn't say I'd made up my mind to go.'

'Then . . . you're still thinking about it?'

'I couldn't come to a decision without finding out how you felt, Rob.'

'Oh, darling!' He seized her by the hands and drew her up to stand within the circle of his arms. 'Don't go!' he begged. 'I don't know how I'd manage if you went so far away! God knows it's bad enough having to be parted from you while you're in the mountains, but at least I can get to you more quickly there than in California. And besides — in Colorado Springs we can be on our own. It wouldn't be the same in San Francisco.'

He felt her nod her head against his chest. 'That's

just what I thought,' she murmured.

'What did you say?' He moved away a little and tilted up her face. He gazed down into her dark eyes, still deep and unclouded although she was no longer a girl. 'You mean you've decided not to go with Greg?'

She nodded.

'Why didn't you tell me at the outset, you minx!'

She smiled and coloured up. 'I wanted to hear you say you needed me,' she confessed, half-laughing, half-embarrassed.

'Oh, Morag . . .' He had always needed her, but never more than now, when everything in life seemed to be changing. Only Morag didn't change — constant, loving, steady.

She sat back in her chair and he took a place on the arm, stroking her hair with a gentle hand. She talked in quiet tones of Greg's going away — to her a greater blow than to Rob, for the bond between Morag and her son was very strong. There was no complaint in her tone, however. Morag McGarth had learned to be grateful for what life had granted her, since at one time her years had seemed to be numbered. Now, every year more was a blessing. And to share them with Rob was more than she could have hoped for at one time.

So she talked of the future with hope and confidence. In his relief and gratitude he was silent; he found comfort in her words. But his future was changed. He had dreamed of happy seclusion with Morag at the house in the mountains, but that was not to be. Cornelius couldn't be left to handle the affairs of Craigallan Agricultural on his own — not yet, not until they had trained up an assistant with hearing, a vice-president, who would be his right hand. Rob must stay on as head of the business for a time yet.

He had wrested a fortune from the lands he farmed
and the grain he handled in such huge quantities now.
He had enjoyed the money, and the power it brought.
But for the first time, he felt it a burden.

Chapter Seventeen

In the summer of that year, Morag's old friend and companion Nellie died. She and Morag were packing, getting ready to move from Craigallan Castle to Colorado Springs for the hot weather. The trunks were ready, the car was to call for them after an early breakfast.

When she didn't appear to sit down at table in their private sittingroom, Morag went in search of her. It was very unlike Nellie to be late.

She found her in bed, peacefully asleep to all appearances. She went up to her and shook her. 'Nellie! Come along, you should have been up an hour ago—' She broke off. The shoulder she had touched was cold.

Her old friend was gone.

No one knew how old Nellie had been, nor her real last name. It was lost in the aftermath of the Civil War, with the burning of the plantation that had been her home.

It was surprising how much her loss grieved the household. Gina, especially, was stunned by it. Nellie had always been there, moving in and out of her mother's household, a privileged person, not exactly a servant, more like a friend. Mama had once liked to talk about the times she had shared with Nellie, as a girl out on the prairie; Nellie's cooking, Nellie's fund of old stories, Nellie's care of pet birds with broken wings or stray kittens . . .

To Gina, Nellie had been a sort of everlasting pillar of the house. Unfailingly kind, she had even slipped food to Gina when she was sent supperless to bed. That quiet tap on the door, the black face at the crack, the black hand offering a tray with a piece of pie and a glass of milk . . . And now she was gone. How could it be?

A surprising number of people turned up for the funeral – fellow-members of the Baptist church in Carmansville, servants from other households, almost all the tradesmen and suppliers who ever came to Craigallan Castle, and even people from Washington. The friends from the black church made up a choir as the coffin was carried to the grave: 'Some day, some bright day, I'm gonna lay down my heavy load . . .' And then, as the casket was lowered into the earth, and the minister intoned the last words of the burial service, they began once more, in a muted, gentle harmony: 'Swing low, sweet chariot, comin' for to carry me home . . .'

Gina's throat seemed to seize up. A great, tearing sob came from her. She felt as if she were going to faint. She turned helplessly, staggering with emotion. An arm came around her. It was Morag.

'There, there,' she soothed. 'There, there.'

'I . . . I can't bear it . . . She's *dead*!'

'Sh . . . dear. Try to be calm. The service is almost over.' One by one Nellie's friends passed by the grave, some casting a flower on top of the coffin, some merely pausing a moment in respect. The members of the Baptist church murmured good words: 'Praise the

Lord!' and 'Safe in His arms!' Rob stood for a long moment at the verge and stared down at the casket. 'Goodbye, good old friend,' he said. His eyes were blinded with tears. She had loved him, and he had loved her — through long years, of hardship and good fortune.

As they made their way back to the waiting limousines, Gina shielded her eyes from the uncaring sunshine. 'I . . . I can't believe she's gone,' she said.

'She was very old, you know,' Morag said.

'Was she? She always seemed the same, to me.'

'My doctor in Colorado Springs said he thought she was about seventy-five, when he took a look at her last year after she was having dizzy spells.'

Morag was talking so as to give Gina time to recover. She was surprised at how deeply the girl was affected. She had her arm linked with Gina's, standing apart from the rest of the funeral party.

'I was awful to her,' Gina burst out. 'I used to snap at her all the time—'

'No, you didn't, Gina. I remember you often playing baby-tennis with her on the lawn at the Washington house—'

'No, but recently! I don't think I've said a kind word to her in the last three years!'

'Don't worry about it, my dear. Nellie knew you loved her.'

'Did she, Morag?' Gina said, earnest and tense. 'When I never told her so?'

'Of course. Even when you were cross with her you always showed you really cared about her.'

Gina accepted this comfort in silence. It had suddenly come to her that if her mother were taken from her at this moment — and so many people were taken suddenly, what with the aftermath of the war and its strains, and the recurring influenza epidemic – she would feel guilty for the rest of her life.

At long last, when the mourners had left after a wake of just the kind that Nellie would have appreciated, Gina sought out her mother in her boudoir. Ellie-Rose was sitting unoccupied, her black hat and gloves beside her on the sofa, her head bent in thought. 'May I come in?' asked Gina from the door.

Ellie-Rose looked up. 'Yes, dear, of course.'

'Mama . . . I want to say. . .'

'Yes?'

'I . . . I'm sorry for the way I've behaved.'

Her mother looked at her. 'You are? What is it you've done?' There was genuine puzzlement in her tone.

The pre-arranged apology died on Gina's lips. Well, if she didn't even *know*, didn't even *care* . . . ! But she'd made a resolution to speak; she felt she owed it to Nellie.

'I . . . haven't been very considerate to you since you came home. I haven't been to see you very often.'

'No, dear. I suppose you're busy in Chicago. Your friends are there.'

My friends, thought Gina. With something like dismay she reviewed them. Fellow jazz-fans. People she met in night clubs. Bootleggers preparing to make a killing when the Volstead Act became law. Bess Gardiner had said to her only last week, about a man she had been dating regularly: 'He's a gangster, Gina. A known associate of those awful men, Frank and Al Capone.'

What was she doing, wasting her time with a man like that?

Well, she had been paying back society for the injustice it had done her. Something like that.

It was absurd, really. All she was doing was hurting herself. She sat down beside her mother and in silence gave herself up to her thoughts. Ellie-Rose didn't disturb her with conversation: she was generally silent these days.

Things have got to change, Gina said to herself. After all, life's precious. Nellie *died*. One minute she was with us, the next she was gone. That could happen to anyone, even to me. And if I were to die tomorrow, what could they say in a eulogy about me? *She was young and pretty and wasted her time in the silliest possible way* . . .

I ought to do something with my life, she told herself. I ought to think about where I'm going.

But it was so long since she'd done anything except react in resentment to outside stimuli that she hardly knew how to look ahead and plan.

For perhaps a quarter of an hour mother and daughter sat side by side in silence, each occupied by her own thoughts. Then the sound of the baby crying roused Ellie-Rose from her reverie. She got up. 'Oh, Gina,' she said, almost in surprise. 'You'll have to excuse me. Bobby needs me.'

'Yes, Mama, of course.'

Ellie-Rose hurried out. Gina sat on, lost in thought as the afternoon sun gilded her dark brown hair. She would somehow change her life; it was decided. The wedding of her Uncle Cornelius was due to take place in three weeks' time. By then she would have made a decision, chosen her new path.

The Gardiner-Craigallan wedding was as quiet as Mrs Gardiner could be persuaded to make it. It took place in the Episcopal Church, as she insisted, and much against her will Bess wore a long white gown and a veil. But they managed to resist all her endeavours to have page boys in white satin, and ten bridesmaids. Bess's sister was maid of honour, Gregor was best man, summoned from San Francisco for this honour. Afterwards there was a reception at the Gardiner house on Drexel Avenue.

It was here that Gina found her new path. One of the guests was a talkative man in a London-tailored suit and a monocle, invited as a friend of one of Bess's sisters. His name, he said, was Charles Cochran, and he was a 'showman'. 'I put on stage shows, darling,' he explained. 'You must have heard of me?'

'No, I . . .'

'Richard Mansfield's manager? Impresario for the Great Hackenschmidt?'

Gina laughed. 'They seem at opposite ends of the entertainment industry, don't they?'

'Yes, by jove, I believe in casting the net wide.' He looked at her with the greatest appreciation. 'Darling, you really are a delicious girl. Has anyone ever told you?'

'Oh, I bet you say that to all the girls!'

'To a great many, I may as well admit. It's my speciality, you know — finding beautiful girls.' He caught up a fresh glass of champagne from a passing waiter, handed it to her. 'Tell me,' he said, 'have you ever thought of going on the stage?'

When Rob heard of her departure, he burned up the telephone wires between New York and London. But to no avail. Gina refused to come home. She had been given a part in the chorus of *Sunny Days* and was learning to dance. London was marvellous. She had made some new friends. Ivor Novello had spoken kindly to her and introduced her to his mother, Madam Novello-Davis – they must know Ivor Novello? Who wrote 'Keep the Home Fires Burning'?

'I won't have it!' Rob roared. 'No granddaughter of mine is going to cavort around half-naked on a stage.'

'I believe Mr Cochran's Young Ladies don't do that kind of thing, Papa,' Cornelius remarked.

'I won't have it! It's obscene!'

'Absurd perhaps, Papa,' said Ellie-Rose. 'Not obscene.'

'Dammit, you're her mother! Can't you do something?'

Ellie-Rose appeared to give it some thought. 'What exactly, Papa?'

'Well . . . she's still a minor. You could have her brought home.'

But Ellie-Rose refused to intervene. If Gina wished to go on the stage, that was her own affair. She even had some training for it; she had after all attended a school of speech and drama for a year, which seemed to show some prior interest in the theatre. And after all, social attitudes were changing . . .

Rob might have gone to London to drag Gina home, but other events intervened. He, to his surprise, was invited to a tête-à-tête with the Mayor of New York. The reason was even more surprising. Filey confided that he was damned nervous about the forthcoming visit of the Prince of Wales of England, as he called him. 'The Government's laid on all kinds of a show for him, and he'll have dinner with the President and so on. But he's coming to New York, Rob, and we're asked to show him the typical New York hospitality.'

'So what's your problem, Joe?'

'See, the old biddies of the Four Hundred have run away with it. I sent over a programme to the Buckingham Palace and his sidekick — what-jacallim — equerry — sends me a note to say that while his Royal Highness is very appreciative of the kindness being shown, he'd like to have at least one evening's relaxation during his stay here.'

'What're you going to do? Take him to see Babe Ruth hit another six-hundred-foot home run?'

'Naw, I don't think he'd care for baseball. D'you know, an English guy I knew once said that back home it was a kid's game called rounders!' The Mayor shook his head at such sacrilege. 'No, what I was wondering was . . . Rob, would you lay on an At Home for him at Craigallan Castle?'

'Me?' Rob gasped, genuinely astonished.

'Yeah, you. That place of yours . . . well, I thought he'd kinda feel at home there. It's like an English castle, isn't it?'

'Scottish, if you don't mind, Joe.'

'Well, Scottish. This prince's kinda Scottish — at least I've seen pictures of him wearing a kilt.'

'Huh,' said Rob.

'But you see, Ellie-Rose was in London through the war, right? And she met him there — at Embassy parties and so on?'

'I believe she did.'

'So she could be hostess, eh? I mean, she's a looker, always was—'

'Oh, now, Mr Mayor, don't let's get ahead of ourselves. Ellie hasn't been too well—'

'Since her bereavement. Sure, sure, I know. But that's a coupla years now, after all. I know she's done very little entertaining, and in a way that makes her a good choice — she hasn't been competing, nobody's going to have their nose put out of joint if she's asked to give the Prince a bit of peace and quiet. What d'ya say, Rob? Eh? Do it for *me*!'

'Give me one good reason why I should do anything for you, hypocrite, letting them put that damned Prohibition Act in force in New York!'

'Well, that was public pressure, pal. I had to bow to it. But the cops have their orders — turn a blind eye where it would be good sense. You can be sure I'm not going to send them to look into *your* cellars.'

He looked appealingly at his old friend, and Rob sat in thought, his cigar burning unnoticed in the ash tray. An evening for the Prince of Wales . . . Surely that must rouse Ellie-Rose at last from her lethargy? It was the kind of opportunity other New York hostesses would give their prize chef for.

'Okay, I'll try it out on Ellie-Rose,' he agreed, 'but I'm not promising anything, Joe. She doesn't take much interest in that kind of thing any more.'

'She will,' prophesied Filey, 'she will.'

He was wrong, however. Ellie-Rose, when asked if she would open the house to the Prince and his retinue for an evening, looked merely surprised. 'Why should they ask me?' she inquired, perplexed.

'Oh, they want to give the poor guy a bit of respite from formality. What they want is a sort of casual party.'

She shook her head. 'I don't think so, Papa.'

'You can't say no, Ellie!'

'Why not?'

'Because . . . because you can't keep ducking out of every challenge.' He drew a deep breath. 'Listen, daughter. Tad is dead. Nothing will ever bring him back. You've mourned long enough. It's time to stop, to take a hold on life again.'

They were sitting over a quiet dinner for two in the Castle. They had no guests, no other members of the family. Curt was off at summer camp still, due back in two weeks. Gina, of course, was in a London theatre. Baby Bobby was asleep in his cot upstairs.

For a long time Ellie-Rose made no reply. At last she said, 'It's not that I'm mourning. It's just that . . . it all seems pointless. We could have had the rest of our lives together but he's gone. What was it all for in the first place?'

'I can't tell you that. Perhaps it was so that you could have a son called Bobby.'

She gave a half-smile. 'If I'd known the price, I might even have decided against having Bobby,' she said.

'It never even entered your mind,' he retorted. 'You wanted his child, even when it seemed likely to bring scandal down on your heads. Now, when Tad isn't here to bolster up your courage, you creep into a shell that no one can penetrate. Are you sure you'll be good for Bobby when he's old enough to want to talk and play? Is he going to enjoy having a mother who's only half-alive?'

She stared at him, then slowly rose from the table. 'Never speak to me like that again,' she said, and for once there was emotion in the tone − something like anger.

'Okay, but let me just finish what I started. If you won't run this party for the Prince of Wales, I'll go ahead without you. I'll get Bess to come from Chicago to play hostess − and a fine mess she'll make of it, so shy and awkward as she is! I don't care if we only sit down to hot dogs and beer, but I'm going to do what I promised — I'm going to entertain His Royal Highness whether you receive him or not. And when your little boy's old enough to hear it, I'll tell him his mother was too chicken to even try real life again!'

She was gone, down the long diningroom and out the door. Whether she had heard his last few words, he couldn't tell. But he wasn't sorry to have said them. Perhaps they should have been said a long time ago.

He started on the arrangements for the party the following day. He had to be in Chicago in a week's time to deal for August wheat, but he could at least set the wheels in motion. He summoned the head of a famous catering firm to discuss ideas, and after a night's thought Alfredo came back with the suggestion that his remark about having hot dogs and beer was by no means without merit.

'You said His Royal Highness was hoping for a change from the formal events,' he said. 'It so happens I'm catering one of them, and I know the other firms who are doing special dinners. The hotels, of course, are going berserk — cakes in the shape of the British coat of arms, brown Windsor soup, every kind of reference to the British Empire that you can imagine. But how would it be if we just gave him an ordinary American home-folks party?'

'Listen, Mr Alfredo, I'm an American home-folks and I never eat hot dogs—'

'No, of course not. I wasn't suggesting actual hot dogs. But how if we give him a barn dance? After all, you are a wheat tycoon . . .'

Rob frowned, then smiled. 'Yeah!' he said. 'I think you've got something there.'

So on that basis, Jack Alfredo began work. He had been instructed to carry on without further consultation until Rob could get back from Chicago, where he was to join Cornelius and Sam Yarwood at The Pit. Dealing was very shaky that autumn. Demand had fallen dramatically. Russia, who usually came in a little after dealing began and bought to replace the failures of harvest, this year did nothing.

'Haven't got a kopek to bless themselves with,' Sam grunted. 'Damn Bolshies! I bet a million or two are going to starve in their marvellous new Soviet Republic next year.'

Rob travelled back to New York in the first week of September, after spending a few days with Morag. He was worried about her now that she was alone in the big ranch-style house he had built for her.

When he got back to Craigallan Castle, a shock awaited him. Luisa, the wife to whom he was legally still married, had moved back in. She came sailing to meet him in a waft of Chanel No. 5 as he entered the big flag-stoned hall.

'Luisa! What the devil — !'

'Rob! *Caro mio!*' She was much given to Italianisms after years of spending her winters in Naples. She leaned close to give him a kiss on the cheek. 'How lovely to see you again so soon.'

'Soon' meant twice in the same year. With winter drawing on? What could be behind it? She *never* came home in cold weather if she could help it.

The reason became evident. He was in his study, catching up on business reports, examining the ticker-tapes, and telephoning with Sam Yarwood in Chicago, when Luisa swept in. She had a sheaf of papers in her hand.

'Now darling, about this party . . .'

So that was it. Naturally, the rumour that the

Craigallans were to be hosts to royalty had reached Luisa. That was why she was here. No prince was going to be entertained at Craigallan Castle without Luisa playing her part.

He looked at her with dismay. Lightless henna-ed hair, full face toned down with rather too much *rachel* powder, lips made into a Clara Bow cupid's mouth . . . Her dress was by Poiret, influenced by his new devotion to 'functionalism': it had no waist to speak of, and reached to mid-calf with only a row of thick silk braid as ornamentation. Present-day fashions were unkind to Luisa, who was made for whale-boned waists and full ruffled skirts.

Yet, after all, Rob reminded himself, she was just like many other American matrons of the wealthy class: determined to stay young as long as possible, determined to be a fashion leader even if the clothes were not suited to her figure. When he thought about it he had no doubt that Luisa was not the only over-made-up old lady His Royal Highness would have to be polite to.

'I'm not against having Jack Alfredo do the catering, Rob. What bothers me is the low-key feeling. A barn dance, I ask you! Whose idea was that?'

'Alfredo's, as a matter of fact. *I* wanted to have hot dogs and beer.'

She looked shocked for a moment then realised it was a joke. 'Well, since he's of Italian extraction he and I will get on very well together. I'll just have a word with him and explain we need something a little more . . . cultured.'

'Such as what?'

'Such as an Italian grape-harvest party − I do agree something "earthy" is a good idea but−'

'Luisa,' Rob said, summoning his patience, 'the

whole idea is to give this boy some notion of what real American life is like. An Italian grape-harvest! You must be joking.'

'Nothing of the kind! I'll telephone Alfredo—'

'Luisa, do me a favour? Mind your own business.'

'But it is my business! Do you think I want to be a laughing stock? The heir to the British throne at my house, and we give him blueberry pie and ice-cream? I won't hear of—'

'Keep out of it! It's like when you wanted to fix up the Castle, *sweetheart* – nobody will take orders from you because I'll warn them I shan't pay the bills if they do.'

'Damn you, Rob! Are you never going to let me play my proper role as mistress of this house?' Her face was suffused with anger.

'No, I'm not. Ellie-Rose is mistress here, always was and always will be.'

'But she's doing nothing!'

That was only too true. Rob went to see her in her boudoir, where she spent so much time cut off from everyone except little Bobby and the nurse.

'Ellie, your mother's going to bitch up everything over this royal party,' he began.

She laid aside the book she had been reading, to gaze at him in perplexity. 'Party? Oh, yes, that . . .'

'Aren't you going to give me any help at all?'

'Papa, I'm not interested in that kind of thing any more.'

'Do you know what your mother's doing? Out of her own allowance, she's ordered a canopy of gardenias for the outside of the front door. Can you imagine? As the way-in to a barn dance?'

She looked at him with her hazel eyes, a level gaze. 'I

don't think it matters. He's probably never been to a barn dance.'

'But he knows damn fine gardenias play no part.'

'Who cares, Papa? Who really cares? Only the gossip columnists.'

Disheartened he turned away. Then he glanced back at her. 'I think there's no way of preventing her from receiving him,' he said. 'She's my wife, after all. She'll make a fool of me in front of everyone I know.'

Ellie-Rose picked up her book again. She didn't open it, however. She sat with her finger in the place. After a moment she said, 'I can tell by your voice how much the idea upsets you.'

'Like a four-point market fall! Look, Ellie – I won't ask anything else of you. But just this once, just once . . . Come out of the tomb, take some part in life. Help keep this party out of your mother's eager hands. I just want a nice, simple, old-fashioned barn dance for the prince. It's not difficult to run. Do that for me and then you can retire back among the funeral wreaths. Will you?'

She had flushed at the unintended sarcasm of his words. 'Is that how I seem to you? A Victorian widow – living among the gravestones?'

'Well, aren't you? You play no part in anything.'

She hesitated. 'It's not that I don't want to. It's just that . . . none of it seems important.'

'This is important to *me*, Ellie. Do it because it's important to *me*.'

With a sigh she opened her book and bent her head over it. He waited, but she said no more. Depressed, he went out.

Late that night, when he was sitting over some business papers in his study, she came in. She was wearing a long dark blue robe, and her ash-blonde hair was tied back with a black ribbon.

'Papa . . .'

'Yes?' He got up quickly, hurried to her. 'Something wrong with the boy?'

'No, he's fast asleep. He's a healthy little thing . . .' She sat down in the chair by the fire. 'Papa, I'm going to make an appointment with my hairdresser tomorrow, and have a manicure. Then I'll take a look at Lord & Taylor — judging by what Mama is wearing, my clothes have gone completely out of date. I'll have to have some things made later on but for the moment I'll just buy a few things. We still have accounts at the department stores?'

'Ellie!'

'I thought it over after you'd gone. I've been very selfish. I'll do it because it's important to you. I can't promise anything after that — the party, I mean. But that at least . . . I'll see to it, you don't have to worry any more.'

The wave of relief that surged over her father was so intense that it actually made his head swim. At last, at long last, the Sleeping Beauty was awakening. And, in fact, because of the arrival of a real Prince Charming . . .

The barn dance party for His Royal Highness the Prince of Wales was a social landmark in New York society. Dowagers and debutantes, wearing the 'simple' country dresses asked for in their invitations, crowded round the prince, eager to be able to say afterwards that they had shaken him by the hand. Solemn financiers, in flannel shirts and workpants, bowed as they had been instructed. He laughed and chatted, teased Rob about the baronial splendours of the Castle — 'We've nothing like this at Windsor' – and made an attempt to take part in the hoe-down. The band of country musicians, specially hired from Ohio, voted him 'a jim-dandy' when he sent a round of drinks to them in compliment for their playing.

Luisa's canopy of gardenias was nowhere to be seen. Luisa herself, in blue checked gingham and sun-bonnet, looked exactly what in fact she was: a descendant of an old Dutch farming family. Ellie-Rose wore grey print and a Puritan collar. Above it her pale-grey blonde hair, cut short by the skilled hands of Pierre of the Waldorf, gleamed like a helmet. Suddenly she was young again, more grave than formerly but still beautiful.

And to complete Rob's pleasure in the event, Luisa stayed only one more week to bask in the compliments that poured in. Then she was off to her winter quarters near Sorrento, leaving him in peace until next spring.

Rob waited anxiously to see if Ellie-Rose would retire into her shell again. He could see it was like the return of a wounded soldier to ordinary life. She had to stretch her mental self, become accustomed once again to little pleasures and indulgences. She had to make channels through which friends could reach her again. It was not a quick process, but it had begun.

He was glad to have that anxiety relieved, for business affairs were going very badly. A strange crisis had blown up. Out in the wheatlands, where he owned great tracts of land, tenant farmers of his were going bankrupt, leaving farms untended. Land in Oklahoma was turning into dust due to over-cultivation. Whole villages pulled up stumps and drove away in trucks and old cars. That wastage and confusion was bad enough, but some of the farmsteads were seized as headquarters by gangs of hoodlums. It was like seeing a garden become a wilderness of thorns and weeds.

'It's got to be dealt with, Papa,' Cornelius insisted. 'I don't want to say, I told you so, but I did warn you to do something about those Oklahoma lands two years ago.'

'Dammit, boy, I was in Scotland with your sister then. I wasn't paying attention!'

'It's no use leaving it to the managers. They're swamped.'

'Say, kid,' Sam Yarwood put in, 'how'd you like to take a whirl at it yourself?'

Cornelius frowned at him. Then he recognised the phrase and nodded. 'I wouldn't mind.'

'You want to travel around the Mid-West sorting out this wreckage?' Rob asked in surprise.

'I wouldn't mind,' Cornelius repeated. 'You know, my first training was in agricultural practice and the use of plants. I've missed close contact with the land. It's over two years now since I spent much time on a farm.'

'Well, I'll be darned!' Rob looked pleased, then hesitated. 'What about Bess, though? Will she like you travelling around Nebraska and Dakota?'

'I'll take her with me,' Cornelius said.

Rob laughed. 'Sometimes,' he said, 'I make the mistake of thinking you don't make decisions fast enough. If you really think Bess would like it, go ahead.'

Bess was charmed and touched when she heard Neil's plan. But more than that, she was proud that he felt he could undertake it if she were there to help.

Since their marriage, Bess had blossomed. She would never be any man's idea of a pretty girl, but she had the glow of a woman who knows she is beloved. Innocent, inexperienced, she had found Neil a wonderful lover, passionate yet gentle. He had taught her much, yet never made her feel lacking in knowledge. When she teased him about how he had acquired all his wisdom in the art of love he would shake his head. She knew there had been someone else, someone who had hurt him badly. And she had made it her life's work to compensate Neil for that hurt.

They were constant companions — in work, in life, in love. If others murmured that she scarcely left his side for fear some other woman would set her cap at this handsome but handicapped man, Bess merely shrugged. She knew Neil would never look at anyone else. She knew he would never have asked any other person — not even a man — to go with him on this trip to the farmlands.

They spent a few days closing up their apartment and planning an itinerary, then they were off. They took the train from Chicago to Mason City, then from there they travelled on by car provided by the Craigallan agent in that town.

'I wonder if you understand what you're setting out for, Mrs Craigallan,' the agent remarked to Bess as he helped her into the big Ford. 'Times are hard out on the prairie. You might meet a lot of resentment.'

'We understand that, Mr Fox. What we're trying to do is see how we can remedy at least some of the problems.'

'Yeah,' Fox said, moving his quid of tobacco to the other cheek. 'But will they understand that in Wichita?'

It became a catch phrase between Bess and Neil: whenever they were working out what to ask a harassed bank manager or silo overseer — will they understand it in Wichita? Their mission was simple: they had to find out who needed money the most and how funds could be channelled towards them. Those who were past saving must be left to die, those who could be shown how to reorganise and reconstruct must be given encouragement.

The state of the land depressed Neil. Harvest was in, the prairies swept on towards the skyline in an unending vista of powdery earth, devilled by little dust storms. Iowa was hot and dusty and dirty. Farmers in patched jeans and straw shaders stood about in the little towns, looking with anxious eyes at the windows of the post office or the grain dealer, where 'Help Wanted' ads were tacked up.

Bess had brought lightweight costumes of corded cotton and straw hats. But soon she began to feel as out of place as a bird of paradise in such clothes, when she compared them with the faded prints the farm women wore. In Lincoln, Nebraska, they called in on old Mr and Mrs Gracebridge for a day or two's respite, and there Bess bought some cotton frocks to make her less conspicuous. But even those were too fine, with their bright new surface and their unfrayed cuffs and necklines.

'Trouble with most of these people,' said Mr Gracebridge, 'they just won't come to terms with real life. They won't accept change, won't adapt. You've learnt that already, I expect, Neil. Won't accept advice, will they? Keep on tilling their lands in the old way until it all gets up and blows away.'

'It's difficult,' Cornelius agreed. 'I'm trying to arrange classes in some of the towns, about soil conservation, but the school teachers say few of the farmers will attend.'

'Darn tootin'! What, go back to school about something they think they know inside out? Naw, they're too stupid, too set in their ways.'

When they drove away, Neil said to Bess, 'D'you think Gracebridge was right?'

'We can't allow him to be right! Neil, it's not just saving what we can of the Craigallan lands. It's helping these folk to save themselves. Some of them have put their lives, and their children's lives, into their farms. They've got to be shown how to make a living.'

He nodded. But he was not optimistic. The changes that had to come about would not be easy, and they would take years. Bess, bright and clever though she was, didn't understand that even if you persuaded the Kansan to turn from durum wheat to corn, it would be half a generation before a visible improvement came about in the tillage. And when it did, it would be time to change again, or to use new dressings, or a new technique.

They had reached Stillwater in Oklahoma when they began to see totally abandoned farms. Until now almost every farmer had clung tenaciously to his home, hoping for an upturn in prices and improvement in trading. But in Oklahoma, they saw a house sagging on its cellars, waiting for the winter storms to bring it to the ground.

It was October, with a reddish sun glinting from behind the lands of the Indian Reservation. Cornelius stopped the car. They got out and walked round the house. To their alarm, a figure suddenly emerged. It was a man in a pink shirt and canvas trousers, his dark hair caught back in a braided band.

'You want something?' he asked.

He spoke with scarcely a movement of his lips, in the

Indian fashion. Bess answered. 'We're just looking at the house,' she said.

He tensed. 'Nobody lives here.'

'No, we can see that.'

'Nearest house is two miles further on, the Cannons' place.'

'What does he say?' Cornelius asked.

Bess told him with finger language. At once the Indian relaxed. 'He is a man of inner hearing?' he asked. 'Come in, be welcome.'

He led them indoors. It was clear he had taken temporary possession. He cleaned a space for Bess on a bench just inside the door and brought her coffee. 'The Wakefords, they owned this farm. They left when they saw the corn dying on the stem. I'm not doing anything against the law, living here.' He looked at them anxiously. 'I can get rabbits and deer — my wife makes things to sell, from the skins.'

'Is your wife here?'

'No, she's home with the children.' He jerked a thumb towards the west. 'Salt Plains Reservation.'

'You've a family? Don't they miss you while you're here?' Bess asked.

'I reckon. But you see, on the reservation, everybody looks out for everybody else. So they make out. It's not like among the white men.' He paused, then when they made no protest he went on: 'Things go bad with the farmers, they don't get together and help each other. It's dog eat dog then. The bank man wants his money, the corn dealer wants his profit, the farmer wants his living, and the plains die . . .'

'That's why we're here,' Cornelius said. 'To see what we can do to prevent that.'

The Indian shook his head. 'Too late,' he said. He

smiled. 'I wish my grandfather had lived to see this day. He always said the white men would go away one day and leave us the plains.'

'But not many have gone,' Bess objected.

'They'll go,' was the reply. 'Ten more years, and they'll all be gone. You'll see.'

When they rose to leave, saying they had hotel rooms waiting for them, he detained them. 'Will you be around for a day or two?'

'Yes, in Perry — why?'

'Sure would like my kids to meet you, Mr Craigallan. You're the first white man I ever met who had some feeling for the land for its own sake.'

'Why, I'd like that,' Cornelius said, never imagining it would come to pass.

But two days later, when they came out of their hotel in Perry to have yet another meeting with a local bank manager, there was an aged truck drawn up in the road. And sitting on the load of kindling it carried, three little dark children in dark cotton shirts — two boys and a girl, the girl with long plaits over her shoulder.

'These my young 'uns,' said John Cross-River. 'I told 'em about you. Show them how you and your lady speak to one another with the fingers. My folks used to do that, you know.' He sighed. 'But we're losing it, we talk at each other now.'

Bess obliged by asking the children their names and translating into sign for Cornelius. They watched in awe. Bess found it sad, that they should be so amazed at what had once been commonplace among their own people, the use of sign language.

'How would you like to come to the candy store and get some taffy?' Bess proposed.

They hung back, looking shy but eager.

'Come on, one stick of taffy for each child,' urged Bess.

They looked at their father. He nodded permission. Cornelius said: 'I think we ought to get on to the bank, darling. Mr Wakeford's expecting us.'

'Would it be all right if I join you later?'

'Of course, I can manage.' This was by no means as certain as he made it sound, for some businessmen were so startled at the idea of trying to converse with a totally deaf man that they almost went into spasm. But Bess was so taken with the children he hadn't the heart to drag her away.

She never did turn up at the bank. When he left an hour and a half later, she was in the toy-shop buying a doll for Josephine, the little girl. The boys already had a wooden truck and a toy metal crane.

'I think you've lost your family to a stranger,' Neil said to John Cross-River.

'She's good with them. How many you got of your own?'

Cornelius shook his head.

'Got no kids?'

'No.'

'That's a shame.'

Yes, it is, thought Cornelius.

That evening, with the day's work over and dinner awaiting them in the diningroom of the little hotel, they changed into fresh clothes. He helped do up Bess's plain silk dress.

'You enjoyed yourself with those children,' he remarked.

'Oh, yes!' She turned to face him so he could read her lips. 'I'm sorry I let you down at the bank. It went well, though?'

'It was okay. But listen, Bess . . . Seeing you this morning made me think . . . it would be nice to have children of our own.'

Her glance wavered away from him for a moment. Then she went to pick up her evening purse. She said something but he couldn't make it out because she was turned away from him.

'What did you say, darling?'

'Oh, nothing.'

But it was not nothing. He saw a glint of tears in her eyes. He went quickly to her, took her purse away, and made her sit down facing him. 'What's the matter, Bess?'

'I thought . . . you remember last year . . . when I wasn't too well?'

'In spring. Yes, I remember. Iron deficiency.' He had trouble with the last word but they both knew what he meant.

'I thought it was a baby, Neil.'

'A baby?'

'I was so disappointed when I was told I was wrong.' She leaned her forehead against his chest, a habit she had when she was upset. He had to tilt her face up to see it. 'I was so sure then, Neil. It was such a knock when Dr Krensky told me to forget it.'

'I'm sorry, Bess. I didn't know. You should have told me.'

'What, and be a complaining, silly wife? I didn't want to bother you with things like that.'

'Well, one day it'll be true and we'll have children of our own.' He saw her face change and he took her hand. 'We can have children, Bess?'

'The doctor says no reason why not.' She withdrew her hand and signed it, for emphasis, and to make sure he understood. 'There's nothing physically wrong. I just don't understand why . . .'

He gathered her up and held her near. 'Don't worry about it, Bess. If we don't have a family it doesn't matter. We have each other.'

He felt her nod in agreement. 'When we get home,' he told her, 'we'll talk it over with Krensky. Perhaps we should settle down a bit more, be like other married couples. Perhaps it's not helping, the way you work alongside of me.'

'But I'd hate to have to give that up, Neil,' she cried, turning in his arms to stare up at him. 'I love to be with you. It makes me feel . . . I don't know . . . part of you.'

'Okay, okay, we'll work something out. When we get back from this trip, Bess . . . We'll work something out.'

Cornelius's absence left Rob rather solitary at Craigallan Agricultural Products. Once again he longed for Gregor to help him, but though he hinted at it in a long-distance telephone call, Gregor refused to be tempted.

'I'm too busy here, Father,' he pointed out. 'Besides, Clare and Lew are well settled in school here, they have lots of friends. And Frannie is really knitted into the social life. We can't uproot ourselves now.' He gave a little laugh. 'I think you ought to consider it the other way round, Mr Craig! Why don't you come out here? There's lots of good land out in the San Joaquin Valley going cheap—'

'Put into Californian land?' Rob interrupted. 'You must be joking! All the Californians do is grow fruit and vegetables! I'm not into the business of producing lettuce!'

He went down to Wall Street to console himself with some quick clever deals on the commodities market. Although the Exchange was jumpy, there was money being made. Farmers might go bankrupt, whole areas of land might be going derelict and even in cities the blight of unemployment might be spreading — but on the New York Stock Exchange fortunes were still being made.

Perhaps it was out of indignation at this very fact that threatening letters were coming through the mailboxes of rich men. 'The people will take revenge!' they said. Or, 'Capitalists, your days are numbered.'

Rob got two of them but paid no heed. Cranks, he thought. They make a lot of noise but never do anything.

He was wrong. On a rainy day in 1922, as he was trying to hail a taxi in company with Sam Yarwood, a bomb went off that blew him through a plate glass window.

Chapter Eighteen

Gina Gracebridge sat by the hospital bed. Her eyes were fixed on the mummy-wrapped figure lying upon it. Head, arms, torso were bandaged. The hands were encased in bits of gauze and gamgee tissue. The lower half of the body was hidden below the pale blue bedspread but protected by a cage to keep the pressure from the limbs.

Gina had come down the gangplank of the liner only two hours earlier. Waved through Customs by officials warned to expect her, she flew into her mother's arms. No thoughts now of resentment, of alienation.

'Is he − ?'

'He's holding his own, darling,' Ellie-Rose said.

'Has he recovered consciousness?'

'Not yet, but Dr Borg doesn't find that worrying as yet. The concussion was severe, and of course he's sedated to hold off the pain of the wounds.'

'Oh, Mama . . .'

It had shaken Gina to find how much she cared about her grandfather. When the cable arrived informing her of the accident she had gone at once to Charles Cochran. 'Please don't be angry, but I must go! He may be dying!'

Cochran had told her soothingly that it was quite all

right, and saw her off at Southampton with a bouquet of white roses.

The family were taking it in turns to sit by Rob's bed. The men did the day-time stints between business commitments, the women the night hours because they could catch up on their sleep during the day. When Gina insisted on taking her turn, Ellie-Rose tried to demur.

'Oh, let me, Mama – I did nothing but rest all the way over on the boat!'

Now here she sat, scared and watchful. In a corner of the room a white-clad nurse was quietly reading a medical textbook. It was two-thirty in the morning on a Thursday towards the end of September.

The figure in the bed stirred. A grunt came from his lips. Gina leapt up. 'Grandfather! Grandfather, it's me, Gina!'

The lids fluttered. Slowly they were raised. The grey eyes gazed at her, unfocused. Gradually, gradually, recognition dawned.

'Na?'

'Oh, *Grandfather*!' She was about to throw herself on him and weep tears of relief and joy when the nurse caught her by the arm.

'Miss Gracebridge, you mustn't disturb the patient. Please sit quietly.' She leaned over Rob and spoke to him. 'Mr Craigallan, do you hear me?'

A faint sound came from Rob's lips, ending in a sibilant. The nurse understood this to be 'yes'. She smiled. 'Splendid,' she said. 'You're doing wonders. Can you see me?'

The same sound.

'Am I wearing blue?'

'N-n-n . . .'

316

'Am I wearing white?'

The sibilant sound.

'Wonderful. Now just lie quietly, Mr Craigallan—'

'Whe . . . Whe . . .'

'Where are you? In hospital. I'm just going to call Dr Borg. Now rest quietly until he comes.' She pressed a bell by the bedhead. Gina, taking advantage of her move, leaned over her grandfather.

'Mama will be here in a minute, Grandfather. She's sleeping in a room nearby—'

'Really, Miss Gracebridge, you mustn't tire the patient by giving him information he doesn't need—'

'Stupid woman . . .' muttered the patient, bringing out the first fully formed words since he recovered consciousness.

Gina was hustled out, laughing to herself in joyful gratitude over her grandfather's remark. She rushed to rouse Ellie-Rose. The news was telephoned to Bess at the Waldorf so that she could tell Cornelius, and to Gregor at Craigallan Castle. The reporters who had been warned to look out for any activity among the Craigallans sprang into action. The early editions carried the news: *Wheat Tycoon Out Of Danger*.

This wasn't quite true when they printed it but it became true. Loss of blood had weakened him to a terrifying extent. Wounds all over his body, caused by flying glass, had wept away his life's blood before they could be staunched. The new treatment of 'blood transfusion' was applied: luckily his blood group, as ascertained by the work of Landsteiner, was a common one and his sons had been able to supply it. Then there had been the frightening danger of septicemia: with so many wounds, infection was a continuing threat for weeks. The coma caused by explosion-concussion had worried the doctors less: they had regarded that as nature's way of ensuring rest to the brain, and they had been justified.

Rob found it difficult to speak at first because of the facial wounds and the bandaging. But six or seven days after he first opened his eyes he managed to inquire what had happened.

'There was a huge packet of explosives in a cart left at the crossing of Broad and Wall Street, Mr Craig,' Gregor told him. 'They found bits of the carcass of a horse, and shoes and bridles. The police think it was a big crate of all kinds of scrap metal with a charge of TNT in the middle.'

'Who did it?'

'Nobody can find out. A printed message was found in a postbox — "Free the political prisoners or it will be sure death for all of you!" and signed "American Anarchist Fighters". But whether it's genuine or a hoax, no one seems to know.'

'Political prisoners? That means Sacco and Vanzetti?'

'They don't say. Anyhow, nobody's going to free them.'

'No.' After a pause to get the strength for the question: 'Sam badly hurt?'

'Pretty bad, Father.'

'He here?'

'No, he's somewhere else.'

It was thought best not to tell him that his old friend had been cut in two by a sword of plate glass, killed instantly.

Thirty-five people died, a hundred and thirty were injured. No prisoners were freed. Nothing more was heard of the American Anarchist Fighters. Detectives followed up clues for months, even years, but the perpetrators were never identified. By Christmas, when Rob Craigallan was gingerly walking about the room to test out his legs, most people had forgotten the event.

Morag came from Colorado Springs to take care of him. It had been decided he must go south for the winter, to Palm Beach, with Morag as his companion. It was she who told him that Sam Yarwood was gone. Rob had a two-day relapse at the news, but recovered again. He still had resiliency and strength, but the long illness had changed him.

To cover the scars on his face, he had let his beard grow. 'Makes me look old!' he said fretfully to Morag.

'Not a bit! You're a braw lad yet,' she assured him, touching the silky growth. It had come in dark reddish-brown like his hair but with a streak of white where one of the worst scars was hidden.

'Beaver,' he said reminiscently. 'When I was a boy, we used to run after bearded men shouting "Beaver!" '

'Nobody's going to run after you shouting rude names, Rob,' she laughed. 'Now come along — ten minutes' walk along the shore for the exercise, and ten minutes' sunshine for the good of your skin. After that it's lunch and a good nap.'

He frowned at her in mock annoyance. 'I believe you women love it when men are sick! Gives you a chance to boss us about.'

'No, darling.' She laid her cheek against his shoulder. 'I'd give anything if it had never happened.'

'Me too. Poor Sam . . .'

'But you're still here and you're going to be well again—'

'Sure thing. Only I keep wondering what the devil Neil may be getting up to all on his own in Chicago, without even Sam to offer advice . . .'

'Neil will be fine,' she assured him, urging him along the beach in the shade of the palm trees. 'Neil will keep everything running fine until you can get back to help him.'

'Help him?' He paused to glare at her. 'Neil helps *me*! I'm the head of Craigallan Agricultural.'

But that was never to be quite true again, not in the way it had been. Although he was back in Chicago to deal for May wheat, he walked with a stick. He didn't gather with the other fellows in the Merchants' Club to chew over the day's business, not in the old way. He liked to get home to dinner, to talk over with Morag the day's events.

He spent his life with her now. He had been frightened by the sudden understanding that everything might be over for him − and he and Morag would not have made the best of the time they had left. In the summer he went to her house in Colorado Springs, in the winter they went to San Francisco. When business dictated his imperative presence he travelled by easy stages to Chicago or New York, with Morag always at his side.

Though farmers and farmworkers were starving, though cities were blighted with unemployment, the great stock market boom had begun. Men with money to invest increased their capital. Men without money made fortunes dealing 'on the margin'. America seemed to produce millionaires as South American republics produced presidents − another was always being hailed. And there was no reason, it seemed, why it shouldn't go on for ever.

Ellie-Rose, having been brought out into the real world by her father's efforts, now had conscience enough to want to do something about its problems. She was interested in helping women obtain their political rights. She was particularly incensed when the Governor of Georgia appointed 'the first woman Senator' in a state legislature. Some women took it as a triumph, but to Ellie it was an insult. Senator Thomas E. Watson having died, the Governor appointed Mrs W. H. Felton to take his place — but the Senate term had only one day to run.

It was the more galling since Nancy Astor, that formidable American expatriate, had been elected to the British House of Commons. Just how a ladyship could be a member of the Commons wasn't exactly clear to most Americans, but they all agreed it was a mighty fine thing.

'The trouble with us,' Ellie said crossly to her brother, 'is we don't really believe women should have visible power. Look at you — you let Bess take an almost equal share in running CAP but you never give her the title of Vice-President.'

Bess, playing with her little nephew Bobby on the floor, looked up. 'I don't want the title of Vice-President,' she remarked.

Neil had his head turned away and was unaware she had spoken. 'I'm quite willing to make Bess a Vice-President,' he said, over her words.

Ellie-Rose laughed. 'I don't know how CAP can manage to flourish when you talk at cross-purposes.'

Bess struggled up with Bobby in her arms, to dump him in Ellie's lap. 'Look after your offspring, Mrs Gracebridge,' she said, wagging a finger at her. 'He's just put one of my beads up his nose.'

It was quite untrue but was enough to break up the party in a wave of giggles and frivolity. But Ellie-Rose was serious about women's rights.

At a meeting in the Palm Garden, she brought herself to the notice of an alert reporter by asking a question. Identified to him as the daughter of a grain millionaire, Ellie-Rose Gracebridge, she was an immediate object of interest. He followed her out and attempted to interview her.

'If you don't mind,' she said, side-stepping him, 'I only came to get information. I've no right to give opinions about politics.'

'It's a long way up-town to come just to ask a question,' he parried.

'Well, one must fill up one's time somehow,' she said, hoping that by acting silly she would put him off.

John Martin was a second generation Italian and had the Italian temper. 'Oh, I see!' he flashed. 'Too early for cocktails, too late for tea, there's a queue for *Lilac Time* and you don't like what's on at the movies.'

'Something like that.' She was glancing about for a taxi.

'Lady, you and your kind make me sick! Nothing to do and all day to do it in! Why don't you stay in your Manhattan apartment and play the phonograph?'

Ellie found his manner offensive and took refuge in further fantasy. 'It's my maid's day off,' she said. 'Winding the phonograph is such a chore, don't you think?'

Baffled, Martin fell back. She got into a taxi and was carried away, taking with her a picture of a pair of dark angry eyes, black Italian hair going grey, a lined and experienced face, and a waving notebook.

Next day, around ten o'clock, a bouquet of red roses

322

was delivered. A note was attached to the green tissue paper.

'After you'd vanished I did some research and discovered you weren't a dumb broad after all — three years in war conditions in London and a husband lost in France entitles you to an apology. Having made it, I'll keep my big mouth shut. John Martin.'

The notepaper had the heading of the Features Department of the *Daily News,* a recently established tabloid which Ellie-Rose despised. Typical, she thought, that he should be employed there.

All the same, she bought a copy of the paper when she next went into the city. She even looked for, and found, his by-line — over a lurid piece about young women forced into prostitution.

They met again over an event run for Cornelius's charity. Bathing Beauties were all the rage now, and Beauty Contests. An entrepreneur had suggested to Cornelius that it would attract money and press attention — sympathetic attention if it could be shown that deaf girls could be as beautiful as any others. Cornelius was reluctant at first, but was at last persuaded by the enthusiasm of the pretty girls in the various colleges for the deaf, who wrote to him when they heard of the notion.

The finals were held in the Biltmore Ballroom. Ellie-Rose attended merely to show support for the charity. But across the room she espied John Martin with a press photographer. She recognised him, looked away, shrugged, and looked back again. After all, there was no reason why she shouldn't acknowledge him.

He made his way round the back of the ballroom to her table. 'Mrs Gracebridge? Remember me? The guy with the instant-judgement equipment.'

'Of course, how are you, Mr . . . ?' It wouldn't do to let him know she remembered his name perfectly well after several months.

'Martin, John Martin. Nice to see you again. I take it your maid's got the evening off again.'

'I beg your pardon?'

'You didn't want to stay home and wind the phonograph yourself.'

'Oh . . . You have a very good memory, Mr Martin.'

'It's my job, Mrs Gracebridge. Say, listen . . . Would you let me do an interview on you some time?'

'I don't think my activities would be of much interest to the *Daily News*.'

He hesitated. 'I . . . er . . . do a bit of work for a non-profit-making magazine. It's about social reform. Now I know a bit more about you, I realise you knew Nancy Astor when you were in London.'

'That's true.'

'Would you chat to me about her?'

'I'd rather not.'

'Why not?'

'I didn't much like her.'

'Oh!' He chuckled and was silent a moment while the master of ceremonies on-stage announced the final parade of the Sweetheart Contest.

'How about Miss Pankhurst? Would you talk to me about her?'

'I'd rather not.'

'Didn't much like her either?'

'Not much.'

'Gee, you're hard to please! Listen, Mrs Gracebridge, I'd really appreciate it if you'd spare me some time when you can. I want to do an article about rich women dabbling in women's rights—'

'*Dabbling?*'

'Why sure. They're not serious about it. All they want is to get rich women into government. They don't want *poor* women to make it to the Senate.'

'That's quite untrue!' Ellie-Rose cried.

'Sshh,' said the people at the next table.

John Martin bowed to her and took himself off. She saw him later interviewing the winner of the contest with the aid of Bess, who translated for her into speech. She wondered if he was aware that the quiet, plainly dressed girl acting as interpreter was one of the 'rich women' he appeared to hold in such low esteem.

He annoyed her so much that she invited him to a meeting organised by the Carmansville Committee for Congressional Campaigning. This was a group trying to get a woman candidate accepted by the Republican Party caucus to campaign for a seat in Congress. Martin came, drank the coffee, ate the sandwiches, took some notes, and wrote a scathing piece for the *News* about 'socialites playing at politics'. He minutely described the inside of Julié Robart's livingroom. She was furious and rang Ellie-Rose to tell her so. 'Next time you ask me to invite a man, I'll make sure he isn't a snake in a pair of trousers!' she raged.

'I'm sorry, Julie. I didn't think he'd do a piece like that.'

'Is he a friend of yours, for heaven's sake?'

'Of course not.' But if he was not, why did she accept a dinner invitation from him two days later?

She went somewhat nervously into the restaurant he had named. She half expected it to be a hobo's diner, but it was a perfectly respectable Italian trattoria not far from the Queensborough Bridge. He rose to greet her as she came in. 'My, you look nice,' he said.

She did. She'd taken special pains with her appearance. She considered herself too old now for extremes of fashion but she was wearing a very simple dark blue georgette dress by Coco Chanel which hung straight from her shoulders like a blue mist. In deference to the hobos she thought she might meet, she had on no jewellery except dark blue earrings.

She was quite surprised to find John Martin wearing a dinner jacket. She was even more surprised when the manager treated him with some deference. A long time later she learned they were distantly related and that Martin was considered to be the intellectual of the tribe.

'I can recommend the cannelloni,' he suggested. 'And the house wine is good.'

'Thank you, I'll have whatever you suggest.'

'Oh, gee, relax, will you? I'm not going to cross-question you. This is purely a social occasion.'

'Oh. That's a relief. I thought you'd want to find out what I thought about Mrs Harding.'

'I can find out all I need to know about the First Lady by telephoning the White House – more than I need to know, probably. I asked you here to talk about *you.*'

'But there's nothing to talk about.'

'No? We're gonna have kind of a dull evening, then.'

'That could well be so,' she agreed. 'And if the cannelloni is tough, the whole evening will have been a disaster.'

'How old are you?' he asked.

'Old enough to have a daughter of twenty-four.'

'Yeah? I've a son of twenty-one.'

'You're married?' she said, suddenly appalled.

'Widowed. She died in the 1918 flu epidemic.'

Ellie-Rose went pale.

'Say, what's the matter?' John said, and put a hand over hers.

'I . . . lost someone I loved in the 1917 epidemic.'

He said no more for a long moment. The waiter came with the cannelloni. When it had been placed, and the Parmesan cheese dusted over it, they sat looking at the plates.

'All at once I'm not very hungry,' he remarked.

'Neither am I.'

'Come on then, let's go for a walk.' To her amazement he lifted the tablecloth to examine her feet. 'You got shoes fit for walking?'

'Not really — but I'd like a stroll.'

They went out into the summer evening. The towers of Manhattan were shining way off in the sunset. He took her arm through his. 'Mrs Gracebridge,' he murmured, 'what are you doing to me?'

It was hard to tell. They quarrelled almost every time they met. If she invited him to a meal with guests at Craigallan Castle he was cross-grained and aggressive. When she went out with him, he was apt to take her to the slums of the East Side and lecture her on social inequality. He was a committed Socialist (spelt with a capital S, as he insisted) — a difficult thing to be in the political climate then reigning.

Her family couldn't understand what she saw in him. Her father grunted that the man was a radical and too old to grow out of it. Her brother Cornelius thought him 'bumptious'. When Ellie-Rose lent him the money to start a small political magazine of his own, Gregor wired her from San Francisco: *Backers are almost always losers*. Curtis was wary of him, perhaps seeing in him a possible stepfather. Only Gina liked him.

'He's sexy,' she said.

Ellie-Rose was shocked by the word. In her circles, although Freud was now the new Messiah, sex still wasn't much discussed — at least not by that name.

'Gina, how can you!'

'Well, he is, Mama. Don't you listen to what anyone says! Perhaps he isn't as goodlooking as John Barrymore but he's just as attractive.'

Gina felt herself well qualified to offer opinions. After spending a couple of years with all the men running after her and never committing herself to one of them, she had decided to get married. The only difficulty was, she had decided to marry someone else's husband.

Clifford Gramm was a stockbroker, young, debonair, and from one of the best families. As he explained to Gina, he had married Alicia because his family and hers expected it. 'Alicia's as bored with the whole thing as I am,' he told her. 'She's ready to break up so long as the money settlement is good enough — and it will be, I'll see to that.'

When Rob Craigallan heard the plan he was outraged. 'No granddaughter of mine is going to marry a divorcee!' he cried.

'Papa, you said that when she insisted on going on the stage — and you couldn't prevent that either.'

'Ellie, you've got to stop it! You can't discard marriage like an old shoe—'

His daughter came to sit beside him and take his hand. 'Papa, if you could have got a divorce, you'd have been happily married to Morag years ago — now wouldn't you?'

'But that's different! Morag and I really love one another!'

'What makes you think Cliff and Gina don't love one another?'

'They don't act as if they do!'

'But, don't you see — that's the way the world is at the moment. This is the age of the sophisticates — cigarettes and cocktails and bright conversation. Sentimentality is considered bad taste. It doesn't do to hold hands and look longingly at each other.'

'I just don't understand the way the world's going,' Rob sighed. 'If we're all going to be shallow all the time, what kind of a foundation is that for building a proper marriage?'

'I don't know, darling. All I can tell you is that Gina's determined to have Cliff. She's old enough to know what she's doing. And Cliff wants her, and his wife wants the divorce. There's really nothing against it.'

Rob shook his head. Nothing would convince him that the right basis for his granddaughter's marriage was the wreckage of someone else's.

But Ellie-Rose was right. Gina wanted Cliff. His wife went to Reno, a quiet divorce was granted, and within two days Gina was the second Mrs Gramm. The wedding was celebrated in City Hall, with a small party afterwards for family and friends. Because Gina liked him so much, she invited John Martin.

And it was after the wedding party, in a mood of confusion and doubt, that Ellie-Rose and John became lovers.

Chapter Nineteen

On a day in June Gregor McGarth put through an urgent telephone call long-distance to his father in the ranch-house in Colorado Springs. It was Monday, June 11th, midday in San Francisco, mid-afternoon in the mountains.

'Mr Craig, there's a big slide going on here on the Stock Exchange. I just heard about it − I was off in the barrios inspecting a new housing area when I saw it on the placards.'

'That so?' Rob said, somewhat irritated at being summoned from his work among Morag's ice-plant hedge.

'Listen, Mr Craig, this is serious. Bank of America has so far slipped ninety-six points and the rumour is it's going down by another ten, perhaps more. And United Security has lost almost eighty.'

The fall sounded horrendous. Rob was jerked out of his nonchalance. 'That's bad. You got much invested in either of those, Greg?'

A pause from the other end of the line. 'Father, you know I'm into real estate for investment these days. It's you I'm worried about.'

'Kind of you, boy. I appreciate it. But everything's okay here.'

He could picture his son frowning at the telephone and wondering if he'd started to go senile. He grinned to himself. Greg was worrying about nothing.

'Listen, Father, don't you think you ought to get off back to Chicago or New York for tomorrow's dealing? This landslip's likely to be reflected in the Exchanges tomorrow.'

'Well, maybe so, maybe so, Greg. But I'm busy remodelling your mother's terrace garden—'

'Father, do you understand what I've just been saying? There's been a catastrophic fall on the San Francisco Exchange which is bound to be reflected in dealing on the eastern side by tomorrow. You must at least ring your broker.'

'I don't think I'll bother, thanks, Greg.'

'Do you want to lose all your money?' Gregor almost shouted at him.

'Certainly not. I wouldn't anyhow — haven't got much in Bank of America, or United Security.'

'But those are only the worst figures — other stocks have been taking a terrible beating! You must know—'

'Yeah, I know, everything will get the jitters. Lucky I got out four days ago, isn't it?'

There was a long, long silence from San Francisco. Then Gregor gave a shaky laugh. 'You old fox! Were you expecting this?'

'No,' Rob admitted, shaking his head. 'I couldn't have told you the date it would happen nor the extent. But I've still got instinct, laddie, even though you think I'm in my dotage. I felt it in my bones that it was time to withdraw when the market was still on an upswing. You're out of touch, Greg, sitting out there arbitrating on Hispano problems. If you looked at the graphs, you'd have guessed a little shake-out was about due.'

331

'A *little* shake-out? Father, banks in Frisco have been closing because of the panic!'

'There's no panic in the east, Greg. Nor likely to be. Thanks for the thought, though. Now you want to speak to your mother before we ring off?'

He beckoned to Morag, who had been hovering after hearing that the call was from San Francisco. She was in fear that one of their grandchildren had scarlatina or the mysterious ailment that was stalking American cities in hot weather these days, infantile paralysis. He listened absently while Morag chatted in relief to her son. His mind was on the likely events on the New York Exchange tomorrow.

The truth was, his withdrawal from buying on the Exchange had not been entirely due to instinct. The United States was in the grip of the most gigantic and longest-lasting 'bull' market ever known in the history of finance. The brokers had more work than they could handle, and dealing was often so fast that the ticker-tape record couldn't keep up with it. Small investors were glorying in a bath of financial sunshine, seeing their savings rise in value as they put them into General Motors or Union Carbide. President Coolidge was right: America was showing the world how to be happy by making money.

What the general public didn't know − nor, for that matter, most of the financial specialists of Wall Street − was that the bull market was being manipulated by a powerful group of speculators. They were men with fortunes at their disposal, money already made in the automobile business or the grain market. They were names to conjure with: W. C. Durant, Arthur Cutten, John J. Raskob.

Rob wasn't one of the inner 'cabinet'. But because he

332

too was a 'wheatie', he got enough hints in the course of conversation with others at his own special market – the Board of Trade in Chicago, The Pit.

But even men of unlimited resources must occasionally slacken their buying. Durant was taking his wife away on vacation, the Fisher brothers had other things to think of for a week or two. So although their brokers had instructions to keep an eye on the run of business they had stopped buying for the moment. And the market was uneasy. There had been warnings in the spring from the Harvard Economic Society that 'business is entering upon a period of temporary readjustment'. Some necessary selling by the Bank of Italy for currency reasons had been seen as a signal of impending trouble.

But it would only be temporary, Rob knew. In this year of 1928, the controllers of the bull market were not about to allow anything very bad to happen. He happened to know that the Democratic candidate for the Presidency, Al Smith, was going to invite none other than John J. Raskob to be chairman of the Democratic National Committee in charge of the election campaign. For reasons that were never clear to Rob, Raskob insisted on being a Democrat. But he wasn't any kind of starry-eyed reformer. He would make sure business interests were looked after by the new President if he turned out to be a Democrat, and he certainly wasn't going to allow a drastic dive on the nation's stock exchanges just before the election in November. If there was one thing likely to make the voters turn towards the Republican, Hoover, it was the sight of the great Temples of Business rocking on their foundations.

So all would be well. But there was no sense in taking

a loss, however temporary. Rob had got out of American Telephone and also Radio Corporation stock. But only for the moment. He had faith in telephone stock because it had all come about through Cornelius's great teacher, Alexander Graham Bell. And he had faith in Radio Corporation because to his mind, radio was a coming thing — soon every home would have a radio set, he was sure.

Meantime, there was no need to take any steps. His brokers, Vinnison Charle and Company, had instructions to take them through any little hiatus in the upward trend of profits. He was here in Colorado Springs enjoying a well-earned vacation while Cornelius looked after the store. Soon he would meet his elder son in Chicago for dealing in the autumn wheat. Ellie-Rose was in London with Bobby, to let the youngster see his big brother Curt take a crack at the Wimbledon championship. Everything was fine. He put an arm around Morag when she hung up the receiver and conducted her to the lower terrace to argue with her about the advisability of a guard rail on the four steps down.

That was the biggest problem on his mind at the moment. If he had been forced to look at matters on a wider scale, he'd have agreed that people who depended on him might not have seen his problems as so small. He had vast areas of land standing untenanted, he had a vast tonnage of grain — wheat and maize — in silo. For farmers, and those who depended exclusively on farming products, times were very hard. But Rob viewed things differently. For the last nine years the world had been shaking down to the business of peace after the end of the war. Russia, once a sure market for wheat, was too poor to buy. Competition from

Australia and Argentina made matters worse. But he felt that there would be a change for the better.

Some little thing would set it off. Japan would occupy the whole of China, perhaps, and need food supplies to fend off the always-imminent famine there. Or Germany would sort herself out and become a factor in European affairs, increasing the demand for farm produce or farm machinery. *Something* would start an upturn in farming finance.

Until that happened Rob would keep his finances intact by judicious dealing on the Stock Exchange. He might, like Gregor, have gone into real estate in some other part of the country, somewhere that had a boom in progress – but Miami had gone down to disaster and so had the Suburban Paradise settlements of many a big city. No, stocks and shares were easier to handle. He'd stick with stocks and shares.

In London the sudden little earthquake from California via the New York Stock Exchange caused Threadneedle Street some uneasiness. Ellie-Rose and Bobby weren't even aware of it. Ellie-Rose was renewing old acquaintances, Bobby was exclaiming in wonder at the shining cuirasses of horse-soldiers trotting to mount guard in Whitehall and Curt, happy and excited, was putting in hours of practice at Ranelagh.

'I don't really think I'm going to make it, Mama,' he confessed when he met her for tea at the Savoy. 'Even Tilden didn't get the championship at his first attempt. No, if I can get up as far as the quarter-finals, I'll feel I've done all that can be expected.'

His mother thought that it was a great deal more than could have been expected during his childhood. So ailing, so delicate – and now he was tall and bronzed and superbly fit. In college he had been a swimming champion, good enough to represent his university in national events. Only later was his ability as a tennis-player noticed – and Ellie-Rose wondered if it wasn't rather too late. True, William Tilden had begun to play seriously at an earlier age than Curt.

Not for the world would she have cast a shadow on Curt's hopes. And his little brother Bobby had no doubts. 'When you get the big cup, will you bring it home to the hotel so I can see it, Curt?'

'I don't think so, chicken. I don't think it's allowed off the premises.'

Bobby's thin face dropped in disappointment. 'Oh, I wanted to *breathe* on it . . .'

'What on earth for?'

'So I could write my name in the mist – then we'd have two of our family on the cup!'

'Mama,' laughed Curt, 'what do they teach this kid in school, eh?'

'They teach him to be a good boy and eat up his sandwich before he grabs at iced cakes,' his mother said, catching Bobby's hand as it was about to fasten on a little square of chocolate fondant. Bobby, frustrated, put the rest of the tiny sandwich in his mouth and swallowed it wholesale, giving himself hiccups. They were still trying to cure him with instructions to hold his breath and count to twenty or sip his tea from the wrong side of his cup, when Gina joined them.

All eyes in the River Room turned upon her as she crossed to their table and dropped into an armchair. She was looking superbly fashionable in a short dress of knit-silk jersey, sleeveless and with a wide collar of contrasting silk that stood away from her beautiful throat. Her neck was exposed in all its slender charm by her very close-cropped hair. At her ears she had big baroque pearls, and her louis-heeled shoes were pearl-coloured too. She carried a white soft hat, as small as a snowdrop bell.

'Whoever spread this rumour that English summers are cold?' she inquired, fanning herself with the hat. 'Any tea?'

'They're bringing fresh,' Curt said, having signalled to the hovering waiter. 'Well, sister mine, what have you bought today?'

Gina had joined them in London to see Curt play and do some shopping. She seemed to know more people than Ellie-Rose, though of a different calibre − theatre people, friends she had made during her short career as a Cochran girl.

Ellie-Rose was worried about her. She rarely mentioned Cliff. Ellie didn't quite understand why Gina had come alone to London − Cliff could easily have taken time off from the brokerage firm. Of course they were scheduled to go to Buenos Aires later in the year to stay with friends of Cliff's but even so − surely he could have spared two weeks or so to accompany his wife for this rather special occasion?

Ellie-Rose stifled a sigh. There seemed to be always something to worry about. Even Curt, whose health was now radiantly established, was a source of anxiety in a way. He was so goodlooking in his rugged, outdoor way − and so successful as an athlete − that girls fluttered round him like butterflies after nectar. As a result he was almost always off somewhere misbehaving − except when in training for a championship. Ellie-Rose dreaded the day when some irate father would come after Curt with a shotgun. It could happen − already some little co-ed from Dubuque had had to be given a large sum of money by Rob to enable her to marry a suitable young man as father for the child she claimed was Curt's.

Ellie-Rose looked at Bobby. What lay in store for him, the youngest of her brood, the Benjamin? At the moment he was a healthy, uncomplicated little boy, quick and intelligent but without any particular gift or aptitude. Her father was wondering whether they ought to send him away to boarding school soon, Granma Morag was arguing strongly against it. Ellie-Rose didn't want to part with him to the care of others, but John Martin told her she must be careful not to be too possessive. According to the Freudians, a possessive mother was one of the worst things that could happen to a boy.

Had life been easier when she was a girl? She tried to cast her mind back, but nothing clear emerged. She had been restless, bored, uncertain; she had married Curtis. Before that she had had a silly affair that almost ended in disaster. Was her life now less beset with problems? The chief of those, if she were to be honest, was John. Their love affair seemed to be a very hit-and-miss business. She loved him, he loved her, they spent half their time arguing and there was no thought of marriage for them. Where would it end? And, almost equally important, when? For a thing so uncertain would almost certainly falter to a halt one day.

She had been quite glad of the excuse to come to London and get away from John. He kept getting very angry these days about some bumptious politician in the land of his forebears, a character called Mussolini. This man's autobiography had been published the previous month – in Italian, which John could read and Ellie-Rose could not. All John had done for the past few weeks was complain about Benito Mussolini — and when she dared to say that her mother, living in Naples, spoke well of him, he lost his temper with her.

Distance might tell her whether she wanted to end the liaison once and for all. She wasn't a girl any more, for heaven's sake — she was the mother of a grown family. She didn't have to put up with the bad temper of a lover just because she was too young and inexperienced to handle him. No, when she got back to New York she might tell John Martin that he could concentrate all his attention on these bothersome *Fascisti* if he really wanted to . . .

That evening, as she was dressing for dinner in the hotel, Gina tapped at the door of her room. 'Can I come in?' she said, already closing the door behind her.

'Of course, darling.' Ellie-Rose watched her in the mirror. They had never been the kind of mother and daughter to have intimate little chats while changing. At the point when it might have been established as a practice, Ellie-Rose had been in London with Curtis, and then when she came home Gina had been going through her rebellious period.

So this visit must mean something important.

Gina picked up the hair band Ellie-Rose intended to wear and tried it on her own black crop. She took the stopper out of a scent bottle and tried a dab of Shocking on her wrist. Ellie chatted about Curt and his practice schedule, about Bobby's visit to the dinosaur in the Natural History museum. Meanwhile she waited to learn the real reason for the visit.

'Mama, may . . . may I ask you something very personal?'

Here it came at last. 'Of course, dear.'

'You and John are lovers, right?'

Ellie-Rose met her eyes in the mirror and smiled. 'Did you come to my room to ask *that*?'

'No, of course not – I knew all that – I just want to get the record straight before I ask . . . before I ask . . .'

'What, Gina?'

'When you make love, Mama – do you like it?'

Ellie-Rose managed not to let her mouth open in an 'Oh' of astonishment. Then she had to fight a wild impulse to laugh. Then, after all these struggles for calmness, she couldn't think of a thing to say.

'The reason I ask,' Gina said, going red with embarrassment, 'is that everybody's talking about how important sex is . . .'

'Not to me, they aren't,' Ellie-Rose murmured.

'No, well . . . You're a different generation, aren't you, Mother? But everywhere I go it always seems to be the big topic – Freud says this and Jung says that . . . It does seem to be accepted as the most important thing in life.'

'I suppose it does, if you go by psychologists.'

'You mean you don't?'

Ellie-Rose laid down her hairbrush and folded her hands in her lap. She took her time about replying.

'Gina,' she said, 'when I was in London during the War I saw people killed in front of my eyes. I saw poor people barely surviving on poor rations. I lost someone I dearly loved—'

'Oh yes – I know that—'

'Wait, let me finish. I'm not being fuddy-duddy when I say sex isn't the only thing that matters. To survive, to pick yourself up and go on – that's the most important thing. The Freudians would say that comes back to sex – the instinct to survive is just the

340

instinct to have sex and keep the race in being. Well, maybe so. But a lot of women who lost their men in the War are leading useful, rewarding lives — with no "sex" in them at all.' She paused. 'Does that answer your question?'

Gina sighed. 'Not really. I was thinking . . . as between a man and a woman . . .'

'You and Cliff, you mean.'

'Oh, Mama!' Gina burst out. 'I love Cliff, I really do! — but he and I . . . I don't know how to explain it . . . that was why I wanted to know about . . . about you and John.'

'I see. From what you hear all around you, you gather you and Cliff are not the ideal partnership.'

'That's it,' Gina said in a burst of grateful agreement. 'He . . . oh, God, it's awful having to talk about it . . . we just never seem to be on the same plane . . . I know it's my fault but I can't . . . seem to do anything about it.'

'Why on earth should it be your fault, darling?' Ellie-Rose said, and turned on the dressing-stool to hold out her hands to her daughter.

'Well, because . . . oh, it's so difficult to tell you . . . I hate all that kind of thing! Ever since I was a girl . . .'

'You were always a romantic little thing,' Ellie-Rose said, squeezing her hands affectionately. 'But life isn't really romantic—'

Gina snatched her hands away. 'Do you think you have to tell me that?' she cried, jumping up to walk restlessly about the room. 'Mama — when I was sixteen, I was forcibly made love to by a man I only met that once. It was . . . so ugly.'

'Gina!'

341

'It shocked me beyond anything I ever imagined. He was so . . . crude. Not brutal, just . . . oh, it was disgusting. He didn't care at all, it was just a way of getting relief from his urgencies. And I . . .'

'But you never told me this—'

'How could I? You were in London — it isn't the kind of thing you can put into a letter—'

'Oh, my God, Gina — I'm so sorry!'

She hurried to her daughter and put her arms around her. Gina submitted, but didn't melt into tears as perhaps Ellie-Rose expected.

'You'll laugh when I tell you, Mama, but I fended men off pretty successfully from then on. I just . . . couldn't bear the idea of what it would come to in the end if I let them get too affectionate. Then I met Cliff, and I thought, "With him it'll be different" . . .'

'And it is, isn't it?'

'It's different in that I know he cares about me. He's terribly unhappy when I don't . . . *respond* . . . Mama, it's ruining our marriage!'

'I can see that it might . . .'

'I wanted to ask you, you see. Am I so different? Is there something hopelessly wrong with me? It seems so unfair if that one experience so long ago has wrecked any chance of . . . you know . . .'

What was she to say? Ellie-Rose looked at the beautiful, unhappy face of her daughter and wondered if the Victorians had not been luckier — their expectations had been less, they didn't measure themselves against dictates from Viennese professors.

'I was wondering if I ought to go to a psycho-analyst,' Gina went on. 'But that seems so neurotic — and I'm not neurotic, Mama, really I'm not. It's just that other people keep on all the time about how important it is, so I suppose it must be. But if they weren't always talking about it I daresay I'd be sort of . . . reconciled.'

'Psycho-analysis,' Ellie-Rose murmured. 'If you feel it might help, I suppose there's no reason why not. But as I understand it, they try to unearth hidden reasons. And you *know* the reason.'

Gina shrugged. 'Sigmund Freud would say I'm hiding behind that. He'd say I had a father-complex or something.'

'Perhaps he would.' Ellie-Rose shook her head. 'I think it's just a matter of bad luck, if you ask me. You started off with a bad fright. If you had met someone like Cliff at the outset, you'd never have had any problem.'

'Mama, what am I going to do? I live in absolute dread of Cliff finding someone else who'd make him happy that way. A lot of my friends would grab him like a shot if he showed any inclination . . .'

'Don't worry about it, darling. That's my advice. Stop thinking you're making a hash of things.'

'Easier said than done,' muttered Gina, with a drooping grimace.

Poor child, thought Ellie-Rose, poor confused unhappy child . . . Where had she gone, that blithe little girl who used to dream about maidens in briar-girt towers and knights in shining armour? Her marriage was doomed.

But Gina's marriage didn't break up. When they got back to New York after the Wimbledon weeks, Cliff was waiting on the dock to welcome her with Cornelius and Bess. John Martin wasn't there — but Ellie-Rose hadn't expected him. Now that the election campaign had begun, John would be stumping the country with candidate Al Smith to report his speeches for his magazine. Political commentary was beginning to be an important factor on radio, and already John had made something of a name for himself with his pithy descriptions of the whistle-stop circus.

As everyone but the most starry-eyed 'radical' expected, Herbert Hoover stormed home in a great victory. Rob was pleased. He had had behind-the-scenes discussions with the programme-planners of the Hoover administration: a new department, under the control of his old friend Arthur Legge, would be given the task of 'preventing and controlling surpluses in any agricultural product'. A pleasant thought to Rob, when he considered the millions of tons of wheat he had in silo.

When, six months later, President Hoover actually appointed the Federal Farm Board, it was a considerable disappointment to Rob Craigallan. Its intention was to deal with future production. It specifically ruled out past production — in other words, anyone who had too much wheat or too many hogs or too large an output of milk in storage was not going to get a cent.

'Goddammit!' raged Rob when he read the preamble to the setting up of the new department. 'What did I put so much money into the funds for — to have the Republicans stab me in the back?'

'Now, now, Papa,' Cornelius said. 'It's bound to work in our favour even if we don't get anything for the grain in the barns. Future output is to be kept down by means of payment for untilled acreage. We can offset that against the wheat we can't sell — and we'll sell it one day.'

'It had better be soon. That grain is getting damned elderly! It'll have to go for stock fodder in the end.' He was gloomy about it. Prices for feedstuffs were lower by far than for human supplies.

By way of compensation for the money he felt he had lost over the new Farm Board's intentions, Rob began to turn his attention more seriously to the stock market. For nearly two years now, a 'bull' market had been in operation. Oh, sure there had been occasional checks, but that was all to the good. When the little old ladies in Hoboken got scared and sold their two hundred shares, men with an eye to the future could buy them up cheap − and then back roared the bull, adding value to each share, ten points, twenty points, money earned simply by standing still at the stockbroker's ticker-tape machine.

Early in September of 1929, the stock market broke. Rob watched it with a cool eye, did nothing, and bought on the morning of the 18th into the shares he liked best: American Telephone, Radio Corporation. On the 19th, next day, the prices of shares had soared to an all-time high. Gratified, Rob waited to see what would happen.

The following week there was something of a slide. Particular shares seemed to take a beating. Steel, for instance, lost a terrifying fifty-five points. But Rob had no money in steel worth speaking of, and the AT&T stood the panic well.

'Papa,' Cornelius said, having come to New York from Chicago on purpose to say it, 'don't you think things are getting damn jittery on Wall Street these days?'

'Sure. That's where the money is, Neil − where there's jitters. These picayune investors get the twitch very easy so that's when to pick up bargains.'

'But Papa, the Standard Statistics group are saying

their prediction is towards significantly lower levels—'

'Standard Statistics is run by a bunch of old women,' Rob replied. 'Besides, since when did I need a stock market advisory service? I've made money all my life on my own instincts, and I tell you that even if shares go down for a month or two, they'll recover well — and that's when I'm going to sell.'

Cornelius argued but was talked down. He went back to Chicago to handle problems over widespread deterioration of the grain in storage. On the morning of the 18th October he received in the mail a clipping from a newspaper sent by his father: Professor Irving Fisher, a highly respected business analyst, had made a speech to the Purchasing Agents Association predicting 'a permanently high plateau in stock prices'. 'If you want to read advisory reports, read this guy,' Rob had scribbled in the margin of the clipping.

There was nothing to do but put the clipping in the waste-basket and agree that in general the market always recovered. All the same, Cornelius got Bess to put through a call to Vinnison Charle, to ask whether his father was still in action on the exchange. 'Mr Charle says yes, though he's left only a general instruction.'

'Which is what?'

'To buy certain stocks any time they lose five points and come on the market in quantities worth buying.'

'I don't know, Bess,' Cornelius said to his wife. 'He's always right . . . But I'm getting worried.'

On Tuesday, October 22nd, the New York Stock Exchange seemed to have steadied itself. Cornelius, looking at the tape in the Chicago office, smiled a little to himself. That sly old possum . . . He always knew what he was about. Yet soon after midday, when Rob in Manhattan was about to go out to lunch with a business associate, his secretary fetched him back from the door.

'Mr Craigallan, have you seen the tape?'

He turned back. The usual snake of used paper had collected beneath the machine. It looked rather more than he expected but he picked up the loop and examined it. He drew in his breath. Activity on Wall Street was so intense that the tape was nearly two hours behind schedule in recording transactions! The operators simply couldn't keep up with the volume of trade – and this within only two hours?

Alarmed, Rob sat down at his desk again. He said to Miss Alleyn, his secretary, 'Call Gavin Selmer and say I'd like to cancel our lunch, will you? Ask him if he's looked at the tape.'

By close of trading at three o'clock, all the gains made in the early-morning recovery were gone. What was more, the out-of-office trading after the Exchange officially closed – what was known as the Curb Exchange – concentrated on selling.

Cornelius in Chicago asked Bess to ring Rob for him.

Ellie-Rose came to the phone at Craigallan Castle. 'Papa's staying at the Waldorf just at present,' she said. 'You know all this activity on the Stock Exchange . . . ?'

'Yes, Neil wants to know what Father-in-law is doing?'

'I've no idea, Bess – except that he's trading.'

'Buying or selling?' prompted Cornelius.

'Buying or selling?' Bess asked.

'I don't know, dear.'

Cornelius had Bess spend three hours trying to track down his father. He wasn't at the Waldorf, he wasn't at the office of Vinnison Charle, he wasn't at the Merchants' Club or the bankers. He wasn't at any of the usual places.

Bess, exhausted, begged Cornelius to call off the search. He hesitated. 'Bess, darling, you know I wouldn't make you stay here working at this if I could make the calls myself. But I can't use a telephone and I've *got* to find Papa.'

They went home to their apartment, however. From there Bess kept up the search. She got him on the telephone about eleven forty-five that evening at the Waldorf, whither he had just returned after a day closeted with a group of old friends who were planning to make the biggest killing on the stock market ever recorded.

'Father-in-law, Neil's been trying to reach you all day!'

'I can guess why, girlie. You tell him not to worry. Everything's fine.'

'Ask him if he's been selling,' Neil prompted.

'Selling on a falling market?' Rob replied when she relayed the query. 'He knows better than that!'

Cornelius seized the telephone from her. 'Papa,' he cried into the emptiness that was all he could sense there, 'don't buy any more! Something's gone wrong – this isn't going to be just a few days' dip.'

'Nonsense, boy,' Rob replied, then laughed. Of course, Cornelius couldn't hear a word of what he was saying. But it didn't matter. He and Cutten and Raskob knew what they were about. They'd been at it a long time – longer than Neil, who was getting cold feet like so many of the greenhorns.

When Bess took back the receiver it was to find that her father-in-law had hung up. 'Come on, Neil,' she urged, 'it's late. Let's forget it for the moment and get some rest.'

Cornelius looked at her. Her angular face was pale behind its freckles. There were shadows under her eyes. He put an arm around her. 'All right, honey. You go up. I'll be there in a minute.'

He sat for a moment after she'd gone then took out a sheet of paper. 'For God's sake come and talk sense to Papa,' he wrote. 'Market fever very high, cold logic needed.' He rang for Larry and asked him to take it to Western Union to send to Gregor. Only Gregor, he felt, could have enough influence with their father to bring him to his senses.

Gregor got the telegram two hours later as he was preparing to go to bed in his cool, airy house in the hills above San Francisco. He looked at it with incredulity. What had got into Neil? Quiet and level-headed, Neil wasn't likely to send signals asking for help unless it was serious. Gregor looked at the clock. In Chicago it would be the middle of the night now, and in New York the early hours of the morning. He'd leave it until after breakfast, then he'd ring and find out what was going on.

When he put through his phone call to Craigallan Agricultural next day, dealing had already been going on on Wall Street for four hours. There was a rush to liquidate stock that even Noah's Ark couldn't float on. Looking at the reports in his morning paper, Gregor had felt a pang of sudden anxiety. Yet his father was a shrewd old campaigner. He was of all men the most likely to have his Ark built and his animals aboard.

Bess had come to the Chicago office with Cornelius. She took Greg's call. 'Greg, we're really worried! Your father and some of his friends have made a plan to buy as the prices go down so as to make a killing when the upturn comes—'

'Well, that makes sense—'

'But Greg – have you seen the slide? I don't know how anything can recover if it goes on like this!'

'But it won't go on like that, Bess. You know the market always recovers.'

'Always?'

'Well, yes . . . In time . . .'

'Greg, Neil is telling me to beg you to come. No matter what you say, there's far too much money going into buying. If the recovery should take more than, say, three months, Craigallan Agricultural will have almost no capital during that time – and you know you can't deal for wheat on our scale without capital back-up.'

Greg thought quickly. 'All right,' he said, 'I'll come. I'll fix things so I can get away today and I'll be in New York as fast as I can.'

He rang home and asked Francesca to pack a bag for him. 'I have to get to New York within the next couple of days,' he said, 'and God knows what may be happening while I'm on the train trying to get there.'

'But *querido,*' Francesca protested, 'we have the Allandas coming to dinner tonight—'

'Put them off. Explain I've had to go to New York on family business.' He knew that would satisfy a Spanish-American couple.

'Is your father sick?'

'Sick? Depends what you mean by that. Let's just say he's got a kind of fever that's going around at the moment.'

He told his secretary to book a berth for him on the New York train. 'The flyer?' she inquired. He was about to say, 'Yes, the flyer,' meaning the express train. Then he paused. If you wanted to get to New York fast, what was the best way to do it?

By aeroplane.

There was a coast to coast service, mostly used for the mail. But passengers could use it, and it certainly cut down travelling time. The plane had to stop several times to refuel, but even so it got you from San Francisco to New York in about twenty hours. He looked at his watch. It was eleven in the morning. He could be in New York, allowing for the time difference, by about noon next day.

When he collected his valise from Francesca and told her his plan, he thought she was going to faint. 'My darling,' she said, throwing her arms about him, 'don't do this! God never meant men to fly through the air—'

'Sweetheart, God didn't mean men to thunder along iron rails either. And it will save me more than two days in travel time—'

'What can it matter if it takes you two more days? Nothing can be so serious in mere business—'

'I think it can, Frannie. Neil is really worried.'

'Then speak to Neil long-distance—' She broke off, remembering that Neil could not use the telephone. 'Ring your father,' she said, starting again. 'If it is he who is causing you anxiety, you can deal with it—'

'I can't get hold of him, sweetheart. That's the whole point! He's holed up somewhere with a gang of cronies, planning to corner the market at a strategic point in the slide — and though he may be right, he could be so wrong that it will wipe him out!'

'Don't go, *amado mio*,' Francesca said, tears in her eyes. 'Don't, don't! You put yourself in danger for mere money!'

'There's no danger, Francesca. And the money isn't exactly "mere".'

There was no help for it. She could see he was determined, and she came from a background where the will of the man is accepted as dominant. She bowed her head and brushed away incipient tears against his shoulder. 'Very well, Gregorio. Go with God.'

He reached New York in time to see the newspaper placards of mid-afternoon Thursday: *Market Dives*. He bought a copy of the *Daily News* and was shocked at the tone of the report. The words leapt off the page at him: 'A torrent of selling . . . Brokers overwhelmed . . . Stampede . . .'

Gregor took a taxi to the offices of Vinnison Charle and Company. There Arnold Charle, son of the William Charle with whom Rob Craigallan had first done business, shook his head at Gregor's inquiry. 'I don't know where he is, Greg. He telephones special instructions.'

'What instructions have you been getting this afternoon?'

'Nothing. The last was about one o'clock − to hold on everything.'

'So are you telling me my father has a big investment in stock that's just lost about three-quarters of its value?'

'Yes. But,' said Arnold, running a hand over his wan face, 'he has always taken the view that the market will recover as it has done before.'

'From this?' Gregor asked, looking at the carpet of ticker-tape on the floor of the office.

'I don't know, Greg. I've never seen anything like it before.'

Greg made for the Waldorf. But the suite was

352

unoccupied, and when he rang Ellie-Rose she told him their father hadn't been there in over a week. Later in the day the news came through that the big New York banks, led by J. P. Morgan and Company, were putting in two hundred and forty million dollars between them to shore up the stock market. They intended to buy to that extent on the market next day, dealing in the leading securities so as to restore confidence.

Gregor could almost hear his father's voice murmuring in his ear: 'Y'see, boy? All you have to do is use what's there! You can always make money dealing!'

But the man himself proved elusive. Although Gregor went to every place where his father liked to spend time, he was nowhere to be found.

Rob Craigallan walked into the offices of Craigallan Agricultural Products in Chicago at nine-thirty the following morning. His son Cornelius leaped up at the sight of him. 'Good God, Papa! What are you doing in Chicago? I thought you were in New York!'

'No, no, that is all well in hand, Neil. The recovery is on the way − I had it from Wiggin of the Chase National Bank last night. So now I'm going to follow on with the biggest bull corner in the history of the Board of Trade − I'm going to show The Pit how to make money!'

'Listen, Papa—'

'No, come on, boy − the market will still be in a dither after what happened in New York yesterday. Let's go and buy it up!'

Cornelius had had almost no sleep for three days. His father's cloak-and-dagger behaviour had driven him almost to the verge of a nervous breakdown. Now here was Rob Craigallan, fresh-faced and confident, sure he knew what he was doing while the rest of the world seemed to be crumbling about him.

Cornelius was still trying to put some words together to express his anxieties when Rob led the way out of the office. There was nothing for it but to go with him. They took a cab to the Board of Trade which was already whirling with activity. Prices of commodities, always vulnerable, were in a state of earthquake after the share slide on Wall Street.

Rob didn't go into The Pit himself. He stayed in the little office in the lobby where Vinnison Charle still did most of their business. He sent instructions to the clerk on the floor, via the dealers' messengers, and heard the results from them as the brokers examined the little dealer's notes they brought back.

Rob was watching the clock. The upturn on the New York Exchange, brought about by the injection of money from the six big banks, must soon take place. The minute it did, grain prices would start to go up. And the minute that happened, Rob Craigallan was going to be worth twice as much money as before. He would have carried through the biggest bull profit in the history of the Chicago Exchange.

But the upturn in New York didn't happen. Prices held, but didn't rise, on Wall Street. The grain price in Chicago continued to go down. Rob was surprised but not worried. There was still Saturday's dealing to work with. He had – on paper – lost money. But tomorrow the loss would be turned into a gain as the money from the big banks worked through the system.

On Saturday he was just a little bit more anxious, so much so that he went down to the edge of The Pit to watch the dealing. Nothing much happened. Dealing was slack. Everyone seemed to be watching and waiting.

Gregor had come on from New York, having been summoned by Bess. He and Cornelius spent Sunday trying to argue their father out of his plan. 'Don't you see, Papa,' Cornelius urged, 'the whole thing depends on your information about the New York banks and the effect it will have on the market. What if it doesn't bring about the upturn?'

'Don't be silly, Neil. Of course it will. Don't you think the banks know what they're doing? Tell him, Greg.'

Greg pursed his lips. Although he had an enormous respect for Rob's instinct, something was telling him that for once the instinct had led his father astray. 'I don't know, Mr Craig,' he said. 'Two hundred and forty millions sounds like an awful lot of money to inject, but have you seen the analysis in the *Times*? They estimate four times that amount of money has changed hands in the dealing—'

'So what? It doesn't matter how much money changes hands so long as confidence is restored and the money goes back to the market in the end. That's the secret.'

Monday came, and Rob Craigallan with his two sons went to the Chicago Exchange. Today was the day. After a weekend spent thinking over what fools they'd made of themselves, the investors would go back to Wall Street and start buying the shares now being offered at rockbottom prices. Wheat would reflect the return of confidence. Rob would see his purchases of Friday turn into a fortune.

It didn't happen. The losses registered in New York were astronomical. The prices at which the bankers' money had steadied the stocks were broken through the minute the trading began Monday morning. In

Chicago, commodities were dragged down to new low levels and everybody was trying to sell before they went lower.

When the clock ticked round to register the end of trading in The Pit, wheat had halved in price. Rob Craigallan had lost every cent he had invested on Friday. And what was more: he had not the money to pay for the buys he had made, because the bottom had dropped out of the New York Stock Exchange so that the stocks he had expected to use as capital were worthless.

The dealers rushed away from the Chicago *bourse* in desperation to get to their own offices and learn what was happening in Wall Street. Only Rob Craigallan lingered in the office of his broker with his sons. The office staff looked at them in perplexity. They were anxious to lock up and get home, to try to recover from the repeated body-blows of the day's trade and to listen to the news of worse things on the radio.

'Come on, Papa,' Neil said. His flat voice seemed appropriate to the occasion – unemotional, cold.

'Where?' muttered Rob.

'We'll go home. Bess will have a meal ready.'

'Yes. Just a minute. I think I . . . I'd like a drink.'

Greg looked at the chief clerk. He fetched the whisky decanter from the inner office and poured some into a glass. Rob reached out his hand for it but as he was about to take it, it seemed as if his fingers wouldn't close. The glass went down on the floor, to spill its amber contents on the mounds of paper and tape that told of the day's tempestuous dealings.

'Come on, Mr Craig,' Greg said. 'We'll have a drink at Neil's—'

Rob nodded and got to his feet. And then, with a

slight shake of his head, he staggered and went over on his side. The chair in which he'd been sitting broke his fall. He hit the ground among the discarded dealing slips and ticker-tape.

'Papa!' croaked Neil, and got down beside him.

The chair rolled away. Rob turned on his back. His head was thrown back, one side of his face distorted under the silky beard.

The clerk gave a cry of alarm. Neil put his hand to his father's neck. There was no pulse.

'Mr Craig!' Greg urged, and tried to help him to his feet with an arm under his shoulders.

Neil stayed his action. They looked at each other. Neil shook his head.

The end, the real end, of the day's trading had come.

Chapter Twenty

Cliff Gramm had been trying to reach Rob Craigallan all through Monday. Gina had no idea why it was so important to her husband but she could see it mattered a lot because, although he'd been home from the Exchange for five hours, he was still looking up phone numbers in his address book.

When the phone rang and her Uncle Greg said: 'Gina? I've something to tell you about Grandfather Craigallan—' she interrupted with a cry of surprise.

'Oh, Greg! Is he there? Cliff s been looking for him. I'll just fetch—'

'No, Gina! Wait!'

'What's the matter?'

'Your grandfather's dead, Gina.'

A finger of cold touched her in some vital innermost spot. The receiver began to slip from her fingers. She made a sound that brought Cliff hurrying to her. He caught the receiver, helped her to a chair. When he saw her safely into it, he said into the phone: 'What the hell's going on? Who's there?'

'It's me, Greg . . . I just told Gina – Mr Craig died.'

'What?'

'About two hours ago. A thrombosis, the doctor says.'

'But . . . but . . . that's impossible! He's the health-
iest, fittest—'

'He had a big shock. It finished him.'

'My God,' murmured Cliff. He looked at his wife,
was relieved to see the colour coming back into her
cheeks.

'How's Gina? What happened?'

'It hit her kind of hard.'

'Yes, her mother took it badly too. Listen, Cliff —
will you take Gina out to the Castle? They might be
some kind of comfort to each other.'

'Sure, I'll . . .' Cliff gathered himself together. In
the midst of this awful tragedy, there was no use
forgetting his own needs. 'Say, Greg — I know this is
an awful time to be thinking of myself, but . . . I've
been looking for Craigallan all day, I wanted to ask
him . . .'

'What?'

'I need some money, Greg. I need it by tomorrow or
our firm's down the chute.'

There was a silence from the other end.

'Greg?' Cliff ventured. 'He would have given it to
me, I know. Are you his executor? Or Neil?'

'We haven't gone into that. The thing is — there
won't be much to stand executor for.'

'What d'you mean, Greg?' Cliff cried. 'Rob Craigallan is — was — worth maybe forty-one million dollars.'

'That was until last week. He decided to play the
market for the bull upturn he thought was coming, and
had it cut down to a quarter of its value by Friday.'

'*What?*'

'And then, certain that the bankers' guarantee would
send it all soaring again, he used it as collateral for the
irresistible deal to any wheatie — the bull market to end

all bull markets on the Chicago *bourse.*'

'But . . . he couldn't − you wouldn't have let him!'

'How could we stop him? We tried everything short of binding and gagging him. The discovery he'd got it all wrong killed him.'

'Greg . . .'

'I'm sorry, Cliff. No matter if you wanted to borrow a hundred bucks even, I don't think we have it.'

'But it can't *all* be gone?'

'Want to bet?'

'Oh, God,' said Cliff. 'Oh, God.'

When he had taken Gina to stay with Ellie-Rose at Craigallan Castle he drove to his father's house on Riverside Drive. Ronald Gramm had been working as hard as his son, trying desperately to raise three-quarters of a million by opening of trading the next day, without which they would be deemed insolvent. One look at his father's face told him he'd had no success.

'I thought sure to get it from Gina's grandfather,' he told him. 'But . . . he died earlier today.'

'*Died?*'

'From shock after losing every cent.'

'Craigallan *lost* his money?'

'So Greg McGarth says. I believe him − it was in his voice.'

Ronald Gramm had been drinking steadily all evening but was not a whit the better for it. He leaned back in his chair and closed his red-rimmed eyes for a moment. 'Well, son,' he said at length, 'your mother owns that little stud farm in Maryland. I reckon the time's come for the two of us to go raise horses and see if we can make a living at it.'

'Won't we be able to save anything, Dad?'

'Worse than that. We'll be in debt. There are clients who'll never be able to settle what they owe us. We've ruined them and they've ruined us . . . No, it's all over, Cliff. Sorry.'

Cliff was a conventional, honourable, hardworking young man. He tried to keep his anxieties from Gina. But in a time when everyone was in near-despair over money, she guessed his secret.

'Oh, darling, don't worry about it,' she begged. 'It'll be all right — you'll see. Things can only get better.'

She gathered him in her arms and comforted him with an almost maternal gentleness. At night they went to bed and made love with a depth and passion they had never known before. Cliff had often felt that he failed Gina somehow — that he didn't bring to her some wonder or joy that she had expected. But now that was over; they were together in this time of ruin — it was as if a rose blossomed among the wreckage, a fragile flower among the thorns.

All at once everything that had worried Gina seemed foolish and juvenile. Facing reality — a harsher reality than any she had ever known — she discovered what was truly important. Cliff needed her. Nothing else mattered. Whether their love-making lived up to standards discussed by her sophisticated friends was unimportant. All that was important was to give comfort and release to her darling.

They would lie with their arms twined about each other, he silent, she murmuring soothing words. She told him everything would be all right. She told him it didn't matter if they were poor. Money wasn't essential. They were both young and healthy. They would get work. She could go back to the theatre. He would find a job.

'Everything's all right, Cliff. We'll manage.'

He nodded and said nothing. He thought of her as he had always known her — exquisitely beautiful, gowned and groomed to perfection. She had been born to money, was accustomed to it. How could she possibly handle the world as it would be in the future? No servants, no credit accounts, no smart parties, no apartment in Park Avenue. No automobile, perhaps. How would Gina acclimatise to the subway and the streetcar? How would she cope with the hardships of life in a walk-up apartment?

As to getting a job . . . As day succeeded day, he began to see it was impossible. His qualifications were in brokerage. The stock-broking business was in ruins. The brokerage firms that survived were cutting down staff to the bone. His own family had nothing — no money, no offices, no prospects. His father and mother were eking out a living on the horse-farm in Maryland — unlikely to do well for years because the moneyed families who bought horses were just as hard hit as the Gramm family.

Cliff was in a daze of despair, only lightened when he and his wife turned to each other in love at night. He was so grateful to her for the intervals of peace she gave him that she became something like a goddess to him. His failure cut at him more keenly every time he remembered that the only reward he could give her was to share his new poverty with him.

One night he drank the best part of a bottle of whisky then went out for a drive on the cliffs along the East River. His car was going so fast when it broke through the guard rail that he knew he'd be dead when he hit the rocks below. He left behind him a widow with an annual income from his insurance policy that would always keep her from starving.

When you have been rich and fortunate then suddenly become poor and unhappy, it's little comfort to know that thousands of others are in the same case. Yet the crash of the Craigallan fortune was scarcely noticed in the general ruin. The loss of the money was awful enough but Gina's widowhood was followed by other miseries. Curt, having been building up towards a Wimbledon attempt for 1930, had to abandon his hopes. Moreover, the girl he had begun to think of seriously was whisked away by her parents when he told them his only source of income would be the salary from his job as physical training instructor at a boys' school in New Hampshire.

The plan to send Bobby to prep school had to be abandoned. The fees were now beyond Ellie-Rose's capability. Her income ceased with the loss of dividends when Rob's estate was dissolved.

Craigallan Agricultural Products was bought as a going concern by Dombrowsky and Laver, but the purchase price was ploughed into the paying-off of the Stock Exchange debts.

Rob's legal wife Luisa arrived in a panic from Italy about a month after his death. The family were holding a council of war at Craigallan Castle, trying to decide what to do for the best. Morag was there, looking suddenly old and frail. When Luisa saw her she drew up to her full height and prepared to oust her once and for all.

'*I* am the owner of this house now,' she declared, 'and I want that woman out, do you understand? Out!'

Cornelius, who had risen to greet her, pulled back. He couldn't hear the venom in her tone, but the words came across to him as clearly as a shout. 'Mama!' he said, shocked.

'Don't "Mama" me! That woman has usurped my place all my life – I want her out of my house.'

Gregor stepped forward from the far side of the big room. 'Mrs Craigallan,' he said, 'apart from the fact that this isn't the time for petty rivalries—'

'Petty? When she's made my life a misery? Let me tell you—'

'No, let *me* tell *you*,' he interrupted. 'This house isn't yours. It belongs with the estate, and the estate is in escrow until all debts have been settled.'

'Escrow? Escrow? What does that mean, for God's sake?' Luisa cried. 'I don't understand legal gobbledy-gook. All I know is that I inherit from Robert Craigallan – that's the law, a wife can't be cut out of her husband's will, and the house is one of the things that can't be taken from her. So this is my house—'

'So you inherit, do you, Mama?' Ellie-Rose said. She had not risen to offer kisses, and now sat up straight looking at her mother with a cold gaze. 'All right then – I'll tell you what you inherit. Debts. Nothing but debts.'

Luisa, rather too hot in a two-piece costume of red marocain trimmed with sable at scarf and cuffs, felt an additional perspiration break out under her cloche hat. 'Debts?' she faltered.

'There isn't any money, Mama. And the house is up for sale.'

'But . . . you can't . . . I won't allow . . . You didn't tell me?'

'I wrote to you, Mama,' Cornelius said. 'The letter probably crossed you on your way here.'

'I don't believe it!' Luisa shouted. She looked from

one to the other. They were all there – her son and his wife, her daughter with her three children, the hated bastard son and his mother and his foreign-looking wife. They all looked back at Luisa. And there was no affection in any pair of eyes.

Luisa felt a strange bubble rising inside her. It was a mixture of hatred and laughter. 'There must be some money!' she shouted. 'I haven't waited all this time to come back to nothing!'

'There's no money, Mama,' Cornelius said.

'But when you sell the house – why, some of the paintings—'

'Papa left most of the works of art to public galleries. And even if they were available, the money would still have to go into the estate.'

'Cornelius, have you consulted a good lawyer?'

Her son stared at her and then shook his head. 'A good lawyer?' he repeated. 'Don't you understand? We could consult Oliver Wendell Holmes and it would make no difference. *There is no money.*'

And all at once it happened. The bubble inside Luisa burst. She began to scream with laughter. 'Oh, it's wonderful!' she cried. 'He was so clever, wasn't he? He despised me, didn't he? So much cleverer than me, so much brighter and keener! And what happens? He ends up a pauper, just like he began! Oh, it's rich, it's rich!' She flung out an arm towards Morag. 'That's the one he always loved! And she can have him now – oh, yes, he's all hers if she wants him! Dead and a pauper, in a pauper's grave! God, how I hated him! And I hate him still, I hate him, I hate him, do you understand? For he's beaten me still – he's beaten me, he's left me poor! God damn him, I hope he's in hell where he belongs!'

She sank down on the floor and beat the ground with her fists. Her grandson Bobby shrank away behind Ellie-Rose and hid his face in her shoulder as if he were an infant instead of a big eleven-year-old. The grown men stood staring at her in horror.

Only Morag made a move. She rose with weariness from her chair. She went to the side of the other woman and captured the beating fists. 'Luisa,' she said, 'Luisa . . . Don't you understand, none of that matters now.'

'It matters to me,' raged Luisa. 'It matters to *me*!'

'Help me, Ellie,' Morag said.

Unwillingly, Ellie-Rose got to her feet and joined Morag. They helped her mother to her feet and led her out. The others could hear her sobbing and laughing as they led her upstairs to lie down.

Gina was the first to speak. 'What's going to happen to her?' she asked. 'She's got to have some kind of income.'

Her Uncle Cornelius sighed. 'I don't know how. There won't be ten cents to rub together when I get the wreckage sorted out.'

'We'll manage something,' Greg said.

'Oh, but, Uncle Greg . . . she's hardly your responsibility.'

'We can't let her starve. He wouldn't have wanted that. He never let her want for anything while he was alive, Gina.'

'No, but . . .' Gina fell silent. She thought of Cliff. Had he thought his death was a final act of responsibility? Grandfather had felt the same responsibility for Luisa. It could not be argued against.

They broke off their consultation to have dinner. The servants were still with them, serving out their notice and unwilling to go because, in these hard times, where else were they to get a roof over their heads? Food was simple, however — the merchants had cut off credit the minute the financial situation became clear. The Craigallan clan sat down to cold meat and salad and ice-cream at a table which had seen roast peacock, sturgeon, and *pêche à la royale*.

The women withdrew at the end of the meal to let the men have a chance to speak in private. Curt, subdued these days, had little to contribute except to insist he wouldn't be a burden to anyone. 'I've got a job,' he said. 'Don't bother about me.'

'Neil,' Greg said, touching his half-brother on the arm to make sure he was facing him. 'How long do you think the rest of the clearing-up will take?'

'Dunno. Another two months, perhaps?'

'And what then? What are your plans?'

'The University of Wichita has offered me a two-year research programme into wheat kernel disease. It's on behalf of the Government of Persia — they're trying to find a way to grow durum red out there.'

'Are you going to take it?'

'Well, it's the best I've been offered. And something else might turn up before the two years are over.' He hesitated. 'I'm not a kid, you know, Greg. I have to take what I can get. I've got Bess to think of.'

'I wanted to offer you something, Neil. Out in California.'

'Oh, no — you're doing enough already.' Greg had already agreed to take Ellie-Rose and Bobby, and Gina too if she wanted to go. By implication he had said he would make some arrangement for Luisa. Neil felt he couldn't impose on his half-brother.

'This is a business proposition. You know that land I

showed you when you came out for Easter last year?'

'The orange valley? Yes, I remember.'

'I wondered if you'd like to come out and manage it for me.'

'Me?' Neil said in astonishment. 'My speciality is wheat! I don't know a thing about oranges.'

'You could learn, Neil.'

'Well, I . . .'

'Listen, I bought that land as a sort of pledge to the local people that I was serious about joining their community. I never thought of doing much with it. It was kind of a . . . a place to retire to when Frannie and I are old, and to leave to the kids when we're gone. But the way things are now . . .'

'Yes?'

'I can't afford to let it just lie. It's got to pay its way.'

'Who handles it now?'

'You met him — Jose Entonche. There isn't his equal in the district for quickness and neatness in gathering and packing. But he speaks English quite poorly and doesn't read it at all. I don't think he's ever going to be able to introduce the new methods of culture — and he'd be the first to admit it.'

'But would he submit to a stranger coming along and giving him orders? A man who doesn't know anything about orange trees?'

'That would be for you to handle. You always seemed to manage well enough with staff problems at CAP. I think you could cut it, Neil. And I wish you would. I need someone I can trust to get on with it while I try and handle the depression that's beginning to grab the food-producing parts of the country.'

'Mmm . . .' said Cornelius. 'I'd have to ask Bess . . .'

'Don't you think she'd prefer it to Wichita?'

Neil laughed. 'She might, at that!'

The auction of the contents of Craigallan Castle was to take place at the end of that week. Next day the men came in to label and arrange the items in lots according to the sales catalogue. Luisa had hysterics again when she saw them at work and had to be taken away to Gina's Manhattan apartment.

Luisa, who had only visited her here once, walked through the spacious rooms with approval. 'You know, Gina, I'd be quite happy to move in here with you on a permanent basis. There's sure to be *some* money coming to me from the will, no matter what the menfolk may say. I can't really be penniless!'

'I think you must face the fact that there really won't be any money,' Gina insisted. 'And as to living here — I shan't be able to afford it myself after another four weeks.'

'But Cliff must have left you enough?'

'No, Grandmama. Really. I don't think you understand. Thousands of people have been ruined. There just isn't any money.'

'Humph,' Luisa said, shaking her head and looking annoyed. 'Well, I can tell you this! If I'm going to starve, I'd rather do it in a warm sunny climate—'

'You mean California?' Gina was surprised. She'd have thought that not even starvation would have reconciled her grandmother to being dependent on Gregor McGarth.

'California? Are you mad? Out at the back of beyond with a bunch of Spanish peasants? I'm talking about Italy, my dear. Italy — where there's sunshine and good wine and people who know how to enjoy life . . .'

'Well, perhaps by and by Uncle Greg and Uncle Cornelius will be able to get together enough to make Italy possible.'

'Will they indeed . . . We'll see.'

She solved the problem for herself. Her jewellery, which didn't belong to the Craigallan estate, was sold for a good price and replaced by handsome paste replicas. With the money she bought herself a one-way ticket on the *Mauretania*. She summoned her two children, Cornelius and Ellie-Rose, to Gina's apartment to say goodbye. 'I shan't be coming back,' she said, 'and since we're now in the church-mouse category, I imagine you won't be coming to visit me. So, this is the last time we'll be seeing each other. We'll write, of course.'

'Of course,' said Ellie-Rose, baffled by the speed with which her mother had made her decision.

'Goodbye, Neil,' Luisa said, offering him her hand. Even over a last farewell, she couldn't bring herself to kiss him. He had always seemed to her alien, 'other' — the handicap of deafness had cut him off from her with a completeness she didn't regret.

'Goodbye, Mama.'

'Goodbye, Ellie.'

'Goodbye, Mama.' They kissed tepidly.

On the way down in the elevator after the farewell Ellie-Rose touched her brother on the arm. 'Neil, I bet she's sorry she wasted the money on coming home in the first place.'

He nodded. 'It's strange, isn't it? I've no feeling of loss . . .'

'No. Whereas if Morag went away . . . ?'

'Poor Morag. I wonder if she'll like California?'

When the plan was discussed in front of Morag, she

never made any adverse comment. She accepted the decisions of others with a kind of passive gratitude. The death of Rob Craigallan had changed her — it was clear to anyone who knew her. She looked older, more tired and thin. Now and again, when friends offered sympathy, she would rouse herself: 'But I'm so lucky compared with others! I've still got my son. I'm going to live with him, start a new life . . .'

But she didn't look forward to it. Even Greg himself knew that. It would be years before she looked forward to anything with any expectation of enjoyment, now that Rob had been taken from her. The one utterance that gave a clue to her feelings had come after Rob's funeral. 'I never thought,' she said to her son, 'that I would outlive him. I used to wonder how he would manage when I died . . . I never imagined I'd have to wonder how *I* shall manage.'

'It will be all right, Mother,' Gregor said. 'You'll like Monterey.'

'Yes, dear. Thank you.'

Something in her voice hinted that she didn't expect to outlive Rob for very long. Gregor put a protective arm about her black-clad shoulders. He would *make* her want to live! Once she was in his home, with her grandchildren, he would make her enjoy life again, no matter how unlikely that seemed to her now.

Ellie-Rose had made her own decisions. She said: 'I've decided not to go, Greg.'

'I beg your pardon?'

'I've decided to stay on the East Coast, not to move out to California.'

'Not go? But . . . Ellie . . .'

'I know, it seems foolish. But my mother gave me the idea. I have jewellery I can sell, too, Greg. And with the money, if I'm careful, I ought to be able to manage. I might get a job.'

'Doing what?' Greg said with understandable scepticism.

'Oh, I don't know. Helping in Neil's charity – even though he and Bess are going to the West Coast, his recommendation ought to carry some weight. And I can speak to deaf people, I can use the sign language – you know I'm adept, Greg.'

'Yes, but most of the workers are volunteers. The pay's awfully poor, really.'

'That wouldn't matter.'

'Ellie, wouldn't you be better off with us?'

She was silent a moment. Then she said, 'I don't want to leave John.'

'But . . . that's always been a very on-again-off-again thing.'

'When I think about leaving him, I just . . . I just don't want to. I'm not a girl any more, Greg. I know how to value affection. I don't want to throw away what John and I have.'

'But what about John? Didn't I hear his magazine had folded?' In the midst of the maelstrom of misfortune, it was difficult even for Greg to keep up with every point.

She nodded. 'Who wants to read a magazine telling us it was all our own fault?' She gave a little laugh. 'That's typical of John Martin, though – never knows when to hold his tongue.'

'You and he – you're not thinking of getting married?'

Ellie-Rose ran a hand through her short hair. It was no longer exquisitely cut, yet somehow it was still becoming. 'He's never asked me. Perhaps he never will.

But I want to stick around, Greg.'

'But what about Bobby?' Greg asked. He had thought his half-sister would jump at the chance of taking her son to the sunshine of California.

She hesitated then shrugged. 'He'll make out,' she said. 'I thought about asking you to take him without me – your mother would look after him, I know. But . . . it's better for him not to be parted from me when all the rest of the world is coming to pieces. I'll get a little apartment, perhaps even a room or two – we'll manage. I want to thank you, though, Greg, for offering to take us. You've turned out to be the anchor of the whole family.'

Her half-brother put a hand on hers. 'I hope things work out for you, Ellie, I really do.'

When she told John Martin her decision, he surprised her by gathering her roughly into his arms. 'Well done, girl,' he said. 'I didn't want to make life difficult by begging you to stay, but . . . I'm sure glad you chose this way.'

'Oh, you fool, why didn't you say something?' she cried, hitting his chest with her fists. 'I thought you didn't care one way or the other!'

'Don't be dumb. You know I love you.'

'Do you, John?'

'Sure I do. I was miserable as hell at the thought of losing you.' He hesitated. 'What d'you think about getting married?'

'Married? To you?'

'To who else, for God's sake? I wouldn't suggest you getting married to Jack Dempsey.' He looked at her. 'What about it, Ellie?'

'But . . . do you really want to, John?'

'Seems kind of a good idea. We're not getting any

younger and times are hard. We could snuggle up together and keep each other warm.'

'Oh, John.' She sighed. 'You're so romantic.'

'Listen, dearie, you're broke and I've got a new job as a radio commentator, pays peanuts. It's no time for romantic notions of champagne and violins. But I love you and you love me—'

'But you never talked about marriage before.'

'You were a rich capitalist's widow and I had principles. Now you're just a broke lady, and I'm a guy with an apartment in Queen's that we could share. What d'you say?'

He was grinning. She said severely, 'Don't look so sure of yourself, you vain Italian *paisano*! I'm not sure I want to be married to you.'

'Suit yourself. I *know* I want to be married to you. And I can wait till you change your mind. Us Italian *paisanos* are famous for that kind of thing.'

The following Monday, after having been open to public view over the Friday, Saturday and Sunday, the contents of Craigallan Castle were put up for sale. Of the family only Cornelius and Bess turned up to see what happened. Greg had had to go back to his post in San Francisco, taking his wife and Gina with him. Ellie-Rose was surveying John Martin's apartment with a view to doing some repainting. Curt had gone to look for a room near the school in New Hampshire. So these two alone appeared to see the familiar belongings go under the hammer.

To Bess it had a macabre kind of interest. But for Cornelius it was utterly depressing. This house and its contents had been the outward sign of success to his father, Robert Craigallan. To have it scattered to the four winds seemed to nullify his father's very existence.

374

Bess, sensing his mood, took his hand and led him out into the gardens of the Castle, already neglected, already returning to the wilderness from which Rob had formed them. Intending purchasers — and sightseers — were strolling about prodding the garden furniture. The weather was hot and still — a typical August day in New York.

Bess drew her husband to a seat under an old maple. 'Neil,' she said, touching him on the arm in the way that meant: 'Look at me . . .'

He turned.

'I've got something to tell you,' she said. 'Under the circumstances I don't know whether it's good or bad.'

He frowned. 'What do you mean?'

'I'm going to have a baby, darling.'

He peered at her in the shade of the tree. He was afraid he had mistaken the words her lips were forming. A baby? The longed-for blessing, always denied to them so far. They had even, until the Wall Street Crash, discussed adopting.

'A baby,' Bess said, distinctly, and made the rocking motion that sketched it for deaf people.

'Bess!'

'Are you pleased?'

'Oh! Bess! I'm—' Words deserted him. He found to his horror that tears had come into his eyes. After all the misery of the past few months, was Fate actually relenting? 'It's wonderful,' he said.

'It presents problems. I'm not an ideal age to be having a first baby, darling. Mid-thirties is pretty late to start. But I want it. I want to give you a son.'

He leaned forward and kissed her freckled forehead. 'Bess,' he said in his strange, flat voice, 'you're so wonderful. I was just thinking — my father's gone . . .

he'll be a Craigallan, you see? He'll bear his name.'

Bess took his hand and pressed it to her cheek. And if it's a girl, she thought, we'll love her just the same. She'll be Neil's child. Darling, dearest Neil.

Into her mind came words spoken by Morag before she left with Greg for the West Coast. 'We're back where we began,' she said, 'looking to the land to give us a living.'

Out there, Bess and Neil would soon join her. They would start again, and the baby would be part of the new life. It was not the life she had expected when Neil first asked her to marry him, but they were together — that was what mattered, nothing else.

A young couple, exploring the hitherto forbidden terrain of Rob Craigallan's grounds, noticed a pair sitting hand in hand on the marble bench, lost in a dream. Probably wishing they could have afforded to live in a place like this, they decided.

But Neil and Bess were not wishing anything like that. They were looking ahead to California, bracing themselves to work for their future, and the future of their child.

A PROFESSIONAL WOMAN

**An epic novel of love and
war, ambition and sacrifice**

Tessa Barclay

'Always spins a fine yarn' Wendy Craig

In 1906, bright, beautiful and sweet sixteen, Christina
Holt is banished from her family because of her
determination to study medicine in defiance of their
wishes. But, once Christina has achieved her aim, all
does not go smoothly and a starry-eyed love affair
leaves her pregnant by a fellow student whom she can
never marry. Heartbroken, Christina must give up her
baby son for adoption.

This won't be the last sacrifice she has to make for her
career - nor the last challenge to her fighting spirit.
Soon after she qualifies as a doctor, the outbreak of the
Great War impels Christina to join the Women's
Service Hospital - a decision that will bring both
professional success and personal tragedy...

**A WEB OF DREAMS
BROKEN THREADS**
'Just what a historical novel ought to be' Elizabeth Longford
'Filled with fascinating historical detail and teeming with
human passions' Marie Joseph
and THE FINAL PATTERN,
are also available from Headline

FICTION/SAGA   0 7472 3552 X

A selection of bestsellers from Headline

THE LADYKILLER	Martina Cole	£5.99 ☐
JESSICA'S GIRL	Josephine Cox	£5.99 ☐
NICE GIRLS	Claudia Crawford	£4.99 ☐
HER HUNGRY HEART	Roberta Latow	£5.99 ☐
FLOOD WATER	Peter Ling	£4.99 ☐
THE OTHER MOTHER	Seth Margolis	£4.99 ☐
ACT OF PASSION	Rosalind Miles	£4.99 ☐
A NEST OF SINGING BIRDS	Elizabeth Murphy	£5.99 ☐
THE COCKNEY GIRL	Gilda O'Neill	£4.99 ☐
FORBIDDEN FEELINGS	Una-Mary Parker	£5.99 ☐
OUR STREET	Victor Pemberton	£5.99 ☐
GREEN GROW THE RUSHES	Harriet Smart	£5.99 ☐
BLUE DRESS GIRL	E V Thompson	£5.99 ☐
DAYDREAMS	Elizabeth Walker	£5.99 ☐

All Headline books are available at your local bookshop or newsagent, or can be ordered direct from the publisher. Just tick the titles you want and fill in the form below. Prices and availability subject to change without notice.

Headline Book Publishing PLC, Cash Sales Department, Bookpoint, 39 Milton Park, Abingdon, OXON, OX14 4TD, UK. If you have a credit card you may order by telephone – 0235 831700.

Please enclose a cheque or postal order made payable to Bookpoint Ltd to the value of the cover price and allow the following for postage and packing:
UK & BFPO: £1.00 for the first book, 50p for the second book and 30p for each additional book ordered up to a maximum charge of £3.00.
OVERSEAS & EIRE: £2.00 for the first book, £1.00 for the second book and 50p for each additional book.

Name ....

Address ....

....

....

If you would prefer to pay by credit card, please complete:
Please debit my Visa/Access/Diner's Card/American Express (delete as applicable) card no:

Signature .... Expiry Date ....